For:
Mom, who said "Dreams Just Require a Net," and then handed me one.
My husband Ron Bueker.
Mike & Janel, Brandon & Kate, Casey &Katie, Ryan & Ashley,
and eight gorgeous grandkids.
My friends, who never stopped believing in T.J.
David Martin, Ron Bueker, & Jim Roelfs for their tech knowledge &
support.
And for Carol and Don Larrick, and LeRoy Peterson, who gave me the gift
of time.

Text copyright© 2016 by Rebecca F. Pittman

All rights reserved. Published by Wonderland Productions.

Graphic Design & Twicket Illustration by Rebecca F. Pittman
Editing by Tara Creel **www.taracreelbooks.wordpress.com**

ISBN 978-0-692-22612-4

T.J. FINNEL

and

THE WELL OF GHOSTS

Book One

REBECCA F. PITTMAN

WONDERLAND PRODUCTIONS

CONTENTS

Don't miss any of these exciting books from Rebecca F. Pittman!

Paranormal Historical: Non-Fiction
The History and Haunting of the Stanley Hotel, 2nd Edition

The History and Haunting of the Myrtles Plantation, 2nd Edition

The History and Haunting of Lemp Mansion

Creative Self-Help: Non-Fiction
How to Start a Faux Painting or Mural Business,
1st & 2nd Editions

Scrapbooking for Profit,
1st & 2nd Editions

Troubleshooting Men: What in the WORLD do they want?
(Dating & Marriage Advice for Women)

Coming Soon!
T.J. Finnel and The Treblin's Secret
(Book 2 of the T.J. Finnel Series)

The History & Haunting of the Lizzie Borden House

The History & Haunting of the Crescent Hotel

Don't Look Now! (Supernatural Thriller)

Sign up here for *Ghost Writings* newsletter:
www.rebeccafpittmanbooks.com

From the beginning of time, man has looked up at the stars in wonder.

Ancient mariners used them as a means to navigate the seas beneath the night sky. Civilizations have worshipped them, astrologers charted them, and crops were planted and harvested based on their telling of the seasons.

But what if, the constellations we see are more than just glittering stars and mythical lore?

What if, they are real, and become mortal beneath the glow of moonlight?

And what if, these entities, both good and evil, found a way to enter our world?

Chapter One

THE DARE

Markus Finnel stood just inside the cave entrance and stared in awe at the sight before him. His best friend, Corey Greenman, was standing a few feet behind him, peering nervously around the boy's shoulder. The other three 9-year-olds comprising Markus's circle of friends waited outside the cave entrance under the sheltered protection of towering pines.

"You have to touch it!" Montie Westcott hissed at the two boys brave enough to make it this far inside the cave. "That's the deal! If ya want to be part of the club, ya have to touch it, and bring back a piece of it!"

The fact that Montie Westcott had never touched "it" (let alone carved out a piece of it), and was cowering outside the cave, pressed like a slice of bologna in a sandwich between his two taller friends, did not seem to diminish his status as head of The Secret Watcher's Club.

Markus took a tentative step toward the object sitting in the center of the cave, moonlight falling upon it from a large hole in the rocky ceiling overhead. He swallowed hard as he took in the decaying boards that someone—or some*thing*—had placed across the object's opening. Large stones had been placed atop the barn wood planks, anchoring each board to the rim of the round cistern that had haunted the townspeople of Coven Bay for a hundred years.

"Are ya gonna touch it?" Corey whispered to Markus, as he wormed his way around to hide behind his best friend's back. "Are ya gonna touch the well?"

The Well of Ghosts sat before the young boys, moonlight playing upon it like a beaconing spotlight. *Come and touch me…it seemed to taunt them. Come…I have secrets within!*

Markus took another tentative step, and Corey held his breath. He stepped away as Markus removed a small army knife from the back pocket of his jeans, and advanced slowly forward. *If something bursts through those boards from the well, it will have to eat Markus first,* Corey reasoned, taking another step back, abandoning in one thought any dictates that fell within the best friend agreement. He could hear the other three boys inching a little closer to the cave entrance to watch the supposed demise of their good buddy Markus.

The well waited patiently in the stillness. It had waited 20 years; another few moments wouldn't matter now. *Closer!* Markus could swear it was whispering to him. He glanced back at the bulging eyes of his friends, paused, took a deep breath, and mustering all of his courage—hurriedly took the final few steps to the well's side. His heart hammering, he quickly dug with shaking hands into one of the weathered boards with the sharp point of his knife, slicing away a thin splinter of wood. As the small blond boy bore down upon the ancient board to cut away his souvenir, the decayed plank cracked and fell into the bowels of the crumbling well. Markus stared, horrified, into the black abyss, the fetid smell of something dead rising from its maw.

"Run!" Markus screamed, unnecessarily, as Corey Greenman had already turned tail and was half-way out the cave entrance. Markus, whose legs were longer, passed him, and tore into the woods, clutching the piece of barn wood in his sweating palm.

"Holy cow!" Corey cried as he caught up to the four boys who were streaking through the dark woods like death was nipping at their heels. The round orb of light from Casey Cane's flashlight pinged about the foliage like a giant bouncing eyeball.

"You did it, Markus!" Corey panted, as he hurried to keep pace with the frantically running boys. "You're the bravest kid I ever knew! Did you see somethin' in the well? Were there ghosts?"

Corey's words tumbled over each other in breathless excitement from the adrenaline rush that came after mind-numbing fear had released its grip on his heart.

"I think I wet myself when that board caved in!" Ryan Smallings said candidly, his words coming in bursts as his chubby form tried valiantly to keep up with the other boys.

Markus said nothing for the remainder of the hurried retreat through Harmon's Wood. He and the others merely crashed through low-hanging pine branches, hurtled fallen limbs, and ripped through briar bushes until they burst from the boundary of the Wood and fell, panting, onto the back lawn of Markus's grandfather's home.

They lay gasping for air, the stars overhead twirling at a dizzying speed. After several minutes, their breathing slowed and they turned their heads in unison to stare at the piece of wood Markus was holding up before him, his eyes still bulging. Reality dawned upon the three members of The Secret Watcher's Club, its newly initiated member, and Corey, who had failed to complete the dare and touch the well. History had just been made in Coven Bay, *heck* in the entire world! Markus David Finnel, age eight (one year younger than the other boys), newest student to enroll at Goreland Elementary, just defaced the infamous Well of Ghosts and lived to tell the tale!

Chapter Two

It Begins...

T.J. Finnel lay in his bed in the darkness, the full moon outside teasing the shadows huddled into each corner of his room. His fingers were laced behind his head as he stared at the moonlit poster of Leonardo Da Vinci adorning his bedroom ceiling. The famous artist's likeness looked down upon the 11-year-old boy fondly, his long gray curls falling from beneath a weathered leather cap. He wore an elaborate blue tunic, his long beard concealing most of its jeweled collar. A white word bubble rising from his mouth said simply, "Got Art?"

As the boy listened to the wind picking up outside his window, he became aware of another noise: a rhythmic creaking of the old stairs outside his bedroom door. The staircase rose from the living room below to the second landing of his grandfather's 110-year-old house where his family was staying. *Creak, creak, creak!* T.J.'s heart began to falter as his eyes moved first to his bedside clock where the digital numbers read 11:45, and then to the handle of his bedroom door, willing it not to move. The creaking sound came closer as the tired floorboards outside his door moaned beneath an unseen weight. He held his breath, sweat pebbling his forehead as he watched the handle with horror.

But it did not turn. In fact the creaking passed by his door and continued a few feet down the hallway toward his little brother Markus's room. A sudden sneeze was heard, and T.J. released his breath in one big blast. It was just his *dumb* little brother! Coming in late again from his secret antics with his *lame* friends who thought they were vigilantes protecting Coven Bay from evil forces. *One of these days, mom and dad are going to catch that kid sneaking out after bedtime,* T.J. thought. He shook his head in disgust and turned onto his side to watch his lizard Popeye through the glass of the reptile's aquarium. The large amphibian tank sat on a long desk beneath T.J.'s window overlooking the back yard. Popeye was stretched out languidly on his rock, his belly rising and falling in contented bliss.

The wind suddenly blasted the side of the ancient house, causing the boards to groan, and the windows to shudder against its savage strength. T.J. glanced up at the dancing shadows skittering across the window glass. He shivered and pulled his blankets higher beneath his chin. *Why did they have to live here in this creepy old house?* he thought miserably for the thousandth time. *Why couldn't his dad find another job so they could live in a normal house again, not holed up here in a musty, decaying wreck that happened to sit just a few yards away from what the locals called the most-haunted woods in America—Harmon's Wood.*

T.J. watched the shadows. No matter how much he loved his Grandfather Dillon, and all he had taught him about science, art, and the stars, he was desperate to leave here. Having to change schools mid-term was an additional icing on his torturous cake. He was the tallest boy in 6th grade. Each day brought an avalanche of taunts, and bullying. The students had been particularly anxious to tell him of the horrors that were housed in the woods behind his grandfather's home. If he heard the name Harmon's Wood, or Well of Ghosts, one more time, he was going to scream. His stomach churned. It was his brother Markus that loved scary stuff and magic, not him. He wanted nothing to do with ghosts and haunted forests. Life was so incredibly unfair!

Sleep finally overtook the tired boy. Even Markus had finally drifted off, after carefully hiding his trophy of wood from the night's terrifying adventure. Images of a bottomless black void, where something was crawling from the well's dark depths, haunted his dreams. He could almost smell the rank odor of decay rising with it. The images reached into the eight-year-old's subconscious and pervaded his sleep. As the moon reached its zenith above Harmon's Wood, the young boy twitched beneath his covers.

The nightmare Markus was experiencing was beginning to manifest in the real world just outside his window within the dark interior of the woods. Something *was* rising from the fetid bowels of the well through the opening Markus had created when he accidentally broke one of the boards. The portal, sealed off for over 20 years, was now open.

The Well of Ghosts shimmered in the moonlight streaming in from the cave opening overhead. But the lunar glow was not the only rays flooding the small cave. A blast of white light shot up from the well, the two remaining boards blocking some of its power. Just beneath those boards, a creature was clawing and catching at the loose stones as it grappled for purchase within the belly of the ancient cistern.

Desperate to reach the well's rim, a forest witch from the Spectre Lands named Morble, dug into the well's interior with her gnarled hands and feet. Two rotted boards overhead still blocked a portion of the opening, but there was just enough room to get through. One of the boards had broken away, leaving only a few jagged pieces anchored by stones. Her matted blond hair caught in the crumbling ruins of the well as she battled to pull herself up. The boards had blocked the full power of the moonlight, making her journey through the two wells harder than usual.

Morble's breathing became labored, and a hissing sound escaped the witch's cracked lips. If not for her need to create more of the Lunar Potion, she would not have gone through all this to enter the Human World, she thought angrily. But the bottle of potion she carried in her pocket was nearly empty. The two drops she had placed upon the ancient symbols on the well's rim back in the Spectre Lands had nearly used up all she had. After tonight, she would have enough of the potion to last her a good, long time, Morble thought happily, as she grabbed hold of another stone. With the Potion and the Dark Orb, the Crone's Kingdom would be within her reach.

Finally, she reached the top of the well and grabbed hold of the broken piece of board. It immediately crumbled beneath her weight and fell past her into the dark void, a heavy stone that had been weighing it down plummeting past her, missing her head by only inches. She barely caught herself before she tumbled after it. Blood was trickling down her wrist from the numerous cuts in her hands. Breathing heavily she reached up again to grab the now exposed rim of the well. With a final heave she crawled from the cistern and sat on the stony edge, looking about her with hooded green eyes as she struggled to catch her breath.

Her fingers felt the distinctive indentations in the stone rim of the well. She looked down to see the symbols of Scorpio the Scorpion, and the twisted shape of a Lamberhook tree carved there. Morble knew that beneath the remaining two boards were 14 more symbols carved into the well's rim. She was back! After all this time, she had found her way back to Harmon's Wood.

Chapter Three

A MIDNIGHT VISIT

Moonlight lay like a shimmering cloak across the lawn behind the Finnel's large, three-story house, bathing the grass in eerie silver. The lush green of the bushes, their rich color leached by the departing sun, now lay in muted tones of blacks and purples where the moon's rays did not quite reach. A few feet back from the house, along the edge of the lawn, stood a thick forest, its towering trees hemming in the people who lived at 1418 Bitterbrush Drive, as an iron fence contains a cemetery.

Harmon's Wood wrapped around the lot where the Finnel home sat like a secret leafed world. It had been the topic of many whispered conversations in Coven Bay. Strange lights and flying objects had been seen coming from the tangle of trees. Everything from ghosts to deformed creatures from other worlds had been attributed to the mysterious sightings. It was not a place people entered willingly.

T.J. Finnel awoke with a start. A sound had jolted him from a nightmare that had been crawling along the corridors of his imagination. He glanced at the clock near the mound of homework he had completed and grimaced. 12:01—it was midnight. He had only been asleep for fifteen minutes after hearing Markus come in. He sighed as he swung his legs over the side of the bed, and stiffly stood up, flipping on the small bedside lamp. The giant lizard rolled onto to its side.

"You've got it rough, Popeye—all 13 inches of you," the tall boy said sarcastically, as he filled the reptile's bowl with dead bugs. "You ever hear of Godzilla? Now *that* lizard could kick your *butt!*"

The reptile opened one bulbous eye, rolled it back in its head and flicked an orange, forked tongue at the boy. It stretched, turned onto its tummy and sighed contentedly.

Shaking his head, T.J. walked to the end of the desk and peered out into the back yard. It looked as though searchlights had been turned on. He cranked open the squeaky window and stuck his head out, craning his neck to look up into the sky above the house. It seemed as if the giant, cratered sphere had drawn closer to the Finnel home.

"Wow! That is one big honkin' full moon!" he said aloud. "That is *way* cool!"

He could smell Coven Bay—the tangy, briny odor that hung like a mist over the forest. The ocean lay in shimmering blue on the other side of the wood's expanse, its frothy foam lapping the beach dotted with small boats mired in the sand. At times, if the wind was blowing in the right direction, he could hear the rhythmic sloshing of the waves as they erased the footprints left by the day's tourists.

Something else was watching the moon as well. Morble, the Forest Witch, peered from the shadows of Harmon's Wood, her green eyes unblinking. A pine bough fluttered in the breeze, temporarily blocking her view as she crouched in the trees only a few yards from the house where a lanky boy was leaning from an upstairs window. A cloud, driven by the wind, scudded across the giant lunar face and the light disappeared, leaving the back yard suddenly drenched in darkness.

T.J. glanced at Harmon's Wood and shivered. He had never liked how close the dense forest encroached on the Finnel's property. On stifling hot summer nights as he lay in bed trying to sleep, he would hear muffled scraping noises coming from the interior of the woods. Images of things crawling from its dark depths, climbing up the side of the house and into his bedroom, had caused him to close his window to a welcoming breeze more times than he could count. He would lay there in the sweltering stillness, his gaze never leaving the dancing shadows that traced their outlines on his windowpane.

Though he loved his grandfather, and spending summers here with him, he was always happy when they packed up the SUV and headed back home. Now they were staying here indefinitely and the boy felt the woods knew it. He hurriedly closed and latched the window.

T.J. ran a hand through his mop of dark brown hair. A soft thud sounded overhead and he smiled tiredly. His grandfather Dillon was up late painting again. It was probably a similar sound coming from the attic that awakened him.

Dillon Finnel was responsible for T.J.'s love of art and science. The two of them had spent many summer nights studying the stars, either through Dillon's giant telescope that resided in his art studio in the attic, or simply lying on their backs in the soft grass, pointing out familiar constellations and discussing the star lore behind them. T.J. probably knew more about what was going on overhead than he did about the world in which he walked.

Another thud sounded from the attic and T.J. checked the clock. It was now several minutes after midnight. Knowing sleep was now beyond him, he stepped into his jeans and slowly opened his bedroom door, peering out into the dark hallway.

He flipped the hall light switch and found it broken. T.J looked at the closed doors lining the dark hallway. The musky smell of tired furniture and yellowed wallpaper permeated the air. The Finnel house was the oldest one on the block. A new subdivision had sprung up around it, making it look like a haunted house in the midst of pristine homes with manicured lawns. Its shadow lay over the small cul-de-sac like a hulking monster.

T.J. stepped hesitantly into the hallway, listening for signs of life. The house moaned slightly, its weathered floorboards shifting back after a day's activity of people pressing upon them. Even Markus' door showed no light coming from underneath.

The house moaned again and T.J. glanced about him at the shadows. A slight breeze had pushed its way through a window frame opening. It fluttered a long, gauzy curtain at the end of the corridor, sending the fabric into a ghostly dance across the darkened hall. T.J. watched it for a moment and shivered.

"Ok...you can do this," T.J. muttered. "It's just an old house with stinky smells and weird noises."

T.J walked quickly across the creaking floorboards to the second door on the left and turned the handle. He looked up the dark stairs at the closed attic door leading to his Grandpa's sanctuary. The door was closed, but a frail slit of light shone beneath the wooden frame.

Dillon Finnel turned in surprise as his grandson burst through the attic door and bolted inside, looking a tad frantic from his journey up the darkened stairs. The elderly gentleman had been working on a large canvas, filling its vastness with brilliant oil paints that shimmered in the moon's light pouring in through the large east-facing window. His finished canvases littered the room while reproductions of paintings belonging to famous Old World Masters lined the walls. There were carvings and bronzes, antique clocks and globes of the world. An old umbrella stand stood in the far, darkened corner, crammed with Dillon's collection of hand-carved walking canes. The room looked like an antique museum that was one-stop shopping.

"Well, Thackery James Finnel, what are you doing up at this hour?" Dillon asked the boy, smiling fondly at him.

Thackery James was the name his parents had saddled him with at birth. Most people referred to the boy simply as T.J., for which he was infinitely grateful; Thackery James sounded like a name given to a pioneer or pilgrim. His mother assured him he had been named after his great-great grandfather Thackery Alias Finnel and it was a huge honor. The way T.J. heard it, old Thackery Alias was known for brewing a questionable liquid in the woods behind his home, and had burned down a famous laboratory. Toward the end of his life he had become a notorious hermit.

"It is the time-honored ritual called 'homework'," T.J. said, grinning crookedly, happy to be in the bright light of the attic studio. His breathing was returning to normal.

The boy hoisted himself up onto the edge of the large wooden table, his lanky legs swinging idly. It was strewn with tubes of paints, bottles of linseed oil, turpentine and several used palettes. T.J. liked the pungent smell of the paints and additives. He loved the reproductions of Leonardo Da Vinci's paintings hanging about the room. Da Vinci's painting of *St. John, the Baptist* hung on the wall in the shadowed corner next to a towering bookcase crammed with dusty books, while a copy of the *Mona Lisa* was propped up on a shelve. T.J.'s love of Da Vinci's art had come from his grandfather's infatuation with the late artist. The painting of *St. John* had been in the Finnel family forever. Though only a reproduction, it looked rich with color and depth.

"Did you get a look at that moon?" Dillon asked, turning back to his painting. His clothes were stained with several hues of paint, and a ratty cloth, covered with every color in the rainbow, was half-stuffed into the back pocket of his baggy brown pants.

"Yeah, I did," T.J. said, hopping down to cross over to the large telescope that dominated the room's only window. He pressed his right eye to the lens and played with the focus. Suddenly the giant moon filled the round glass and he gasped at its enormity. Jagged craters jumped out in stark relief and he felt as if he could reach out and touch them.

"Wow", he said, his voice filled with awe. "I think a little green guy is waving at me!"

His grandfather grinned. "Well, wave back. We wouldn't want to be thought unfriendly folk."

T.J. waved at nothing in particular and swung the telescope to zero in on the stars of the Big Dipper. He never tired of the mysteries of the massive darkness overhead. After several minutes of checking out the Crab Nebula and Saturn's amazing rings, he stepped away from the scope and walked over to peer at his grandfather's work. Something was nagging at him, however. Something he couldn't put his finger on.

"Which constellation is this?" he asked, studying the night sky his grandfather was so carefully painting. Silver stars glittered on a cobalt blue background, while a sailing vessel was being tossed about in rolling waves beneath the painting's night sky. His grandfather was famous for his ocean scenes and his dedication to the detail of the sky's constellations.

"You tell me," Dillon challenged, as the boy cocked his head and stared at the configuration of stars his grandfather had just painted.

"Hmmmm…," T.J. mumbled, "this is a hard one. It's not Aries. It isn't Canis Major or Minor." He chewed his lip in frustration. He took a lot of pride in his knowledge of the star constellations, but this one was tricky. His hand snaked up to the bookshelf behind the canvas's easel, reaching for one of the many books on the Galaxy. Dillon playfully smacked it with the wooden end of the brush. The boy dropped his hand in resignation. "I give up," he said finally, sounding none too pleased.

"This is not a well-known constellation," Dillon said smiling. "It is a very old one called *Toucana, the Toucan*. It was also known as *the Parrot* to some cultures. The story goes that it would never shut up so the other constellations got together and threw it out of the Galaxy." The artist laughed, his blue eyes crinkling, as he dabbed a brilliant burst of light around one of the stars. "You have to hand it to the Arabs and the Egyptians," he said happily, streaking his thick gray hair with a glob of blue as he pushed his bangs from his forehead. "They could tell a good story. Most of the ancient constellations were founded on tales from Mesopotamia and as far back as the Druids. There was even a star cluster called *The Clock* long ago. Many of the very old constellations were those of witches and dark creatures, deeply steeped in superstitions. Originally there were 44 known constellations, now we claim 88. Still, many, many of them simply fell out of sight."

A muffled scratching sound came through the open window and

T.J. whirled around to face it, his heart hammering.

"What was that?" he asked nervously.

Dillon cast a casual glance toward the window. "Just some forest creature," he said shrugging. "Probably a raccoon or a rabbit."

T.J. edged over to the window and looked out nervously over the top of the telescope. The trees of Harmon's Wood cast long, irregular shadows across the moonlight-soaked grass, making it appear as if a dark giant was crawling toward the house, his lengthy arms almost reaching the back patio. He shivered and backed up a step.

Dillon glanced at his grandson and said, "T.J, it's just some trees. There are bound to be little things living in the bushes and nesting in the branches. You and Markus used to play there when you were little, when I brought you along with me while I painted landscape scenes. Harmon's Wood has been here forever, and though there have been a lot of rumors about it, there were never reports of capturing the Bogey Man out there," he teased, trying to play down his grandson's abnormal fear of the woods.

"What about that old well?" T.J. asked. He felt this arms pebble with goose flesh at the thought of it.

Dillon turned to study his grandson. T.J.'s fear of the woods had begun around the boy's seventh birthday when he and Markus had been playing hide-and-seek among the trees. T.J. was also afraid of being stuck in small places, the dark, being alone, and new situations.

"That well has been out there in those woods forever...for as long as I can remember," Dillon said. "Townsfolk like to make up stories about it, but I've never seen anything other than some lights. That could be anything...such as fireflies, low clouds, or kids messing around."

T.J. did not look convinced. The moonlight had just reflected off something peering at him from a tangle of bushes at the woods' boundary. It looked like two shining eyes watching the house!

Unwilling to look like a big baby in front of his grandfather, he backed away from the window and swallowed.

"Yeah, well….plenty of people think Old Man Harmon could *be* the Bogey Man," T.J. said finally, his dry tongue sticking to the roof of his mouth. "He's batty! He hardly leaves that old house of his over on the Bay."

"Some people like their privacy," Dillon said softly, preoccupied with his painting. "I was surprised when Tabor Harmon finally gave in and sold the county this parcel of his land for a new housing development. For years he refused to have any houses around him other than the abandoned one his brother owned over there near the Cove. Ruther…that was his name…Ruther Harmon. I believe his second brother owned this house for a while—uh, Thaddeus—his name is. One day Thaddeus just up and disappeared. I finally bought this place dirt cheap after it sat here empty for several years. Some of the furniture and boxes he left behind are still in the next room," Dillon continued, adding a touch of white to a cresting ocean wave.

"Anyway…Tabor Harmon still owns over 100 acres. Selling off that section of woods out there you are so fond of was the biggest surprise. The Harmon's were notorious for guarding that patch of trees for centuries. Suddenly, Harmon just up and told the county to tear it all down, and build their 'con-founded modern crap'…unquote," Dillon said, smiling to himself as he stepped back to study his artwork. He laid the brush on the palette, and wiped his hands on the rag he pulled from his back pocket. "But when the economy hit a bad patch, all the construction stopped….and there it sits…Harmon's Wood, still intact."

"Yippee," T.J. muttered.

"I should be finished with this painting in a couple of days," Dillon said with satisfaction. "I want to hit the sky with a final wash, and add a little more iridescence to the stars, but all in all, I quite like it."

"Is it going to be one of the six paintings you are showing at my school's Art Fair?" T.J. asked, a dull quality sounding in his voice.

He was not looking forward to the annual art exhibit at his school. He would be thrilled when it was over! His grandfather had been asked to supply six canvases of his latest work as a huge promotion for the fair. The other art would be provided by the local students. Dillon Finnel's name in the art world would be a huge drawing card—at least the school faculty was hoping it would be. T.J. was still adjusting to being the new boy at school and the constant teasing. The last thing he needed was a spotlight on him due to his famous grandfather's art contribution.

"I'm not sure yet," Dillon said, cocking his head to study the canvases lining the room's walls. "Actually, I'm planning on surprising you with the six paintings I've chosen. But, if you have a favorite you want shown, let me know."

"I want the dragon," T.J. said, grinning.

"What is it with you and that dragon?" Dillon said, laughing. "Draco the Dragon is not the biggest constellation, ya know! It's only the 8th largest. Hydra the Water Snake wraps more than a quarter of the way around the celestial sphere!"

"Dragons are cooler," T.J. said, simply.

"Ok, you win," Dillon said. "Time for bed, my skittish friend," he said, placing a protective arm around his grandson. They were the same height, which always surprised Dillon as he was 6-feet tall and T.J. was only a 6th grader. While the Finnel's were a tall family, T.J. was by far the tallest for his age, something that caused the boy no end of anguish.

T.J. walked to the attic door and turned back to his grandfather who was busy cleaning out the day's brushes. The acrid smell of turpentine filled the room.

"Love ya, Grandpa," T.J. said, looking fondly at the elderly man. "You don't care that I'm not good at sports and all that other stuff. I'm tired of the gym teachers being bummed that I can't play basketball...as tall as I am, and all. And then Dad..."

Dillon put the brush into its holder and crossed over to his dejected grandson.

"Teej," he said, using the family's pet nickname for the boy, "we all go through an awkward stage, especially at your age. It takes us a while to figure out where we fit in, but I will tell you something. The ones who make the biggest impact on this world are the ones who never did *fit in*. And I think it was because they *were* different that they tried harder in life and shown as bright as that moon out there! Even Einstein had trouble in school and was thought to be odd." He squeezed the boy's shoulder fondly. "The only person you have to impress is *you*. Those other people out there don't think they fit in either…some are just better at faking it!"

He winked at the boy and hugged him.

"Now getteth thyself to thy bed chamber!" He flicked the white rag at T.J.'s backside, shooing the boy toward the door.

T.J. paused before he began descending the stairs, and looked back at his grandfather who was staring at him affectionately.

"Did you go through an awkward stage?" the boy asked.

"Yep…," his grandfather said with a straight face. "It started about a week ago."

T.J. heard the elderly gentleman chuckling to himself as the boy disappeared into the darkness of the stairwell, shaking his head good-naturedly. He left the attic door open so its light would filter down the stairs. As the comforting glow of the room above him receded, he quickened his step and took the last few steps two at a time.

T.J. exited the doorway, and quickly crossed down the dark hall. Entering his room, he shut the door behind him, double-checking the lock. He heeled out of his Levis and straightened his boxer shorts. Pulling back the covers to his bed, T.J. crawled under the blanket, electing to sleep in the same shirt he had worn all day. He lay in the soft light from his bedside lamp for a moment, and looked up again at the poster of Da Vinci's placid face.

"Did you ever go through an awkward stage?" T.J. asked the poster. He sighed heavily.

He reached over and shut out the bedside light, his thoughts cloaking his tired brain with an unrelenting heaviness. The house sighed with him, its weary boards settling in for the night.

Somewhere at the edge of the forest, the thing from the well watched the upstairs window at the rear of the house as the soft glow of light was extinguished. The windows were all dark now, including the large one at the top beneath the eaves where a large telescope sat. The light from that room had gone out only moments before. Morble looked up at the full moon and the twinkling stars overhead, and then turned to face the woods. The magic path was here somewhere. Now that she was sure the humans were down for the night, she could use the Glimrocks to find it.

Chapter Four

LUNAR POTION

An owl, nestled in a towering pine, swiveled its head to watch the strange, stooped-over figure walking slowly beneath it. The bird's golden eyes reflected the speckled moonlight filtering in through the canopy of trees comprising Harmon's Wood.

Morble looked about her carefully for prying eyes. Her sharp eyesight had seen the owl following her movements, but it was not an owl for which she watched. It was a green-bodied, winged creature called a Siglet, with red tufts of hair, and a stinger. Siglets were the Crone's spies from the Spectre Lands.

The Crone was the most-evil and powerful constellation in the Universe. She ruled the 2nd Dimension, called the Spectre Lands, from a crumbling castle near the Black River. Her eyes were extremely powerful, and by placing one of them into the opening of the Dark Orb, an ancient map was released, viewable to whoever was holding the Orb. The map showed the hidden symbols for the five wells, one residing in each of the Five Dimensions. Someone could only travel the portals if they knew the two secret symbols on the wells' rims. These travelers were called Well Riders. Once a Rider knew the two symbols, he, she, or *it*, would then need to drop Lunar Potion upon the well's carvings beneath the glow of moonlight, thus opening the portal. But now everything was in chaos—-someone had taken the powerful Orb, along with one of the Crone's eyes.

Knowing Morble had been in possession of the Dark Orb, and the Crone's missing eye, the Siglets had been following her throughout the Spectre Lands, and she was sure they would know she had traveled through the well here to the Human World. Morble watched the treetops and patches of sky above her for any telltale movement. When none were worthy of her notice, she drew a leather drawstring bag from the pocket of her ratty robe.

"Let's see where it's hiding," she hissed, as she opened the pouch with long, gnarled fingers. "I can hear and smell the Bay, so I must be near."

The Forest Witch from the Spectre Lands carefully upended the pouch, and let seven jewel-colored stones fall into her wrinkled palm. They sparkled in the spotty moonlight that was falling in patches through the leaves overhead.

"Find Luthor!" she croaked in a throaty voice.

She tossed the stones to the forest floor and waited. At first they merely lay there in a heap, their rainbow colors dazzling in the fragmented light. Then suddenly, they began to quiver and jump. One by one they moved, and scurried about in circles upon the hard-packed ground. Finally, they arranged themselves into an arrow that pointed off down an overgrown path.

Morble's eyes narrowed to slits as she focused on the almost indistinguishable path at which the Glimrocks were pointing. The passing of time had changed it all. She would not have recognized the small trail she had trod so often, so many years ago. She stooped painfully and gathered up the stones, replacing them into the bag, and drawing the opening closed. Pocketing the pouch, she began the cumbersome job of clearing the briars and entangled brush, as she moved slowly down the hidden pathway.

An hour later, the trail came to an abrupt halt as the woods suddenly gave way to the rocky cliff side overlooking Coven Bay. The night breeze blew the biting, brine smell of the ocean into the witch's nostrils. Moonlight played among the cresting waves like scattered diamonds. *The magic path,* she thought happily. She grinned as she reached into her pocket and once more withdrew the bag of Glimrocks.

"Find Luthor!" she hissed excitedly, and tossed the rocks out into the air before her. They hung in the night sky high above the Bay below, quivering in the moonlight. As Morble looked on with bated breath, the Glimrocks began to grow. The stones became the size of large boulders. They hung there for a moment, and then began to organize themselves into a path leading through the air above Coven Bay. The last Glimrock touched the rocky face of the cliff across from where Morble waited; a cliff cut off from the rest of Harmon's Wood by a huge crevice, essentially turning the sector of land into an island.

Morble clutched the empty leather bag as she tentatively stepped out onto the nearest Glimrock. It rocked slightly beneath her bare feet but held steady. Swallowing hard, she looked down at the crashing waves below. Taking a deep breath she stepped onto the next rock. Her left foot slid on its slick surface, and she caught herself before pitching forward over its edge into thin air. She stood there, panting in the moonlight, the ocean waves waiting over a hundred feet beneath her.

Pressing her thin lips in determination, she took another tentative step to the next rock, and then the next, until she had made her way carefully across the suspended stones. With a huge sigh of relief, she stepped from the final rock onto the firm, and rocky ground of the waiting cliff side.

Morble turned and looked at the floating stones. Garglon had taught her how to use the Glimrocks as a magic path that could defy gravity. Not many knew the secret. Bending, she reached out and laid her weathered palm onto the face of the nearest Glimrock. It shimmered and began to shrink, the other rocks following suit as they floated over to where Morble waited. Once they were all within reach, she gathered up the now small stones, and turned toward the waiting forest.

"Find Luthor!" she cried, as she tossed the magic rocks to the ground.

They pointed into the woods to where a cluster of ancient oaks rose up before her. On each side of the stand of trees were massive boulders precluding further passage. Her green eyes glittered with eagerness. *This,* she recalled. The rocks were pointing to one large oak in particular—the massive one to the right of the stand.

Morble's face dissolved into a fissure of wrinkles as she smiled broadly. Her pointed teeth turned the ugly smile into something feral. She panted with anticipation as she scooped up the stones and replaced them into the pouch. As she dropped the bag into her deep pocket, her fingers curled around the only other object nestled there. Carefully she withdrew a long slender vial. Lifting it up to where her eager eyes could see it, she turned it gently in the moonlight. Only a small bit of liquid remained in the glass container.

"We will find Luthor, and all will be well," she whispered, looking about her again for signs of anything watching her. She held the vile of Lunar Potion up to where a stream of moonlight hit it, and watched in fascination as the small drops of liquid lit up like a searchlight, swirling in iridescent green within the frail glass. She had saved the last of it in order to get to Luthor. There was no other way. If she had used this entire Potion to travel through the well back to her true home in the Glimmer Lands, there would be nothing left to further her plans. The only other vial of Lunar Potion was hidden safely away in the Crone's castle in the Spectre Lands.

There was a reason the Potion was so valuable. Not only did it release the powerful portals of the five wells, but it brought to life anything the Potion touched when moonlight played upon it. It was also used in the rituals involving the Dark Orb.

It will all be mine! Morble thought, her gray skin becoming mottled with color from the excitement pulsing through her brittle veins. *Tonight, will be the start of the Dimensions falling beneath me.*

Morble stepped up to the massive oak and ran her long finger along its bark. For several minutes she felt into each scar of its face, and probed each knothole. As frustration was overtaking her, her finger touched on a protruding knot that moved slightly. Hissing with excitement, she leaned closer and pushed hard against the round knob encased in the rough bark. It suddenly gave way, and a small, hinged door, the size of one found in a doll house, swung open. Carved into the bark behind it was an ancient keyhole.

Being careful not to drop the small vial of Lunar Potion, Morble gently pulled open the glass stopper, and leaned toward the tree. Breathing heavily, she tipped the bottle up so that the remaining little drops of liquid fell into the mouth of the keyhole. The potion puddled into the bowl of the marking. Morble looked above her at the brilliant stream of moonlight, and stepped aside to let it fall fully upon the tree's hidden secret.

Moonlight struck the carved keyhole, and the Lunar Potion exploded with light. The tree trembled, dry leaves spiraling to the forest floor. A low groaning sound could be heard from deep within the massive trunk. The witch stepped back just as a giant door swung out from the tree's base, exposing a dark, web-infested interior.

Morble recapped the empty vial and dropped it carefully into her pocket. Her breath came in erratic bursts as she ducked her head, and stepped into the tree's hollow center. She was brushing cobwebs from her eyes when the moon slid behind the treetops on its way toward the west. Harmon's Wood was suddenly thrust into utter darkness. The tree's magic door slammed shut behind her.

Chapter Five

AN AWKWARD STAGE

T.J. awoke with a groan as the morning light poured through his bedroom window. Images of the day ahead at school caused his stomach to churn as he thought about the usual routine of hiding from the Marek brothers, who seemed determined to snuff out his life; disappointed coaches who eyed his long legs and dreamed of track medals, only to find the kid ran like a wounded wildebeest; kids making fun of his height, and his geeky love of the sciences and art...the list of atrocities tumbled about in his brain like gleeful acrobats. He stared up at the poster of the emotionless face of Leonardo Da Vinci.

"Well Leo, if I could travel into the past right now, I would be helping you discover some new war weapon, or the means for man to fly....*anything* that would get me out of school today."

He yawned again, a dull headache from lack of sleep knocking on the doors of his temples. He thought about his conversation with his grandfather the night before, and peering at the stars through the telescope. Something had bothered him as he swung the scope across the night sky. T.J. suddenly sat upright, his head protesting the sudden movement. That's it! That's what had been nagging him! *There were missing constellations in the sky last night...total voids where the star clusters should have been! But which ones?* he thought anxiously, as he tried unsuccessfully to capture the images he had seen through the glass eye. He had to tell his grandfather as soon as he saw him.

T.J. swung his long legs over the side of the bed and stood, stretching his lengthy arms over his head as his mind tried in vain to remember which stars were no longer there. He walked to the lizard's aquarium and switched on the sunlamp. Popeye opened a reluctant eye, and then slowly crawled toward his sunning rock, where he would spend the remainder of the day bathing in the warmth.

"I gotta get me a dog," the boy sighed, as he grabbed up his pants and crossed the room to his bedroom door.

The intoxicating aroma of fresh, hot pancakes wafted up the stairs from the kitchen below as T.J. stepped into the hallway, zipping his jeans, and running his fingers through his thick hair in an effort to tame it. His stomach rumbled in appreciation, and he felt his spirits lift slightly. Markus's door was open to his right, so he assumed his younger brother was already at breakfast.

T.J. descended the creaking stairs and crossed through the large living room. The furniture was old but comfortable—years of people's imprints pressed into the tired fabric. His grandfather's famous paintings of constellations and sailing ships hung about the walls in a variety of frames. Magazines dedicated to the art world were strewn everywhere.

"Good morning, my amazing son," his mother said brightly, as he entered the homey kitchen. She was standing at the stove flipping pancakes in a sizzling skillet. The small dinette table in the corner of the room had been set for five people. Maple syrup, butter, and a huge pitcher of orange juice rested in the center. Sunlight poured in from the Bay windows where the table was nestled, bathing the room in a warm glow. His grandmother's collection of Elvis Presley plates was seen adorning the walls.

T.J. crossed over to his Mom, and leaned over the frying pan, inhaling deeply. Marsha Finnel laughed, and leaned over to kiss him on the cheek.

"Hey! Careful, Woman...you are invading my personal bubble!" T.J. said playfully.

"Woman? Personal bubble? Excuse me?" Marsha grabbed her son and planted a huge kiss on his cheek. He laughed and gave her a hug, while trying to steal a pancake from the stack waiting on the nearby plate. Marsha pulled her son away from the hot stove. She tousled his dark brown hair while gazing at him fondly.

"Teej, you look tired," she said in a concerned tone. "Aren't you sleeping, Sweetheart? Please tell me you aren't going to school in the shirt you slept in!"

The tall boy looked into the green eyes of his equally tall mother. Marsha Finnel was 5'11" tall, with perfect posture. Her strawberry blond hair was pulled back in a sleek ponytail, and she smelled lightly of gardenia perfume. T.J. adored her. He had inherited her green eyes and crooked front tooth. His dark hair, and a propensity for freckling, was courtesy of his father. His 8-year-old brother Markus sported Marsha's blond hair, but looked at the world through their father's brown eyes. It had always struck T.J. as ironic that he resembled his tall, brunette father more, when Markus was the one who was his Dad's Mini-Me.

As if to underscore the thought, the sudden TWANG of a hollow ball bouncing on the concrete driveway out front echoed through the kitchen. T.J. slumped, and slid into a chair at the table.

His mother glanced at him with concern, and then said with forced gaiety, "So are you wanting a grown-up pancake this morning, or Mickey Mouse?"

"Which one isn't going through an awkward stage?" T.J. mumbled.

"What?" his mother asked in surprise, turning to face her dejected son.

"Just hit me with the mouse ears," T.J. grumbled. "I am feeling the need 'to regress to a simpler time of life'," he said in a mature tone, quoting a line from a movie he had recently seen.

His mother turned to face him. "Sweetie, I know you are having a hard time with stuff at school, and…well, feeling your Dad doesn't understand you. Cut him some slack. Losing a job at his age isn't easy. And then, having to move in here with your grandfather until he finds another one was a huge blow to his ego. Marketing and advertising are all he knows, and there just aren't any jobs available right now." She flipped the mouse shape over in the pan, and continued. "My salary at the Flower Shop can't support a mortgage on its own. It's only temporary, and I think your grandfather likes having us here...after losing your grandmother last year so suddenly. I promise; it will all work out. Now, please go tell your dad and little brother that breakfast is ready. I'll call Dillon down from his sanctuary," she said.

T.J. shot her a panicked look. "I'll go get Grandpa—I have something really important to tell him," he said hastily. "You can go call Dad and..."

"Teej, you have to deal with this," his mother interrupted. "I can't intervene all the time. You and your dad are going to have to come to terms with your differences. Now, please, call them in."

T.J. shoved his chair back with a bang, and stomped from the room. He felt as if his mother had betrayed him, offering him up as a sacrifice to the enemy camp. A magazine fluttered to the floor as the boy swept past an end table in the living room, and swung the front door open wide.

"No, Markus," he heard his father say, as he stepped out onto the porch. "Like this...dribble with first your right, then your left. If you use the same hand all the time, the other team will know where to block you. You need to learn to move with both hands so you can suddenly switch and cut around the guy...."

Before David Finnel could finish his sentence, his young son had flipped the basketball from his right hand to his left, cut quickly around his father's spread legs, and dribbled to the basket, laying the ball into the net with perfect precision.

"Whoa HO!" his father cried in delight. "THAT'S IT! That's my son!"

T.J. groaned, took a deep breath, and crossed the sidewalk to the edge of the driveway.

"Mom says to come in for breakfast," he said quietly, and turned quickly on his heel to head back for the house.

"Here!" his dad called, bouncing the ball across the driveway toward the boy. "Take a shot!"

T.J. turned quickly, the ball hitting his knee, and bouncing into the front yard.

"No...I, uh...Mom says we have to hurry up, so not right now, K?" He retrieved the ball, and prepared to toss it back to his father.

"Just shoot the dang thing!" his father demanded, sounding peeved. "It's one lousy shot. Just focus on the net and picture it going in." The muscular man waited expectantly from the center of the driveway, his hands placed firmly on his hips. Markus was watching uncomfortably, still dressed in his zombie-covered pajamas.

"Dad, I don't want to ...," T.J. began.

"Shoot the dang ball!" his father ordered, his face marbled with red.

Tears stung T.J.'s eyes as he swallowed several times. He felt his palms sweating against the pebbled surface of the basketball. He hated his life!

He swallowed again, his heart beating against his ribcage. The pungent smell of the ball's leather filled his nostrils. Shakily, he bent his knees slightly the way his father had taught him, lifted, and pushed the ball off into the air with trembling hands. His heart hammered as he watched it sail past the basket without even coming close to the rim, take an awkward bounce on the pavement, and land with a crash in a juniper bush. The boy bit his lip and turned quickly, running toward the front door. He could hear his father's elaborate sigh and mumbled words.

"Grab the ball, Mark," his father said angrily. "Let's eat, and you need to get ready for school."

T.J. burst through the open door, and took the stairs to the upstairs hallway two at a time. His confused mother peeked around the kitchen corner, and called, "Don't you want your pancakes?"

"I'm not hungry," he yelled back, his voice choked with pain. He slammed his bedroom door, and threw a book from his desk across the room, narrowly missing the sleeping lizard.

T.J. looked about the room wildly, wanting to punch something. His eyes lit on a gold plaque hanging near the window, pronouncing him the winner of the Young Inventor's Award at the Science Fair at Goreland Elementary. It was something of which he was immensely proud, as he had only been attending the school for a few weeks when he won the award with his invention of a magnet that could pull objects through obstacles that would typically block magnetic waves. He stripped the plaque from the wall and carried it to the window. Turning the creaking handle as fast as he could, he swung the glass open wide, and hurled the plaque out into the back yard. It plopped into the damp grass, and lay glinting in the morning sun.

Chapter Six

LUTHOR'S GHOST

Morble felt her way along the winding, rough-hewn steps. They led from the entrance inside the oak tree, down into the tunnel that ran beneath the ground. She kept one hand on the cool wooden wall of the stairwell secreted inside the tree. As she descended farther into the earth, the damp became more noticeable. Everything smelled of moist dirt and rotting tree roots. She was used to darkness, but this was something else again. The blackness was complete. All she could do was inch her way forward down the narrow steps, pebbles and broken roots biting painfully into the soles of her bare feet. If she were in her star form, and not this horrible visage the Spectre Lands had turned her into, she would be able to see in the darkness.

After what felt like an eternity, the steps ended abruptly. Morble almost fell as her foot slid a few inches ahead of her into what she knew from experience was a long, descending tunnel that would finally lead her to Luthor. Still holding onto the wall, she inched her way along. There had been no time to pack a torch for this part of her journey. The trip through the wells would have lost it anyway. Her twisted fingers found it hard to hold onto things.

Something scurried across her bare feet and she jumped. She could feel small things crawling along her arms and burrowing into her robe. Morble shivered but kept going. There were worse things to deal with than rodents and bugs.

After long minutes traveling the pitch-black corridor, her foot suddenly banged painfully into a wall. Reaching out blindly she felt along the obstruction. She had reached the end of the tunnel. One final task and she would be home. Running her fingers across the face of the wall she could not see, she felt for the three protrusions Morble knew would be there. After several moments of searching, she found them.

They were the same as she remembered: three small bones protruding from the wall. She could feel the slick surface of the epiphyses—the knobby end of the bone. Placing a finger on top of each, she pressed them all at once. They sunk into the wall and then sprang back. Morble pressed the middle one, released, and then finally pressed only the bone to the left. The wall shuddered. She waited expectantly, stepping back a few inches, as a loud scraping sound erupted, echoing through the dark tunnel. Light shot out from what she could now see was the wall sliding open. Cobwebs from the other side stretched and snapped, as small spiders scurried.

Morble blinked in the sudden brilliance of light coming from the other side of the wall. When the white dots finally stopped spinning before her eyes, she stepped through the opening, and into what had once been her secret sanctuary.

The crude hut had been home to witches for the past one hundred years—the amount of time the Well of Ghosts had been active in Harmon's Wood. The well in the Human World had been the portal for evil constellations throughout the centuries to enter this dimension. It changed locations every hundred years.

The young girls of Salem, Massachusetts, in the year 1692, discovered the well in the woods outside their small village. There, beneath the shimmering stars overhead, they secretly worshipped the evil constellations; the dark trees echoing their strange words as they tossed herbs and crude concoctions into the ancient well. Tituba, a black woman from West Africa, who worked as a house slave for two of the girls, taught them the rituals. One night, as they swayed to the chanting, Tituba poured drops of a shimmering liquid onto two of the symbols carved into the well's rim. Suddenly the symbols glowed in the moonlight, and a dazzling white light shot out of the cistern. The girls screamed, and jumped back in fright, as strange creatures began climbing from the well. Little did the girls know, Tituba was opening the portal from the part of the Galaxy known as the Spectre Lands, allowing the evil constellations to enter through the well and into the Human World. The malevolent forces spread throughout the tiny New England hamlet, possessing the girls. Chaos ensued. The Witch Trials that followed took the lives of many innocent villagers on Gallows Hill. Finally, the well in the woods of Salem disappeared in 1714, reappearing in New Orleans.

During the century the well resided in New Orleans, voodoo, witches and priestesses reigned. Bijous echoed with the ritualistic chanting beneath full moon nights, where the sounds of drums and the jangling of *gris-gris* could be heard.

When the well moved in 1814 to England, the great witch Harriet Hart came through its portal and tormented the English countryside with storms and plagues. Finally, in 1914, beneath the glow of the Dark Moon, the well moved to Harmon's Wood.

Every hundred years, beneath the advent of the Dark Moon, the wells in the 5 Dimensions moved. These Dimensions were the Glimmer Lands (where the constellations who were *not* evil-worshiping lived); the Spectre Lands (the realm of evil ruled over by the Crone); the Treblin, also known as the Toad Kingdom (home of amphibian-like creatures who dwelled underground); the Human World; and the Void (a black, cosmic dumping ground from where nothing ever returned). The secret symbols carved into the wells' rims changed whenever the portals moved to another location, so only the person possessing the Dark Orb and its map would know where the wells had gone, and which symbols now opened their portals. Shortly, the Dark Moon would rise again, and the wells would once more change locations, keeping each Dimension's inhabitants captive there for another century.

Morble walked carefully through her sanctum. Cobwebs dangled from overhead tree limbs that had forced their way through the dirt walls of the small hut. What had appeared to be bright light shining from inside was only the starlight coming in from a hole in the thatched roof of the crude dwelling. After all the time in the tunnel, any light had been blinding to the weary forest witch.

The smell of strange herbs and damp soil permeated the air inside the hut. Morble looked about at the destruction brought on by the passage of time. Her worktables were covered with spider webs and dusty bug cocoons. The pieces of broken thatch from the ceiling lay in moldy clumps about the floor. Wooden jars lay upside down, their contents spilling out and decaying; broken pottery, once housing precious herbs, lay everywhere.

She walked to the small opening in the west wall and looked out. The dropped edge of the cliff was only a few feet away. The circle of blackened stones still lay in the clearing; tall pines that had born witness to the nightly rituals remained standing like sentinels. It was there the coven of witches had danced and celebrated the solstices. She could still smell the sickening, cloying smoke that rose from the fire within the circle of stones. Unholy things had been added to the fire, along with the strange herbs and twisted roots they had grown in the hut.

Garglon had brought her here the first time after Morble had found the powerful witch in the Lamberhook Forest of the Spectre Lands. Garglon had taken her on as an apprentice, not knowing who Morble truly was, or her insidious plans for the 5 Dimensions. When the Crone captured Luthor, and all of the pods she could find that would be used in creating him again, Garglon and Morble were forced to come here to the Human World where they could begin anew. They had planted the only remaining pod from Garglon's garden to grow a new Luthor.

"So many years ago," Morble whispered to the silence around her.

As she looked out once more at the ring of blackened stones, she remembered the night of the Summer Solstice. Thirteen witches were dancing beneath the moonlight, circling the fire and tossing in their special blending of herbs, dead animals, and potions. Garglon lead the procession. She was second only to the Crone in power and magical ability. Garglon and the Crone had been sisters once, long ago when they ruled the night sky, before the evil constellations were cast out into the Spectre Lands. Over time they became mortal enemies, as they vied for control of that dark, deformed Kingdom.

"Right there we danced," Morble said aloud, her raspy voice filling the stillness. "And there, Garglon met her fate!" A cruel smile twisted the witch's face.

Morble looked out, and remembered the moonlight lying on the ocean waves below that night, as the witches danced and chanted. She could see humans far away on the lonely beach pointing up in horror at the firelight and dancing figures. Then...when the ritual was complete, and the other witches were returning to the hut for the feast of the Solstice, Morble had seized her chance.

As Garglon looked down with cunning upon the frightened humans below, Morble stepped forward and shoved the powerful witch over the cliff side. She could still hear the screams of her unsuspecting mentor as she plummeted through the darkness into the crashing waves below. Morble had watched as the churning water pulled the powerful witch beneath the surface. Water, the purest element in the Universe, had been used since witches first found their way into the Human World. In Salem they had called it "Swimming the Witch." Whatever definition it was given, water was the only known way to destroy a witch.

With a deep breath, Morble shook off the past and looked over the hut for the subject of her journey here.

"It has to be here," she whispered to the damaged walls. "With Luthor standing guard, no one could have gotten close to it." She continued to mutter to herself as she stepped over the debris scattered about the earthen floor.

Near the back of the small room were towering plants, most shriveled and bent from lack of care and light. Morble stepped past the broken pots holding only dead stems and rotted pods. She had been lucky that someone had broken the board blocking the well's portal, or she would not be here at all. With the rise of the Dark Moon coming soon, there was no time to lose.

Morble moved a dead plant labeled *Sibeard's Tooth* to one side and gasped. Towering above her head, its sticky white pods a profusion of whiskers, stood the tall, spiny plant she had been seeking. *Luthor's Ghost* was inked on the small tag still tied to one of its stems.

"Luthor!" she cried, throwing her arms about the hideous plant. He was alive! Against all odds the plant had survived! She looked up to see starlight shining down upon the plant through one of the holes in the thatched roof—and she knew: the nightly moonlight, and occasional rain coming through that opening, had kept her most precious plant thriving, even after all these years.

Luthor trembled in her embrace. She was sure of it. The plant remembered her! Finally, she pulled away, Luthor's sticky tendrils catching at her hair and robe.

"We have much to do!" she said to the plant excitedly. "There are spies about and we must hurry."

At the mention of the words "spies", Luthor's pods suddenly became infused with a green liquid, turning its once white heads into a luminescent emerald color.

"No Luther!" Morble warned, knowing the green color meant the pods had filled with poison. "I don't think they were able to follow me here. We must be on the watch."

She watched the pods from a safe distance. One touch of the gel that would drip from the pod's opening meant instant paralysis, and death. Luthor seemed to hesitate. Finally the green liquid withdrew from the pods, and they returned to white.

"Soon," Morble said, stroking the plant as if it were a precious pet. "Now, are you still guarding it? Did you keep it safe?"

As if in response, Luthor's largest pod near the top of the plant turned toward her, its long, sticky whiskers quivering, and undulating like small snakes.

Holding her breath, Morble bent before the plant, and began digging around its base. The pot holding the towering organism was large, its moist dirt spilling over the sides as Morble probed the soil with long, tapered fingers. One of her broken nails suddenly hit upon something hard, and her breath caught. With her heart hammering, she dug down around the object and unearthed a small silver ball.

"It's still here!" she cried out, her voice rising through the hole in the roof, and floating out toward the Bay. "I knew my Luthor would keep it safe!"

Morble straightened, pain shooting through her tired back. She held the ball in one hand, and brushed the caked dirt from its surface with the other. Taking up the hem of her ratty gown, she rubbed the metallic surface until it gleamed. She turned it in her hand and held it up to the starlight.

"The Dark Orb," she whispered, reverently. "Only you could protect it from the Crone's reach, Luthor. You never fail me!" Morble said with feeling.

She tenderly laid the ball into the deep left pocket of her robe. Then, turning back to the plant's pot, the witch once again dug into the moist dirt. After several moments, she pulled a rotting bag from its soil. The bag fell apart as she opened it. A stream of red light shot out into the room. The witch looked down at the red crystal eye resting in her hand. Its black pupil stared back at her. Quickly, Morble grabbed a small wooden box from the debris scattered about the floor, and thrust the glowing red crystal inside it, slamming the lid shut. Her breathing was labored as she looked out the window toward the Bay. She prayed fervently one of the Siglets had not seen the red, telltale light shining out from the Crone's missing eye.

"I have the Orb and the Crone's eye," she hissed. "All that's left is the Potion."

Morble walked across the earthen floor to a mud wall where a crude stone carving of Medusa hung. Writhing snakes, frozen in stone, wrapped about the statue's face. Though once beautiful,

Medusa's face now showed only cruelty, and hatred. Morble looked into the blank eyes and smiled. She reached up and pulled on the ends of two of the carved snakes. Medusa's jaw suddenly dropped open, and a metal ring appeared, attached to a short length of chain. Morble pulled upon the ring, and a small bottle dropped into the statue's jaw.

"Not much, but enough," Morble stated, after she had uncorked the small bottle and studied the remaining contents of Lunar Potion. "After tonight I will have enough of this potion not only to return home to the Glimmer Lands, and reclaim my Kingdom and my beauty, but I will be able to stop the Crone, and capture the 5 Dimensions for myself!" She pulled the small empty vial from her pocket, and carefully poured the shimmering liquid from the bottle that had been hidden inside the mask of Medusa into it.

Morble decided to waste no time. There was much to do. She pocketed the small vial of Lunar Potion, and the box holding the powerful Crone's eye. The witch turned back to Luthor.

"I will make this as painless as possible," she whispered to the plant, dread threading her words.

Luthor trembled again at the sound of her voice. Retrieving a small burlap bag from a box of used herb pouches, she stepped gently to the towering plant.

"I only need three for now," she said softly, in a cracked voice.

With trembling fingers Morble gently plucked three of the white pods from Luthor's stems. Each time one was broken away from his protruding limbs, he trembled, and a high, keening sound came from the pods. The witch carefully placed them into the pouch, the sticky pod whiskers making it difficult to force them into the bag's interior. Finally she closed the opening and tied a bit of twine around it to hold it securely.

"I will return, and when all is ready, I will take you back with me where you belong!" she promised, as she backed away from the plant. Luthor hung his giant head, the starlight overhead bathing his luminescent pods in a pale glow.

The witch found an old torch lying in a heap of dried leaves at the back of the hut. She had collected matches from the humans in her journeys here, and located a packet in a jar on the wooden table. Pocketing the matches, and making sure the vial of Lunar Potion, the small box with the Crone's eye, and the Dark Orb were secure in the pocket of her robe, she grabbed up the torch and turned to face Luthor.

"I will be right back! I promise!" she said, as she touched one of his leaves lovingly. The leaf responded by lifting slightly as if to wave farewell.

Morble stepped hurriedly into the tunnel and paused. She pulled the packet of matches from her pocket and lit one, touching it to the dried straw tied tightly about the torch head. The flame sprung to life. She knew the straw, bathed for years in oil, would burn long enough to guide her back to the ancient well in Harmon's Wood.

The witch hurried through the tunnel and up the wooden steps until she arrived at the hollow of the giant oak, her shadow thrown by the torch flame scurrying along behind her. She pressed on the tree's secret door and stepped out into the night. Morble retraced her steps across the suspended Glimrocks after tossing them out into the darkness above the Bay. Once reaching the other side, and retrieving the stones, she scurried through the forest, looking constantly about her, knowing the torch light was giving her away if one of the Siglets had followed her here. Morble watched the tree limbs overhead as she hurried on, her bare feet tripping from time to time over rocks and fallen branches. She would never get used to the curved bones that twisted her once-dainty feet into these hideous extremities.

Just when she could see the cave ahead where the well was waiting, something flew at her. The creature attacked her face with its sharp talons, leaving a deep gouge in her right cheek. She shrieked and looked up to see the green-bodied Siglet circle to come at her again. Clutching the burlap pouch holding her precious pods, she tried to dart into a stand of trees where the winged creature could not get at her. But before she could, he dove at her again, grabbing the pouch with its claws. She clung to it fiercely as she swung the torch at the Siglet's head, the flame reflected in its brilliant blue eyes. A tuft of its red hair ignited, and the Siglet's face burst into flames.

Shrieking, it released its grip on the pouch, but not before the bag tore, as one of its talons ripped into it. Unnoticed by Morble, a pod fell toward the opening, hanging only by a long sticky whisker. As she clutched the bag and ran for the trees, the pod finally lost its grip, and fell, undetected, into the weeds. Morble hurried on as the Siglet shrieked at her from above, its eyes badly burned.

Without hesitation, the witch ran into the cave, and tossed the torch to the ground. She pulled the small vial of Lunar Potion from her pocket and poured two drops onto the well's symbols of Serpens, the Serpent, and the marking of the twisted shape of a Lamberhook tree. The fragile slip of moonlight shining through the cave's opening overhead hit the wet symbols. They shimmered in the lunar glow. Suddenly a stream of blinding white light shot out of the well, signifying the portal was open.

Morble carefully replaced the vial of potion in her pocket, clutched the damaged pouch of pods to her bosom, and leapt into the light, disappearing into the well's depths.

Chapter Seven

Harmon's Wood

Tabor Harmon walked across the weathered boards of his front porch and paused, surveying the day with distrust. He grimaced as he saw the two Finnel boys walk by at the end of his long driveway on their way to school. The small, blond kid caught sight of Tabor and waved, as he always did, and Tabor ignored him...as *he* always did. The tall kid chose to look away as they passed by. He liked it better when Dillon Finnel's grandkids only stayed for the summer. Now he had to endure them walking past his place every weekday morning and afternoon, when they took the shortcut to-and-from Goreland Elementary.

Tattered unopened newspapers littered Tabor's weed-choked front yard like decaying bones in a neglected cemetery. The driveway that curled snake-like past the dense woods had sprouted tufts of grass through the cracks and ruts that would have challenged a visitor's car, if visitors ever traveled to his door, which they did not. Tabor Harmon made it clear through the abundance of *No Trespassing* signs tacked to every available tree trunk and rotting fence post lining his property that the welcome mat was not out at his residence on Coven Bay.

He stepped carefully down the two crumbling stone steps that led to the overgrown sidewalk where more newspapers lay in various stages of decay. Tabor had left notes for the paperboy to desist in his delivery of the *Coven Bay Tattler*, but the familiar thud of the rolled paper hitting the driveway or side of the house aroused the old man from his slumbers every morning precisely at 6 am.

Tabor had no phone; there was no one to call. He had no car;

there was nowhere he cared to go. Lloyd Filbert delivered groceries to his doorstep once a week. He was a young freckled-faced boy that Jamison's A & P employed. Though an occasional apple was missing from the grocery order, Tabor liked that the boy never knocked or bothered him…simply left the bags of meager food items, collected the exact amount of change (which always included a dollar tip) that sat waiting for him in a cracked flower pot on the front porch, and departed.

The morning sun was brilliant, and Tabor shielded his bleary eyes. Cataracts had greatly affected his vision in his left eye, making the world seem a little scary. Anything coming at him from his left would have the advantage. He didn't like the sunlight, much preferring to sit in his home with the curtains drawn and the doors securely bolted. But if he had to deal with the woods, sunlight was preferable, and today, he would have to deal with the woods.

Harmon's Wood had been in Tabor's family for longer back than anyone really knew. While it had always been the source of rumors, the past one hundred years had thrown the woods into the spotlight. Instead of mere innuendo, people were reporting they had actually *seen* apparitions in the woods, strange shapes flitting about the trees, and moonlit bonfires from the cliff across the Bay. When Katie Barley over on Deerfield Drive told a reporter she had seen a toad-like creature emerge from Harmon's Wood, people took notice. While toads are hardly news-worthy, those that are 6-feet tall and wearing a fancy robe, are. It seemed full moon nights brought out the more fantastic sightings.

The people who once visited the elderly gentleman, back when he wore clothes that were freshly pressed, and the Victorian house had a glistening coat of paint, had stopped dropping by years ago. Even on nights when only a sliver of a crescent moon shone over the trees, the woods frightened the town people. The tearing down of massive portions of the acreage to build a new subdivision of middle-class homes had made the woods seem a little more civilized, but still the people moving into those new homes watched the trees bordering their back yards with trepidation.

Tabor rubbed a hand over his tired eyes and walked tentatively to the edge of the forest. Even in the brilliant sunlight, it appeared dark and unwelcoming. He paused and listened for sounds. He stooped, stepped over a piece of fallen barbed wire attached to nothing in particular, and tried to peer beneath the low-hanging pine branches. He tossed a small pebble into the darkness, half-expecting it to be tossed back by some unseen creature. When nothing happened, he pushed a pine branch gently to the side, one arthritic hand holding onto a leaning fence post for support. When nothing lunged out at him, he stepped into the woods, his heart hammering.

The cool temperature drop as he entered under the impenetrable canopy of leaves overhead sent a shiver through him. He pulled his ratty sweater tighter about his frail frame, and pushed a strand of silver hair from his filmy eyes. He could feel his pulse jumping in his throat. *"Which way should he go?"* he wondered, looking about him at the unrelenting tree trunks. Each view looked the same…East, West, North, or South, it was a continual parade of thick branches, bushes and boulders.

He had seen the glare from his bedroom window the night before. A bright funnel of light had shot out of the trees like a beacon. Tabor had watched it in horror, wondering what it meant. Hours later he had seen something odd moving through the trees. It looked as though someone with an old-fashioned torch was roaming through the woods, as though searching for a way out. In the past, when Tabor had seen strange lights in the woods, he had never had the courage to come here and see for himself, not in the dark, not all alone. But the lights last night had unnerved him. No one from this generation would have used a torch…not with flashlights at the ready. And what was that bright blast of light? For the first time Tabor wondered if UFO's were using the woods as a landing site. He wasn't sure if aliens used torches, but you never knew. He had to know once and for all what was going on in his woods.

Tabor decided to lay a trap, something that would show him what was haunting his property. He carried a small brown grocery sack in his left hand. It shook as his arthritic fingers wrapped tightly around its neck, sending his loose-fitting watch twirling about his wrist. Stumbling often, the old man wandered farther into the woods, looking for signs that something had been there. The farther in he ventured, the darker it became, and he reluctantly removed a flashlight from his sack. He was hoping not to use it, as it would alert anything hiding in the bushes as to his whereabouts. His fingers trembling, he turned on the switch, and a brilliant ray of light shot into the foliage; lighting everything around him in a round halo of white.

He stopped, swallowing hard. He swung the beam this way and that, but all he saw was more of the same...trees, bushes and rocks with an occasional footpath disappearing into the brush. Tabor pressed on, focusing the beam on the forest floor, looking for footprints, parts of a spaceship...anything.

Suddenly the old man stopped. He could just make out a tall, deformed shape in the frail sunlight piercing the treetops up ahead. It was bending toward him and moving. *An alien!* Tabor thought in horror.

Just as he was about to turn and run, the object swayed slightly in the breeze which was ruffling the treetops overhead, and he realized it was only a sapling, bowing in the wind.

Tabor stood there for a moment, catching his breath, listening to an occasional flapping sound he had been hearing from overhead. Hoping it was only a forest owl that frequented the woods, he swung the flashlight beam upward, searching the thick canopy of trees.

The Siglet ducked behind a cluster of leaves. Tabor's eyesight was too weak to catch it. The spy from the Spectre Lands had returned to look for the pod he had seen fall from the witch's bag. His badly burned eyes made it hard to see in the forest's darkness. He would watch for a while, and see if perhaps this old human stumbled upon it.

Tabor was becoming more concerned. He had no idea how much time he had spent in the dark interior of the forest. It was hard to believe it was daylight on the other side of the towering pines.

Up ahead, an opening in the treetops let in a beam of light directly over an outcropping of rocks. Crossing to the boulders, he snapped off his flashlight. The rare stream of sunlight bathed the large stones in a soft glow. The sun didn't seem as bright as when he had entered the woods, and he worried that the afternoon was upon him.

Tabor stopped, and rubbed his eyes. It looked like an opening to a cave. The sunlight was shedding a soft glow deep inside, and it encouraged the old man to step shakily into the rock's entrance. He could see a beam of light streaming in through an opening in the cave's roof. Tabor followed the ray down with his eyes, newly disturbed dust dancing in its light, and was surprised to see it showcasing a well.

Since Tabor was a small boy he had heard fairytales from the people who rocked him to sleep of a magic well in Harmon's Wood. It was supposed to possess mystical powers that could take a person to other amazing worlds. He stood in the soft light, staring in awe at the crumbling structure before him.

It had been a long time since he had seen it, or the interior of the woods. Once, when he was a young teenager, he had let a group of the local boys dare him into taking them to the well. The woods where the well sat was private property, belonging to Tabor's family. It was Halloween and the well was known for being haunted. Tabor had not been happy about going there. In fact, it had taken several hours to find it as the opening to the cave was overgrown with thick briars and brush. The three boys had stood there, moonlight peeking through snarled branches overhead where an opening could be seen in the cave's roof, and dared each other to throw a stone into the well's opening. Finally, one of the older boys had stepped forward and tossed a small rock into the black void of the open well. Nothing happened for several moments. And then suddenly, a noise had sounded from deep within the stone hole. It sounded like someone gurgling, as if they had swallowed too much water. As it grew louder—and closer—the boys began backing up toward the cave's entrance. Suddenly, something filmy and white shot from the well, shrieking like a Banshee. The boys had fled the cave in terror. Tabor never returned to the Wood. But the well's reputation had continued to grow.

Now as Tabor stood there staring at the crumbling structure, he wondered if perhaps this well was the site of the mysterious lights. He was too turned around to know where in the forest he was, but if he were near its center, then this could very well be the location for which he was looking.

The sunlight was growing fainter; the cave dimming slightly. Tabor was surprised to see broken boards anchored to the well's opening by large stones. The center board was completely missing, leaving a sizable hole. He peered nervously into the blackness of the well, and immediately backed away. It looked as if the thing had been boarded over at one time. *Why? As a safety precaution to keep kids from falling in, or to keep things from coming out?* he wondered, panic plucking his heart. *And who had boarded it over?* It was then he noticed the strange symbols carved into the stone rim. Tabor backed away in fear. *Dangit! He had told that gal-durned construction company to go ahead and raze over this area for their second plat of new-fangled homes! What was taking so long? If they demolished the dang cave along with this well, it might all be over! No more ghost stories, or lights in the woods!* he thought heatedly.

As he stepped back, his shoe hit something and he looked down. His heart hammered. It was a torch! This had to be the torch he saw moving through the woods the night before. The flame had gone out, and the blackened straw stub, attached to a long tree limb, lay on the cave floor, abandoned. Where had the person gone that had been carrying it? He glanced at the well's opening and shivered. There was no time to lose!

Tabor hurriedly set his grocery sack on the cave floor and opened it wide. He pulled out a small bag of flour and walked cautiously around the well. He did not want to be standing too close to it if something decided to come out. With trembling hands he held the flour sack and opened the top. Carefully he began shaking its white powdery contents around the well, and out onto the floor leading toward the cavern's exit. He was careful not to step into it himself. Next he removed a thin roll of wire and a pair of wire cutters from the sack, and carried it to the cave's opening. Unrolling a length of wire that would run the distance across the cave's mouth, he snipped it off and secured each end by twisting it around a heavy rock. Now he had a trip wire should anyone exit the well, or come toward it in the night. If, in the morning, there were prints in the flour, or the wire had been snagged from beneath the rocks holding it in place, he would know someone, or some*thing* had been here. The tracks in the flour might even tell him what.

The Siglet outside watched curiously from a nearby tree as the sunlight was fading quickly, knowing a large moon would soon replace it.

Tabor's heart began pounding, and perspiration was beading up on his forehead as he threw his items back into the sack and turned toward the cave's entrance. He stepped gingerly toward the trip wire, not wanting to snag it with his shoe. Just as he was about to reach the wire, and head out into the woods, he thought he heard a sound coming from the well. He wheeled around to face it, his eyes bulging.

Quickly he fumbled for the flashlight. As his trembling fingers searched for the *On* switch, he heard it again....a scratching sound! Moaning in fear, Tabor shoved his thumb against the switch but as he did, his sweaty palms lost control of the flashlight and it fell from his hands, rolling into the flour on the cave floor. The old man dove for it, grabbed it, and began backing up toward the exit, as he frantically fumbled with the switch. Suddenly, his heels hit the trip wire and he found himself falling backwards, his arms windmilling around him in an effort to right himself. He landed with a thud on his back just outside the cave's door, his head hitting a large rock. The flashlight fell from his hand and rolled a few inches away. The loose watchband flew from his wrist and landed farther inside the cave. His world went black.

As the moon began its ascent, claiming the night on the heels of the vanquished sun, the Siglet watched it from the pine tree branch through an opening overhead. He felt the welcome glow reach down to him as the moonlight bathed the creature in its brilliance. He looked down with scarred eyes upon the prostrate form of Old Man Harmon who lay on the forest floor beneath him.

When Tabor Harmon opened his eyes, pain shot through his head. The throbbing that began at the base of his skull was spreading to the back of his eyes. Dark tree limbs circled above him like a spinning ceiling fan. His stomach felt queasy. He could feel the painful intrusion of every rock that was pressing into his back and legs. As he lay there, looking up into the dark curtain of leaves above him, he suddenly remembered where he was. The queasiness in his stomach turned to gut-wrenching spasms. It was night, and he was alone in Harmon's Wood. Even worse, it was night, and he may *not* be alone in Harmon's Wood. The world overhead spun around and in one of the revolutions, he thought he saw a pair of squinting blue eyes looking down at him from a tree branch overhead.

Tabor pulled his arms toward his shoulders, bending his elbows to lift himself slightly from the ground. The pain in his head exploded. He moaned loudly, pressing a hand to the base of his wounded scalp. His fingers came away stained and sticky with blood that looked black in the lack of light. As the wave of nausea passed, he sat up fully and looked around slowly, not wanting to turn his head too quickly. He was lying in front of the cave's entrance, moonlight falling onto the well before him like a spotlight.

The old man struggled to his feet, and stepped a few inches into the cave to retrieve his flashlight. He could not find his watch. His head screamed with pain as the room spun dizzyingly around him.

Tabor grabbed the flashlight and tried to turn it on. He had to find his watch…and his way home. The old man turned to face the cave's exit, still fumbling with the switch. Outside was the dark forest with its uncertain pathways.

A gurgling sound erupted from the well, echoing throughout the small cave. Tabor turned, his head exploding from the sudden movement. A brilliant light suddenly shot from the depths of the well, flooding the room with its brilliance. The old man screamed, both from fright, and from the pain the light caused his throbbing head. He stumbled back until he was pressed against the rough rock wall.

Tabor's heart pounded in his throat as he watched the well's opening in horror. Something was coming out of it! Long green fingers with knobby knuckles were reaching out of the opening, grabbing at the well's crumbling edges. A pair of spindly arms followed as the thing tried to pull itself from the hole. Tabor thought his knees would give out from under him as a bald green head appeared, covered with warts and a shimmering dampness. Large, orange, luminescent eyes finally peered over the edge of the well's rim, their black pupils dilating in the light. The creature's pinched nostrils flared as it took in the strange odors of the cave. Tabor pressed himself into the shadows of the rocks, praying the thing had not seen him. Outside, the Siglet blinked in surprise as he watched the happenings in the cave, nearly toppling from the tree where he was perched. The Treblin's portal had been breached!

As the toad-like creature pulled itself from the cistern, the other boards anchored to the opening cracked and fell into the well's depths. All that remained of the boarded cover was some splinters of wood weighted down by stones. Tabor's heart was pounding. He was shocked to see the creature was dressed in a flowing robe, an ornate clasp holding the folds together at the thing's throat. It was also carrying a long stick—some strange carving of a head at its top. Clambering clumsily over the well's rim, the creature's giant web-like feet landed with a plop into Tabor's dusting of flour. The

* * *

powder "poofed" up in a cloud and the toad-like beast sneezed. To Tabor's amazement, the carved head that sat atop the cane sneezed as well!

The green creature started toward the cave's exit, still sneezing and snorting from the floating particles of self-rising flour. It was leaving enormous webbed tracks on the powdery floor. The thing was at least 6-feet tall, and walked slightly hunched over. As it reached the place where Tabor was hiding in the rocks, it stopped, its nostrils opening wide as it sniffed the air. The old man's knees were knocking, and he was trembling fiercely. Suddenly, the creature whirled toward him, its giant orange eyes flashing. Tabor screamed and swung the flashlight up to shield himself. As he did so, his thumb hit the *On* button, and the flashlight shot out a blinding stream of light. The amphibian-like face let out a high-pitched squeal and stumbled back, covering its eyes. The stick it had been carrying fell to the flour-covered floor. Still shrieking, the thing turned and darted for the well, flour swirling around its flapping feet. Without hesitation it dove headfirst into the opening, the dazzling light emanating from its depths swallowing him whole.

Tabor was shaking uncontrollably. Minutes passed as his panicked eyes stared hypnotically at the well's opening into which the thing had disappeared. When it didn't look like the creature was going to come back out, the old man swung the flashlight's beam onto the stick lying in the flour before him. Moonlight from the cave's opening was also falling upon the strange object. Its head looked like that of a troll, and it was blinking at him with enormous blue eyes.

Sounds were still coming from the well. Tabor had images of other creatures coming from its depths and lunging at him with long green arms.

The cane's troll head suddenly wrinkled up its nose, and sneezed. Green mucous flew through the air, splatting on the rocks next to where the old man was standing.

"Me no like this white stuff," the troll head said, wrinkling its nose in disgust. "You pick Twicket up now, ok?" the head asked hopefully, smiling broadly at the old man.

That was all Tabor needed to get his legs to work. He jumped over the stick and ran for the cave exit, his head and heart pounding. He stepped over the fallen trip wire, and darted into the night. The last thing he heard from the cave was the sound of another sneeze and a splatting noise.

Chapter Eight

A FATAL MIX-UP

Markus Finnel walked through Harmon's Wood with slightly less gusto than he usually did. This time he wasn't collecting frogs, looking for sparkling rocks for his magic tricks, or playing Ghosts in the Treetops with his friends; a game where his buddies from The Secret Watcher's Club would take turns hiding sheets high up in the branches, and then time the others as they ran through the dense forest with flashlights trying to find them. Now...a well...with *real* ghosts had been found, and he, himself, had accidentally opened and released *heck knows what* on Coven Bay.

The eight-year-old boy gripped his baseball in his left hand, while his right held tight to his brother's flashlight. He brought along his magic ball (a baseball spray-painted silver), for comfort, as well as his need for a possible weapon. It was one of two silver balls Markus used in his Disappearing Treasure trick.

Markus walked slowly through the woods, eyes to the ground in search of the army knife he must have dropped during his hurried retreat from the well. He had looked everywhere in his house, and the back yard, but not found it. He had risked sneaking out of his room after his family was asleep to look for it. It must be in the woods somewhere along the route the boys took that night, he reasoned, as he strained to see into the tall weeds, and scattered leaves. He kicked an empty soda bottle into the bushes and continued on, occasionally knocking crumpled raisin boxes, and other discarded trash from the path with his shoe.

Markus stopped and swung his flashlight beam up toward the canopy of tree limbs overhead. The sound of fluttering wings had been following him for the last several minutes. The noise would stop when he did, and resume as he walked on. The beam of light flashed through the dark greens of the unrelenting treetops, but the boy couldn't spot anything out of the ordinary.

He continued on, playing the light into each stand of reeds and tall grass. The light caught on something white, and he stopped. Markus leaned closer to the thick patch of weeds. *What was that thing?* he thought, as he pressed the flashlight beam closer to the object. He was gripping the silver ball tightly, thoughts of crushing the thing with it if he needed to, entering his mind. The strange object was oblong, with fibrous veins running through its parchment-like skin. One end tapered off into what almost looked like lips.

Gently, Markus set the ball down on the ground near his feet, parted the weeds with the flashlight, and reached in with his free hand. His breathing was coming faster as he carefully picked up the object. It was light and felt as though any pressure would smash it. It was also sticky, and the boy wrinkled his nose in disgust. As he tried to pull it from the weeds, the thing's long gummy whiskers caught on the foliage's reedy stems. Markus finally tugged it loose and held it up, keeping it a safe distance from his face.

Even in the dark, the white object had a kind of eerie glow. When the boy shown the flashlight beam full upon it, a high keening wail came from within, and it seemed to shrink in on itself. Markus nearly dropped it in his fright. Instead, he hurriedly turned off the flashlight, and set the light on the ground. The thing's wailing ended abruptly. He stood there in the darkness of the woods, licking his lips over-and-over, trying to decide what to do with the strange thing he was holding. It reminded him of the pods that took over human's bodies in an old horror movie he'd seen late at night on Nightmare Theater, called *The Body Snatchers*.

A rare patch of moonlight was falling upon the wood's path a few inches away. Markus stepped softly over to it, and slowly held the pod up to the light. He flinched as he waited for it to start wailing. But this time it did not scream; it seemed to fill out as though someone had blown air into it. Then, before the startled boy's eyes, it began to glow a luminescent green. As it did, the pod and whiskers began to fill with the pulsing color. The smaller end of the object that Markus thought resembled lips, suddenly parted, and a shimmering green liquid began to ooze slowly from the opening toward the boy's hand. Markus shrank back in horror, images of body-snatching racing through his mind. Panicking, he tried to throw the thing away from him, but its sticky whiskers stuck to his hand.

"Let me go!" he yelled aloud, but the thing's long tendrils were wrapped around the boy's fingers.

As Markus flung his hand this way and that in an effort to rid himself of the pod, the thing's green liquid suddenly stopped flowing. Markus had reached down for the silver ball. He would smash the thing. But the pod suddenly turned bright white as it neared the silver ball. All traces of green disappeared before any had dripped onto the boy's hand. Its lips parted, and a shimmering white liquid, the likes of which Markus had never seen, fell in drops onto the silver ball, coating its metallic surface.

Markus jumped back, the thing still entangled around his fingers. He accidentally dropped the ball. It rolled into the patch of moonlight and began to glow. Suddenly the ball jumped into the air, and began to spiral around in frenzied animation. Markus stopped his frantic attempt to rid himself of the pod thing, and watched wide-eyed as his baseball shot up into the trees, streaked through the bushes, and finally flew off toward the boundary of the woods near the boy's grandfather's house, leaving a white trail of light behind it. "Crimination!" Markus breathed, his jaw hanging open. Slowly, he looked again at the pod, its white light staining the tree trunks around him. He stood there thinking for a moment. This thing did something to his baseball. He wasn't sure what, but it was the best magic he had ever seen! It didn't like the light from the flashlight, but it came alive under the moonlight. And, for some reason, it changed from green to white when it got near his silver baseball.

As an experiment, Markus stepped back from the ray of moonlight until he and the pod were once more in the forest's shadows. As he suspected, the thing's shimmering inner light went out, and the opening from where the liquid had spilled, closed again. It sat there, looking weird, but harmless. Biting his lip, he took one giant step back into the moon's ray, and watched in fascination as it began to glow white again. As the lips began to part, the boy looked around frantically for something with which to capture the shimmering white liquid. Whatever it was, it was miraculous, and he had to have it for his magic show!

That bottle he had kicked out of the way! Where was it? Markus retraced his steps until he saw the discarded soda bottle, lying half-hidden by the tall grass it had rolled into. He eagerly snatched it up and tried to clean the dirt from its surface by rubbing it against his T-shirt. Quickly, he ran with the bottle and pod back to the stream of moonlight, and waited for the thing to begin glowing again. Moments later, the mouth opened and Markus saw the luminescent white liquid begin to flow slowly from the thing's lips. He held the bottle's mouth to just below the dripping, shimmering stream, and watched as it slid down the inside of the glass container. The bottle began to glow as the liquid filled it. Markus licked his lips in anticipation as he watched the magic drops fill the bottle to about three, or four inches, before the flow suddenly stopped. The boy shook the pod lightly to see if he could coax anymore from it. Instead, the thing's light suddenly went out, and before the boy's startled eyes, the pod turned black and crumbled to dust.

Markus jumped back, flinging the rotted debris from his hand. He wiped his palm on his pants and watched as the black dust disappeared on a breeze. His heart hammering, he looked again at the bottle of magic liquid that was still glowing…in fact, it was now swirling in a hypnotic stream of iridescent light. The bottle began vibrating in Markus's hands. Fearing it would try to fly off as his baseball had done, he gripped it tightly.

Overhead, the boy heard the sound of flapping wings again. He snatched up his flashlight, turned it on, and hurried down the path leading back to his grandfather's house. *The flapping could be a ghost from the well,* his frightened mind whispered. He picked up his pace until he was running to the forest's opening and the happy sight of the Finnel house up ahead. Stopping only to pick up his silver baseball, lying in the shadowed grass near the house, the boy darted through the side door and into the welcoming shelter of the kitchen.

The next morning, Dillon Finnel walked into Harmon's Wood, the sunlight warm on his shoulders. That warmth disappeared as soon as the artist was inside the shelter of trees. He was looking for pine cones his daughter-in-law Marsha needed for a floral arrangement she was making for a client. He had invited T.J. to come with him, thinking he would show the boy that there was nothing to be afraid of in Harmon's Wood, but T.J. turned him down. He had come straight home from school the day before and stayed in his room the remainder of the afternoon, foregoing dinner. Dillon had tried to stay out of the conflict between his son and his grandson, but he realized now he would have to talk to David about the stress he was putting on the boy.

The woods smelled wonderfully of earth and pine sap. He walked along, stopping here and there in the dim light to select the perfect pine cones. Much later, as he rounded a bend in the path he was following, he realized he wasn't quite sure where he was. He had never ventured this deep into the woods. Up ahead was an outcropping of rocks and he walked toward it, curious to see what they might offer. As he neared the large boulders he was surprised to see an opening with soft light glowing from within. Dillon set his bag of cones on the ground and stepped closer, his hand resting on the rocks as he bent over and peered into the opening. It was a cave with sunlight filtering in through a hole in the ceiling. He took a hesitant step inside and stopped.

The light was shining down on what appeared to be an old well. He had never seen the ancient structure, only heard the rumors. But what was that white stuff all over the floor around it? He looked closer and saw the tracks in the powder, showing enormous web-like feet. They were leading from the well and ending directly in front of him, and then turning, and sliding back toward the crumbling cistern! A stick with a stub of burned straw tied to it lay off to one side. A few feet from it laid an even stranger-looking pole, only inches from his feet. It had some kind of strange carving at its top so that it resembled an ancient walking cane. Dillon had a collection of canes in his studio, and he excitedly bent to pick up the stick.

The artist stared at the small green head with the frozen expression adorning the cane's top. It was highly detailed right down to the bulbous nose and small warts that dotted the thing's bald scalp. Its eyes had been painted a brilliant blue, and they seemed to twinkle at him. The large ears were pointed, and the wide grinning mouth almost touched them as it spread across the comical face. Dillon turned the stick in his hand, his fingers feeling indentations in the wooden cane. Squinting in the soft light of the cave, he studied the pole the head was attached to, noticing for the first time that there were symbols and numbers carved into the hard black wood.

A brown sack lying on its side near the cave's exit caught his attention. Still holding the cane, he stooped over and opened the sack. There was a small empty bag of flour inside, along with a spool of thin wire, and some wire cutters. *Well the flour explains the white powder on the cave floor*, he thought. Dillon noticed a small crumpled piece of paper in the bottom of the sack and pulled it out.

Smoothing it open he saw that it was a grocery delivery list from Jamison's A & P. The delivery was being made to Tabor Harmon.

Dillon looked at the cane, and looked back at the delivery slip. The walking stick must belong to Old Man Harmon, though what was going on with the flour and wire was a mystery. The artist looked back at the strange footprints in the flour, and shivered. Something was very odd here. Nothing he knew of could have made footprints like the ones he saw stamped into the sprinkled flour. Dillon left the primitive torch where it lay. He replaced the items in the brown sack and walked toward the cave's opening, carrying the grocery bag and the troll-head walking cane with him. As he did so, Dillon noticed a piece of loose wire lying in the entrance to the cave. *What had Old Man Harmon been up to?* he wondered. He stooped and picked up his burlap bag of pine cones.

Following the labyrinth of paths for what seemed like hours, tracking the occasional footprints, and drops of what looked like dried blood, the artist finally saw light ahead where the forest was coming to an end. He stepped through the final stand of trees, and looked out at the towering Victorian house before him. It was dilapidated, the paint peeling and yellowed. The front porch sagged under years of use, resembling an old man's toothless grin. Broken shutters clung to the side of the house, exposing dirty windows with tattered curtains hanging at odd angles.

Ignoring the *No Trespassing* sign tacked to the tree near the driveway, Dillon stepped over rotting newspapers and quietly walked up the two stone steps to the porch. The old boards creaked beneath his weight, and he prayed Old Man Harmon would not grab a shotgun and start shooting.

Taking a deep breath, Dillon tapped lightly on the weathered door. Minutes passed and just as he was about to knock again, the door suddenly flew open. Dillon found himself staring into the angry face of Tabor Harmon, a deer rifle in one hand.

"You can't read?" Tabor barked, trying to make out Dillon's face with his one good eye. "You want a bullet in yer backside?"

Dillon held out the brown grocery sack, and Tabor looked down at it, not recognizing it for a moment.

"It's just me, Mr. Harmon...Dillon Finnel...your neighbor. I think you may have dropped this in the woods," Dillon said quietly. "I found it near a cave. This walking cane was there as well, so I wanted to return them to you."

Dillon held out the cane and the bag. Tabor gasped, and jumped back, fear contorting his face. "Get that thing away from me!" he croaked. "Get it out of here!" He backed further into the shadows of the house, his frightened eyes riveted on the cane in Dillon's hand.

"But the delivery slip in the grocery sack says these are....," Dillon began.

"Get it out of here!" Tabor shouted, slamming the door in Dillon's face. The artist heard a dead bolt thrown.

"Are you alright?" Dillon called through the closed door. "I saw what looked like blood drops and..." The sound of a metal security chain sliding into place on the other side of the door concluded the one-sided conversation. Backing away, the artist saw a thin hand pull aside a yellowed lace curtain in the window near the door. The muzzle of the deer rifle was pressed to the glass, aimed at Dillon's mid-section.

Sighing, Dillon turned and walked down the steps. He left the sack of items on Tabor's porch, but took the walking cane and bag of pine cones with him. Following the broken driveway, he made his way to the seldom used road, and turned toward home.

Chapter Nine

TWO WORLDS COLLIDE

It was late, and the Finnel family was asleep; all but one eight-year-old boy who was tiptoeing up the steps to the attic of the old house. Unlike his brother T.J., the dark did not bother him. He just needed a couple of things from his grandfather's art studio.

Markus reached the attic and flipped on the light. Moonlight was pouring through the window that covered the east wall of the room. The fear from the night before had left him as Markus concentrated on how amazing his magic show would be now that he had this mysterious liquid.

The boy walked softly to the large table holding his grandfather's plethora of paints, additives, and brushes. He set down his precious bottle of magic gel he had secreted from Harmon's Wood. The minute the moonlight shining through the window hit it, it began to swirl and light up hypnotically. Markus took a moment to bend over and study it through the murky glass of the soda bottle. As the bottle began to vibrate, the boy moved it away from the moonlight and it became still.

"This is going to be awwweeeesoommmme!" he said ecstatically to the empty room. "Now, where's the black paint?" Markus whispered to himself, as he pawed through the hundreds of paint tubes. "I just need some black and some silver."

Markus had found a perfect stick to use for his magic tricks. But if it was to become a wand, he needed to paint it black with silver tips. He had used up all the silver spray-paint on his two baseballs.

As he pushed through the many paint tubes, something suddenly smashed into the giant window overlooking the work table with a loud *CRASH!* Startled, Markus jumped, his elbow hitting the soda bottle containing the magic liquid. Before he could catch it, the bottle fell over, spilling the potion onto Dillon's palette of fresh oil paints. Markus watched in horror as the white shimmering liquid flowed into the paints. He grabbed up the bottle and looked into it with dismay. A lot of it had spilled out, and was now mingling with the oil paints on the palette.

BAM! Something hit the window again. The boy leaped back as a large green-bodied creature with red tufts of hair and a scarred face dove at the window. It seemed frantic to get in. Markus had never seen a bird, or *anything*, that looked like this deformed creature attacking the glass. Its face looked badly burned.

Markus grabbed up a dirty rag and hurriedly wiped the oils from the bottle's side where it had fallen into his grandfather's wet paints. He tossed the rag down, and looked fearfully at the window. Forgetting the paints he had come for, the boy raced from the attic, looking over his shoulder in terror. He hastily flipped off the light and bolted down the attic stairs.

The Siglet flew off in search of other ways to get into the house and retrieve both the bottle of potion the human child was carrying, and the silver ball he had seen the boy rescue from the grass before he could fly to it. Wouldn't the Crone be pleased if he brought back to the Spectre Lands not only the Lunar Potion, but also the Dark Orb?

Moonlight fell upon the work table of Dillon Finnel. His paints began to shimmer in the moon's stream of light. The soiled rag Markus had used to wipe the shimmering paints from the side of the bottle suddenly perked up beneath the moon's glow, and began to dance across the table. It cavorted across the length of the wooden surface, doing moves a rock star would envy, until it danced into the shadows at the fair end, where it suddenly dropped and lay motionless.

T.J. paused and wiped his sweating brow. He brushed a few cobwebs from his shirt collar and sighed.

"Geez, Grandpa," he said, breathing hard, "Saturdays are supposed to be a day to relax!" T.J. tossed a paint rag at his grandfather's head, while smiling broadly.

Dillon looked at his disheveled grandson and laughed. They had been rearranging his art studio all afternoon, moving bookcases, and taking down paintings. The artist needed a large wall for a new mural project he was undertaking for the local museum. A giant section of canvas would need to be attached to the wall while he worked on it. As all of his walls were covered with either bookcases or paintings, he had enlisted T.J.'s help to clear things away. Dillon noticed the boy's mood brighten as the hard work distracted him from his thoughts. They even discussed the missing constellations T.J. swore were absent from the night sky. Dillon promised to check it out.

T.J. stopped before the large easel holding the canvas of *Toucana, the Parrot*. It sparkled in the sunlight with fresh paint.

"Do you want me to move this?" he asked his grandfather, pointing at the easel.

"No, I rather like the light through the window there," Dillon answered. "I almost finished it this morning. One or two more strokes and it's done."

"What do you want me to do with the all these walking canes?" T.J. asked, lifting the umbrella stand from the dark corner in which it had been sitting. "Hey! You got a new one. Who's the funny-lookin' little green guy?"

Dillon glanced at the canes and hesitated. He was not ready to talk about the cave, or the giant web-like footprints he had seen there. Something about this cane scared Old Man Harmon out of his skin. T.J. was already frightened enough about the woods outside.

"Oh, just lying around somewhere," Dillon said evasively. "Just put the umbrella stand over there across from the window. And let's move Da Vinci's painting of *St. John* next to it. That should open up the north wall enough to tack up the canvas for the mural."

The two of them gently lifted the giant painting of Leonardo's famous painting of *St. John, the Baptist* from its wall hook, and carried it over by the stand of canes. Dillon grabbed a hammer and a picture frame hook and drove it into the wall. He and T.J. lifted the painting up, and brought it down carefully until the wire hanger on the back caught on the protruding hook. Dillon adjusted it a few times until it was level, and then stepped back to admire it.

The afternoon sun set Da Vinci's famous painting's colors ablaze. The young man in the painting with the mop of curly hair seemed to be smiling at them. He sat on an outcropping of rocks outside a jagged cave entrance, one bare leg crossing the other at an angle, his left hand holding a wooden staff. He wore only an animal skin about his waist, leaving his chest bare. Dillon had always thought the odd thing about the painting was that the youth was pointing with his right hand toward the dark entrance to the cave, and grinning, as though he knew a secret. Da Vinci had an affinity for pointing fingers in his paintings, most of them pointing toward nothing at all….or so it seemed.

"How long has this been in our family?" T.J. asked, staring at the dazzling colors.

"Forever," Dillon laughed. "It has been passed down from way back in the Finnel lineage. I was told it is one of the best reproductions ever done of the original. Amazing, isn't it?"

T.J. nodded and bent closer to study it.

"It looks like it got burned a little," he said, noticing a scorched mark in the lower left-hand corner of the painting.

"I noticed that as well," Dillon said, glancing over at. "Considering it has been moved around from Finnel home, to Finnel home, for hundreds of years, I'm surprised it looks as good as it does."

T.J. turned his attention to the two remaining bookcases that needed to find a new home. "South wall?" he asked, as that was the only place left that could take on the two book-laden cases.

He and Dillon duck-walked them across the floor, panting and tugging until finally they were shoved into place. T.J. fell into the artist's chair that sat before the easel.

"I think you have earned yourself some dinner, young man," the artist said, slapping the sweaty boy on the back. "Sushi or vegan sandwiches?"

T.J. wrinkled his nose. "Tacos or burgers," he said hopefully. "Pizza is also good...and chicken, ice cream sundaes, and I hear baby back ribs are especially popular!"

"Let's think a little healthier," Dillon said smiling.

T.J. stuck out his bottom lip in an exaggerated pout.

"Noooo...," Dillion said. "...not the lip!"

T.J. made his lip and chin quiver, as he emitted pitiful, whimpering puppy sounds.

"Oh for Pete's sake!" Dillon said laughing. "Ok, ok, ok...but no greasy fries! I think the others went to help your mom with her floral deliveries, so it's just you and me, kid."

T.J. smiled and headed down the attic steps, wiping his dirty hands on his pant legs. Dillon looked around the studio with pleasure. This would work out fine. In fact, he liked the new placement. The painting of *St. John* was much more vibrant in the light coming in from the window than it had been in the dark, stuffy corner where it had been hanging for years. He pushed his hair from his sweaty forehead, and followed his grandson down the stairs.

The afternoon shadows played across the artist's studio, the day bidding farewell in a blaze of sunset colors; oranges, purples, and pinks tinted the gold-gilt frames of the paintings adorning the walls. It lasted only a few minutes. Then the brilliant pastels faded, and night reclaimed the day.

An abundance of stars perforated the black sky, like pinpricks in velvet fabric, letting in the light. A large yellow moon was rising over the treetops, its light illuminating the countryside, and playing happily in the waves of Coven Bay. It was enormous and looked as though it had lost none of its fullness from the full moon of last night, and the night before; indeed news anchormen were calling it *Full Moon Rising, Part 3!* Though extremely rare, there had in the course of history, been two or more full moon nights back-to-back. Scientists attributed it to a freak gravitational pull of the planets. Superstitions abounded when the phenomenon occurred, calling it a Phantom Moon, or the harbinger of something evil coming.

The moon crested a large stand of elms, its light pouring through Dillon Finnel's studio window and into the workroom. It played fully upon the umbrella stand of walking canes, and the painting of the constellation of *Toucana, the Parrot,* that was now beginning to shimmer with a luminescent glow. The troll-head walking cane Dillon had found in the cave, lying on the flour-covered floor, was wrinkling its nose and trying to avoid the direct stream of moonlight that bathed the stand of ornamental walking sticks. His giant blue eyes were taking in the contents of the room, and wondering just exactly where he might be. This was definitely not the Toad Kingdom, and Mudlin the Toad Sorcerer was nowhere to be seen.

As the giant lunar light poured its rays upon the stand of walking canes, a loud sneeze erupted from the center of the sticks. Suddenly, a green stream of mucous shot across the room, and splatted heavily on the painting of a tree frog. A few seconds later, a second sneeze sent another blob careening through the air to land with a *BLOP* on one of Dillon's paint palettes.

Twicket had been trying to hold in the sneezes, but it was of no use. As the little troll watched wide-eyed from his place in the umbrella stand, the painting across the room from him was beginning to change. It shimmered in the moonlight. Suddenly, the stars in the painting's night sky began to swirl and pulsate. As Twicket watched, the painting, depicting a constellation of an ancient chattering bird, began to come to life. *Toucana, the Parrot,* whose wings were, even now, turning from stars to feathers, began lifting from the canvas.

* * *

Chapter Ten

THINGS WITH WINGS

Dillon Finnel entered his attic studio the following morning and looked around once more with satisfaction. The new arrangement of bookcases and paintings he and T.J. had configured looked a lot more organized. He crossed to his work table and picked up his brushes to begin his final work on his painting of *Toucana, the Parrot*.

The artist stopped and stared in shock at the painting. The night sky he had so diligently filled with the stars of the constellation of the Parrot was completely empty.

"What in the world?" Dillon muttered, as he leaned closer to the painting. "That's impossible! I was working on it yesterday, and they were right there!"

As he laid his brushes down on the work table his eyes fell on a bright green glob of what appeared to be snot. Wrinkling his nose in disgust, he reached for a rag, and wiped the vile splatter from the corner of his paint tray. Odd things were going on in his studio, and he was at a loss. He turned again to look at the vacant sky of his latest painting. Shaking his head in bewilderment, he looked absently about the room. Everything else looked as he had left it the day before. Dillon's eyes fell upon the painting of Leonardo Da Vinci's *St. John* painting hanging on the wall across from him. The morning sunshine played fully upon the beautiful painting of a young man in a fur loin cloth, sitting near a cave and pointing at it. As Dillon stood appreciating the painting in the sunlight, he noticed the dark entrance to the cave in the rendering was cracked with age. The painting had been in the Finnel family forever and he felt it his responsibility to keep it in perfect shape. As he reached for his paints to touch-up the painting, he turned back to stare once more at the empty sky of his *Toucana* painting. It was not his imagination—the constellation he had painted of the bird was gone.

The artist picked up his palette of paints, and a medium-sized squirrel-hair paint brush, and stepped over to the famous painting of *St. John*. Carefully he layered on the dark umbers and blacks to add just enough of a shimmering coat to cover the cracked surface of the cave's entrance. As he was stepping back to eye his work, he heard a rustling sound coming from the spare room where the elder Harmon brother had put all his extra furniture when he lived in the house. Dillon paused, eyeing the door leading to the cluttered storage room, and waited.

There it came again. Something was definitely moving on the other side of the partially open door. Dillon set the palette and brush down on his work table, and walked slowly to the doorway. All he could see was darkness through the partial opening. Taking a deep breath he pushed the door open the rest of the way, and looked into the cobweb-laden room.

At first, all he could make out were the shadows of hulking furniture pieces covered in sheets. A tall bureau stood off to the side, and he could just distinguish stacks of newspapers, and other trash piled about the room.

Suddenly, a shadow atop the bureau moved. His eyes darted up to the space where he could swear something atop the tall wardrobe had just shifted from one end to the other. He waited. The shadow waited along with him. His eyes were bleary from staring at the same dark spot. Suddenly, it moved again. In fact, the shadow made a scratching sound as it scuttled across the wooden bureau top. Dillon stepped back, his back pressing against the door jamb, eyes glued to the place where something was coming toward the edge, as if preparing to jump down.

But the thing did not jump. It *flew!* With wings flapping, the shadow launched from its place near the ceiling and soared down toward the petrified man, landing finally on the back of an old wicker rocking chair. Its sudden weight caused the chair to rock back-and-forth, almost toppling over.

Dillon backed into the bright light of the studio, and reached quickly to grab the doorknob of the spare room in preparation to slam the door; capturing whatever it was on the other side. Before he could swing the door closed, a broken voice sounded from the rocking chair.

"Awk! Hold on there, buddy! This bird ain't stayin' in no dusty hole! Now be a good boy and get me somethin' to eat!"

Dillon jumped back, nearly taking his swivel chair with him as he tripped over it. The shadow-thing was talking!

Night entered the artist's studio through the window abutting his work table. The moonlight once again filled the room, showcasing an altered painting (where once the constellation of an obnoxious bird had been), a stand of walking canes, and the painting of Da Vinci's *St. John.* Dillon had finally gone to dinner, after checking to make sure the talking creature on the other side of the attic storage room door was locked in. He wasn't positive what it was…but he had a growing concern that it might be something he didn't know how to deal with.

Sounds of people preparing for bed filtered up the back staircase to the attic. As moonlight washed over the stand of walking canes, once again, the sound of two missile-propelled wads of green mucous could be heard flying through the studio to splat upon some unsuspecting object.

"Me tired of sitting here with these wooden heads," Twicket mumbled, green snot dripping from his nose. "Nobody ever up here at night to talk to Twicket. Me want to go home to Mudlin."

The little troll head looked out at the empty studio and sighed. He had tried talking to the other canes in the umbrella stand, but they merely stared back with frozen wooden eyes. He glanced about the room as the moonlight poured in, noticing two doors, both firmly shut. Occasionally he heard scratching noises coming from the other side of the small door by the bookcases. It sounded as if something was trying to unlock the door. He blinked his enormous blue eyes nervously; hoping whatever it was could not get out.

Just then, a noise sounded from the large painting next to him. He turned quickly to look at the painting of some young guy wearing an animal hide, seated near a cave. As the troll watched, he could see the image of the cave in the painting glowing eerily beneath the moonlight. The entrance to the cave in the masterpiece suddenly filled with a white light until it shot out into the room like a searchlight. Twicket watched wide-eyed, as a white ghost-like shape began emerging from what looked like an ancient well painted inside the cave.

"Me want to go home now," the little troll whimpered.

Chapter Eleven

GORELAND'S GHOSTS

T.J. flung his heavy backpack into his school locker. It had not been a good day at Goreland Elementary School for T.J. Finnel. It had been an even stranger morning at his grandfather's house. T.J. had entered the kitchen, hoping to find French toast or waffles, anything but eggs (he hated eggs), before he faced another fun-filled day at school.

His mother started in on what looked to be an on-going complaint about noises she'd been hearing the night before.

"I don't think you're telling me everything, Markus," his mother said, standing before the young boy, with both hands on her hips. "I heard a large bird flapping around in the upstairs' hallway last night. I got up a couple of times to look, and even had your father check the downstairs. We can't find anything. If I find out you are bringing a bunch of pets in here from the woods, there is going to be a lot of trouble raining down on that golden head of yours!"

Dillon was suddenly jumpy, and gulping down breakfast as if it was his last meal.

"Gotta get back to the studio," he exclaimed with cheeks bulging. "Lots of work to do." He shot a nervous glance at his family, and finally sprinted from the room, almost knocking T.J. to the floor.

Marsha Finnel sighed. "It's going to be a long day," she said wearily, handing a plate of eggs to her son. "You don't look like you got much sleep again, Teej," she said.

"I kept hearing noises outside my door," he said, feeling sheepish in the bright morning light.

"Did you check it out?" Markus asked, grinning, knowing his big brother was afraid of just about everything. "Maybe the flapping sound Mom heard was a vampire bat!" Markus had heard the sounds as well...something flying around in the hallway. Fearing the thing that had slammed into the attic window had found a way inside the house, he had secretly locked his bedroom door and pushed a chair under the doorknob.

"I gotta get to school, Mom," T.J. said heatedly. "Thanks anyway for the *eggs*. Come on, Markus. Let's go! We'll be late."

Things at Goreland Elementary weren't going any better. So far, T.J. had managed to offend three teachers, and had narrowly avoided a fight with the Marek brothers in the hallway outside the gym. The Marek brothers were two angry blobs of freckled rage and red hair that dominated the halls of Goreland, tripping students, stealing lunches, and basically leaving a wake of destruction in their paths. The fact that the third Marek brother had moved on to Junior High was the only bright spot for the beleaguered students. T.J. had accidentally slammed into Thad Marek when something pushed him into the back of the chubby boy, sending Thad's open bag of chocolate chip cookies flying. Students had chased the rolling goodies down the hall, plopping them into their mouths with glee, and then running before either of the monstrous brothers could catch them. T.J. had not fared as well. The two angry bullies had grabbed the tall boy and shoved him into the girl's bathroom. T.J. fled the porcelain sanctuary, accompanied by high-pitched screams, and flying rolls of toilet paper. His next stop had been the Principal's Office with Mrs. Globstein, the girl's P.E. teacher, acting as tour guide. She had been washing her hands at the bathroom sink when T.J. was tossed into the area like a lamb to slaughter.

T.J. was still trying to figure out what had been happening to him at school all morning. Several times he had smelled some kind of foul odor which was usually followed by the sensation someone had tripped, or pushed him. Each time he spun around, there was no one there. Students were beginning to notice his odd behavior as he suddenly slammed into walls, or fell face down in the middle of the floor. The tormenting followed soon after.

"Hey T.J.!" a boy called as he walked past T.J's open locker. "Whatsa matter? You got ghosts following you around, or are ya just clumsy?" or, "Hey, Finnel! Can I borrow the ghost of Abe Lincoln for my history test today? Parts of the *Gettysburg Address* are still a little fuzzy for me!" The kids laughed and walked off.

But it was the afternoon recess that had really cooked his goose. Teams were chosen for softball, and as usual, T.J. was chosen last. He was put way out in left field where the team captain, Dennis, felt he could do no harm. No one was going to hit a ball that far anyway. T.J. stood in the afternoon sun, picking at the stitching on the glove he'd been given; a glove much too small for his long fingers. He could care less if the score was tied 6-6. He sighed and wished the day would end. As he stood there, thinking of going home and looking through his grandfather's telescope that evening, searching for missing stars, he heard a loud *"thwack"!* Tony Fastino had just stepped up to bat and using every bit of his 200-pound weight advantage, socked the ball high over the heads of the infielders.

"On *noooooooo!"* yelled Dennis, T.J's captain. "It's headed for Finnel!"

In a complete panic, T.J. looked up to see the white orb sailing toward his head. Shouts of "Catch it, Stupid" came from every direction, as he closed his eyes, ducked his head, and held the glove above him; more in an effort to protect himself from getting *bonked* than in really trying to catch the ball.

Then it happened! He felt something cold and filmy slide into his mitt. He opened his eyes to see the ghost of a man with long hair, and wearing old-fashioned clothes. His transparent hand was sliding into the glove and trying to wrestle it from T.J.

"Let me see that!" the ghost shouted, trying to steal the leather mitt from T.J.'s hand. "What is it? What's it for? What's it made of?"

It was then the foul stench T.J. had smelled all day at school hit him. It was coming from the man who was trying to steal his baseball mitt. In an effort to keep the glove from the ghost, T.J. shoved it higher into the air. The ball landed with a solid "plop" into the outstretched glove. The two teams stood in total shock, jaws dropping. "He caught it," they said in dazed disbelief. "He actually caught it!"

Cheers erupted from T.J.'s team, but before he could take it all in, the cheers stopped, and gasps could be heard as the teammates froze, their eyes locked on the glove floating only inches above T.J.'s hand. From the infield no one could tell the tall boy's fingers had slipped out of it, but when the ghost finally grabbed the mitt, ball and all, from T.J.'s hand, the crowd could see something was wrong. The glove floated up and over T.J.'s head before gliding eerily across the outfield. It finally plopped to the ground when the ghost suddenly tired of it, as he walked through the tall grass tossing the ball up-and-down in the air. No one had seen him but T.J.; all everyone else had seen was a leather baseball glove gliding mysteriously through the afternoon sun, and a white ball rising-and-falling like a hands-free Yo-Yo.

The rest of the day had not been pretty. The ghost seemed intent on following him around; his foul odor a constant companion. Several girls had asked T.J. if he had given up on showers and deodorant.

The worst of it was when the ghost had taken to making loud burping sounds whenever T.J. was asked to answer a question in class. His teachers were not amused, but the student body was laughing at him everywhere he went.

Finally, in Math class, the most embarrassing incident occurred. T.J. was called on to come up to the board and work out an equation, as the teacher and class looked on. Math, along with science and art, was T.J.'s strong suit, and he sighed with relief when he saw that the problem on the board was an easy one...at least for him. He picked up the chalk and began working out the complex equation. He had just reached the summation when he felt his hand holding the chalk suddenly grabbed with terrific force. He turned to see the ghost who had stolen his baseball mitt, holding on tightly to his hand. The chalk took on a life of its own as it began putting up strange equations. Not only were they strange, but Latin phrases were quickly scribbled next to them...and the letters were backwards!

"What is the meaning of this?" Mr. Hardgrave sputtered. "That is not the problem I put up!"

As the complex equation continued to fill the board, T.J. tried to free his grip from the runaway chalk stick. Mr. Hardgrave erupted from his seat near the chalkboard, and attempted to grab the chalk from the boy, his face effused with color. The ghost refused to release it from T.J.'s hand. A struggle ensued as the classroom exploded with laughter. Finally, the ghost released the boy's hand, and sailed undaunted out the classroom door. Mr. Hardgrave fell backwards as the chalk came free, his toupee flipping onto his face. Puffing and trying to regain his composure, he shoved the hair piece back onto to his balding head, and cleared the offending scribbling from the board with one, hard continuous swipe of the eraser. He turned to face T.J. The laughter ended abruptly as the students waited to see the boy's fate.

"To...the...Principal's...Office...right...*NOW!*" he sputtered, straightening his tie as he struggled to calm his breathing.

T.J. snatched up his backpack beneath the grins of his fellow classmates and hurried from the room, his face ablaze. Tears stung his eyes as he walked briskly once more through the deserted hallways toward Mr. Jacobs' office. The interview lasted thirty minutes. T.J. had no way of explaining what was happening to him. It ended with a warning that if the behavior was ever repeated, he would be suspended from school. As he left the office, Miss Fredrickson, the receptionist, winked at him and asked if perhaps they should keep an empty seat available for him, as he had already been to see Mr. Jacobs twice in one morning.

Now, as he stood by his open locker, listening to the sounds of students laughing, he wished fervently he could just go home.

"*Oooooooooooooo!*" moaned several kids as they walked away down the hall. "*Oooooooooooooooooooooo!*" The imitated ghost sounds echoed eerily in the cavernous halls. Soon, everyone had joined in, the walls reverberating with the wails of a haunted house.

Several kids laughed as they slammed their locker doors and walked off to class. T.J. pressed his lips together, and leaned into his locker to hide his reddening face.

"No use trying to hide in there!" called a boy as he passed. "You're too tall!"

Again peals of laughter echoed through the hallway. If elementary school was *this* fun, he couldn't *wait* for Junior High when the kids were *really* supposed to be mean!

T.J. reached into his locker and carefully withdrew something long and shiny he had hidden behind a stack of books on the top shelf.

"Hey Dude, I've been looking for ya," a voice boomed near T.J.'s elbow. He jumped, nearly dropping the metal object he had just removed from the locker.

"Don't sneak up on me like that," T.J. said, somewhat irritated. He looked down at his young friend LeRoy Larrick, who was several inches shorter, and one year younger.

"What you got in your hand?" LeRoy asked, trying to peer around T.J.'s body as the taller boy blocked his view of the mysterious object.

"Nothin'," T.J. said evasively.

"Come ooonnnn!" LeRoy begged. "You have to show me what it is...I'm your best friend."

T.J. grinned. "And that means I have to share all my secrets with you? Says who?"

"It's in the best friend's agreement package," LeRoy said, squaring his shoulders and trying to look important. "It's right after "all best friends must share candy, comic books, video games, treasure maps, and unused sandwiches.""

T.J. laughed, looked around to make sure no one was watching, and then grabbed the smaller boy by his sleeve.

"Ok. Come on...I'll show ya."

LeRoy allowed himself to be dragged down the hallway until they stood before Room 211—Mr. Roelf's science classroom. Once again, T.J. looked around for prying eyes, and then hurriedly opened the door to the room, and pulled LeRoy in behind him. He shut the door and stood listening for voices. When all remained silent, he turned to his friend and said in a soft whisper, "It's a special magnet I created." He held the slender metal object out to LeRoy's waiting hands.

"What's so great about it?" LeRoy asked, turning it over and studying it from all sides. "It looks like a fat pencil."

"Watch!" T.J. said mysteriously.

He held the magnet out in front of him and aimed it at the large clock on the wall above Mr. Roelf's chair. Several small metal objects on the teacher's desk twitched as the magnetic wave passed over them on its way up to the clock. Suddenly, the hands on the clock jumped, vibrated, and moved slightly. As T.J. moved the magnet slowly in a clockwise position, the clock hands moved with it. Within seconds he had moved the time ahead by 15 minutes. As the importance of this scientific feat dawned on young LeRoy, a broad smile creased his face.

"That's brilliant!" he yelped. "You can make the class end sooner!"

T.J. beamed and simply said, "Yep. Early recess tomorrow will be courtesy of Mr. T.J. Finnel." The boys left the room with heads held high, feeling as though Goreland Elementary had just lost a few points to the mere mortals that made up the student body.

T.J. hurried to his locker, grabbed his sketch pad, and ran off to Mrs. Wagner's art class. He shoved his thick bangs away from his eyes. Only two more hours and he could finally go home. "Surely, nothing else could go wrong today," he muttered dismally, as he pushed open the door to Room 349.

T.J. loved the smell of the art room. It always had the odor of clay, warm crayons, and tempera paints. Numerous paintings were taped to the walls about the room, giving it a warm feeling; colors of every hue shed a vibrant glow to the surroundings.

Many of Mrs. Wagner's students were very talented. Then there were some, like Mathew Tansels, who were a little…strange. Mathew had a fondness for painting things with multiple heads. The assignment for today's class had been to copy any painting done by a famous artist. T.J. was curious to see what Mathew came up with for that one.

T.J. slipped into his seat near the window and opened his art pad, hoping fervently that the rest of the day would go by without incident. He pulled out a detailed copy of Leonardo Da Vinci's famous painting, *St. John, the Baptist*. He had copied the one hanging in his grandfather's art studio. It was a very hard painting to do, and T.J. was proud of his vibrant colors and deep shading. Many of the art students commented it was an unfair advantage that his grandfather, Dillon Finnel, was a famous artist.

"His grandpa probably paints all his homework assignments," was a phrase T.J. had heard more than once.

Mrs. Wagner was in the next room adding linseed oil to the paints for the day's project. She reentered the art class, wiping her fingers on a soiled cloth. The pungent odor of turpentine followed her. She laid down the cloth and several tubes of oil paints on her desk, and then picked up the paintings that were being passed to the front of the class. When she got to Mathew Tansels' painting, she paused, bit her lip, cocked an eyebrow, and sighed elaborately.

Mathew had copied the famous painting by Peter Paul Rubens called *Portrait of Carlo Doria on Horseback.*

"Mr. Tansels?" Mrs. Wagner asked in frustration, as the other paintings were being handed in. No one was ever called by his or her first name in Mrs. Wagner's class. She said they were growing men and women now that they were in 6th grade and should be treated as young adults.

"Yessss?" Mathew called innocently.

"What have you done to your painting?" she said indignantly, holding up the artwork for all to see. Giggles filled the room. "Your fixation with heads is starting to get to me!"

"You said to be original," Mathew said with a grin. "I was being original!"

"And just how is giving the noble horse in this painting *two* heads *original?*" she hissed.

"You mean someone else painted it with two heads before I did?" Mathew exclaimed, feigning surprise. Muffled laughter echoed around him.

"You know *very well* what I mean!" the teacher spat. "You have ruined a world-famous painting with your childish attempt at humor!"

Mathew cocked his head to one side and studied his painting as it shook in Mrs. Wagner's trembling hand.

"I think a two-headed horse is awesome," he said. "What if you came to a fork in the road and didn't know which way to go? The horse could look both ways at once. Or, what if a bird poops in one of the eyes, and one horse head goes blind from the rare Bird Poop Eye Virus, so the other head has to take over and lead old Carlos to the nearest veterinarian just in time to…."

The classroom erupted in laughter. Mathew paused and beamed, basking in the glory of the appreciation of his fellow classmates.

"*ENOUGH!*" shouted Mrs. Wagner, the painting quivering in her hand.

Mrs. Wagner's face had turned a deep purple, which contrasted horribly with her bright red hair. Veins were now showing in her forehead, causing an abrupt silence throughout the room. Her skinny frame shook as she tried without success to calm herself; her blue eyes looked ready to shoot out flames. From the back of the room it looked as if her eyeglasses had actually fogged over. Several students slid down into their chairs, waiting for what was sure to be one of the teacher's famous tantrums. They were soon spared when

Principal Jacobs suddenly entered the room.

The short, round principal walked to the front of the class, while looking around at the subdued students. He could sense tension in the room, and the sight of Mrs. Wagner's flushed face confirmed it. Then he saw Mathew's painting, still gripped in the art teacher's hand. At the sight of the two-headed horse, he sucked in his cheeks in an effort not to smile. But his quivering nostrils and trembling chin gave him away.

"It would appear Mr. Tansels has taken on Renaissance art," Mr. Jacobs said, a twinkle in his eye. He and Mrs. Wagner had butted heads more than once on the subject of stifling a young person's creativity with too much criticism.

Mrs. Wagner shot him a glacial look, threw the painting on her desk, and stepped aside to let Principal Jacobs make his announcement. After gathering his composure, he looked around the room, cleared his throat and addressed the class.

"Students, as you know, every year at this time, we are proud to showcase Goreland's creative talents. Our art show this year will be held Friday evening, May 2nd in the main court. Refreshments will be provided, and we encourage you to invite your families, friends and favorite politicians."

He looked about the room expectantly, but no one laughed. It was an election year and everyone was sick of the relentless political ads bombarding TV and radio. He cleared his throat again and continued.

"Yes, well…we are honored this year to have a very special guest artist. Dillon Finnel, grandfather to our own T.J. Finnel here," he said, making a sweeping gesture in T.J.'s direction, "has consented to display six of his latest canvas works!" His voice raised in excitement as he looked about the room for enthusiasm. When the faces remained wooden, he frowned, glanced at T.J., who was hunched miserably in his seat, and continued with his announcement. "As you are aware, Mr. Finnel is a world famous artist and has appeared on television with his wonderful paintings of the night sky and ocean scenes. I was thrilled when he accepted our invitation to show his latest work. Frankly, I didn't think we had a ghost of a chance getting him."

The classroom erupted in laughter with ghostly wailing noises interspersed. The principal looked confused, and noticing T.J.'s red face, decided to wrap it up.

"Please pick up copies of the invitations as you leave today and hand them out to all you wish to invite," Principal Jacobs said, a bit dejectedly. "They are on bright yellow paper and you will find them near the library. Mrs. Wagner will help you select your best work to be spotlighted that evening. Remember, sculptures, mosaics, and other art are also welcome if you prefer not to offer a painting."

He glanced behind him at Mathew's two-headed horse rendering and bit his lip once more. With a short bow to the art teacher, he turned and walked hurriedly from the room.

Mrs. Wagner took a deep breath, pushed a strand of wiry red hair from her cheek, and eyed the class warily. After a few moments of awkward silence, she let her gaze wander over to T.J. who was still holding his painting in his hands.

"Is that your homework assignment?" Mrs. Wagner asked quietly, obviously trying to regain control of her emotions.

T.J. nodded. The art teacher walked over to him and held out her hand. He reluctantly handed it to her as several students next to him craned their necks to see what he had painted.

Mrs. Wagner studied the painting, while sniffing indignantly from time-to-time. She rubbed her nose and pressed her lips together.

"Interesting," she said haughtily. She turned and carried T.J.'s painting to the front of the classroom, and pinned it to a large easel for all to see.

"Mr. Finnel has chosen to copy a painting by the famous Leonardo Da Vinci," she blurted with authority. "Leonardo di ser Piero da Vinci was born April 15, 1452, and died May 2, 1519. He was an Italian Renaissance genius, known for his contributions as a painter, sculptor, architect, musician, mathematician, engineer, inventor, geologist, botanist, and writer," she boomed, placing her hands behind her back, and strolling importantly back-and-forth in front of the easel. A few sighs escaped the lips of the students as they realized they were in for another long, boring lecture.

She continued, "His only rival for the title of Renaissance Man during this time was the equally famous and talented Michelangelo."

"*Hogwash!*" a husky voice blurted next to T.J.'s ear. The boy jumped, and turned to see the ghost who had been tormenting him all day, standing next to him. He wore long tunics and a leather cap—his hair hung in flowing waves. And, quite frankly, he smelled!

"Michelangelo *my* rival? Ha!" the ghost said. "The man spent more time ducking the Pope than he ever did painting!" He floated over to the windowsill near T.J.'s desk, and sat down upon its edge; his dirty sandals resting on an old radiator there.

T.J.'s eyes flew open wide. That's why the ghost looked so familiar. This was the last face he saw each night before he drifted off to sleep; the face adorning the poster pinned to the ceiling above his bed! He hadn't recognized him at first because the ghost was an older version of the poster's face. The smelly guy was a Renaissance genius—Leonardo Da Vinci!

"Mr. Finnel has chosen one of Da Vinci's famous paintings from 1511," Mrs. Wagner intoned.

"*1513!*" Da Vinci shouted. "*1513,* you dolt!"

"Shh!" T.J. hissed at him. No one else had heard, or seen the ghost.

Mrs. Wagner turned to eye T.J. "Is my teaching somehow interfering with your day, Mr. Finnel?" she asked acidly.

The students were all staring at him with suppressed smiles.

"No Ma'am," T.J. said in a low mutter, hunching into his chair.

Mrs. Wagner eyed him for a moment longer, and then returned to her subject with zeal. With sweeping gestures she pointed out her own paintings that covered the wall behind her desk. Many of her landscapes and portraits hung there; most rendered in oil paints that shown dully under the room's fluorescent lighting.

"As you can see by my *own* work, shading adds depth, and without depth, the painting looks flat, as is proved here in Mr. Finnel's painting. Though he made a valiant effort in trying to capture Da Vinci's feeling for light and dark, he did not quite carry it off!"

"The woman is an *imbecile!*" Leonardo's ghost cried out. He was half-way off the windowsill. T.J. was hoping the ghost would sit somewhere else, as the faint breeze coming through the opened glass was carrying the artist's rank smell over to him. T.J. twitched his nose.

"But then, in Mr. Finnel's defense," Mrs. Wagner continued, "Da Vinci owed much of his talent to his apprenticeship to famous artists of the time. He was not, particularly, original. Most of his early work was fairly basic stuff."

"*WHAT?*" Da Vinci's ghost cried. He sprung from the window, his fists clenched in rage.

"Oh," T.J. muttered, cowering in his chair. Kate Filton made a face as she sniffed something foul wafting past her nose. She looked around and frowned at T.J. Placing a finger under her nose, the pretty blonde slid her desk a little farther away from him.

"It isn't me..." T.J. started to whisper, and then shrugged in defeat.

The famous artist's ghost, trembling with anger, advanced toward the teacher. "You frizzy-haired Banshee!" he cried out. "You know NOTHING of art! You...you... bag of bile and witless gas!" T.J. grimaced, and braced himself.

Mrs. Wagner faced the class, and lifted her chin high, looking totally pleased with herself, completely unaware of the ghost. "I will conclude by saying that it is my humble belief Da Vinci should have stayed with his sketches and left painting to the Masters, such as Michelangelo and Titian! Many of Leonardo's works lacked vibrancy."

"*AHHHHHHH!!!!*" The ghost erupted and leapt at the pompous

unsuspecting teacher. He whipped her paintings from the wall in one odor-filled gust of wind. "And it is *my* humble opinion that my father's *goats* could paint better than you, you Harpie!"

"*What in the world…*" Mrs. Wagner cried out as several of her framed works went sailing through the air. Students dove beneath their desks as the artwork flew about the room like Frisbees shot from a cannon.

"You want to see vibrant *color?*" the ghost cried. He streaked over to the freshly mixed oils the teacher had prepared for the day's work and snatched up a tube of cobalt blue.

"No, no, *nooooo!*" T.J. yelled jumping to his feet, waving his arms in the direction of the angered ghost.

Mrs. Wagner looked in surprise at the boy, and then turned her head to peer anxiously into the space near her where T.J. was desperately waving. Surprised students looked at the spot as well, their eyes bulging, seeing only the tube of blue paint sailing toward the teacher's head.

T.J. bolted across the room in an effort to grab the floating tube from the air. Just as he touched the paint, the ghost dove at the frenzied teacher, squeezing the full tube of oil paint as he did so. With a loud "pffftttt" sound, a large blob of brilliant blue hit Mrs. Wagner full in the face. She shrieked and wiped a large smear of paint from her eyes, while sputtering and spitting tiny blobs of blue everywhere. She took a deep breath, nostrils flaring and exploded.

"*T.J. FINNELLLLLLLLLLLLL!*" she screamed, as students bolted from the destroyed art room.

Chapter Twelve

IF PAINTINGS COULD TALK...

Dillon Finnel tried to put the disturbing occurrences of the past three days from his mind as he hurried to create the final paintings for the Goreland Art Fair. He wanted the presentation to be perfect. This was T.J.'s school and he knew his grandson was nervous for some reason about the showing.

The missing stars in his painting of *Toucana, the Parrot* had finally been found out when Dillon realized the voice chattering at him from the storage room was none other than that of the missing constellation. He was at a loss to explain how the bird came to life and exited the painting. To top it off, Markus had come up to the attic looking for something he could use as a magic cape. He opened the storage room door, and found the chattering parrot where Dillon had once again placed it after it escaped, and flew around the house on two occasions. The crafty bird had figured out how to open the old latches on the attic doors. It had squawked incessantly at him through the door while the artist tried in vain to concentrate on his paintings. Now, due to Markus's relentless begging, *Toucana* was housed in a tall bird cage in the kitchen. Dillon was actually relieved to have the parrot out of his hair. Only he knew why a tropical parrot had ended up in Coven Bay...although he still didn't understand *how!*

Dillon placed the six tall paintings around the room. He had chosen several of his favorite ancient constellations to depict in the night skies of the paintings. He had not had time to paint Draco for T.J. It was, instead, a surprise he was saving for the boy's birthday present.

Dillon reached up to the top shelf of his bookcase where he kept all his books on the constellations and the Universe. He pushed two large volumes aside, and reached behind them to pull out a small slender book he had hidden there. The cover was brittle, the leather cracked and peeling. As he carefully thumbed the yellowed pages, drawings of crude, ancient constellations flashed before his eyes. These were the oldest star clusters in the Universe; many of them considered evil. They fascinated him, as all superstition and rituals did.

The artist looked at several pictures in the book, and then glanced at the various paintings he would showcase in the Art Fair. He had kept them hidden so he could surprise T.J., and the public, with something a little different than his usual selection of subject matter. He studied the paintings, and deemed them worthy. They looked exactly like the drawings from the book he was holding. The last thing to do was a final wash of luminescent blue to sink the colors of the ocean and sky. Returning the book to its hiding place on the shelf, the artist dipped his large fan brush into the sparkling paints on his palette, and ran a thinned wash across the surface of each.

Dillon's paints seemed to take on a shimmer he had not seen before. Perhaps it was the new medium he had been adding to extend the paints' drying time. Whatever it was, he liked it. The paintings seemed to breathe with life.

Just then, T.J. entered the room, a look of total frustration on his face. He marched over to his grandfather, hands on his hips, and glared at him. Da Vinci's pranks at school over the past two days had gotten worse, and the ghost seemed to know T.J.'s grandfather. The boy had waited long enough to confront his grandpa with his frustration.

"Would you like to explain to me what is going on?" he said, trying to sound like a grown-up. "You've been acting really strange. You get jumpy every time you get near that loud-mouthed bird in the kitchen. You've been hiding out up here, and now, some smelly ghost is following me around school, who just happens to claim he's Leonardo Da Vinci! You wouldn't know anything about all this, would you?"

Dillon stared at his grandson and swallowed several times. He took T.J. by the arm and led him away from the paintings as he wanted them to be a surprise.

"Teej...settle down. I don't know what to tell you. All I know is something strange is happening to the paintings." Dillon paused, searching for the right words. Finally he said, "First my painting of *Toucana* is messed with so that the constellation of the bird is totally missing—-and shortly after I noticed it, I find a parrot in that room over there."

Dillon waved a hand toward the storage room door and paused, waiting for T.J.'s reaction. The boy stared at his grandfather as though he were wearing red lipstick and a blue wig.

"The motor mouth bird in the kitchen came out of your painting?" T.J. asked, his words slow and unbelieving. "That parrot—-who, by the way, is telling all of us to call him "Harper"—who is living in a bird cage Markus bought for $2.00 from Kaitlin Moore—-is actually the stars you painted in that picture over there?" T.J. pointed dramatically to the painting labeled *Toucana*.

"It's the only thing that makes sense. OK, maybe makes sense is not the correct way to put it—but, yes, I think...somehow...the bird came out of the painting. And furthermore..." Dillon swallowed again, his face looking as if he had eaten a bug. "...the ghost of Leonardo Da Vinci came out of the well I found in that painting over there. He's been...well...giving me some advice on lighting with my paintings for the past two days."

Dillon stopped talking. T.J. stood in the middle of room, eyebrows raised, mouth frowning, and eyes repeatedly blinking. He glanced over at the painting of *St. John*, and did indeed see a well set way back in the shadows of the painting's cave. His grandfather's wash of paint over the cave entrance had illuminated the faded well and made it more obvious. His head was spinning.

"I don't feel so good," he said finally, and sat down in the chair.

"I feel your pain," Dillion said, perching limply atop his work table. "I've gone through three bottles of Aspirin."

Images of the nightmares T.J. had been enduring at school due to the ghost's antics ran through the boy's mind.

"Can we stuff him back in the painting?" T.J. asked hopefully. "How 'bout we turn the painting to the wall—you know—so he can't get out of the well?"

"Not until I find out what's going on," Dillon said. "Something is happening to the paintings in this room, and I have to know! Leonardo is sneaking out and running about town like a kid in a candy shop, looking at all "the magnificent inventions of this century!" I'm afraid he is not as much of a secret as I had hoped."

"You should have told me!" T.J. declared, hurt that his grandfather, whom he considered his best buddy, had kept something as big as this from him. Plus, a heads-up would have helped him deal with it at school. He felt blind-sided.

"I'm sorry," Dillon said sincerely. "I definitely should have. But, the fact is…something strange is going on…and…we have a ghost staying here."

"Then tell him I know "who I'm gonna call" and it ain't Batman!" T.J. got up and walked from the room in a daze. Even though the antics had only been going on for a few days, it was a mess.

The afternoon was fading. The tired artist looked about his studio, his eyes falling on the umbrella stand. He walked casually over to it, and picked up the wooden troll-head walking cane he'd found in the cave. The troll's motionless large blue eyes stared at him. Dillon had often wondered what about the cane had scared Old Man Harmon so. He looked again at the strange carvings on the troll's staff. He twisted his mouth in confusion, and replaced the wooden cane back into the stand.

Wearily, Dillon dropped into his chair and rubbed his tired neck muscles. He would need to get going on the mural for the museum soon, he thought. The ancient castle scene he wanted to paint was fresh in his mind. He shifted uncomfortably to one side, and finally moved his cell phone from the back pocket of his pants to his shirt pocket. As he sat there picturing the mural's elements, his tired eyes shut, and the elderly man slipped off into a much-needed nap.

Darkness filled the art studio as Dillon slumbered on. The sounds of dinner being made two stories below him did not awaken him. Even the distant sounds of the parrot's non-stop chattering from the kitchen failed to penetrate his sleep. He dreamed of castles and tangled country-sides. His imagination struggled to come up with something truly unique for the museum's medieval exhibit; something dark and foreboding that would lend atmosphere to the setting, he thought in his dream-state.

A large moon crested the tall pines of Harmon's Wood and shown down through the window of Dillon's studio. It lit up the palette of oils, and shimmered across the paintings. Before it had made its way to the stand of walking canes, one of the tall paintings for the Art Fair stirred beneath the lunar glow. The cluster of stars in the fresh oils began to swirl, a shape slowly taking form. Moments passed. A hideous face took shape and turned toward the window as it began lifting from the canvas. Its bright red eye pierced the moonlit room and came to rest on the slumbering, elderly man in the chair across from it. Robes of swirling grey fabric billowed from the painting as a disfigured creature stepped from the scene and floated soundlessly to the floor. Her white hair writhed around her misshapen face. The features looked as if the skin had melted and run down in ruined folds, revealing exposed bone and cartilage. One withered eye socket sat next to a blood-red eye, its crimson beam staining the room around it. The creature reached out with skeletal fingers toward the unsuspecting artist.

The sound of distant thunder shook the house as the moon rose higher, its light filling the rest of the studio. It fell upon the umbrella stand of canes. The troll-head walking cane wrinkled its nose in an effort not to sneeze under the glare of the strong light, but it was no use. Taking a deep breath, Twicket unloaded two loud sneezes, propelling the green slime across the room, where it narrowly missed the bent figure reaching out for the sleeping man.

Dillon awoke with a start at the sound of the loud sneezes, and crashing thunder. Rain began to pummel the windows. Just as he opened his eyes, the thing from the painting lunged at him, grabbing his arms with steel-like strength. Before the artist could cry out, she pulled him back with her into the painting. Twicket watched in horror. The last thing to be seen of the famous artist was his shoes disappearing into the painting labeled *The Crone*.

Chapter Thirteen

PHANTOMS AND PAINTINGS

The wind rustled the early summer leaves of the towering maples lining the sidewalk to Goreland Elementary School. Hundreds of parents and children were making their way to the large glass doors leading into the main hallway. A fluttering blue banner was draped above the entrance with the words Goreland Elementary Art Fair splashed across it in neon-orange lettering. The late afternoon shadows stretched across the lawn, reaching like phantom fingers for the ankles of the hurrying crowd, as the sun began slowly making its way behind the hills. A few clouds slithered soundlessly into place above the school.

"Hurry up, T.J.," Mrs. Finnel called to her 11-year-old son for the third time, as she scurried up the steps to the school. She tried unsuccessfully to wedge her way through the anxious crowd waiting to press through the open doors. Newspaper releases touting the unveiling of Dillon Finnel's newest artwork from the supernatural realm had fanned the excitement of the local people into a frenzy. Out-of-town guests were also arriving, cramming their cars into the limited parking spaces, finally spilling over into the baseball field.

"Just go on in," T.J. called as he hung back on the sidewalk, hands pressed miserably into his jean pockets. "I'll be there in a minute." He kicked a stone into the grass and seriously considered going home.

All the newspaper publicity and fanfare concerning his grandfather's latest masterpieces had only made his life at school a walking-breathing-could-it-get-any-worse-nightmare. After the giant debacle in Mrs. Wagner's art class, rumors had been circulating that the ghost of Leonardo Da Vinci was haunting T.J., and even tutoring Dillon on his paintings. Ghost calls from the students followed T.J. everywhere. Miniature spirits made from toilet tissue had been molded and hung from his locker door. The most imaginative addition had been a disembodied rubber hand protruding from the vents at the top of his locker holding a small sign that read "Finnel's Phantoms!"

As T.J. stood in the cool grass, watching the late afternoon sun sink behind a nearby hill, he tried to take in all that was happening at the Finnel home: an annoying ghost, a chattering bird that used to be a cluster of painted stars…it was a lot to take in. He had gone to his grandfather's studio in the attic before leaving for the Art Fair to see if he needed help with anything. Men from the school had been to the house earlier to collect the six paintings for the exhibit. His grandfather was not in the studio, in fact he was nowhere in the house. T.J. assumed he had gone over to the school early to make sure everything was set up to his liking.

Suddenly, T.J. heard the familiar "*Oooooooooooooo*" moaning coming from behind him. He turned to see the Marek brothers standing there, chocolate smeared around their mouths as they inhaled two large candy bars. They smiled broadly, exposing several bits of almonds and chocolate chunks wedged into the gaps between their teeth.

"Funny!" T.J. said, his voice dripping with sarcasm. "That's really original. I mean, gosh, you guys must have stayed up nights thinking of that one!"

Thad Marek nodded his head in agreement and took another massive bite out of the candy bar. "Yeah," he said, spitting chocolate as he spoke. "Pretty cool, huh?"

T.J. sighed, shoved his bangs from his forehead, and turned to walk off. Chad Marek, a shorter and stockier version of his younger brother, grabbed T.J's arm.

"Your Grandpappy's been in all the papers," he told T.J. unnecessarily. "Even made a big deal about the delivery men comin' to your house and getting' the paintings...all secret-like, like it's some big freaky deal! " Chad continued, "How many of his spook paintings are in there? Like, are there gonna be heads floatin' around and creepy stuff like that?"

T.J. jerked his arm free and glared at the grinning bullies. Inside he was quivering. No one ever stood up to the Marek brothers, but he was sick of being pushed around. The last kid who fought back, after having his head pushed into a school water fountain, found himself enjoying a close-up view of a boy's room toilet as well.

"Get lost!" T.J. threatened, pulling himself up to his full height. He had taken all he was going to take. His knees were shaking and he felt as if a freight train were loose in his stomach. Chad eyed him with curiosity for a moment, wondering if the boy would really take on both of them. He looked around at the throng of potential witnesses, and deciding it wasn't worth ruining a perfectly good chocolate bar over, he shrugged, elbowed his brother and the two ambled off. The sound of "*Ooooooooooooo*" could be heard floating over their shoulders. Some of the students heard them and laughed, as they glanced back at T.J. while making their way to the main doors of the school.

"T.J.!" His father was suddenly standing next to him. "Come on! Your mother wants all of us in there when they unveil the paintings. We're a little stressed right now. Your grandfather hasn't shown up yet and he is the guest of honor. We have been calling his cell phone for the past thirty minutes and only getting his voice message."

"Dad, he'll be here." T.J. said, still shaking. He had dodged a major bullet with the Marek brothers. Then he saw his father's worried face.

"Look, he's probably just stressed about all the publicity," the boy continued. "Maybe all this ghost business is getting to him," T.J. said.

"I don't want to hear another word about *ghosts!*" David Finnel hissed, as he pulled T.J. into the crowded throng of people. "This whole thing is a danged embarrassment!"

A large woman, with the biggest purse T.J. had ever seen, bumped into him painfully. She glared at him as if he had been the one to cause the collision. She fumbled in the purse, while stepping on several people's heels and toes, and finally, withdrew a digital camera from the bag's massive depths. Sighing with relief, she forged on, pushing parents and students out of the way like a determined linebacker.

Inside the school, people were angling for a good spot near the small stage that had been set up at the back of the cavernous indoor courtyard. Dark clouds hung above the school, allowing only sporadic light to shine through two wide skylights directly above the area where six large paintings, draped with black cloth, stood waiting on sturdy easels. Around the room, hanging from partitions, were hundreds of drawings and paintings, divided into the three age groups of the older elementary school students. Primitive sculptures were standing on tables and podiums, each labeled with the child's name and age. Proud parents snapped pictures of their children standing next to their projects, self-conscience smiles frozen on their faces.

Chris Tansels, Mathew's father, was busily shooting footage of the event, mainly his son's sculpture of a three-headed phoenix rising from a soda can filled with ashes. The name on the can said ASHES COLA in bright blue acrylic paint. Mathew had burned several sheets of newspaper and used real ashes to surround the base of his artwork, as well as having it spill from the top of the clay soda can. Each time someone pushed open the large double doors leading into the courtyard; the faint breeze caught the ashes and lifted them into the air where they floated about the heads of the excited crowd. Mrs. Wagner, the art teacher, followed the airborne debris until she stood before Mathew's sculpture.

Mathew had kept the clay model at his home, and had secreted it into the art display before Mrs. Wagner had a chance to view it, and stop him. She stood there now, eyeing the crude bird with three heads; all six protruding eyes painted in a vivid red, its three beaks stuffed with ash. The plaque beneath it (a crude cardboard sign lettered in black marker) read **"Phoenix Rising from Ashes"**. Mrs. Wagner's first reaction of fury as she studied the sculpture, finally waned, and her lips began quivering to suppress a grin. "You have to give him credit," she thought. "The three heads are in proportion, the colors work, and it is...well...clever." She sighed elaborately, shook her head in resignation, and walked off into the crowd to study the art work she deemed more worthy.

"Attention! May I have your attention, please?" barked a voice from the stage. The microphone sent out an ear-splitting squeal. Mrs. Phillips, the assistant principal, laughed nervously and stepped back a little from the microphone. "We'd like to welcome all of you to a truly special night. Not only are we privileged to have our very own students' talents displayed this evening, but, thanks to the enormous graciousness of the Finnel family, we are able to showcase the latest paintings of the great Dillon Finnel!"

A thunderous round of applause echoed throughout the courtyard.

"We are also thrilled this evening to have the Finnel family here with us," Mrs. Phillips continued, "and, to have their son, T.J.'s artwork in our show as well. As many of you know, T.J. is one of our very own 6th graders here at Goreland, and his younger brother Markus is attending here as well."

The muffled sound of moaning ghosts could be heard coming from several students as they held a hand before their mouths and whispered, *"Ooooooooo"*. Parents looked around in confusion as the rest of the student body giggled. T.J. clenched his jaw and eyed the nearest exit.

Mrs. Phillips checked her notes and continued, "So, if you'll join me in thanking the Finnels, we would like them to come up on stage at this time as we unveil these amazing paintings."

T.J's eyes bulged from his head and he turned a panicked face to his mother who was standing next to him, along with his father and little brother.

"I am *not* going up there!" T.J. hissed into his mother's ear. "I mean it...no *possible* way!" He began backing up, until he ran into the large women with the huge purse who had bumped into him on the sidewalk. He turned to see her reddened face glaring at him with impatience.

Mrs. Phillips held her notes before her and intoned into the microphone, "If we could have Marsha Finnel, David Finnel, T.J. Finnel, Markus Finnel and of course, Dillon Finnel, who was so wonderful to let us have his paintings here this evening, come on up."

David Finnel whispered something to a nearby teacher, and the woman, looking extremely disappointed, mounted the short stairs to the platform. She murmured a short sentence into Mrs. Phillips' ear. The Vice Principal flinched, turned back to the microphone, and addressed the crowd.

"Reluctantly, I must inform you all that Dillon Finnel is unavailable to be with us at this time," Mrs. Phillips said. A grimace tightened her face as she waited for the crowd's reaction.

A murmur of disappointment rumbled through the throng of people, as T.J.'s parents, with Markus in tow, made their way to the stage. T.J. was heading toward the doors leading out of the building. His height made it impossible to blend into the crowd. Chad Marek stepped in front of him, and with a sneer on his face, said, "Stage is thattaway, Ghost Boy!"

"Thackery James!" The boy turned to see his father glaring at him as he paused on his way to the platform. *"Get over here!"* he hissed.

With an enormous sigh, T.J. turned and walked over to his father, who then took the boy by the sleeve and propelled him toward the three steps leading to the stage. As T.J. took the first stair, he felt like a condemned man ascending to the gallows.

The Finnel family stood on the podium next to Mrs. Phillips, and waited for the murmuring to stop.

The Vice Principal looked nervously at the disappointed crowd and tried to recover her composure. Mr. Jacobs, the school principal, hurriedly stepped up to the microphone.

"Welcome everyone," he said, beaming at the crowd. Mrs. Phillips gratefully stepped aside. "Without further delay, let's look at these wonderful paintings. I myself have not yet seen them, as I just arrived from a convention in Detroit. If they are anything like the ocean and night sky renderings Dillon Finnel is so famous for, we are in for a real treat. As you all know, Mr. Finnel has been declared the foremost artist in the country for his detailed depictions of the constellations in his paintings. He painstakingly researches each piece of work to make sure the scenes are authentic; in fact they are sought after by avid collectors. There are rumors that his intense focus has even included a...uh...how shall I say...*unusual* expert recently who has been stepping in to advise him on his creations."

"More like *floated* in to help him," muttered Thad Marek from the front of the crowd. He pushed a cream-filled doughnut into his mouth and grinned through the vanilla filling. Several people around him laughed. T.J. bit his lip and kept his head down, staring at his tennis shoes.

"Ahem...yes, well...," continued the principal. "I think we are all ready for this long-awaited moment. So, Michael, if you will please have the teachers un-veil the paintings."

A murmur of excitement spread through the audience as the crowd jockeyed for a better view of the six easels. Michael Durrand, the history teacher at Goreland, stepped up to the first painting, as five other teachers each took their places next to the large, draped rectangles.

The crowd was pressing forward, cameras and video equipment ready. The large woman who kept running into T.J. had effectively shoved her way to the front, and was checking her camera.

Principal Jacobs waited until the teachers were in position before the six easels. With a flourishing wave of his handkerchief, he gave the signal. Each teacher dramatically whipped off the black draping, exposing six, five-foot-tall paintings on their original canvases.

A gasp sounded from the crowd, followed by an eerie silence. T.J. angled past his father to get a better look at what the astonished faces were gaping at.

Each of the pieces glistened with fresh oil paint; colors so vivid the objects in the paintings seemed to breathe. Moonlight was falling sporadically onto the paintings through the skylight overhead as the clouds occasionally blocked out the lunar face. The paintings seemed to be vibrating with a subtle energy. But it was the drawings attached to the side of each painting that was causing the audience to stare horrified at the latest art pieces from Dillon Finnel. They depicted strange creatures, with deformed bodies, and hideous faces. Nervous murmurs were coming from the crowd.

"Cool!" Markus chirped, as he sped past his startled family and hopped down from the stage. He hurried over for a closer look at the paintings before Mr. Finnel could grab him.

Several mothers in the audience were pushing their young children behind them in an effort to screen them from the artwork. The teenagers in the crowd were hooting with appreciation, while the school faculty merely stared in amazement, not quite sure what to do next.

"Mommy? Something's moving in that picture over there," a small girl exclaimed nervously, as she pulled at her mother's skirt.

The woman turned to peer at the painting to which her daughter was pointing. It was the usual scene of a sailing ship tossing about in the waves beneath a star-encrusted sky. But along with Dillon's usual clustering of stars depicting the sky's constellations, these paintings also had drawings clipped to each piece of art, showing what the stars looked like if they were *mortal,* as in the star lore. The painting the child was pointing to showed strange green creatures with pink wings, and shriveled goblin-like faces flying through a velvet sky. Their eyes were a piercing blue, and they had red hair protruding from their balding heads, and running the length of their backs. Small stubs with stingers, like a giant bee, were painted as tails. A small gold plaque attached to the picture was labeled *The Siglets*.

"Nothing's moving," the woman soothed her daughter with a slight tremor to her voice. "You just think they are because it's a strange picture, Sweetie," she said, although she had just glimpsed movement in one of the painting's constellations.

"I want to go home," the child said, as she clung to her mother's legs, keeping an eye on one of the flying creatures at all times.

Some of the adults had stepped up to study the other paintings, a mixture of expressions on their faces, ranging from frightened to confused. The majority of the collection seemed to focus on the ancient constellations no one had heard of. They appeared a little more grotesque.

"Perhaps Finnel has been keeping company with some dark ghosts lately," one man whispered to his wife. A few people overheard him and turned to look at the art with new thoughts forming in their minds. Had the artist's association with a ghost finally taken him into more sinister areas? As if to underscore their dark thoughts, the moonlight was suddenly blocked out entirely by the gathering clouds. The subtle movement in the paintings ceased.

One of the renderings depicted a very ugly hag—her face showing one blazing red eye. Where the other eye had been was now an empty, shriveled socket. *The Crone* was spelled out on a small gold plaque beneath the painting. Another was of a large orange cat seated before the Egyptian Pyramids. The tag attached to this painting simply said *Theops*. The final three paintings bore constellation names the people recognized: *Cassiopeia (The Queen); Capricornus (the Sea Goat);* and *Canis Major (Orion's Hound).*

T.J. wasn't surprised to see that the painting of *Toucana* was not among the collection.

Several people began leaving the school building, glancing nervously back at the shimmering paintings. These were not the masterpieces for which Dillon Finnel was famous. These had a dark, almost evil interpretation, and one got the dizzying sensation they were coming to life. Mr. Jacobs, noticing the crowds were thinning, quickly took the mic in hand.

"Uh, ladies and gentlemen, we would like to encourage you to view all of the students' artwork before you leave this evening. Several have been awarded prizes for their outstanding efforts and we would like to draw your attention to those. Please feel free to roam about the room and enjoy this special event. We have refreshments in the media center for your enjoyment as well."

Chad and Thad Marek made an immediate dash for the hallway to the media center as the crowd broke apart to tour the exhibits. Flashes continued to pop from cameras and cell phones in the other areas of the large court, parents hurriedly posing their children in front of their masterpieces. Mathew Tansels, whose three-headed phoenix creation had been awarded "Most Original Art Piece", was extolling his win to his father's video camera, as he pointed to the blue ribbon pinned to his clay soda can. His mother beamed with pride. Mrs. Wagner overheard Mathew's documentary and slapped her forehead, grimacing. She had been out-voted four-to-one on the young artist's award during the impromptu voting by the Committee that night.

"T.J., why don't you show us your painting," Mrs. Finnel said, as she led the family down the steps from the stage. She was anxious to get out of the spotlight.

T.J. led his family through the crowd of parents and students. As they threaded their way through exhibits, whispers followed them. Markus was the only one who seemed to be enjoying the attention. He smiled broadly and waved to a few friends.

Markus Finnel's dream was to become a famous magician. Though only eight, he was most at home in front of a crowd of people. Being up on stage this evening had been something he had dreamed of. He should have brought a few card tricks with him, he thought, disappointed it hadn't occurred to him before. But then, he didn't know they would all be called to the stage. From now on he vowed to have a traveling magic show with him at all times. This thought thrilled him, and he bounced ahead into the crowd.

"Something seems to be happening up ahead," Marsha Finnel commented, as they rounded a large table of sculpture exhibits.

Markus had noticed the commotion too, and pushed through the people, not wanting to miss anything. When T.J., along with his mother and father, finally caught up with his little brother, they stopped abruptly and stood gaping, along with a dozen parents and students.

Everyone was standing in the 6th grade art section. Here, the paintings of seventy-five students hung on ten separate partitions, each labeled with the artist's name, age, and the medium with which the painting had been rendered. The astonished crowd was focused on T.J.'s copy of the self-portrait Rembrandt, the famous 17th Century artist, had painted of himself. T.J. caught sight of his painting and his heart began to falter.

"Oh crraaappp!" T.J. moaned to himself.

Chapter Fourteen

INTO OUR WORLD

As T.J. and the shocked throng of people at the school Art Show looked on, the distinguished face of Rembrandt, one of the world's foremost artists, began to change. First a large red clown's nose appeared where the gentleman's regular nose had been. The rims of a pair of large black glasses began to show around the painting's eyes. The shocked murmurs of the watching crowd grew. No one saw the ghost of Leonardo Da Vinci, palette in hand, flourishing his brush as he worked to transform T.J.'s painting. As T.J. watched in horror, the famous ghost quickly added orange curly hair, spilling out from under Rembrandt's hat, and enlarged the man's ears to gigantic proportions. As a final assault, he painted the lips a bright purple.

All this had been quickly done. Even the students who had teased T.J. mercilessly about his ghosts stood with open mouths as they stared at the ridiculous painting. Mrs. Wagner, who had pushed her way through the crowd to see what all the fuss was about, came to an abrupt halt before the disfigured painting. Her face became infused with the color of over-ripened eggplant, and the vein in her forehead, which had been a pale red twig beneath the surface of her tight skin, was now the size of a branch, threatening to burst from her face. She turned toward T.J., who was praying the floor would open up, and dump him immediately into the belly of the basement beneath the elementary school.

"Is this your idea of a *JOKE?*" she exploded, not caring who heard her. "How *dare* you make a mockery of this art show!"

"Oh look," Da Vinci's ghost said, as he wiped his painted fingers on his already soiled tunic. "The windbag is back. I think a bright red nose would do wonders for her as well. The drab female could use a little color…something to match that red vein that looks like a road map across her forehead. What do you think, boy?"

"No!" T.J. cried out.

"No?" Mrs. Wagner shouted. "Then what would you call it? These students have worked hard for this evening's showing. I want that picture removed immediately! I will take your conduct up with the school board on Monday!"

"Why so upset?" Leonardo's ghost asked innocently. "Rembrandt was always dull. The man wore funny little hats that would have looked better on a child's doll. And those mustaches! You could hide a day's lunch in them! I was just having a little fun with him, that's all."

The ghost floated off through the crowd, his foul odor trailing after him. Several people sniffed the air and frowned; closely eyeing whomever was standing next to them.

T.J. turned suddenly and bolted for the boy's bathroom on the other side of the partitions. This evening had been ten times worse than he feared it would be. He would never hear the end of this. He slammed into the bathroom door and ran toward an open stall. Several boys who were loitering near the sinks jumped as the boy banged the stall door closed.

The ghost of Leonardo followed T.J. into the bathroom, eyeing the gleaming porcelain sinks and metal doors with interest. This new world was exciting to him. It was like Christmas morning every time he turned around.

T.J. bolted his stall door and leaned upon it, his head hung in dejection. He was trying to figure out just how long he could hide out in the boy's room.

The sound of a toilet flushing filled the room. T.J. thought nothing of it, until it flushed again, and again. Then he heard the familiar laugh of the ghost who had been tormenting him. He rushed from the stall and approached the one next to him.

"What are you doing in there?" he whispered hoarsely through the closed bathroom stall.

"What do you think I'm doin'?" called the indignant voice of a small boy. "Get away from my door, you Sicko!"

Embarrassed, T.J. crossed to the next stall and could immediately smell the ghost's rank odor—and if you could detect it over the other foul smells emanating from the toilets, that was really saying something. The toilet was flushing over, and over. T.J. could see water flying out from under the metal door.

"Knock it off!" T.J. hissed through the door. "What are you *doing?*"

"Making the white paper go down the hole!" Leonardo shouted out with delight. "You can put one end of the paper into the bowl, and when you push down the handle the swirling water unwraps the whole thing as it empties!"

"NOOOOO! Don't do that!!! You will clog it up and....." T.J. did not finish. At that moment a sound very much like a belching whale sounded, and the toilet erupted, sending water and globs of wet toilet tissue flooding out into the bathroom from beneath the stall door.

The small voice called out from the next stall. *"What the crap are you doing?* These are my church pants and my Mom will *kill* me...."

He was interrupted by the sound of five exploding toilets. Water washed out onto the tiled floor as though a dam had broken. Boys bolted for the door, slipping and sliding as they went. Anguished cries rose above the bathroom stalls as the imprisoned victims grabbed up their soggy pants, and made a hasty retreat.

Parents stared in disbelief as seven young boys slogged out into the courtyard, their shoes squeaking, and their pants leaving a trail of water. Toilet water spread out through the open bathroom door and into the courtyard. People moved hurriedly to avoid stepping in it.

T.J. was the last one to exit the bathroom. His tennis shoes made a squashing sound as he moved quickly through the astonished crowd of people. Without looking up, he made his way along the far wall until he reached the double doors leading outside. Leaning his shoulder into one, he shoved it open and hurried out of the building. Just as the door was swinging closed, he heard Mrs. Phillips's voice booming over the loud speaker.

"Mr. Hiverson? Could we have your clean-up crew over to the boy's bathroom in the courtyard, please? *Pronto!* And the person responsible for carving the three-foot-tall face of the *Mona Lisa* out of Cook Grimson's butter bars, please report to the kitchen!"

A ray of moonlight penetrated the skylight, finally appearing from between the clouds, which had hung around for most of the evening. It fell like a spotlight on the paintings by Dillon Finnel, all except the rendering of *Cassiopeia, the Queen*, which was at one end of the display, and outside the reach of the moonlight. The other paintings sparkled with an eerie glow, and several people who had been standing close to the easels began to back away; a strange uneasiness overcoming them. It was at this time the remaining body of guests hurriedly left, nervously glancing over their shoulders as they did so.

David and Marsha Finnel grabbed Markus. As they made their way toward the exit doors, T.J.'s mother glanced apprehensively at her father-in-law's paintings. The artwork titled *The Crone* seemed to be coming to life; the ocean waves were actually tossing, and she thought she saw a seagull sailing through the mist. The crowd had thinned out considerably, leaving the refreshments largely untouched.

The Finnels caught up with T.J. outside as he tried to conceal himself behind a giant oak near the parking lot.

"I want to walk to Grandpa's," T.J. announced. He knew his father would be angry about the antics associated with his Rembrandt painting.

In truth, T.J.'s father was steaming. David Finnel had overheard whispered conversations all morning as he walked the small town of Coven Bay looking for a job. There were growing rumors that his father was keeping company with a ghost. Tonight's antics at the school seemed to confirm something was going on. The Principal had even hinted at it from the stage tonight! And to top it all off, his father, the guest of honor, didn't even show up. Being the laughing stock of the town was not something he enjoyed. He was having a hard enough time finding a job.

"Honey, it's dark out," T.J.'s mother objected. "I don't want you walking through that dark ole park at night."

T.J.'s mother was looking back at the school doors as if worrying something from her father-in-law's paintings might come after them. She watched as Mr. Hiverson propped them open to allow the rush of people to leave.

"Marsha, it's only thirty minutes to Dad's house," Mr. Finnel said irritably, as he led the way to their car. "Quit babying him. Let him walk if he wants to."

Marsha glanced over at Markus who had stopped to talk to some friends. T.J. was inching away toward the park entrance, out of ear shot. She lowered her voice and spoke to her husband across the hood of the car.

"Look, I know you've got a lot on your mind...we all do. But beating T.J. down is not how to handle it. He's not you. He doesn't care about sports. I get that Markus is more inside your comfort zone because he loves playing ball as much as you do, but T.J. needs you to accept him and love him. I can't keep watching you hurt him."

David stared at her for a moment and she saw his shoulders sag. A deep sigh welled up from within him. He looked as if life had defeated him.

"I'm sorry," he said tiredly. "I'm not sure why I come down hard on him. I'm under a lot of stress. I just don't seem to know how to relate to him. I don't know...maybe...a part of me is a little jealous of him."

"Jealous?" Marsha said in shock. "Of T.J.? Jealous of what?"
"How close he and Dad are. I never got all the science, artsy stuff...and the stars he's so crazy about. Dad and I never, well, *clicked*. We were very different. Being here was the last thing I wanted. Plus, it's embarrassing for me to have Dad see me not taking care of my family."

Marsha seized this rare opportunity when her husband was finally opening up to her to voice her concerns.

"David, your dad loves you. He knows jobs are scarce right now...for everybody. Just cut T.J. some slack. He's a great kid!" She paused, glanced again at the open doors leading into the school courtyard, and said, "But listen, there's also something else we need to focus on....the paintings...something is wrong with them...," she began, but the exhausted look her husband shot at her quelled her need to take it any further. She sighed and got into the car. Markus bounded over and jumped into the back seat.

"So what's up with Grandpa?" he asked. "Why didn't he come?"
"Markus...," his father said, ignoring the question, "...have you seen your grandpa today? Do you know anything you're not telling us?"

The boy panicked, remembering his magic liquid and spilling it onto his grandfather's paints. He knew better than to be messing around in his studio; it was off-limits unless his grandfather was there with him. If he confessed, he would be in trouble. They would probably take the swell stuff in the bottle away from him as well. And if he told about the creature that attacked the window when he was up there, it would be admitting he had been in the attic to start with...and he was back in trouble. *Besides, what could any of that have to do with Grandpa not showing up tonight at the school?*

"I haven't seen him today," Markus said truthfully, and left it at that.

T.J. ran across the street toward the park entrance. Some other kids were using the park as a shortcut home as well, their shapes resembling dark ghosts flitting ahead of him. Pieces of their conversation trailed back to him on the breeze. He could hear the voices of Serenity and Ashley Portman:

"Those were the creepiest..." "How'd you like to have him for a grandfather?" "T.J.'s just as weird..." "Can't even play sports..."

Short bursts of laughter floated on the air as T.J. walked beneath the rusting arched entrance bearing the name Grimlett Park in twisted metal letters; the words looking as though a giant spider had spun them from black, iron thread.

Back at the school, the last remaining guests were brushing cookie crumbs from their shirtfronts and taking one last look at the strange paintings. The faculty was picking up discarded paper cups and straightening tilted artwork. The cloud cover outside had passed. Moonlight was playing brightly through the skylights upon Dillon Finnel's paintings.

The constellation of stars in the painting titled *The Siglets* began to swirl, several bodies taking shape. As one man turned his back to leave, the pink wings of one of the creatures in the painting fluttered, and pulled slightly out of the landscape. It turned its green squat head and looked out into the room with blue, sparkling eyes.

Mr. Saunters, the Audio/Visual teacher, was disconnecting the PA system. He failed to notice the green-bodied creature spring from the oil painting and take flight. It instinctively headed for the skylight, the huge golden moon visible through the window. With a dull *thunk* its wings hit the glass, and it bounced away. Emitting a thin, high-pitched squeal, it circled and followed the scent of night air to the open school doors.

"What was that?" Mrs. Phillips asked, looking up from the courtyard floor.

"What was what?" Mr. Bryman, the English teacher asked, as he helped coil the cable to the speakers.

"That screeching sound."

"Probably the mic again," he said, yawning widely. "Let's pack up and get out of here," he said. "Maybe we can live down this whole evening by doing a smash-up job on the end-of-the-year carnival."

Mrs. Phillips was watching a large, flapping shadow disappear out the entrance doors, while another Siglet exited the painting.

"Well whatever we do, I think we should shut the doors. Some large birds are getting in here," she said nervously, as she finished up. No one hurried to close them as the tired teachers left the area.

Mr. Hiverson, the school custodian, shut the indoor courtyard lights off, section-by-section, until only the ones by the double doors remained on. The moonlight still shone through the skylights onto the artwork below. Shouts of "good night" and the sound of slamming doors could be heard down the school hallways, as teachers retrieved their belongings from their rooms, and departed through the side exits. Mr. Hiverson was busily sweeping the courtyard floors by the open doors, anxious to get home and put his feet up.

Dillon Finnel's middle painting squirmed in the moonlight. The lettering adorning the bottom of the artwork read *The Crone*. Stars in the constellation shimmered as the canvas began to glow. The image in the painting vibrated, as its twisted form began to lift from the painting. It was the figure of a hunched hag, wearing a long, gray tattered gown. Her white hair, matted and hanging in stringy disarray, framed a face that was startling. A cavernous hole, where once a mouth had been, hung open in a silent scream.

The creature paused in the painting, her red eye watching the bent back of the janitor; moonlight casting the man's shadow behind him as he tiredly swept the gritty floors.

Curling crippled fingers into fists, the Crone stepped from the painting and floated silently to the tile. She glided soundlessly over to the man who swept with a wide arc at the cookie crumbs, and shattered leaves that had blown in through the open doorway. The janitor's keys glistened in the moonlight; jingling from his back pocket as he moved about. The key ring held over fifty keys to the doors of the school, and several other buildings in town he took care of after everyone had gone home. Mr. Hiverson's keys could unlock virtually any business in Coven Bay.

Suddenly the sound of a barking dog shot through the large indoor courtyard, echoing off the polished walls. The janitor jumped and turned toward the sound. It had come from the stage area. "How in the world did a dog get in here without my seeing it?" he muttered, his heart pounding. The animal sounded ferocious. He walked gingerly toward the direction of the incessant barking, brandishing his broom in front of him like a sword.

As Mr. Hiverson neared the noise, he realized it was *not* coming from the stage; it was coming from the third of Dillon Finnel's paintings titled *Canis Major,* which was now reverberating with the sound of a madly barking dog. He watched in astonishment as the stars in the painting suddenly morphed into the image of an enormous canine. The large animal in the painting turned its head to look out upon the room, drool dripping from its chops. His hackles were raised, and his eyes were squinted in fierce concentration.

Mr. Hiverson fell back, his broom clattering to the floor. Before he could recover, the large black dog leapt from the painting, his jaws snapping, as he took off out the open doors.

The Crone took advantage of the distraction and moved into position behind the frail janitor. The old man whirled around to face the tall floating creature, her mouth gaping open before him. A terrified scream came from him as he stumbled back, one frail hand pressed to his heart. He could not take his eyes from the hideous sight of the hag's glowing red eye.

The Crone floated closer to the cowering man. Mr. Hiverson felt as though his soul was being sucked from him by the strange red light emanating from her eye as the room spun in dizzying blackness. Only the red stream of light penetrated it, as it fixated on the old man's bulging eyes. The Crone could see images shooting toward her as she sucked Hiverson's memories, adding them to her own. Beginning with the last thing the old man had seen, they went backwards. Thus, the image of a large black dog leaping from the canvas shot toward her, followed by a vision of the janitor sweeping the floor, and cleaning up the boy's bathroom after the evening's toilet explosion. She saw him setting up chairs for the Art Fair, and then a vision of the old man pulling a ring of keys from his back pocket and unlocking the door of a red brick building earlier that day, flashed toward her. *Coven Bay Library* was chiseled into the stone plaque above the building's glossy red doors. Through Hiverson's memories, the Crone saw him sweeping the worn wooden floors in a room where books were piled high to the ceiling in rickety bookcases. The janitor neatened piles of magazines, and finally stopped to straighten a pile of old maps scattered about on the long reading table in the center of the library room.

Maps! The Crone thought excitedly. These could be of use to her! She needed to find the well she was sure Morble had come through. Her missing eye and the Dark Orb must be here somewhere. At that point the old man's visual memory began going farther back, beginning with the prior day. This did not interest the Crone at the moment. She had seen what she needed.

Moaning in pain, the old man withered before her. As his knees buckled beneath him, he saw with horror his vision was becoming tunnel-like. He felt the ring of keys being lifted from his back pocket. The light around him was shrinking to a pin-point of brightness. The last thing he remembered was his sight leaving him. He was totally blind.

Chapter Fifteen

LOOK WHAT FOLLOWED ME HOME!

T.J. was aware something was moving behind him in the bushes as he made his way through the dark shadows of Grimlett Park. The anger and embarrassment that had propelled him into the park, and away from his disapproving father after the Art Fair disaster, had dissipated under a new feeling...fear. He had tried to keep close to the group of kids ahead of him, but they had broken out into a sprint, and disappeared through the tall oak trees, dotting the park like towering tombstones, leaving him alone in the shadows.

There seemed to be sounds coming from everywhere. A twig would snap, or a dry branch rustle each time he moved a few feet along the path. Several times he would stop suddenly and whirl around, expecting to see the Marek brothers sneaking up on him. But the only thing moving were the restless leaves as a light breeze moved the clouds in hurried wisps across the bobbing moon. A fierce rainstorm the night before had ripped foliage from the branches of the towering elms, boldly guarding the two gated entrances that led into, and out of, the park.

"I know that's you, Chad and Thad!" T.J. called out, not quite as confident as he tried to sound. "Why don't you goons get a life? Go scare Old Man Harmon...he's more your speed!"

T.J. eyed the dark bushes for a few moments and then moved on, glancing nervously over his shoulder as the noises continued. Twice he thought he heard the sound of jingling keys. For the hundredth time he cursed the fact they were now living in his grandfather's house. If they were still living at home, he would have taken the opposite route, leaving the park far behind.

Then he saw it. A tall dark figure in flowing robes darted behind a large oak. Heart pounding, T.J. froze and strained to see the thick base of the tree in the blackness. Perhaps it had been a trick of light cast by the cloud-streaked moon, he reasoned. Voices seemed to whisper on the breeze; brittle leaves blew across the black grass, tumbling over each other like cackling witches.

Something suddenly flapped near his hair, the breath from its wings actually moving his bangs. Instinctively he swatted at it. Looking up, he saw a large shape, wings beating the air, and circling back around. It was much larger than the bats that frequented the park at night; larger than the birds he was used to seeing around here. Without looking back, he began running toward the arch at the other end of the park. The sound of other flying things accumulated overhead, and he doubled his speed. He could see the street lamp shedding its yellow glow on Hawthorn Drive. If he could make it to the light, he would be only about fifteen minutes from his grandfather's house.

The pounding of his running feet filled his head as he darted around swing sets, their chained seats moving eerily in the night breeze as though phantom children were pumping their short legs. He hurdled a teeter-totter, caught his soggy shoelace on one of its handles, and came crashing to the ground, his tooth biting painfully into his lower lip. The copper taste of blood salted his tongue as he jumped up quickly to stare behind him. His ribs hurt and his pounding heart felt as if it would burst out of his chest. Something off to the right slipped hurriedly behind a group of pines, long garments sweeping the crackling leaves behind it. The soft sound of keys clinking against each other reached the boy's ears.

Suddenly a bright red eye peered at him in the darkness. He froze to the spot. It couldn't be that of an animal as the eye was up too high. It was coming closer to him, a strange glow piercing the night.

Taking great gulps of air, T.J. could feel his heart pounding in his throat. A twig snapped. No longer believing it was Chad or Thad

Marek, he turned and made a dash for the park arch, and the welcoming glow of the streetlight beyond. He was too scared to look behind himself to see if the eye was following him.

He shot out of the park and sprinted across Hawthorn Drive, streaking past the Coven Bay Library. He cut through Mr. Bigmen's front yard and up Bitterbrush until he finally came to his grandpa's driveway at 1418. He heard the sound of beating wings overhead as he ran into his grandpa's side yard, and raced for safety through the back kitchen door.

His mother looked up in surprise as T.J. burst into the kitchen. She was standing at the oven, removing a steaming pan of lasagna. It had been cooking while the family was at the Art Fair. The house smelled wonderfully of basil, tomato sauce, and cheese. Marsha Finnel turned off the time bake on the stove, and paused to look in dismay at her disheveled son. Leaves and twigs were tangled in his thick brown hair, and his face was badly scratched. His lip was three sizes bigger than normal.

"What in the world are you doing?" she asked, setting the pan on the burners. "Is your mouth bleeding?"

Slipping off her oven mitts she crossed the kitchen to her son and tipped his head back to get a better look at his face.

"Please tell me you weren't fighting with those awful Marek boys, Thackery James Finnel! This night has been hideous enough without you brawling like an alley cat."

She pulled him over to the sink, wetted a paper towel, and pressed it gently to his swollen lip.

"Well?" she asked, as she tossed the red-stained towel into the garbage. "Who were you fighting with?"

T.J. was looking past her shoulder out the kitchen window into the darkness. Something had definitely moved on the other side of the glass.

"Thackery James, I'm talking to you!"

"What?" he stammered, keeping his eyes on the window.

She turned to look behind her.

"What are you staring at?" she asked, leaning across the sink to peer out the window that faced the street outside. "Did whomever you were fighting with follow you home? Well, we'll just see about that!"

She grabbed a broom and headed for the back door that led into the side yard.

"No! Mom, wait!" T.J. yelled, making a grab for the broom as she marched past him. "Don't go out there!"

"I'm not afraid of some eleven-year-old who thinks he's the Hulk!" she barked. Flinging open the kitchen door, she disappeared into the darkness.

"Hey, cool lip!" Markus said, suddenly entering the kitchen from the back stairs. "Chad or Thad Marek give you that? Where's Mom? I'm starving!" He poked a stubby finger into the lasagna's melted cheese topping, and jumped back, blowing on his burned fingertip. "Kinda hot," he said sheepishly, sucking the injured digit.

"Go get Dad, Mark," T.J. ordered, as he flipped on the outside porch light.

"Why?" he asked him, leaning over the lasagna and inhaling deeply.

"Just do it!" T.J. darted out into the side yard, searching the sky overhead for flying shapes. Just then his mother came around the corner of the house, broom dragging behind her.

"The little coward took off," she said, as she passed T.J. and entered the house.

"Who took off?" T.J. asked in alarm, as he followed her in, locking the back door behind him.

The large parrot began squawking from inside his new cage standing in the corner of the kitchen.

"Awk, coward took off, coward took off!"

"Shut up, Harper!" T.J. barked. The parrot clamped its beak closed with a "snap".

"Who took off?" Markus echoed as he grabbed a large spoon from the silverware drawer.

"I don't know," Marsha Finnel said. "I just saw his shadow run into the front yard. By the time I got there, he was gone. This boy must be quite a bit taller than you, Teej," she said. "His shadow didn't look like any eleven- or twelve-year old boy I've ever seen…and he had some kind of blinking red light."

She crossed to the sink and lathered up her hands. "You boys go wash up. Markus David Finnel, don't you dare stick that spoon into my lasagna! You go wash your hands and call your father for dinner while I dish up the food." She glanced up at the clock above the sink where Elvis was gyrating along with the sweep hand. "Goodness, it's already after nine o'clock." She glanced at her older son. "And, T.J., please don't tell your father you got that lip in a fight tonight," she continued. "He's still pretty upset about the whole evening."

"I didn't get in a fight," T.J. muttered to himself.

His mother looked at T.J. fondly and ruffled his hair with her hand.

"T.J., your Dad has a hard time with all these ghost rumors. He's afraid all this hocus pocus stuff will affect his getting a job someplace. We've had three calls from your school about odd things happening around you, and now your grandpa is missing. He still isn't answering his cell phone Do you want to explain what was happening with your painting tonight at school?"

"You won't believe me if I tell you," he said dejectedly. "I'll tell you later but just know that the stuff happening at school is not my fault!"

As T.J. saw the worried look on his mother's face, he sighed.

"I'm sure Grandpa is fine," he said, going back to a safer subject. "He's probably down at Coven Bay sketching the boats in the moonlight at Fairgate's Tavern, talking ships like he always does. He loses track of time when he's working on something. Remember when he missed his own birthday party last month? I guess the Art Fair just slipped his mind."

Even as he said the words, he knew they didn't ring true. His grandfather would never miss the art exhibit. He had been working on those paintings for months. T.J. walked away, a scowl furrowing his forehead. His hands were dirty and covered with scrapes. Entering the guest bathroom, he slammed the door behind himself and locked it. He just wanted to be left alone for a few minutes.

He snatched up the soap bar and looked into the mirror. Outside the locked door he could hear his mother screaming at Markus to stop leaving the front door wide open.

T.J.'s reflection surprised him. His face was streaked with dirt, bits of leaves dotted his hair like snowflakes, and his bottom lip looked like a fat garden slug. He tested it gently with his tongue; the inside tissue felt like raw hamburger.

Sighing, he flipped on the hot water to full blast. Steam rose in wisps before him, streaking the mirror with mist. He lathered his hands and winced as the hot water found every cut and scrape on his palms and knuckles. Fearing the pain in his lip would be too intense to handle a washing, he opted to gently dab it with a moist cloth.

As T.J. stared at his lip in the mirror, he saw a glint of red near the window to his left. Whirling around, he searched for any sign of movement. *Had it been on the inside or outside of the window?* he thought, his heart hammering.

Jerking the faucets off, he bolted for the door, flipped the lock over, and throwing it open, raced into the hallway and toward the kitchen. As he rounded the corner he collided full force into Markus who had just come in the front door, leaving it open again as he called his father to dinner.

"Crimination!" Markus yelled, as he pulled himself off the floor. "What are you running from, you big door-knob?"

"Mark! Come here, quick. Look in the bathroom and tell me if you see anything," T.J. gasped, as he jerked his younger brother toward the open door.

"Oh no you don't!" Markus cried, trying to free his arm from his brother's grasp. "I know this joke! You've got a big brown floatie in the toilet you want me to see. No way I'm goin' in there!"

"No, honest. You can stay out here in the hallway. Just peek in and tell me if anyone else is in there."

Markus looked at his brother as though he had just sprouted moose antlers.

"If anyone *else* is in there?" he repeated after T.J.

"Yeah. Anyone or any...*thing*."

"Ok. You got a fat lip and a bonk on the noggin' tonight," Markus said sagely. "Let's let it go at that, goof-ball. As for me, I'm goin' to dinner. It's probably one of your ghosts the kids at school says are followin' you around. Maybe the ghosts like potty humor!" He bolted down the hall before T.J. could grab him.

"I don't have 'ghosts'!" he yelled. "I just have the one smelly one!"

Swallowing hard, T.J. poked his head into the bathroom. Everything looked as it usually did. The towel he had dropped in his hurry to escape still lay on the floor. *Had it just been my imagination? Maybe that spooky painting of Grandpa's at the art show is getting to me. Probably just Da Vinci messing around,* T.J. thought, as he walked off down the hall.

"T.J.! Dinner!" his mother called from the kitchen.

"Awk! Din-din, T.J. Din-din!" cried the irritating parrot.

His father came into the house through the open front door, slamming it behind himself. He had been looking around the yard for any sign of Dillon, even though he was sure his father was gone. What concerned him most was that his dad's old Lincoln was still parked in the gravel driveway. He walked past his oldest son without a word. Crushed, T.J. shuffled into the kitchen, taking his place at the dinette table.

The round kitchen table sat in a corner flanked by Bay windows overlooking the back yard, side yard and front of the house. T.J. picked at his food as he quietly watched the shadows cast by the white glare of the porch light onto the lawn chairs and patio furniture. The lights from the neighboring house came on, and he could see the outline of the fence separating the modern home next door from the Finnel's antique.

"So...," Markus mumbled, his mouth stuffed with lasagna, "...can I stay up a little while more since it's late already, and watch some TV?" He glanced at the clock. Nightmare Theater would be starting in an hour.

"We'll see," his mother said tiredly. "But no scary shows!"

Markus was undeterred. If his parents were still awake when his favorite show came on, he would simply go to his room, retrieve his binoculars, and watch the show through the window of Corey Greenman's room across the street. Corey's parents had no TV restrictions, and the kid was happy to angle the television set to where Markus could see it—and enable the closed caption feature.

"Well," Markus said, ripping into the garlic bread with gusto, "I like the new paintings...very cool! They would make a good backdrop for my magic shows."

T.J. moaned and said nothing. Just then something moved across the patio. T.J. saw the shadow from the lawn chair break apart and expand, as some tall thing moved across its path. He followed its movement across the back yard until he could no longer see it from the window nearest him.

"What are you looking at?" his father asked him absently. "And what happened to your lip?"

Marsha sighed. She could not believe her husband had just now noticed their son's lower lip was the size of a polish sausage.

"Nothing," T.J. said, meaning both his lip, and what had captured his attention outside the window, but his heart was racing.

David caught the look his wife was giving him. He reached over to T.J.'s face and tipped it back to get a better look at his son's lip.

"That's a respectable fat lip ya got there," his father said, a kinder tone threading his words. "Put some ice on it after dinner, ok?"

T.J. ran his tongue over the raw tissue on the underside of his lip, and nodded, managing a grateful grin, and then looked back outside.

Markus, who had seen the shadow move as well, suddenly slid his chair back and bolted for the door, wiping tomato paste from his lips onto his sleeve as he went.

"Markus Finnel, you get right back here and eat your dinner!" his mother scolded.

"Something's in the back yard," Markus said excitedly. "Maybe it's a new pet!"

"No more pets!" Marsha cried, but the boy was already racing across the room.

Before T.J. could stop him, Markus had thrown open the kitchen door, and raced out into the yard.

"Markus, shut the…," Mrs. Finnel began. "Oh for Pete's sake. I hope he doesn't hurt whatever poor thing he comes across," she said, watching the action from the kitchen window. "I swear this family is getting stranger every day."

Sounds of the eight-year-old crashing wildly through the bushes and garden in his effort to capture a fleeing animal could be heard from inside the kitchen.

Markus's scream suddenly split the air.

"Guess new pet has teeth," Harper, the parrot, chuckled.

Mr. and Mrs. Finnel were on their feet in a second and running for the open door. But before they could pass through it, a flock of creatures suddenly flew into the kitchen with high-pitched squeals.

Chapter Sixteen

THE SIGLETS

"David!" Mrs. Finnel screamed, as a dozen or more green-bodied creatures, with pink wings and red tufts of hair running along their backs, crashed into kitchen cabinets, and perched on light fixtures.

Markus entered the open door, chest heaving, and clinging to a large cat.

"They look just like the ones in Grandpa's painting," he panted. "The ones called *The Siglets!*"

The shriveled faces with glittering eyes peered at the four Finnels. Then, as if on cue, they began to tear apart the house. Canisters of flour spilled onto the floor; the lasagna pan was up-ended as it crashed to the tile, leaving a trail of tomato sauce running down the front of the oven. One goblin-faced creature was riding a wet bar of soap down the length of the kitchen counter top. Another was jumping up and down on an overturned plastic bottle of blue liquid dishwashing soap. Spurts of blue gel hit the cabinets, walls and appliances; a small blob sailing through the bars of the parrot's cage, and hitting Harper squarely in the left eye. The parrot stiffened, sucked in its beak, and dramatically wiped the sticky liquid from his inflamed eye with his wing.

"Awk...funny...*really* funny!" He flipped the blue gel away from his wing, where it then landed on Markus's nose.

A loud grinding noise filled the air, as forks in the running sink disposal twirled around, and around. Other sounds of destruction could be heard coming from the living room, as books were torn from bookshelves, and vases were tossed to the floor. Thuds and crashing noises came from upstairs.

"They're in my room!" T.J. yelled, bolting for the back kitchen stairs leading to the second floor landing. "They might hurt Popeye!" The boy hesitated at the base of the stairs, his heart pounding. The thought of his lizard being torn apart by the flying creatures' sharp claws finally gave him the courage to run up the staircase.

"T.J.! You get back here!" his mother screamed, but the boy had disappeared up the stairs. "David, do something!" she screamed, as another flying creature tore through the dining room, opening the doors to the hutch where Agatha Finnel's fine china was kept.

"Meoarrrrrrrrowwwwwww!"

Suddenly the guttural sound of a large cat echoed throughout the kitchen. Mr. and Mrs. Finnel turned toward the sound. It was coming from the enormous orange-and-black tabby Markus was holding. The cat's fur was bristling; its eyes squinted in concentration as its tail twitched furiously.

"Go get 'em, Kitty!" Markus yelled, as he lobbed the cat toward the kitchen. The air-borne feline hit the tile floor, skidding to a stop before the frightened face of a green-bodied creature whose blue eyes threatened to bulge right out of its head.

Terrified squeals filled the house as the cat pounced, chased, and scratched its way through a half-dozen scampering goblins; their pink wings beating against walls and windows in their haste to flee the room.

"For a fat kitty, he's gotta lot'a spring in him!" Markus said proudly, as the plump feline leapt atop a kitchen counter.

More creatures came flying down the staircase with T.J. in hot pursuit, wielding a giant tennis shoe. Mrs. Finnel ducked as one after another of the Siglets beat a hasty retreat out the open back door. She looked up to see one of the creatures clasping her red ruby broach in its claws, the gold chain dangling.

"My broach!" she yelled, as she watched in dismay as the Siglet flew out the open door carrying the glittering jewelry.

"Hey! Gimme back my ball!" Markus yelled, as another Siglet made for the yard with the boy's round silver-painted baseball clutched in its sharp claws.

The cat managed to pounce on one of the winged creatures, but it bit the feline's paw and hastily scampered under the table, and then out the door before it took flight. The last the Finnel family saw of the Siglets, they were flying crookedly over the side fence into the evening sky.

"Well that got 'em!" Markus said proudly, scratching the ears of the panting cat. "Good Ole Kitty! He's a good Kitty, yes he is...he's a Hero, aren't you? I think I will call him Walburg!"

"Oh yeah...AWK...the kitty whose stomach looks like he ate the neighbors is the Hero!" Harper squawked. "How 'bout the blind parrot? Huh? How 'bout the poor feathered friend who will have to spend his days on a street corner with a tin cup and a seeing-eye Finch?" Harper spit out the last bit of blue gel soap onto the newspapers lining his cage. His left eye was swollen almost shut—the only part showing was bloodshot and watery.

T.J. crossed over to his little brother who was cradling the heaving cat. A blue velvet ribbon encircled the animal's neck, barely visible in the mound of fine hair. A small gold name tag twinkled beneath the kitchen light, as the boy lifted it out of the fur, and read the single word: *Theops*.

"I think you might want to rethink Kitty's name," T.J. said, showing the tag to Markus. "What we have here is yet another escaped constellation from the 'Strange and Unusual World of Dillon Finnel.' This cat is from one of the paintings at the school tonight."

Mr. Finnel, overhearing his son, stormed over and grabbed the cat's name tag from T.J.'s hand. He stared at the lettering sparkling in the light. His chest heaving, he let the tag fall, and marched over to the sink, heatedly turning off the garbage disposal. The sudden silence made their ears throb. Mrs. Finnel quickly shut, and locked the back door.

"I don't understand what just happened," she moaned, surveying her ruined kitchen.

"I'm telling you, Mom, those were the little green guys from one of Grandpa's paintings!" Markus set the cat down, and turned toward the windows overlooking the back yard. It was too dark to see anything that fell outside the porch light's reach.

Theops sat down next to the birdcage and began grooming himself. He was tenderly licking a small scratch on his right paw when he felt something wet plop onto his head. The cat looked up to see Harper whistling innocently from his perch near the bars overlooking the feline. Theops squinted at the parrot suspiciously, and then ran a paw over the wad of spit that lay atop his furry head.

"Mom...," T.J. began timidly. "I don't know how to tell you this, but Markus is right. Grandpa told me Harper over there is...well...part of one of his paintings that somehow came to life. He's from a painting of the stars called *Toucana*." He paused, waiting for the fireworks.

T.J.'s mother and father turned in unison to look at the parrot who stared back at them in feigned innocence. Harper shrugged his feathered shoulders and smiled.

"See?" Markus shouted triumphantly. "I told you! This is so awesome! Does Grandpa have any paintings of vampires?" he asked hopefully.

"Markus, please," Mrs. Finnel said, still staring in shock at the parrot who was grooming his claws.

"Fine! We will just have to ask Grandpa," Markus stated, plopping a blob of lasagna dripping from the light fixture, into his mouth.

A soft *pffttt* sound came from the direction of Harper's cage. The parrot looked down to see a dollop of spit resting on his freshly groomed claws. Theops wiped his mouth with the back of his paw, and sauntered happily away.

"I don't know what's going on here, or what those were," Mr. Finnel said angrily, as he wiped down the blue gel from the cabinets, "but if you think I'm going to buy the story that the bird over there is from a painting…," he stopped, a nervous tremor showing in his face. "As for those flying things, I hope I never see them again. What a mess! How bad is it upstairs, Teej?" he asked his oldest son. He needed to focus on something he could control right now as his mind swam trying to understand the night's events.

T.J. was silently watching the back yard. A red eye was staring at the house from the protection of the forest. It blinked and disappeared. It then appeared again to the right of the patio. His heart hammered. He was about to turn to tell his parents, when he realized how his father would react if he told him about more phantoms hanging around the house. When the eye did not reappear, he pried himself away from the window.

"We should probably make sure the doors are locked," he said, almost to himself, feeling his body tremble. Chasing flying pink uglies was all the adventure he wanted for one evening.

"I already did…," his mother muttered, trying to remove tomato sauce from the oven door, "…if I could just get Markus to keep from leaving them wide open." She turned her attention to her older son. "Teej? Your father asked you how badly the upstairs got hit?"

"It was weird," he said absently, turning back to watch the window. "They were going through all the rooms…it's like they were looking for something. Then they flew into Markus's room, and grabbed that silver-coated baseball of his. One of them was clawing at his floorboard." Markus's eyes flew open wide.

"They took my mother's ruby broach that I had made into a necklace," Marsha whined. "What would they want with it? It isn't a real ruby. My mother loved that thing, and now it's gone!" She wiped her eyes and scrubbed harder at the drying tomato paste.

Mr. Finnel went upstairs to check the damage, and to see if anything else was missing.

"And why steal a dumb ole baseball?" T.J. asked.

"It's not dumb!" Markus retorted. "It's part of my Disappearing Treasure act! It's supposed to be silver." He suddenly bolted for the stairs leading up to his room to check on his hiding place for the magic liquid he had stashed beneath a floorboard.

Forked lightning suddenly slashed the sky, splashing the yard with brilliant light. At that same instant, T.J. saw the robed figure dart from behind a large pine into a grouping of oak trees near the garden. Suddenly, a huge *boom* sounded from the clouds, shaking the house.

"Goodness, that came up fast!" Mrs. Finnel gasped. "T.J., you and Markus check all the windows."

But, T.J. didn't move. He watched as treetops thrashed about wildly in the sudden gusts of wind. Rain began pelting the patio in huge ricocheting drops. Then, with a flash so brilliant, it made him squint, a huge bolt of lightning struck the twenty-foot poplar tree a few yards from the window. Sparks flew as it split the trunk in two; branches dangling toward the ground like broken Popsicle sticks.

"What in the world was that?" Mrs. Finnel cried, rushing to the window to stand next to T.J. "It sounded like a cannon!"

T.J. merely pointed to the smoking tree with trembling fingers. Its split trunk was glowing with small orange flames.

"Oh gracious!" she screamed. "David! David! Get down here. The tree's on fire!"

Small flames, fanned by the wind, began crawling up the poplar's branches, as Mrs. Finnel ran for the garden hose. T.J. stood like a statue staring at the burning tree. A blinking red eye watched it as well from its hiding place back in the shadows of Harmon's Wood.

Chapter Seventeen

THE GREAT ARTIST IS MISSING!

The fire department had come, and gone; curious neighbors were ambling back to their homes. The Finnel's yard was a soggy mess; muddy tracks from the firemen's boots marked the patio like a bad finger painting.

"I can't believe this whole evening!" Mrs. Finnel wailed, as she turned on the hose to full blast, and began spraying the boot prints. "Did we win a contest for family most likely to be wiped out in one night?"

"Mom? A phone's ringing," Markus said happily, as he picked up a piece of burnt tree limb.

"And I'm the only one who answers phones around here because *why*?" she asked angrily.

"Right! I'll just get that phone for ya, Mom," Markus called, as he sprinted for the house. A few moments later he was back. "It's Grandpa's cell phone number on Dad's Caller ID, but he hung up when I answered it."

"How odd! But thank goodness he is trying to get in touch with us!" Mrs. Finnel breathed. "We've been so worried about him. Your father is cleaning up the mess upstairs. Why don't you tell him his dad just tried to call."

She finished cleaning the patio and turned off the hose. Everything smelled of burnt wood, damp earth, and wet cement. As she pulled the patio furniture back into place, she surveyed the ugly remains of the once beautiful poplar tree. Showcased in the washed moonlight, it looked like something from a black-and-white horror film.

In the darkness, something near the forest's edge suddenly moved; a quick flash of swirling fabric off to her left, briefly glimpsed out of the corner of her eye.

"T.J.?" Mrs. Finnel called meekly. "Is that you, Sweetie?"

The silence was unnerving. After the sirens, shouts of firemen, and gushing hoses, to suddenly stand in the still darkness with something moving through the tall pines, was enough to cause Marsha Finnel to begin slowly backing toward the kitchen door.

Something in long grey robes swept through the dead leaves of the forest floor.

"Teej?" she whimpered.

A hand grabbed her arm. Screaming, she jumped back, knocking over a patio chair.

"Crimination, Mom! You tryin' to give me a heart attack?" Markus yelled, slamming into the door.

"Give *you* a heart attack?" she screamed, her hand on her chest, heaving violently. "Don't you *ever* sneak up on me like that again!"

A neighbor's head peered over the fence. "Everything alright over there?" she called meekly.

"We're fine, Mrs. Clayson," Mrs. Finnel called. "I just saw...a...a...spider!"

"Goodness, you people have had quite a night," she said, as her curly gray head disappeared below the fence line. A moment later, her back door closed with a soft click.

"I was tryin' to tell you that Dad wants you," Markus said defensively. "Next time I'll wave a white flag first!" He marched into the house.

With a nervous glance over her shoulder into the far reaches of the yard, Mrs. Finnel righted the patio chair, and entered into the cozy glow of the kitchen, hurriedly locking the door.

"Awk...I'm fillin out my papers," Harper squawked. "I demand to be moved to a new family; someplace without Crispy Crème kitties, burning trees, and black-in-white comics. They've been makin 'em in color for some time now, ya know!" The parrot looked at her in disgust.

"Harper, the last thing on my mind right now is whether or not the newspaper lining the bottom of your cage has full-color entertainment value!" Mrs. Finnel snapped.

"Fine! Take out your frustrations on the adored family pet! Does anyone care that I am blind for life? No....just 'Shut Up, Harper', 'We're busy now, Harper', 'Go read Junk Mail, Harper!'"

"What do you want?" Mrs. Finnel asked her husband, ignoring the bird.

Mr. Finnel was leaning on the counter, tapping a pencil nervously on the Formica. T.J. entered the room just in time to hear the next conversation.

"Markus told me Dad was on the phone. When I called him back, someone picked up, but wouldn't say anything...just dead air. I called out his name a couple of times and then he hung up without saying a word. Something is really wrong here. I've tried five times to call him back on his cell, but it goes straight to voice mail. Markus, your grandpa didn't say anything when you answered the phone earlier?"

"Nope," Markus said, thinking back to the call. "I said, 'Hey Grandpa', cuz I saw his name on the Caller ID. He didn't answer or nothin'... then it sounded like he hung up."

David Finnel mulled over the information, chewing on his lower lip.

"Your Dad wouldn't have missed the art show tonight for anything," Marsha said. "Even if he does space out things sometimes when he's working—when he didn't show up, I was shocked. Should we call the police?"

David sighed and pushed his thick bangs from his forehead. It was a nervous trait he had inherited from his father, and now his own son had picked it up as well.

"Not yet," David said. "If he tried to call, he will probably try again. This family has had enough publicity without bringing in the police right now. There's one other thing," David said softly, not wanting to add to the look of concern on his wife's face. "The school called, and said there is a problem with Dad's paintings; something about vandalism concerning some of them. The constellations that were painted in some of the skies are missing...just big voids left in the artwork." He swallowed. *"The Siglets, Theops, The Crone, that Goat constellation,* and *Canis Major* are all missing."

Marsha felt a small tugging sensation in her stomach.

"You believe it now, right Dad?" Markus asked, staring at his father mockingly. "I told ya...Grandpa's paintings came to life. How come ya won't believe it? I find this kinda odd comin' from the guy who's been tellin' me there's a Bogey Man, and, "if I pick my nose, a booger will eat my finger.""

Dillon eyed his young son, and frowned. He looked back to his wife and continued.

"Mr. Saunters thinks some smart-aleck art student painted over them. How do I tell him Dad's flippin' paintings are running around town? No, I *don't* want to admit it! Even when I heard people in town talking about it, I thought this whole ghost business was a joke. How do we explain Harper the Yakker over there, a cat from Egypt, and those flying things he named *The Siglets,* that just blew-up our kitchen? Lord knows where the other missing things are! The school is returning the paintings tomorrow." He turned suddenly to look at his oldest son. "T.J.? What do you know about all this? You're always hanging out with Dad."

T.J. paused, choosing his words carefully. He was tired of his father finding fault with him.

"I don't know. I was just helping Grandpa arrange his studio a few days ago. He seemed fine. He started acting weird after Harper showed up out of the painting."

"Sure! Blame the bird!" Harper screeched. "You can't be happy for me? You try being stuck in a painting!"

"I looked for him earlier today to see if he needed help for the Art Fair, but he wasn't here," T.J. finished.

David Finnel eyed his older son for a few seconds, feeling there was more to the story.

"And this ghost that everybody says is helping him paint...what do you know about that?" David asked.

T.J. bit his lip, and then cringed from the pain.

"Grandpa said he came out of that old painting in his studio...the one by Da Vinci." T.J. grimaced, and watched for the explosion.

"He said *what?*" his father asked incredulously. His voice was quavering. He was nearing information overload.

"The painting of *St. John*," T.J. said. "It's got a well in it and..."

"Never mind," his father suddenly bellowed. "I can't take anymore!" He ran his hands through his hair and paced the room. "What a night!" he moaned. "We will have to move to another town just to get away from all of this gossip and mess!" He took several deep breaths, and gradually straightened his back. "Well, it's late. I'm going to drive over to Coven Bay, and see if he's hanging out at the Tavern. Don't wait up, I'll be back shortly. I'll tell you this much...Dad has a lot of explaining to do."

Marsha kissed her husband's cheek. "I think I will finish cleaning up this mess, and then cover Harper for the night. A nice long bath sounds wonderful!"

"You don't really think more of them are running around do you?" her husband suddenly asked. "I mean more than the ones from the Art Fair?" His mouth drooped and his forehead was furrowed. The whole thing was just too abnormal to deal with.

"I don't know," Marsha said, her voice ragged. "Let's hope not in this house, at least. T.J., would you check your grandfather's studio before you go to bed, and see if anything looks...different? You know his paintings better than any of us," Marsha said to her son.

T.J. paused, the thought of going into a possibly haunted attic room where who-knows-what was flitting about didn't make him happy. Then he saw his father's expectant look, and sighed. "Sure," he said simply, and headed for the back stairs.

"On second thought, I will finish cleaning up tomorrow," Marsha said. "I'm beat. I'm just going to cover Harper and let Calgon take me away!" She picked up the long drape for the parrot's cage.

"Awk! Sure! Cover poor Harper! Leave him alone down here in the dark with monsters lurking everywhere!"

Mrs. Finnel draped the cloth over the cage as they had done every night since they acquired the noisy bird. It allowed Harper to sleep, so as to not keep everyone up all night with his squawking.

"Harper, go to sleep," Mr. Finnel said, his voice thick with exhaustion. "There are no monsters."

"Call me crazy, but I consider twelve winged vampire goblins, and the cat that ate Cincinnati 'MONSTERS'," the parrot spat. "Lemme sleep with you guys!"

"No," Mr. Finnel said simply, grabbing his jacket.

"Pleasssseeeeeeee!" said the muffled voice from inside the cloth-covered cage.

"No!"

"I'll call the Humane Society!" the bird threatened.

"'Nite, Harper," Mr. Finnel said, as he headed for the door.

"Check your oatmeal in the morning, Hero!" the parrot screeched. "Beware of things cleverly disguised as walnuts!"

The kitchen door shut with a loud click. Marsha shut out the lights, leaving only the stove light on for her husband when he returned.

Chapter Eighteen

TWICKET

T.J. paused at the door leading to the attic staircase. He ran a finger over the deep gouges in the wood's thick paneling. It looked as though the Siglets had been desperate to get through the closed door that led up to his grandfather's studio. He opened it and stepped through, stopping to look up into the shadowed stairwell. The door at the top of the stairs was closed and it was extremely dark. He thought about backing out and fibbing to his parents...telling them he had found nothing unusual in the attic; but if his father double-checked and found something, he would be in for it. His heart was pounding, and his lip throbbed. He began climbing the steep staircase. Every few steps he would stop and listen. The only sounds he heard were water gushing from the faucet over the old claw-foot tub in his parent's bathroom down the hall, and his mother tossing her shoes on the floor.

Finally he reached the top step. Softly opening the attic door, he reached hurriedly around the corner, and flipped the light switch. The overhead light bathed the room in welcoming brightness. T.J. stayed where he was and looked cautiously into the room. Nothing seemed out of order. The six large canvases that had been taken to the school exhibit had left a void against the west wall, but other than that, it looked normal. He felt his heart swell as he acutely noticed his grandfather's absence.

The boy crossed the room to where a few paintings leaned against the wall. He pulled several aside and studied them. The constellations seemed to be in place. Aries was still there, Aquarius,

Hydra, and Lyre. As he began to thumb through the next batch, he thought again of the paintings at the exhibit tonight. He figured the Finnel's were probably ruined in this town. Life at school would be unbearable. Jokes about his Rembrandt painting, and flooding the boy's bathroom, would haunt him the rest of his life.

T.J. glanced down absent-mindedly at the painting in front of the next batch of canvases. He didn't recognize the constellation painted there. He tilted his head to read the title at the bottom of the five-foot tall painting. *The Gemini Twins* was written on a small card attached to the canvas. He stared at the constellation in the painting. It didn't look right. Then he realized what was wrong. The constellation was only *half* of the entire star cluster depicting the Twins. Why? Why only one Twin remaining?

To make sure, T.J. took down one of Dillon's books on the Galaxy and flipped to the illustration of the Gemini constellation. He looked at the book's image. He was right! Half the stars in his grandfather's painting were missing!

T.J. was too busy trying to figure out the missing half of the constellation to notice the changing light coming in through the window from outside. Dark clouds were hiding the moon, allowing only a soft glow to highlight their fluffy edges.

As he stood there thinking, he noticed a stream of light travel across the attic room floor, until it climbed the side of his shoe, and bathed his laces in moonlight. The clouds shifted position again and moonlight filled the room, bathing the paintings, the umbrella stand, and the portrait of *St. John* that Leonardo used as his private travel hub.

T.J. looked up in surprise at the large window. A giant moon was playing with the dancing pine trees just outside the house.

A loud sneeze suddenly sounded from the umbrella stand and T.J. ducked as a wad of green mucous sailed past his head, splatting on the bookcase behind him.

"What the…..?" T.J. began, as another sneeze exploded, propelling another glob against the window, where it hung quivering for a moment, before sliding down the glass, leaving a trail of green slime.

"Me done now," a voice from the umbrella stand said, sniffling. "Bright light always make Twicket sneeze two times."

T.J. turned in surprise. His eyes darted around the room, taking in the paintings, looking for anything that was talking and would have launched a mucous attack on him. Something moved amidst the carved walking sticks in the umbrella stand across from him. With eyes bulging, T.J. crossed to the stand and peered nervously at the display of custom walking canes. He glanced across the ornate carvings of eagle's heads, lizards, a carved owl, a Masonic-looking symbol, and finally came to stop on two large blue eyes blinking up at him.

"You pick Twicket up now, ok?" the troll head asked hopefully. "These other guys no talk to me," he said, glancing at the frozen wooden carvings surrounding him.

"What the heck are you?" T.J. asked in shock, bending to peer at the cane more closely.

"Me Twicket," the cane said, as if it should be evident.

"Yeah, great, but *what* are you?" T.J. asked, feeling silly.

"Me just Twicket. Mudlin drop me in cave. Can you help Twicket get back to Toad Kingdom? It kinda boring here."

T.J. reached into the stand and gently picked the little troll up by his cane. Twicket's smile spread across his green face while his large ears quivered happily.

"Ok, I don't know who *Mudlin* is, I have NO CLUE what a Toad Kingdom is, and I want to know how come you can talk," T.J. said, turning the cane in his hand to study the little head from all angles. Maybe there was an *On* switch somewhere; something that explained how it worked.

"Why wouldn't me talk?" the troll asked surprised. "You talk. Mudlin talk."

T.J. looked at the strange carvings on the troll's cane. They appeared to be some kind of symbols and numbers.

"What's this mean?" T.J. asked pointing to the symbols.

The troll just stared at him, an odd expression on his face.

"Okkkkk....what kind of wood is this?" T.J. asked, looking at the glistening cane with its strange black color and deep burling.

"Lamberhook," Twicket said, bored with the conversation. "Me made from Lamberhook tree. Same tree witches brooms be made. Me hungry."

"Hungry? You don't have a stomach! You're just a head!" T.J. exclaimed.

"You rude for a ugly boy," the troll said, narrowing his eyes.

T.J. started to retort, and then thought better of it. He didn't need to get into a spitting contest with a wooden troll head.

"Fine...what do you eat?"

"Me partial to beetles and needle worms." Twicket offered.

T.J. frowned. "You like dried lasagna? There is plenty of it sticking to the cabinets downstairs."

"Me no know what that is, but me willing!" Twicket said, a rumbling noise sounding from the back of his mouth.

"What was that?" T.J. asked in surprise.

"Me tummy growling!" Twicket said with disgust. "What you think?"

T.J. stared at the strange little cane he was holding. Even with a dead artist's ghost following him around, and paintings coming to life, he was having a hard time getting used to talking to a walking stick—especially one with hunger issues.

T.J. sighed. "Ok, I will get you something to eat but first tell me something. Today——or tonight, did you see anything weird in here? I mean did you see my Grandpa or anything strange going on?"

"You grandpa tall old guy who found me in cave?"

"Uh, sure...Yes," T.J. said hopefully.

"Me no see in day, only in moon." Twicket said grumpily. "Old guy get pulled into painting of ugly lady last night. Me still hungry." He eyed the boy with impatience.

"He WHAT?" T.J. exclaimed, and then looked toward the attic door in a panic. He didn't want his dad walking in on this.

"Crone," Twicket said simply. "She queen of Spectre Lands. She come out of painting and snatch old man. He in deep doo-doo now!"

T.J. stood staring at the troll incredulously. This wasn't happening! His mind was swirling. If his grandfather was in the painting, then maybe they could get him back. The painting was still at the school, and it was locked up for the night. He would have to wait until tomorrow when the school was bringing them back.

"If I show you the painting, will you help me get my grandpa out of it?" T.J. said in a pleading voice. "You seem to know all about this "Crone". Where are these Spectre Lands you just mentioned? *And why is it you can talk?*"

The troll sighed, a rumbling sound coming from his mouth. "Me told you. Me made from Lamberhook tree. Lamberhook wood made from special potion...come to life when in moonlight. Spectre Lands..."

"I've never heard of a Lamberhook tree," T.J. said, cutting the troll off. He was beginning to feel as if the little cane was jerking him around.

"You hear of witches?" the troll said with an elaborate sigh.

"Of course. Everyone has heard of witches," T.J. said defensively.

"What witches ride on?" Twicket asked, a sour expression on his face.

"Brooms, why?"

"Brooms made from Lamberhook trees, dumb boy! When broom in moon, broom fly. No fly during day. Some wands made from Lamberhook too. Now you feed Twicket! Then take home, Ok?"

"This is nuts!" T.J. said, pushing his bangs from his forehead.

"Nuts good!" Twicket said, the grumbling sound gurgling up from this throat.

Half-an-hour later, T.J. sat on the edge of his bed, holding Twicket in his hand, with his back to the door. Questions tormented his head as he studied the strange carvings on the troll's cane. He kept brushing crumbs that were falling onto his pants' legs, as Twicket hungrily munched on crackers and peanuts. T.J. was having trouble grasping all that was happening. The creepy paintings of the ancient constellations kept running through his mind; he had never seen his grandpa paint anything so strange. Many people might argue that for a man who collaborates with a ghost, a few eerie art pieces would not be out of the norm. But it was a drastic jump from painting ocean scenes with night skies filled with realistic constellations, to something from the Addams Family Reunion. He had never heard of constellations with names such as *The Crone,* or the *Siglets.* And now, one of them had actually pulled his grandpa into a painting!

He felt something looking at him and whirled around on his bed to see Leonardo Da Vinci's ghost watching him with interest. He was seated on T.J.'s desk, looking down on the large aquarium with the huge lizard lounging on a heated rock. .

T.J. stared in amazement at the famous artist he had always read about. He still could not believe Leonardo Da Vinci's ghost was following him around, and now sitting here in his room. T.J. lowered Twicket to where his legs were blocking the artist's view of the cane.

"I was looking for Dillon," Leonardo said mildly. "I thought you might know where he is." He stroked his long gray beard and tapped at the aquarium glass to arouse the lizard. The creature rolled onto his back, stretching languidly. "This is a rather boring pet," he intoned.

"We don't know where Grandpa is," T.J. lied, ignoring the man's comment about his lizard. "He seems to be missing. Dad's out looking for him over on the Bay." He wasn't certain whether to tell the ghost about the troll's story of Dillon being pulled into a painting. But then again, a ghost might prove helpful when dealing with the supernatural. He sat still, thinking over his options.

Leonardo looked vexed and said, "Well, we are wasting a perfectly good moon. They are the best for painting lessons, you know?" He stood and stretched, and then his gaze fell upon the poster of himself on the ceiling above T.J.'s bed.

"Got Art?" he said, tilting his head sideways to study the poster. "What does that mean?"

"It's just playing on some advertising saying we have here," T.J. said. "It started with 'Got Milk'?"

Leonardo straightened and looked at the boy, a puzzled expression on his face. "Do you have a shortage of milk in this century?" he asked.

"Úh...No...," T.J. faltered. "Can I ask you...I mean...Grandpa told me a little...about you coming here...out of the painting, and all. I guess I didn't expect you to be a...you know...prankster...and to...well...smell bad." T.J. pressed his lips together with embarrassment, pain shooting through his lower lip. He flinched.

The ghost raised an eyebrow and studied the young boy before him. He cleared his throat.

"Why, pray tell, would a man with my obvious talents and advanced IQ not be able to configure a few well-timed pranks? Do you consider me boring? Do I strike you as a dullard?"

"No!" T.J. exclaimed, hoping to redeem himself. "You just come across as, well, focused and scholarly in everything I've read about you."

"Do the books mention the time I replaced Raphael's brown paint with sheep dung?"

"Nooooo," T.J. said quietly.

"What of my famous stunt of sculpting a dolphin for the pond of the Medici that actually spouted dead herrings? It was the talk of Florence for years!" he said proudly.

"I guess I missed that one," T.J. said sheepishly.

"Fireworks in the Pope's chamber? Exploding pottery during market day?"

T.J. merely shook his head.

"As for my "smelling bad", I am actually one of the few people of my era that bathe once a month. I am a pleasure to be around!"

T.J. coughed. "So, why is it the other people at school can't see you? You're pretty much wrecking my life," he said, grimacing.

"I choose when to appear and when not to," the ghost said. "Now...back to what I was talking about..."

Just as the ghost was about to go on touting his renowned escapades and hygiene practices, a crash sounded from the back yard. With nerves jangling, T.J. got up and tiptoed to his window overlooking the back patio. The storm was over, no breeze to be seen, but a lawn chair lay on its side.

Deciding to tell the ghost that there was a chance his grandfather had been pulled into a painting, and to beg him to stop following him around school, T.J. turned quickly back to the artist, but he was gone. With an elaborate sigh, T.J. looked out the window for the cause of the chair crashing. As he watched, eyes darting everywhere at the shadows crawling out from beneath trees and bushes, a very large one suddenly moved across the grass. As it slid across a swath of moonlight, T.J. jumped. It was the figure he had seen in the park; the tall thin shape covered in hooded, grey robes with flowing sleeves and tails. It stopped just beneath his window, paused, and then suddenly looked up.

The boy jerked, as the emaciated face and a red, piercing eye leered at him. Her mouth hung open in gaping horror, pouring down over her pointed chin. Suddenly the red eye from the hag shot out a blood-colored stream of light, aimed directly at T.J.'s face.

T.J. darted to the side of the window, his back pressed against the wall, chest heaving. Twicket was still in his hand. He accidentally banged the little guy's head against Popeye's table.

"Hey!" the troll cane yelled. "That me noggin you bangin'!"

T.J. was afraid to turn and look out again. He was sure now; it was the gowned figure in his grandfather's painting from the art show tonight...the one called *The Crone.*

"If she's here, then maybe Grandpa is too!" T.J. whispered to the troll. He suddenly remembered the red light he had seen in the bathroom downstairs. "Maybe she's been here all night," he breathed. "Maybe she's hiding him in Harmon's Wood!"

Chapter Nineteen

HEADLINES AND HAUNTINGS

The following morning, Brandon Jacobsen pumped his Speedboy racing bike down Bitterbrush Drive; the last street on his paper route. It was Saturday morning and third base was waiting for him over at Grimlett Park. Hurriedly he flung the *Coven Bay Tattler* in the general direction of the seven porches left on his list. Moments later, seven residents were grimly plucking their newspapers off rooftops, bushes, and low-hanging branches. Finn Gumpson had to climb the rickety ladder to his son's tree house to retrieve the paper he could see peeking at him from the edge of the fort's platform. Collette Hill found hers nestled snugly in a pot of petunias.

"DILLON FINNEL'S PAINTINGS SHOCK COVEN BAY!"

the headline screamed, as people slipped the rubber bands from their papers and read the strange story over breakfast.

"It says here that pieces of the paintings are missing," old Mrs. Clayson read in hushed tones to her bored husband, as he wolfed down runny eggs.

"Uh, huh," he mumbled.

"Ashlynn Jo Henderson said some strange goat was in her garden this morning eating her pole beans."

"Uh, huh."

"Janel Freedman at the school says she saw something green with pink wings fly out the auditorium door after the Goreland Art Fair, and Caroline Steinspein said a giant dog chased her across the parking lot!"

"Uh, huh."

"She says it looked like something from one of those creepy paintings!"

"Uh, huh," Mr. Clayson said, slurping luke-warm coffee.

"Well...just last night Marsha Finnel next door was in her back yard screaming!" she continued, her small eyes crinkling with excitement. "When I poked my head over the fence and asked her what was wrong, she said she'd seen a spider!"

"Prob'ly did," he muttered.

"I think she saw those flying green things from her father-in-law's painting!"

Finally Morton Clayson set down his fork and looked across the table at his wife of fifty years.

"Are you trying to tell me you think paintings can come to life?" he asked, brows furrowed.

Her curly gray head bobbed excitedly. "I do, Mortie! I really do!"

He shoved his chair back with a screech and rose to his feet.

"Where are you going?" she asked in surprise.

"To lock that painting of your dead mother into the basement closet!" he said, exiting the room.

Mr. Finnel crumpled the newspaper in disgust and launched it at the kitchen garbage can.

"How can grown people be so ignorant?" he barked. He was exhausted from being up all night looking for his father all over Coven Bay. He'd even rang the doorbell at Old Man Harmon's house. There had been no answer. Hearing the old man kept a deer rifle, he was afraid to go any farther than the dark porch.

"Calm down, David," Mrs. Finnel urged. "They didn't come right out and say the paintings came to life and attacked people."

"They did everything but!" he raged. "'Experts could find no brush strokes to indicate anyone had painted over the missing figures'," he quoted from memory. "Well, what does that leave? If no one covered them up, then it says the creatures from my dad's fruity imagination are flying around Coven Bay! And OH, it gets better!" His voice had risen to a high-pitched squeal. "Two people are reported suddenly blind after last's night art show! *BLIND!* How the heck do we get blamed *for that?*"

"WHAT?" Marsha Finnel exclaimed. "Blind? *Who?*"

"Mr. Hiverson, the school custodian, and an elderly woman who runs the local library by the park. Are you ready for this? She claims a creature in a long dress came in and was stealing the old maps of Coven Bay last night when she confronted it. Here, read it yourself," he said, picking up the crumpled paper and smoothing it out.

Marsha took it from him, and noticed the reporter mentioned the librarian being interviewed spoke with a lisp. In an effort to be realistic, the interview had been typed as she had given it. Marsha read it aloud:

"I wasss cleaning up late lassst night when I sssee ssssomething red ssshining in the Documentsss Room," Mrs. Carnavay said. "I think to myssself, itsss sssome darn kidsss looking for treasssssure mapsss again, even though the doorssss wasss locked tight. Sssoo I go in there and what do I ssseee? The ssside door isss ssstanding open and thisss *thing* isss rolling up some mapsss of the old Harmon's Wood area. I recognizzzed the mapsss immediately. Ssso, I yell, SSSTOP! The thing hasss a ring of keysss in itss's handsss, which I guessss isss how it got in. It turnsss to look at me and it hasss only one glowing red eye! I dang near peed myssself!"

Mrs. Carnavay requested tissues at this point, the article stated, blows her nose and then continued: "Asss I backed up, the eye got brighter and nexxt thing I know, I can't ssseeee!" The article ended describing Mrs. Carnavay's terrified demeanor.

Marsha stood there dumbfounded, the paper hanging limply from her hand.

"The rest of the article goes on to say there were reportings of green flying creatures over Grimlett Park last night. Good grief! We will have to move to Africa to get out of all this mess!" David Finnel said in exasperation.

"Dad!" Markus sputtered through a mouth crammed with French toast. "They flew in our kitchen and wrecked the place! How can you stand there pretendin' you didn't see 'em?"

"I am not pretending I didn't see them!" he barked. "But now every weird thing that happens around here is going to be blamed on Dad's paintings!!! AND, to top it off, he is still missing!"

"David, this has gone far enough," Marsha said, her lip quivering. "We have to call the police. Most of the town already knows Dillon didn't show up at the art exhibit yesterday. It made the headlines this morning in the paper. It's no secret he is missing!"

"Crimination!" Markus yelled. "He can't just disappear. He has to be around here somewhere! So, we just keep looking for him. Right, Harpie?" Markus leaned his chair back and tried to stuff a soggy piece of syrup-drenched toast into the parrot's cage.

"Awk! Don't feed the parrot leftovers," the bird squawked, pushing the limp toast back through the bars until it plopped to the kitchen floor. "And don't call me *Harpie*, you little juvenile!"

T.J. laughed tiredly. The Saturday morning light, along with the promise of a weekend off from school had dispelled much of last night's fright. True to his word, Twicket did not talk during the daylight so T.J. had left him hidden in the corner of his room under a jacket. He glanced out the Bay window at the woods, the morning light only slightly dispelling their terrifying presence. Somewhere in the dense foliage some hideous creature was trying to get at him.

What if it *had* gotten to his grandfather? The thought sobered him and his stomach turned. He thought about the article his mother had just read. What if his grandfather was now *blind?* The thought of the great artist seeing only darkness for the rest of his days sent a shudder through the boy. He looked down miserably at his half-eaten breakfast.

Just then something attacked the window near T.J.'s elbow. The boy jumped, nearly toppling from his chair.

"Crimination!" Markus yelled, knocking over his glass of orange juice. Harper let out a terrified squawk.

A large black dog, drool flying from his snapping jaws was jumping at the Bay window, his front paws clawing at the glass.

"Where in the world did *he* come from?" Marsha said, grabbing a mop from the corner as a weapon.

"May I introduce the latest all-star attraction from the Finnel's Crazy World of Art?" Markus said, as he backed away from the window and the ferocious dog.

"What does that mean?" David asked heatedly, watching as spittle dotted the glass.

"Unless I miss my guess, Lassie out there is none other than *Canis Major*, the dog in Grandpa's painting," Markus said. You know...one of the missing playthings from the school show?" Markus was enjoying Harper's terrified expression at having the large black dog separated from him by only a thin pane of glass.

"I prefer the view of the garbage can wayyyyy over there by the stairs now, please," the bird said, a loud swallowing sound coming from its beak.

The dog suddenly dropped its paws to the ground and whirled around, staring at the woods behind him. The hackles stood up on his back as a low guttural sound came from his throat. He lowered down on his haunches, and then lunged off the patio, tearing toward the trees as he barked ferociously. With grass flying from beneath his paws, he disappeared into Harmon's Wood.

"This has gone far enough," Mr. Finnel said, his face marbled in red. "How in the world do we get all these...these...creatures back into the paintings and end this mess? We have to find Dad, and I mean NOW! If he did it, he can undo it! I'll be lucky if I get hired as the town sewer cleaner after this!"

He snatched up his coffee mug and refilled it, slurping loudly as he mulled over his next move.

T.J. placed his elbows on the table, watching the woods in case the dog returned. He glanced at Harper, frowned, and then leaned over to peer at the cage bottom.

"Hey, Harper! You finally got some colored comics," he said, noticing the colorful paper lining the parrot's cage.

"Look again, Whistle Face!" Harper barked. "Those are pictures of dead ducks from *Field 'n Stream!*"

"Oh, Dad!" Markus cried, looking into the cage. "That's gross! There are pictures of dead birds all over his cage!"

Theops got up from his place beneath the table where he had been curled into a comfortable ball, and crossed to the bird cage. Under Harper's stare, the cat glanced at the ghoulish bird photos and snickered. The large feline turned with his tail arrogantly in the air. With a yawn, he lay down again next to Markus' feet.

"He wanted colored pictures, so I gave him colored pictures," Mr. Finnel said, trying to hide his smirk behind his coffee cup. "Besides, I didn't know they were dead birds...I just thought they were sleeping. Anyway, I agree with Markus on this," David said. "Let's look for your grandpa today and if we can't find him, then we call the police. We have enough publicity to last us! Besides, your grandpa called last night, didn't he? He was alive and dialing a phone. I'm not sure why the call got cut short, but we do know he is alive...somewhere! His phone battery probably just ran out. We'll find him."

T.J. got up from the table, balancing his empty milk glass on his plate. "When is the school bringing the paintings?" he asked. Hopefully he and Twicket would find his grandfather in the painting, without T.J. having to tell his father the old man had actually been jerked into it. *That would go over great!* he thought. He knew in his gut he would have to tell his father about the Crone hanging out in the woods eventually. Things had gotten so far out of control that at this point he needed an adult to help him out.

T.J. glanced out the Bay window at the towering trees. He was sure Harmon's Wood would be the next place his dad would want to search.

Chapter Twenty

PICK A CARD...

"I have to stay here and wait for your grandfather's paintings to be delivered from the school," Marsha Finnel said, as she began clearing the breakfast dishes. "But after that, I will help look for him," she said glumly. It was obvious she wanted the police to take over at this point.

"What time are they bringing them?" T.J. asked again.

"They said they would call when they were on their way," Marsha said. "Reporters are hindering them getting out of the school parking lot." She glanced over at her youngest son to see if he had finished eating.

"Markus, clean up that sticky toast you dropped on the floor, young man!" she demanded. Theops had ambled over to the messy toast, sniffed it, and sauntered away.

"I didn't drop it, Harper did," he said, as he bent to pick up the soggy mess with a paper napkin.

"You don't want to see your 9th birthday, do you Comic Boy?" Harper hissed through the bars next to Markus's ear.

"Ooooh, I'm so scared!" Markus said with a fake shudder. "Threats from the Mafia Bird! What are you gonna do? Cut the head off my stuffed pony and put it under my blanket?"

"Cut it out you two," Mrs. Finnel snapped.

Markus poked at the parrot with the handle of his fork. Harper slapped it. The fork spiraled over the boy's head and landed with a clatter on the countertop.

Mr. Finnel stood there mulling things over. "What if we *can't* get those creatures back into the paintings now?" he asked dismally. "What if this nightmare is just starting?"

T.J.'s hands trembled as he washed his plate and glass in the sink. Everything was happening so fast. A movement outside the window in front of him caught his eye. His grip slipped and a dish clattered into the sink.

"T.J.," his mother yelled, "Be careful! You two have broken enough of your grandmother's good dishes to last a lifetime."

"I think you better see if we can check into a hotel," T.J. said nervously, as he leaned across the sink, pressing his face closer to the window.

The other three Finnels crossed the room to stand next to him, and peered out the glass facing the front street.

"*What the...?*" Mr. Finnel began.

"Wow! We're famous!" Markus yelped.

Dozens of reporters were crossing Mrs. Clayson's front yard and marching up the Finnel's driveway. Large zoom-lens cameras swung from their necks. A white news van with the call letters WCBN pulled up in front of the Finnel's mailbox.

"Don't answer the door!" Mr. Finnel ordered, as he pulled the kitchen curtains closed. "Stay away from the windows!"

"Tax Audit?" asked the parrot.

The phone began ringing at the same time the front doorbell pealed.

"No!" Mr. Finnel yelled, as Markus dove for the phone.

"Hello?" Markus answered. "Finnel's House of the Strange and Unexplained! Oh...it's you, Corey," he said disappointedly. "Yeah. We just saw them. I think it's cool, but my dad is kinda ticked."

David snatched the phone from his young son's hand. "Corey, we can't talk right now, ok? He'll call you later." He slammed down the phone on Markus' young friend.

"You answer that doorbell Markus and I'll have you cleaning Harper's cage for a year!" his father yelled. Harper sighed.

"What are we going to do?" Marsha wailed. She could hear reporters pounding on the windows in the living room.

"You could charge 'em for the show," Harper squawked from his cage.

"Show? What show?" Marsha said irritably, turning toward the parrot.

"The one Houdini Junior is giving in the front yard! AWK!" Harper clamored.

"WHAT?!" Marsha cried, rushing to the kitchen window. "DAVIIDDD!" she screamed, as David joined her and peered outside.

T.J. was trying to see past both of them. He could hear reporters shouting. Explosions from camera flashes were going off all over the place. Markus's black magic hat could just barely be seen through the throng of people. David Finnel made a dash through the dining room, heading for the front door. T.J. followed him. David unbolted and flung open the door; the noise level was terrific.

"Hey kid!" one reporter shouted at Markus in an effort to be heard about the cacophony of voices. "Where's your grandpa? You see any spooky paintings in the house...you know...stuff flying around, or crawling out of Dillon's artwork?"

"Yeah...we got a parrot that flew out of Grandpa's painting. He's a nuisance and won't shut up. Here, pick a card, any card," Markus said to a nearby reporter, ignoring the questions that were being flung at him. He was wearing his magic cape, and had a newly-created wand tucked behind his ear. "I had a really cool baseball trick, but these flying green guys took one of the balls," he explained, as a reporter obliged him and chose a card from the fanned deck Markus offered him.

"Flying green guys?" a reporter asked eagerly, scribbling lines into a notepad.

"Can we get a picture of the parrot?" a woman yelled eagerly.

"Anything else missing besides your baseball and your grandpa?" yelled another reporter.

"Markus David Finnel! Get over here!" Mr. Finnel screamed above the crowd. The reporters turned, noticing him and T.J. for the first time, standing on the front porch. They turned on them like a pack of hungry wolves.

"Any word from Dillon?" they screamed, as they ran toward the pair, trampling Agatha Finnel's flower beds.

"Get off this property," David screamed, his face purple. "T.J., grab your brother and get in the house!"

T.J. swallowed hard, eyeing the surging mass of reporters and photographers. Several cameras flashed in front of him until dots were swimming before his eyes. Putting a hand over his face, he stumbled through the crowd, people grabbing at his arm and jamming microphones toward him.

"You are holding the Ace of Spades," Markus said triumphantly, as the reporter looked at his chosen card. Suddenly the magician felt his arm jerked away and he turned to see T.J. angrily trying to pull him toward the house.

"Wait!" Markus yelled. "This is my best trick!"

"Not really kid," the reporter said, eyeing his playing card. "I got the 9 of Clubs here."

"This is *my* best trick," T.J. growled. "Make the lame little brother disappear!"

T.J. hauled Markus through the crowd. Reporters were yelling at them, while trying to block their way.

They finally made it to the porch where David was standing, blocking the front door from a few journalists who were trying to see inside. He pushed his two sons behind him, and looked out over the frenetic crowd.

"Listen to me!" he yelled. "Stop yelling and listen to me!"

The crowd's noise abated slightly as Mr. Finnel struggled to gain his composure.

"I will tell you what I know if you promise to go away and leave us alone!"

The cries erupted anew from the reporters as they all began to scream out their questions.

"Where is your dad?" "Did a creature get him?" "What happened to Mr. Hiverson's eyesight? And old lady Carnavay's?" "Is there Black Magic going on?" "Is Da Vinci's ghost really working with Dillon, or is this all a big publicity hoax?"

David held up his hands and the crowd quieted to hear him.

"My father was called away on an important errand, that's all! No big mystery, no spooky stuff. As for things flying around Coven Bay...we do have seagulls, ya know!"

The crowd erupted in angry disbelief.

"Seagulls? *Green seagulls with pink wings!* You Finnel's are nothing but a bunch of nut jobs! Meanwhile people are getting hurt!"

The reporters surged toward the house and David had no choice but to back up. He pushed his sons through the open front door, and hurriedly followed them in; bolting it behind him.

"Crimanation!" Markus yelled. "Wait till the kids at school hear about this!"

Chapter Twenty-One

IN SEARCH OF DILLON

The next morning's headlines glaring from the *Coven Bay Tattler* in bold black print, added fuel to the media circus:

"FINNEL FAMILY'S HAUNTED HOUSE! A TALKING PARROT NOW ADDED TO THE CREATURES ESCAPING FROM THE GREAT ARTIST'S PAINTINGS!"

"The family residing at 1418 Bitterbrush Drive may eat their cereal each morning like the other families that call Coven Bay home, but how many of the rest of us share the morning paper with a talking parrot that once resided in a seascape painting?" the article began.

"According to young Markus Finnel, a tropical parrot is now in residence at the Dillon Finnel home, one that 'flew out of' his grandfather's painting. This reporter did a little research into the constellations that Mr. Finnel is so famous for painting, and while it took some impressive digging, I found a very ancient constellation listed in *Galaxies Through the Ages*. This constellation is called *Toucana* and depicts a Toucan, or Parrot. It is my belief, this is the painting that came to life, and now eats his Post Toasties with the Finnel family every morning.

"And as Coven Bay watches the ongoing circus of events that surround this family, the question still remains, where is the man who started it all? *Where* is Dillon Finnel?"

A large black-and-white photograph accompanied the article. It showed a startled Harper, beak open and eyes bulging, staring through the bars of his cage as a camera flash erupts through the window next to him. A smaller photo revealed Markus holding out a fanned deck of cards to a group of reporters. Beneath his picture was the caption: *"Magic...but what color?"*

"What does that mean?" Markus asked his mother as he studied the picture of himself with pride. This was the best morning of his life! He had made the front page of the *Coven Bay Tattler!* His journey to fame as a master magician had begun.

Marsha Finnel was rubbing a hand over her tired face. She had bags beneath her eyes and was on her third cup of coffee. She was living in a walking nightmare and she saw no end in sight.

"It means could it be *black* magic, Markus," she said, her voice drained. "The term 'what color', is their way at hinting that we are all witches!"

"Oh...COOL!" Markus said, as he darted from the room with his newspaper. "Wait till Corey sees THIS!" his voice echoed from down the hallway.

T.J. entered the kitchen and noticed his mother's haggard expression.

"You ok?" he asked, sitting down at the breakfast table and grabbing a piece of toast from a plate. "Where's Dad?"

His mother brushed a strand of hair from her face and stared at him with hollow eyes. "He has gone off to look for your grandpa," she said wearily. "He had a sudden idea that Dillon may have gone into Brighton to buy more art supplies, though how he got there without his car is beyond me. I think David will search the outhouses of Willard County before he'll bring in the police and more publicity. Most of the reporters followed his car this morning, so at least it is a lot quieter today. The school tried to deliver the paintings yesterday and decided against it when they saw the circus on our front yard. They said they may try again today." She picked up a piece of toast and nibbled on it.

In truth, T.J. had seen his father leave from an upstairs window. He had waited to come down until he was gone. Not meaning to eavesdrop, he had overheard a whispered conversation earlier between his mom and dad, as they sat in the living room below the upstairs landing.

"David, what's happened to us?" he heard his mother say. "Will this ever end? I got a call this morning after the latest edition of the *Tattler* hit the streets. My boss at the floral shop was hinting they may need to cut back on staff. Basically, I was being told ahead of time that my services will no longer be required." Her voice cracked, as she struggled to fight back the tears.

"Oh Honey, I'm sorry!" David said.

T.J. could tell his dad did not know what to say to make her feel better. With his father out of work, they had been depending on his mom's small salary at the floral shop.

"As soon as Dad gets back, it'll get better," David promised, trying to sound convincing. "People will get bored with the whole thing once stuff quits happening. We'll get rid of all the paintings he worked on showing the...uh...you know...creepy stuff."

T.J. listened, and added secretly to himself, *"We'll put Leonardo back in his well, too."* T.J. had thought of doing just that earlier; hiding the famous painting with the well portal in it. But he worried about sealing off the famous artist's escape route should he be here, and want to go home. The last thing he wanted was to be stuck with the ghost's pranks for the rest of his life!

"Ok? It'll work out," David had said, trying to convince himself as much as his wife.

Later T.J.'s dad had taken off in the car, a herd of reporters trailing after him.

T.J. sat across from his mother and felt helpless. Things kept getting worse.

The rest of the day was relatively quiet compared to the previous day's onslaught. At 6 o'clock that evening, a large van pulled up, and two men from Goreland Elementary began unloading the six paintings belonging to Dillon Finnel. The paintings had been kept locked in the van inside the school's warehouse in an effort to contain things. Only someone knowing the combination on the keypad could unlock the warehouse doors. As the men carried the canvases, they were careful to keep the artwork draped in the black fabric with which they had been first covered at the Art Fair, in an effort to thwart the remaining reporters from snapping photos of the missing constellations, and adding more to the sideshow. Disappointed photographers had to content themselves with pictures of six tall canvases ominously draped like coffins.

T.J. showed the men to the attic, and once again felt the sadness of entering the empty art room belonging to his grandfather. The men leaned the paintings against the wall. T.J. couldn't help but notice how one man took his time. He was carefully looking around the room, taking in all the other paintings and items that comprised Dillon Finnel's studio. Finally, the last painting in place, the two men left. T.J. could hear his mother thanking them from the first floor. Moments later he heard the front door shut. Muffled echoes of reporters screaming questions at the men could be heard from the front yard.

With his heart pounding, T.J. took a corner of the black fabric draping on the first painting and pulled it back just enough to peek beneath. He could see the small card attached to the painting that read *The Crone*. His hands began to sweat, but he had to know. Pulling the draping back farther he hurriedly looked at the painted night sky in the scene. The stars were missing! There was no doubt in his mind now. *The Crone* was alive and well and living in Harmon's Wood! But where was his grandfather? If he was in the painting, he had no clue how to get him out. He hoped Twicket did.

T.J. carefully put the cloth back in place, making sure all the paintings were entirely covered. The room had an eerie feeling to it. He was aware of the painting of *St. John* across from him. It looked harmless; the young prophet was seated on a rock, pointing toward a dark cave. T.J. stepped to the painting and slowly touched the well. His fingers felt only textured canvas.

He looked about the familiar room where he had spent so many wonderful hours with his grandfather. T.J. could almost believe nothing had ever happened here. Then he looked again at the six dark canvases sitting in the corner and his heart dropped, leaving a feeling like a huge weight had shifted into the pit of his stomach. It was all a very real nightmare!

The afternoon sun was setting. The last place T.J. wanted to be after dark was in the studio with all the paintings. Well, almost the last place. His mother had declared that if his grandfather was not found by dark, she was calling the police…no arguments, no more delays! He quickly stepped to the large windows and pulled the curtains closed. It was time to get Twicket to help him.

T.J. left the attic room, making sure to close the door behind him. The darkened stairs didn't seem as daunting when all he could think about was his missing grandfather. He walked dejectedly to his room and took his jacket from the troll head cane. Twicket blinked up at him in the moonlight.

"Ok, troll face," T.J. said, snatching the cane up. "The paintings are back. You need to help me get my grandpa out of *The Crone*."

"What?" Twicket said, shocked. "Me no know how to get old man back! Me never said me could! Me not going near Crone face!"

"But you know all about her," T.J. argued, a sinking feeling in his stomach.

"Me know she ugly and bad, me no know how to get stuff out of magic paintings!"

T.J. set the cane back in the corner to the sounds of Twicket complaining about being hungry again. He left the room and headed down the second set of stairs to the first floor. As he passed through the living room he turned to see Markus practicing his magic show to the captive audience of ten stuffed animals he had placed about the room in chairs. T.J. quickened his pace, hoping his little brother had not seen him.

"Teej!" Markus called excitedly. "I gotta a new trick to show you. It's the best ever!"

"Not now, Markus," T.J. said. "We have more important stuff

to think about."

"Just a few minutes, Teej? Please? Please, please, pleeeeeasse!" Markus begged.

Sighing elaborately, T.J. turned and walked into the living room. He nudged a ratty-looking bunny rabbit with enormous eyes out of the way, and sat down next to it on the sagging sofa.

"Hurry up!" he said miserably.

Markus the Great smiled broadly. He hurriedly arranged the objects on the coffee table that had been draped with a blue sheet from his bed. His black top hat sat in the middle of the table, surrounded by jars, beacons, metal rings, multi-colored handkerchiefs, and a white, stuffed rabbit. One of Dillon's art easels was standing next to the table holding a large sheet of poster board. The sign read:

Markus the Great

Brings you:

Marvelous, Magical Illusions of Wonder!

Tickets:

50 ¢

"Just so you know," T.J. said, "I'm not paying for this performance!"

Markus looked disappointed, but continued on.

"Ladies and Gentlemen!" he intoned. "Welcome to Markus the Great's Marvelous, Magical Illusions of Wonder!"

T.J. looked about at the stuffed faces around him, and wondered which the "ladies" were, and which were the "gentlemen"?

"Today...before your very eyes, I will show you magic straight from the mysterious Orient!" Markus exclaimed dramatically. He swirled his red cape for emphasis.

"Hey...isn't that Mom's old red table cloth..?" T.J. began.

"You will be *amazed*...," Markus continued, ignoring the rude question, "...amazed enough to tell your friends and bring them to the next show where there *will be* a fifty-cent charge!" He looked meaningfully at his big brother.

Noticing T.J.'s restlessness, and his furtive glances toward the dark skies outside the window, Markus hurried on.

"First, the amazing metal rings!"

Markus grabbed up three large metal rings, and clanged them together with a flourish.

"You will see that I hold before you three ordinary rings. Now watch, as I magically cause them to join together in one long chain!"

The young magician gripped one ring in his hand, as he picked up the other two, and clanked them against the middle one. One ring fell from his hands, and rolled across the living room floor. The other failed to penetrate the one he was holding in the other hand.

T.J. sighed and prepared to rise from his chair. The moon was rising higher outside. He wanted to talk to his mother (who was in the kitchen), about Harmon's Wood, and the Crone. It was time to tell her what he knew, and he would rather confide in *her* than his dad. He had no idea how to see if his grandfather was still in the painting, and Twicket wasn't being of much help in that regard.

"Wait!" Markus cried, abandoning the rings. "I can see this is an audience not satisfied with traditional magic. Therefore...," he said, as he reached into the magic hat and withdrew a soda bottle filled with some kind of liquid, "...therefore, I have saved the best for last! May I present The Magical Hopping Bunny!"

"Markus, I have to go," T.J. said, his hands pressed into the soft cushion in preparation to rise.

Markus ignored him and dramatically picked up the white stuffed rabbit from the table.

"An ordinary stuffed rabbit?" he asked mysteriously. "I think not! Two drops of the magic potion and he comes to life!"

T.J. had risen to his feet. He sighed out loud as Markus drizzled two drops of liquid from the dusky soda bottle onto the head of the rabbit.

"Great! Now you have a sticky rabbit," T.J. said sarcastically, shaking his head. But just as he turned to leave, Markus set the damp bunny onto the table, positioning it so that it sat within the stream of moonlight just now penetrating the large living room window.

The toy suddenly perked up its long ears and sat upright. T.J.'s eyes popped from his head. Before he could speak, the stuffed rabbit began hopping about the table, doing backflips, and one cartwheel before finally jumping into the magician's top hat, where he thumped about for a moment, and became still.

"How did you do that?" T.J. asked in shock. "Is that a wind-up toy?"

Before Markus could stop him, his brother had leapt toward the table, and snatched up the magic hat. He pulled the rabbit from its interior and held it up, letting the hat fall back onto the tablecloth. T.J. had his back turned to the window, blocking out the moonlight. He turned the rabbit over-and-over in his hands, but could find no key or switch. He shook it, watching as the thing's ears flopped lifelessly back-and-forth.

"I don't get it," he said irritably. "How did you make it jump?"

"A magician never shares his secrets," Markus said dramatically, snatching the rabbit from his brother's hands. "If you want to see more amazing magic, kindly tell your friends, and attend the next performance…bring cash!"

With that, Markus the Great began folding up shop, keeping the stuffed rabbit from the reach of moonlight. He closed up his suitcase of magic tricks, and swept from the room, his red cape billowing behind him.

T.J. stood there with his hands on his hips, mouth still gaping. Ten pairs of plastic eyes stared at the frustrated boy from their places about the room. He finally turned and walked toward the kitchen.

"Mom?" T.J. called, as he stepped into the kitchen and found her stirring tomato soup at the stove. "I kinda need to talk to you." It was then he realized his mother was crying.

"Not right now," Marsha said, keeping her back to the boy, as she tried unsuccessfully to keep her voice even. She sniffed and wiped her nose on a napkin. "Would you please tell Markus to wash up for dinner? Your dad is on his way home. He couldn't find your grandpa. We are finally calling the police…it's been three days now. We should have called them sooner."

"But Mom…," T.J. began.

"Teej! Not right now…PLEASE!" Her voice was near hysterics.

The boy walked back into the living room and stared out the front window toward the street. He watched the moon highlighting the rooftops and trees. It was now. It was time. Scared or not, his family was falling apart, and he knew more about what was going on than any of them. They weren't listening to him anyway. T.J. turned and headed up the stairs to his room where he would get together the things he would need. He would look for his grandfather where he had seen the Crone. He would go inside Harmon's Wood.

Chapter Twenty-Two

MANDOLIN BRANDY

A round orb of light pierced the darkness of Harmon's Wood. T.J. walked reluctantly beneath the canopy of leaves, his flashlight barely illuminating the shifting shapes of the forest. A backpack hung from his shoulders, crammed with everything he could find to make the journey into the trees bearable. In his right hand he gripped Twicket. The troll had been protesting the trip ever since T.J. snatched him up from his corner in the boy's bedroom.

"Me no want to have 'adventure'," the troll complained for the third time, using the word T.J. had tried to entice him with. "Me just want to go home to Mudlin."

"Look, I didn't want to come in here alone, and you seem to know things about that Crone thing. If you would have known how to look for Grandpa in the painting, we wouldn't be out here! Help me out, and I'll see what I can do to help find your Mudlin Dude," T.J. said, as he pushed through yet another low-hanging tree branch.

"Him not called *Dude*," Twicket said indignantly. "Him very powerful wizard."

"Whatever," T.J. said, his eyes darting fervently along the trail for any signs of movement.

The boy came to an abrupt halt, his heart hammering. A few feet up ahead, something stepped from the bushes out onto the path. A patch of moonlight fell upon the figure through a clearing in the trees.

"Do you see that?" T.J. whispered hoarsely.

"Not till you turn me head around," the troll said drolly.

T.J. turned the cane in his hand until Twicket's face was pointed toward the strange-looking creature. From where T.J. stood, it appeared the figure was that of a girl. She was slight of build, almost waif-like, and had startling green eyes. Her hair was a profusion of red with orange highlights. As she crossed slowly over to the boy, T.J. could see that the odd dress she wore shimmered in the moonlight. The girl wore simple slippers on her dainty feet, and a small bracelet adorned her slender wrist.

"The moon is up," she said mysteriously, in a voice that sounded like tinkling bells. "I can help you, if you will help me."

T.J. stared at her, open-mouthed. She was now standing directly opposite him and was a good twelve inches shorter.

"I…uh…don't know what you mean," he said feebly. "How do you know I need help with anything?"

She smiled a very thin, all-knowing smile as her green eyes twinkled up at him.

"You are seeking your grandfather, are you not?" she said lightly. "I can explain it later, but I think it best if we get going."

"Going? Going where?" T.J. said, his voice sounding anxious. "Do you know where my grandfather is? Is he alright?"

The girl glanced at the moon rising higher in the night sky, staining the clouds with gold. She watched it for a few seconds, a wistful look upon her face, and then looked back at T.J.

"I think I know where he is," she said carefully. "I cannot say if he is alright, but we have to hurry. There are many lives in peril right now, not just his."

She turned and began walking back in the direction from which she had come. Glancing back at him, she paused.

"Are you coming?" she asked, as T.J. stood watching her, his mind in a tailspin.

"Mind telling me where we are going?" T.J. asked, as the beam from his flashlight bobbed among the bushes. His heart was jumping as he constantly looked around at the dark shapes that were everywhere.

"She isn't here," the girl said finally.

"Who?" T.J. asked, looking at her in surprise.

"The Crone. She came here to find the Dark Orb. So did the Siglets. They have followed it home."

"Ok, just hold up," he said heatedly. "Who the heck are you, and how come you know so dang much? Where is my grandpa?"

She looked up at the boy and smiled. The first stars were appearing in the night sky above them. She glanced up at them, her eyes dancing.

"My name is Mandolin Brandy," she said sweetly. "You can call me Mandy if you like. I don't know as much as you think...about this place at least. This is my first time here. I do know quite a bit about the Crone, and most of the constellations, for one simple reason—I am one."

T.J. stared in disbelief at the small girl before him. Her hair seemed to sparkle in the soft glow of evening.

"You am one...I mean you *are* one...WHAT?" he asked, afraid of the answer.

"Your grandfather's paintings brought us here," she said, tilting her head to look up at him. "I don't think the Crone or Siglets would have bothered coming from the paintings if they hadn't thought the Dark Orb was here. The Crone always knows in which dimension the Orb is, since it, and her eyes, are the most powerful talismans in the Universe. The Siglets are her spies, and I'm sure she sent them out of the paintings to look for the Orb. Somehow she found the location of the well, and thus came to this area of woods. I'm guessing something happened so that she couldn't get back into the painting to go home."

T.J. thought of the school locking the paintings into the van inside the school warehouse.

"Frankly, I think the Orb was here, but not anymore," Mandy said.

T.J.'s mind flew to the article his mother had read aloud about the librarian saying something in robes with a red eye had stolen a map of Harmon's Wood. The Crone was looking for the well!

"Wait!" T.J. cried. "What is a Dark Orb?"

"It's a powerful object that holds the ancient map of the Universe," the girl said quickly, not wanting to waste any more time. "It is used to find the symbols of the wells, unlocking their portals. It's important we find the Orb, get it back, and get everything else in place before the Dark Moon rises."

"The Dark Moon?" T.J. said sheepishly. "Why do I NOT want to know what that is?"

"The Dark Moon marks the 100-year date, at which point all the wells will change locations," Mandy said hurriedly. "The secret symbols carved on the rims will change also. Wherever anyone is when the wells change is where they will stay for the next 100 years; unless they know the well's new location, and the new secret symbols that will open its portal. Only the person with the Dark Orb and map will know those two things. They will also need Lunar Potion to pour onto the symbols beneath the glow of moonlight. Once the wells and symbols change, there will be no going home for many of the constellations. There will be no getting your grandfather back either. If you want him back, you will have to trust me, and do what I tell you to do, no matter how frightening!"

T.J. blinked repeatedly, his mind spinning. Dark Orbs, Dark Moons, Lunar Potion, maps, and constellations? He was suddenly living in a graphic comic book!

"You're telling me...," he paused, choosing just one of the million questions flooding his overwhelmed mind, and feeling totally ridiculous, "...that you know where Grandpa is, and it has to do with Orbs and stuff? Twicket here told me he saw Grandpa being pulled into the painting of the Crone."

"Then we have no time to lose," Mandy said quickly. "If we are going to save him, the Glimmer Lands, and quite possibly all the dimensions, we have to hurry."

She glanced up at the top of the trees as the large moon peeked above Harmon's Wood.

"Glimmer Lands? What are you talking about?" T.J. shouted. "WHERE ARE WE GOING?"

"To the well," she said, as she turned and strode off through the tall weeds.

"Hold up!" T.J. hollered. "What well? If you mean the one I think you mean, you are going by yourself!"

She stopped and turned to look at him, placing her hands on her hips in vexation.

"Do you want to get your grandfather back or not?"

"You're telling me my grandpa is in a *well?* A real well....not a painted one?" T.J. shouted.

"If your little green man said he saw the Crone pull your grandfather into a painting, then he is probably at the other end of the well...in a...uh...different place, and we need to go *now!*"

"Me name Twicket...not little green man," the troll said importantly. "And me no want to go to other end of well either." Twicket's bright blue eyes peered suspiciously at the strange girl.

"What do you mean 'other end of well'?" T.J. asked the troll, his stomach knotting up.

"Me no mind well ride if me heading back to Toad Kingdom," Twicket said matter-of-factly. "But me no dummy. Me think me know where you going to find Orb. Spectre Lands! Me rather you put Twicket down in weeds, and me take me chances with forest critters!"

"What's going on?" T.J. asked Mandy, who had turned and walked back over to them, looking none too happy. "I'm lost!"

"This...," she said dramatically, holding up a small bottle of liquid, "is called Lunar Potion. Whatever it touches becomes animated under moonlight. It's why the paintings came to life...it's why I am here. It's how your grandfather got pulled into a painting. How your grandpa got hold of any and put it in his paints, I don't know! I found some of the liquid glowing in a bottle in your little brother's bedroom. I took the liberty of borrowing some of it and putting it in this. I'm not sure how he got hold of it, but we are very lucky he did. I'm pretty sure Morble was here to look for the pods that create it, and had the Orb with her. It's the reason the Crone and Siglets were here looking for it. But Morble's gone back to the Glimmer Lands, and the Crone and Siglets have gone back to the Spectre Lands...and it's most likely where your grandfather is now."

The moon rose higher in the sky, its light striking the small bottle in the girl's hand. It began to shimmer and vibrate. T.J.'s eyes grew large as he stared at the magical liquid. This was why his brother's stuffed rabbit was jumping about. This stuff truly was magic! *How the heck did Markus get his hands on it?* T.J. wondered.

The bright stream of moonlight also shot into the troll's blue eyes. A loud sneeze erupted from the troll head, sending green mucous shooting through the air. Before T.J. could react, a second sneeze shook the cane, and green slime hit the boy's hand holding the walking stick.

"EWWWWWWWW!" T.J. shouted, nearly flinging the troll away from himself. "GAD, can't you control that nozzle of yours?"

T.J. switched the troll to the hand that had not been assaulted with slime, wiping the goop onto his pants' leg.

"Me no can help it," Twicket said, sniffing indignantly. "It new moon. New moon, new sun, anytime new light first hit Twicket's nose, me sneeze two times. Get over it!"

T.J. started to rebut, but Mandy jumped in.

"Please! We have to get going," Mandy said urgently, as she stared at the moon and glowing bottle. "I will explain it all, I promise, but first let's get there. We only have three days before the Dark Moon."

"You expect me to climb into a well?" T.J. asked incredulously.

"You kinda a wussy boy," Twicket said, smirking.

"And the well is a passage to some place called *what?*" T.J. asked, ignoring the troll.

"The Spectre Lands," she said, turning to walk away. She could not bring herself to tell the boy there was a chance he might end up deformed after he entered the Spectre Lands through the well, like all the constellations who had been sent there by the Crone, Scarflon, and the evil Queen, Cassiopeia. Mandy was pretty sure she would become some vile creature as well once they entered the dark realm. Getting the Orb back was all that mattered. If they succeeded in their quest to find the Dark Orb and map, they could return everyone home. T.J. would be himself again when he traveled through the well back to the Human World anyway. *Why scare him away now?* she reasoned.

"Me want to go home," Twicket moaned.

"Wussy troll," T.J. muttered.

"Where is home?" Mandy asked the little troll, as they walked through the woods toward the cave. T.J. was dragging his feet, in total misery.

"Toad Kingdom," Twicket whined. "Mudlin there. You take Twicket home, Ok?"

"We will need to know the correct symbols on the well for the Treblin," Mandy said apologetically. "If we hurry and get everything we need before the wells change their location and symbols, we have a shot at getting you back home, and getting T.J.'s grandfather back. Right now our only chance is to go to the Spectre Lands, and gather up the necessary stuff. So...are we going to keep talking all night, or get going?"

T.J. looked up at the moon and swallowed hard. He thought of his grandfather and all he had done for him. He had taught him more about the galaxies than any schoolbook could have. He was his best friend in the world. He looked at the troll head who was watching him closely.

"Me think we have no choice," Twicket said uneasily. "It don't hurt. You go in well, it get really dark, you feel whoosh, smell bad stuff, and then be at other end. Climb out of well there. Me no like going to scary place either, but me want chance to be back to Mudlin."

Mudlin again, T.J. thought. His head hurt from the surge of information, and the terror of what lay ahead. Mandy was walking faster now, looking determined to go with or without them.

"Ok!" T.J. yelled, not just to the girl, but to the world at large, that he felt was totally against him at the moment. "Wait up!"

Twicket had stopped taunting the boy and now looked around with huge blue eyes, his rubbery lips pressed together in trepidation. No matter how much he wanted to get back to the Toad Kingdom, and Mudlin the Toad Sorcerer, a trip through the well that ended in the Spectre Lands would make anything faint of heart.

"You're sure the Hag Princess is gone?" T.J. said, looking about him nervously.

"Yes," Mandy smiled. "I saw the Crone go into the well to find Morble and get the Dark Orb back. I tried to follow her in since she had added Lunar Potion to the well's symbols, but the Siglets hovered around until it was too late. By the time they went in, the moon had gone behind the trees. Since your grandfather wasn't with her, I'm pretty sure she took him to the Spectre Lands through the painting, and then returned to look for the Orb, and her missing eye."

"That's why those Siglets attacked our house? They were looking for that Orb-thing? All they took was Markus' silver baseball, and my mom's ruby broach."

"They probably thought the silver ball was the Orb, and the broach was the Crone's red eye. Well, they are gone now," she said. "Let's hope Morble has the real ones."

Mandy led them through the twisting trails, her shimmering dress and hair sending off a soft glow. T.J. watched her in the flashlight's beam.

"So, which constellation are you?" he asked, feeling foolish.

"Guess," she said playfully. "I will give you a hint. On any constellation in mortal form, you will find a mark somewhere on them with the symbol of their sign."

"Were you in one of Grandpa's paintings?" T.J. asked.

She nodded softly.

"Why can't we just go into your painting instead of the well to get Grandpa back?" T.J. asked hopefully.

"Because I came from the Glimmer Lands," she said simply. "The Crone came from the Spectre Lands, and that's where she took him, if she pulled him into her painting. We need to use the well. Sorry."

"Then, let's go home and go through the Crone's painting!" T.J. suggested. He wanted anything other than a well ride.

"There's no time for that!" Mandy said. "The other side of that painting could be the Crone's dungeon."

"If you constellation, then you disappear in daylight," Twicket said suddenly, eyeing the girl. "What we do when we no can see you in morning?"

"The moon is always out in the Spectre Lands," she explained. "And, constellations coming into your world, whether through a well, or a painting, are different," she said. "Once we have been in another dimension for at least two days our composition changes and we become real, or mortal. Either way, you will see me."

"That explains Harper, the cat, the dog and the Crone," T.J. said. "I have seen all of them in the daytime."

"What's a Harper?" Twicket asked.

"An annoying parrot that used to be a constellation until he jumped out of Grandpa's painting...he never shuts up," T.J. said.

Mandy laughed. "You mean *Toucana!* That's why he was thrown out of the Glimmer Lands in the first place. No one could stand him." She laughed a sweet tinkling laugh, and hurried along ahead.

"I remember Grandpa telling me that," T.J. said sadly. Then a thought occurred to him. "Speaking of daylight and moonlight, why didn't *you* talk today?" T.J. asked the troll. "You've been in Grandpa's study for days!"

"Twicket Lamberhook wood," the walking cane said with impatience. "Me tell you already. Lamberhook only alive under moonlight. You no could get witch broom to fly in daylight if you smack its bottom with a hot stick! *Me no made of stars!* You no catch on too fast!"

They rounded a large pile of boulders and Mandy came to an abrupt halt. Before them was a cave, its opening aglow from the moonlight streaming in through a hole in the rocky roof inside.

"Here we are," she said, her voice losing its bravado.

"It's in there?" T.J. asked, as the well's details came into view, the moonlight playing upon it, spotlighting the portal to other worlds. A sudden memory shot through T.J.'s mind; dark and unwelcoming. He had been here before!

The boy swallowed and stood there, reluctant to make the next move. Twicket said nothing; he just looked at where Mudlin had left him that night beneath a full moon.

Mandy finally stepped through the cave opening and walked slowly to the well. Most of the flour Tabor Harmon had sprinkled about was gone. T.J. stepped to the other side of the stone cistern to view the carvings on its rim. His shoe became tangled in a mound of thin wire, crumpled on the ground. He stooped and picked it up, pulling it towards himself from where one end lay beneath a large rock at the cave's opening. He jerked on it, and the wire came free of its anchor.

"What the heck is this for?" he said aloud as he wound the wire into a ball. Shrugging he reached behind himself, and stuffed it into his backpack.

The boy walked around the well and stopped. He saw moonlight glinting off something metal lying in the weeds. Stooping he picked up an old gold watch, its band scratched and dirty.

"What is it?" Mandy asked, stepping over to him.

"Is it food?" Twicket asked hopefully.

T.J. turned the watch face over. There were faded letters etched into the metal.

"It says Tabor Harmon. 25 years of faithful service. JHW Industries," T.J. said. "What in the world is Old Man Harmon's watch doing here?"

Without a word, all three heads turned, and looked into the depths of the well. T.J. swallowed.

The boy pocketed the watch and leaned over the well's opening, looking down into the bottomless blackness.

"Be careful you no drop Twicket in there!" the troll yelled.

"I think we are going in there anyway," T.J. said, feeling his knees tremble. *How in the world did I myself get into this?* he thought, feeling as frightened as he had ever been. His heart was thudding against his ribcage.

Suddenly he saw images of a well with him struggling to get out of it. He could hear someone calling to him from far away…"T.J? Where are you?" Perspiration ran along his neck as he saw the scene play out in his mind.

"Are you ok?" Mandy asked the boy, noting his frozen stare, and horrified expression.

"What? Oh…yeah…I don't know….what that was," he said, trying to recall the brief nightmare that had flashed through his mind.

"Don't forget to add potion to symbols! Me no going in well without potion added!" Twicket wailed. "Me no end up in Void where no one see Twicket's pretty face ever again!"

T.J. looked at the warty green head with enormous ears, and said nothing.

"I will add the potion, Twicket," Mandy said. "Relax…you aren't going to the Void."

T.J. began to ask what "the Void" was, but changed his mind. He couldn't handle any more information right now, and besides, it sounded horrifying.

Mandy ran a trembling hand over the etchings that marred the stone rim's face. T.J. stepped over to her, looking down at the markings.

"What are they?" he asked, brushing bits of dirt from several of the deep gouges.

"They are a puzzle," Mandy said. "You have to know which of these images to use when traveling to the other wells. They are secret symbols."

Mandy unscrewed the lid from the bottle of Lunar Potion.

"In order to travel to a dimension of your choosing, you have to add Lunar Potion to two symbols on the well's rim. Each of the 5 Dimensions has an image representing its land, and a symbol of the Zodiac. Only someone possessing the Dark Orb and the map it contains knows the two symbols for each Kingdom."

"So how come you know the symbols?" T.J. asked suspiciously. He still didn't know who this Mandolin Brandy actually was.

"I have seen the potion added to the symbols before," she said mysteriously. "I know the image for the Spectre Lands is the twisted Lamberhook tree, and I know its Zodiac sign is Serpens, the Serpent."

T.J. thought this over for a moment, and then said, "Wait a minute...Serpens is not a Zodiac sign."

Mandy looked at the boy with renewed interest. "Very good," she said smiling. "You know your stars. Serpens was at one time a member of the 12 Zodiac signs, along with others. Over the years, they were changed into what you humans know today. The well is very old."

"So what happens if you put the potion on the wrong sign?" T.J. asked, running his fingers over the strange carvings.

"If you don't match the Zodiac sign with the correct symbol for the dimension you want to travel to, you will end up in the Void. There is no use trying to cheat it," she said.

Mandy carefully dropped small amounts of the Lunar Potion onto the two symbols and hurriedly recapped the bottle. Before T.J. could question her, the two carved symbols began pulsing with light as moonlight played over them. Suddenly, the well's interior exploded with a white stream of light, nearly blinding the three standing near it. A repugnant stench belched up from its center.

"Whoa!" T.J. exclaimed, clamping his nose. "That's nasty!"

"Ok," Mandy said, looking at T.J. and Twicket with a grim

expression. "It's now or never."

"Me choose 'never' now," Twicket said, chewing his full lips, while twisting his nose in disgust at the smell swelling up from the well's depths.

Mandy made sure the lid to the Lunar Potion was secure, and handed it to T.J., who dropped it into a zippered pocket of the backpack. Taking a deep breath, she sat on the well's rim, twisted around, and then slipped into the opening, hanging onto the rim with both hands. She hung on for a second, looked at T.J., pressed her lips together, and let go. She disappeared into the well's belly.

"Holy crap!" T.J. said, peering with squinted eyes into the white light emanating from the well. "Oh man. I'll take the Marek brothers over this!"

"Hurry, Wooshy Boy!" Twicket barked. "If moon go, we no go anywhere!"

"Stop calling me that!" T.J. yelled, his nerves at the breaking point. He swallowed several times, and felt as though he might throw up. Taking a huge breath he crawled onto the well's rim, holding Twicket tightly in his left hand

"Ready?" he asked. Twicket's cane shook from the boy's quaking hands.

"Maybe we think it over..." Twicket squealed.

T.J. took a deep breath, held it, clinched Twicket tightly, and jumped in.

"Hollllyyyyyy Crrapppp!" echoed up from below.

Chapter Twenty-Three

THROUGH THE DARKNESS

T.J. awoke with a throbbing headache. His arms felt cold and he could feel a light breeze blowing across his face. He reached for his covers, his mind a sleepy haze, and felt his fingers curl around…dirt. It took a moment for this unexpected surprise to register as the dark clouds inside his head began to dissipate slowly. As his consciousness started its hazy swim up to the surface, he became aware of a dank, sour smell filling his nostrils. He blinked several times, and opened his eyes. It was pitch black with only a breeze showing signs of life. He pushed up on his elbows from his reclining position. A shock of pain ran up his spinal column. Something was poking him in the back, and he winced as he straightened. Reaching behind himself he felt cold, hard stone! *Ok, I am not in bed!* he thought in a panic. *Where the heck am I?*

Suddenly memories of walking with some strange girl through Harmon's Wood came flooding back to him. Twicket was jabbering away, calling him a "Wussy Boy". A cave in the forest with moonlight flooding in through a hole in the ceiling. The girl….Mandy!...that was it…Mandy….adding drops of some potion onto the well's rim. Light flooding out of the well…and….and…*OH MY GOSHHHHHHHH!* he thought, "*I went into the well!*"

Something next to him was snoring—a deep mucous-filled rattle that echoed off the stone walls. Twicket! T.J. realized he was still holding the annoying cane in his hand. His head spun as he remembered the terror he felt as he dropped into the blinding light in the well. There had been a loud rush of wind around his ears. The light was so bright he could see nothing but a white glare as his body fell into what seemed like an eternity of space. The rushing sound was as loud as a freight train barreling past him. He had smelled odors that defied description...the kind of smell you associate with road kill, or fresh dog poop ...only worse.

He remembered clutching Twicket for dear life, certain that when they hit bottom they would be crushed to death by the impact. But there hadn't been an impact, he recalled, the memory pushing through the remaining cobwebs in his head. The rushing sound had ended, and he was looking *up*....not down....but *up* at the mouth of a well waiting above him. He was floating in the belly of it, and looking at a stream of moonlight falling onto the opening of the stone cavern above his head. He could make out rough stone walls, and that was about all. He had reached for the well's rim, his shoes pushing against the crumbling rock wall of the cavern's interior. Finally, he grasped the edge, pulling himself out, using Twicket to keep his hands from slipping. The strange thought that he had done this before had been banging around in his head. The last thing he remembered was tumbling to the rough ground outside the well.

It is so dark in here! the boy thought, looking around only to see more shadows. A pale thread of moonlight filtered down from an opening in the cave's ceiling overhead, illuminating only a few inches before his face. Twicket's snores were echoing near him. *Mandy! Where is Mandy?* T.J. wondered. He was too afraid to feel around himself for fear of what his fingers might touch. Gathering his courage he whispered her name, which came out as a frightened squeak.

"Mandy?" he croaked, trying again. Silence. "Mandy....are you here?"

Something off to his right moved in the darkness. He grabbed the sleeping cane and gripped it with both hands, his breathing coming in short blasts.

"You choking Twicket!" came a sleepy voice from the blackness.

"Twicket!" T.J. gasped, happy to hear another voice even if it was the troll's. "Where are we? Do you know?"

"Where you think we be?" Twicket asked sarcastically. "Only place smell like this be Spectre Lands! Smell like somebody's feet died!"

"Are we still in the well?" the boy asked, every nerve fiber in his body screaming.

"No…we be in cave with well," Twicket said quietly. "Me can see entrance to cave over there."

"You can see? How can you see anything in this dark?"

Twicket sighed. "Me need to get you book on creatures from other dimensions," he said rudely. "Me *troll!* Trolls live under the ground. We born to see in dark!"

T.J. digested this information for a moment.

"Ok, well can you see Mandy anywhere?" T.J. asked, his heartbeat slowing slightly, as he realized the obnoxious troll with his night vision would be tremendously helpful. It beat trying to navigate blind.

"Uh, me no think you wanting to be seeing Mandy," the troll said thickly.

"Why not?" T.J. asked in alarm. "Is she hurt?"

Twicket looked over at the small lump curled into a ball a few feet away. He could see the girl's back and her mass of red hair. Her arms were wrapped tightly about her, one hand visible as it clutched her upper shoulder. Twicket swallowed as he saw the gnarled fingers, and purple scales of the girl's hands. Her elbow stuck out at an odd angle as though someone had twisted it backwards. Mandy's bare legs protruded from her torn dress. They too were encased in purple scales, and there were strange horns sticking out of her ankles.

"Why NOT?" T.J. demanded again, his stomach once again coiling into a tight knot. *Why wasn't Twicket answering him?*

"Me be thinking," the troll said quickly. "You have Lunar Potion in pack, right? We forget about Orb, and try go to Toad

Kingdom! Me know Toad Kingdom symbol on well is small toad. Zodiac sign we guess at! We puts drops on all the Zodiac signs all at once, and then we go home. You like Treblin! Toads be very funny to hang out with! They hilarious!"

"You're forgetting something. The portal will dump you into the Void if you don't know the two symbols. That's what Mandy said. It won't let us put potion on all of them! Anyone could do that!"

"Anyone with Lunar Potion," the troll muttered hotly. "Me say it worth try."

"And if you are wrong, we end up in that Void place you like so much? NO! Besides, I have to find my grandfather, and if Mandy is right, we need the Orb for any of us to go home! Now tell me....what's wrong with Mandy?"

Twicket looked over at the creature still lying on its side near the well. Suddenly she stirred, moaning softly. Her gnarled fingers straightened slowly as if in pain. She unfolded her arms and pushed her deformed hands onto the floor in an effort to sit up as she drew in her knees, and turned slowly to a sitting position. The troll drew in his breath as he took in her face. Half of it was hidden by her matted hair, but the half showing was twisted and misshapen. Mandy's nose was no longer human. It had two thin slits for nostrils. Her dainty chin had been replaced with a quivering blob of shimmering gills. The eye he could see was bulbous.

Before Twicket could answer T.J., Mandy felt her legs with her hands and let out a low howling sound. The pain and horror in her cry was heart wrenching.

"What was that?" T.J. screamed, his right hand jerking back toward his side, getting ready to launch himself from where he sat. The back of his hand struck something soft. His fingers enclosed around a strap and buckle. His backpack! The image of his flashlight jumped into his head, and he quickly flicked open the latch. He dug around inside the pack, feeling the few contents he had hastily thrown into it when he left his grandfather's house. That seemed like an eternity ago. His fingers grasped the cold metal handle of the flashlight, and he pulled it quickly from the slick fabric bag. His thumb found the *On* switch, and taking a deep breath, he pushed it.

Light shot out into the cave room illuminating the well, and blinding Twicket, causing him to scream.

"Me eyes!" the troll wailed. The small green face began twitching uncomfortably, his nose twisting this way and that, as his giant blue eyes watered.

"Ahhhh...ahhhhhhh...AHHHHH...CHOOOO!" Green mucous flew from the troll's mouth and nose, coating the wall across from him with slime. "AAHHHHHHHHH......CHHHHHHHOOOO!"

T.J. hurriedly swung the beam away from the walking cane's face. As he did so, its light swept across a purple creature who suddenly hunched over, and turned away from him. The boy screamed, dropping the flashlight. It rolled across the floor, coming to a stop a few feet away, its beam playing on the thing who was now screaming his name!

"T.J.! Turn it off! Please....turn it off!" Mandy begged. The last words came out as a pathetic plea.

The huddled mass began to sob; the scaly purple shoulders were shuddering in the cruel glare of the light. It was hideous to look at...but the voice! The voice had been Mandy's! T.J. was frozen to the spot, unable to look away.

"Mandy?" he finally choked out. "Is that really you? What's happened to you?"

Twicket was looking at the girl sadly, his nose still twitching from the sneezes.

"Spectre Lands happen to Mandy," Twicket said with emotion in his voice. "Things come here through well get ugly."

Mandy's sobs filled the room. She lifted her head slightly, and T.J. recoiled at the sight of the quivering blob that was now her chin. It had fibrous slits that breathed in and out like a fish. The girl peeked at the boy through strands of snarled hair, trying to hide her face as much as possible. She stopped sobbing, and straightened in surprise.

"Nothing's wrong with you!" she gasped, the chin wobbling in rhythm with her words.

"Thank you," T.J. said lamely, still repulsed by the girl's deformity.

"No...I mean....why aren't *you*...why didn't the well change *you?* Why are you still...*you?*"

T.J. looked down at his hands...the same hands he had seen every day of his life. Other than some scrapes and bruises, they looked the same.

"I don't know," he said quietly. "Does everything that comes here through the well turn...um...ugly?" he asked, using Twicket's description, though it seemed a tad cruel under the circumstances.

"YES! I have never heard of an exception!" the girl cried out. "I don't understand it. I mean I am happy for you, but...." She looked down at her grotesque arms and legs that had once been so lovely, and began sobbing again.

"If you knew that, then why did you force us to come here?" T.J. said tersely. He was just beginning to realize Mandy had brought him here thinking he would be turned into some horrible creature; his sympathy for her waned.

"I had to! We have to find that Orb!" she wailed. "You want your grandfather, and I want my friends back...and...my...uh...all the other constellations sent here against their will!" she said, pausing between words. "The Dark Moon is coming in three more nights and it will be too late after that! Whoever has the Orb will control everything! You had a small taste of what it will be like for your world if creatures from here keep showing up. They have been to your world before, and done unspeakable things to your people...you don't have *any* idea!"

"It lucky wooden troll heads no turn ugly," Twicket said appreciatively.

"It couldn't get any worse," T.J. mumbled hotly.

T.J. finally pushed himself up off the hard floor, leaning heavily on Twicket's cane, as he was still a little disoriented after the trip through the portal.

"You crushin' me head!" the troll cried.

Ignoring the cane, the boy picked up the flashlight and shone the beam along the dirt floor of the cave. As he swung the light across the stone walls, he stopped. A portion of one of the walls was shimmering, its face shifting in and out of a black swirling mass.

"What is *that?*" T.J. asked nervously, keeping the flashlight beam trained upon it.

Mandy looked at the shimmering wall. She struggled to a standing position, and stepped over to it awkwardly, her new horned feet making her progress unpredictable.

"Watch," she said, as she stepped in front of the swirling haze.

Suddenly the black morphing shadows shimmered into one cohesive surface, mirroring Mandy's reflection back to her. As her image appeared on the wall, that now resembled some contorted mirror, a name began to appear in the reflection above her head. In black, spidery writing, the name *Worken* appeared.

"What's a "Worken"?" T.J. asked, looking at the mirror-like surface in amazement.

"I'm Worken," Mandy said whimpering, as she took in her hideous appearance. "When you come here through the well, you are given a new shape, and a new name. It's the Crone's way of erasing your old life. Well, I refuse to change my name for her!" But the quiver in Mandy's voice did not sound as sure.

T.J. stepped in front of Mandy and stared at his reflection in the mirror. He was the same tall kid he saw staring back at himself in the mirror each morning. He was almost disappointed when no name appeared for him. It was like not getting picked for sports all over again!

"This is so weird that nothing happened to you," Mandy muttered, nervous she would set him off again.

T.J. stood looking into the strange mirror for a few moments, the walking cane still in his hand. He looked down to see Twicket smiling at himself in the wavering reflection. The troll was making goofy faces and baring his teeth, obviously delighted with seeing his image.

"Oh brother!" T.J. said in disgust.

Twicket pouted as T.J. stepped away with him from the mirror and walked the few steps to the well. He peered into its black interior, watching as the black abyss swallowed up the beam from his flashlight.

"I won't stay here and wait for that Dark Moon of yours to show up," the boy said gruffly. "You have the three days to try and find that Orb and my grandfather. If it looks like we are running out of time, then we will try the well to get out of here before that moon rises and the wells change locations. Maybe Grandpa isn't here at all. Maybe this whole thing was a trick of yours to get me here to help you. Do you know the symbols we need to return us to the well in Harmon's Wood?"

"Hey!" Twicket yelled. "Me want to go home to Mudlin!"

T.J. ignored the troll as he waited for Mandy to answer. The cave was silent for a few moments before she spoke.

"No," she said looking away from him. "No...I don't."

Chapter Twenty-four

THE GLIMMER LANDS

A week earlier in the Glimmer Lands...

Cassiopeia sat before her gold-gilt mirror twisting her long blond hair into perfect braids. The reflection staring back at her was no longer the disfigured visage of Morble, the Forest Witch from the Spectre Lands, but that of the reigning Queen of the Glimmer Lands. The trip through the well from the Human World back to her home here had left the horrible form of Morble behind.

Watching her reflection carefully, she wound the two plaits into perfect ovals atop her head and secured them with a diamond comb. The Queen carefully patted an errant strand of hair into place until all was perfect. A final touch of brilliant red lipstick to her full mouth completed the picture. She turned her head from side to side, admiring the reflection before her. She touched the angry cut in her right cheek left there by the Siglet's talon. With an experienced hand, she covered it with makeup until it barely showed. Her beauty was restored, and tonight she would be well on her way to ruling the 5 Dimensions.

She had made more Lunar Potion from one of Luthor's pods, and hidden the remaining one away. Unhappy that she had dropped a pod by the well in the Human World when the Siglet attacked her, she reasoned if someone found it, it wouldn't matter. The pod would turn green with poison within seconds of anyone disturbing it that it did not trust.

The bedroom chamber door of the castle suddenly opened, and a towering man in flowing fur-lined robes swept into her sitting area.

Cassiopeia eyed him with disdain as he leaned over her shoulder, kissing her affectionately on the cheek. Stifling her annoyance at being interrupted, she locked eyes with his in the mirror's reflection.

"What is it?" she asked coldly. She returned her gaze to her image, adjusting the gem-encrusted crown she had placed lovingly upon her head. The light captured its brilliance, spraying sparkles into the highlights of her fair hair.

"I thought we might go for a walk in the garden," he said, stuttering slightly as he always did in her presence. Everywhere else he was known as Cepheus, King of the Glimmer Lands—the great leader of the constellations. Here, in her cold, demeaning rejection of him, he was nothing more than an infatuated low-life being spurned by the town beauty. "I missed you while you were away. It's a full moon this evening. The stars are already in the courtyard dancing!"

The "stars" referred to the constellations making up the Glimmer Lands. While earthbound humans looked up in wonder at the night sky, and saw only clusters of stars with strange names and stories, here in this Star Kingdom called the Glimmer Lands, they lived and breathed, taking on their mortal forms when the moon bathed the realm in its brilliance. By day they disappeared, becoming an almost indiscernible outline of soft, shimmering stars. Cassiopeia and Cepheus ruled the Kingdom as King and Queen, their constellations two of the most ancient star clusters in the timeline of the Universe.

The Queen put down her hairbrush, turning to stare coldly at him.

"Is there any word of your brother?" she asked, her voice dripping with sarcasm, one eyebrow elegantly arched in mockery.

Cepheus swallowed, his face contorting with pain.

"Of course not," he hissed. "He is still missing. Why do you do that? Why do you delight in torturing me?"

"Oh....I don't know," she said, sighing dramatically. "I suppose because it amuses me. You must admit—it is funny in its own way. The mighty twin Kings! Destined to rule the Universe together in fairness, reason, and *justice!*" she said, tilting her chin high as she taunted the giant man before her. "And now look…," she continued, pouting with fake emotion, "Scarflon has disappeared. Tsk, tsk, tsk," she said clucking her tongue. "What will you do without your twin and his magnificent mind?" She turned back toward the mirror smoothing her hair with her long tapered fingers. "There are times, my dearest, when I wonder if I married the wrong brother!"

The King inhaled sharply, his face effused with purple.

"Is that what you want?" he shouted. "Scarflon is dabbling in black magic! Nothing good can come of it! My brother was not always like this. We both wanted the Glimmer Lands to be the greatest Kingdom in the Universe. Now he's missing!"

Cepheus paused, taking a deep breath in an effort to control himself.

"I only recently learned of his visits to the cave with the well," he said, pacing the room. The Queen shot him a quick glance. "It's that Orb! All of this happened when he got hold of the Dark Orb and that ancient map! He has always been hungry for power, even when we were kids. I told him the power of the well has always been something to be feared. If he opened the portal to other dimensions we may all be doomed." The King's voice dropped, heavy with sadness and loss. "When I learned about his visits to the cave, I tried to warn him. He pretended nothing was going on. He didn't realize the power he was dealing with. I greatly fear he may be dead."

Cassiopeia turned, and smiled wickedly into the mirror. "It's just too easy goading you," she said haughtily. "There is nothing wrong with wanting….*more*," she said, putting emphasis on the last word. "Scarflon was always more ambitious than you. *So* he wanted the keys to the most powerful magic in the Universe. We are royalty, Cepheus, and we have the means within that Well Room to rule the 5 Dimensions and here you are, whining about some silly dance in the courtyard! Go dance, you puppet King. Go dance with your *loyal* constellations. I have other plans tonight."

Cepheus stared at her, a mixture of pain and anger on his face. He started to speak, and then abruptly turned on his heel. She watched him carefully in the mirror. He did not see the Queen smile with satisfaction as she watched him leave the room, slamming the heavy chamber door behind him. A small star cluster known as the Lynx scurried out of the way before the door could hit him, as he attempted to enter the grand bedroom. The small creature crossed slowly over to the Queen where he offered her a golden goblet of wine on a silver platter.

"I suppose you heard everything," she said acidly to the small feline who looked very much like a miniature striped house cat with a bobbed tail. The Lynx however walked upright and sported a red suit jacket.

Cassiopeia snatched the goblet the Lynx was holding up to her. His whiskers quivered nervously as he waited to be dismissed. Instead the Queen regarded him with interest as she sipped her wine.

"Scarflon is gone," she said to the Lynx, whose small bright eyes watched her carefully. "Only I know what has happened to him," she purred with satisfaction. She took another sip and dabbed at her full red lips. "With the Dark Orb, the Crone's eye, the ancient map, *and* the Lunar Potion, it will soon all be mine! Men are so easy to manipulate. Just think, before the night is over I will have toppled the Twin Kings, and opened the portal to the Toad Kingdom, all beneath the power of the full moon."

She looked at the opulent room around her, forgetting the small servant at her feet. "And whoever owns the Dark Orb and the map, rules them all!"

Laughing evilly, Cassiopeia replaced the goblet onto the silver tray and kicked at the Lynx to announce he was dismissed. The creature hurried across the floor, and disappeared behind a velvet curtain, leading to a secret passageway into the back dining hall where Sagittarius, the Archer stood guard.

A dark shadow fell across the room, as the moonlight pouring in through a tall window was suddenly blocked from view. Cassiopeia ran to the arched opening and looked out to see the enormous body of Draco the Dragon flying through the night sky. He circled around the castle spires, his massive wings blocking the moonlight intermittently. Their heavy flapping sounded like thunder as they rose and fell just inches from the castle walls. The Queen could feel, and smell, the dragon's rank breath as he passed near her tower window. Light sparkled from his iridescent blue scales, his pale green eyes glistening. Long orange tendrils hung from each nostril, rising and falling with the dragon's blasts of hot air.

As the giant monster glanced toward the Queen's window, Cassiopeia hastily hid behind the velvet drapes. Seeing nothing, the dragon finally lifted into the sky, his long, forked tail nearly toppling the spire of the north battlement. The Queen watched him until he was lost from view. *He is keeping watch for the Crone,* she thought. A smile twisted her face into a vision of evil cunning.

The dragon's distant thrumming was suddenly replaced by a flurry of wings, as a large black crow flew in through the open window of Cassiopeia's sitting room. He alighted upon a tall, ornate perch near her dressing table and shook himself, puffing out his blue-black feathers. The Queen hurriedly sat next to him.

"Corvus," she cooed excitedly, reaching up to stroke the bird's smooth chest with her long, lacquered nails. "Is everyone away from the cave? Tonight must be flawless. With Cepheus gone, there will be no Twin Kings to rule this dominion anymore! My time is finally here, and everything is in place!"

The Queen stroked the bird's wings slowly. "You are the only one I trust, Corvus," she said, her long fingernail dangerously close to the crow's left eye. Corvus edged away from her along his perch. "You have done well to bring me the information and things I sought, and you will rule beside me tonight, as we begin our destiny into greatness. I suppose I could leave you behind, but what would become of you?" she asked cruelly. "You are the Queen's spy. Everyone knows it, and therefore no one trusts you. What a pity. I'm afraid I am all you have, my constellation of feathers and pluck!" She flicked his beak with red-varnished nails. The bird let out a sharp cry of pain.

"Oh dear, am I being too playful?" she asked sarcastically. "Well...I'm sure we understand each other, don't we Corvus?" She stroked his right wing while eyeing the bird closely. "I don't suppose you know who told Cepheus about Scarflon working with the Dark Orb?" Her long nails inched up toward the bird's eyes again. "It appears he knew his twin brother was dabbling in the Dark Arts. Now *who*, I wonder, let him in on *that* little secret?"

The large crow edged farther away from her, his black, beady eyes watching the Queen's every move.

"What am I saying?" she said, her voice an icy hiss. "You would tell me if you knew." She ran her fingernail over the crow's beak and up between his eyes, tapping him painfully on his head with her pointed nail. She rose abruptly from her chair.

"It pains me to be the bad Queen," she said insincerely. "It seems I am always forced into this position by other's actions. Like those silly sea nymphs! The nerve to suggest they were more beautiful than *I*...their *Queen!* Well...the Nereids aren't here any longer, are they? I do hope they are enjoying their new found ugliness in the cold dark waters of the Spectre Lands." Her face contorted in an evil scowl. "Those glittering, insipid little stars and all the other pathetic sea creatures that rejected me here can live out their days in the dark waters of Apparition Bay. It really doesn't pay to...how shall I say it...*displease* me!"

She sighed contentedly as she picked up a flowing black cape. "If someone hadn't boarded over the well in the Human World, keeping me away from the Dark Orb I hid there, I would have been farther along. At least 20 years in the Human World is only one year of time here. Still, it was a nuisance to wait. But now, they will all bow down to *me*. And....on *that* note....let's go dethrone the King!" Her laughter echoed throughout the castle bed chamber.

The Queen threw the long velvet cape about her shoulders and pulled the hood gently over her crowned head. She picked up a large velvet bag, its crimson color blood-red in the candlelight of the chamber.

* * *

"You are such a creature of habit, Cepheus," she hissed to herself, as she opened the large bed chamber door and peered out into the long hallway. "Always going out on full moon nights so you can be one with the common little star clusters you reign over. Well, this is one time your humble actions will cost you!"

Pulling the bag's drawstrings tightly, she closed the velvet opening. She walked hurriedly through the door and out into the castle's depths.

Cassiopeia crossed quickly through the cavernous great room, barely glancing at the giant portraits of the Twin Kings hanging in golden frames. Her eyes did drift up in approval of her own likeness, hanging (appropriately) alone at the head of the room. She stepped from the back hall doorway of the castle and out into the night air. Glancing around carefully, she made her way along the garden wall, keeping to the high hedges and seldom-used footpaths. The velvet hood of her long black cape was pulled over her head, shielding her face. Corvus flew overhead, his inky-black color melding into the dark shadows beneath the weeping willows flanking the castle walls. Music could be heard coming from the front courtyard as the constellations laughed and frolicked in the delicious white glow of the full moon.

A spray of leaves suddenly spiraled to the garden floor, several catching in the Queen's hooded robe. She hastily pressed herself into the shadows of the stone wall, and held her breath. A snapping noise sounded from a few of the high branches. She waited several seconds; wondering if one of the constellations had followed her. Images of the ones who could fly swept through her mind. Pegasus? Cygnus, the Swan? Aquila, the Eagle? Perhaps Draco, the Dragon had returned, though she was sure she would have heard his heavily beating wings. Not all who soared overhead were from the Glimmer Lands. Cassiopeia knew the Crone from the Spectre Lands had sent spies flying here in the past. Reports of winged constellations terrorizing the humans had also reached her ears.

As the Queen stood there in hiding, fuming at the interruption, an unpleasant smell wafted down to her. It was the rank odor of dirty clothes, stale seawater, and rotten breath. An annoying clanging was also sounding from overhead.

"Barnacle!" she hissed to herself. "That insufferable pirate ghost and his flying ship!"

Corvus was circling at a distance, watching as the large pirate ship scudded jerkily across the treetops, while a fat fish sailed along behind. A frayed rope tethered the fish to the back of the ship, like a faithful dog following its Master. The boat's filthy sails were tattered and hanging at odd angles, while a crusty frying pan clanged noisily against the brass riggings on the main mast. As the boat hovered above the hiding Queen, Barnacle suddenly appeared at the port bow and upended a bucket of vile water over the side. It sloshed through the trees nearly hitting the royal lady below. Cassiopeia jumped back as the brackish liquid just missed covering her satin shoes.

Barnacle had been a very ancient constellation, back when pirates ruled the Galaxy's High Seas. He was a stowaway from the Island of Jamaica and had never been of high rank. The other nautical constellations had tired of him, largely due to his foul odor, and his habit of helping himself to the other pirates' treasure. He kept a large fish constellation called Volans as his pet, often riding on the grouper through the night sky in search of lost trinkets from other ships that may have fallen overboard.

The pirate ghost had not been lucky in his pursuit of silver and gold. He was caught pilfering a gold bracelet once belonging to Serena, the Sky Sorceress. After being found out for the theft, Barnacle was kicked off the large constellation flagship and stripped of his star power, leaving him only a pirate ghost throughout eternity. He had commandeered a broken-down star vessel called *Vela* he found abandoned in Apparition Bay; a dark body of water in the Spectre Lands, and tied his faithful, floating fish to the keel.

"Ye Ok back thar, Volans?" the pirate ghost called in his broken Cajun accent to the sleeping fish. The grouper floated languidly on the night breeze, and merely burped in response.

Barnacle adjusted his dirty suspenders hanging limply over his lanky frame, as he pulled the bucket back over the side, tossing it noisily to the weathered planks. His long greasy beard caught in the rotting rope. He jerked his matted hair from the hemp, freeing several dead bugs, and scraps of spoiled meat, from where they had been trapped in the tangled knots of the beard's braids. A dirty bandana covered his head, allowing only a long, ratty strand of hair to hang from the back. His baggy pants were stuffed into holey boots, while a stained and torn grey shirt fluttered in the night wind. A broken pistol dangled from a faded leather belt.

"Keep a sharp eye out fer that dang dragon, Volans!" he barked. "He's a lot more dangerous when he's mortal than when he's just a bunch of stinky stars! Full moon nights are always treacherous, Matey!" Barnacle spat over the side for emphasis, the blob of quivering jelly-like bile splattering only inches from the Queen's hiding place.

"Ughhhhh!" she groaned, pulling her feet closer to her, her face red with anger.

As the Queen pulled her skirts away from the shimmering spit, her large ruby ring caught the moonlight. Barnacle grasped the ship's railing and nearly fell overboard in his eagerness to see what treasure was winking up at him.

"Volans!" he hissed. "Do you see it, Fishhead? Aye, tis treasure fer sure. Where's me hook?"

The ghost scurried about the ship, as the Queen grew more and more agitated. She was wasting precious time. Her plans could not go through without the full moon, which was already at its high point in the night sky. But she dared not move. The pirate had a clear view of the garden exit. No one was to know of her secret mission.

A shout of joy sounded from the ship, as the ghost found what he was looking for. He carried the fishing pole to the ship's railing and carefully held it over the side, releasing the long fishing line an inch at a time. Something round and wet was attached to the hook, and it swung in wide arcs as the breeze played with it, as a cat would pat a dangling ball. Barnacle let out more line, until the round object pierced the last strands of tree branches, and came to rest only inches from the Queen's face.

Cassiopeia jumped back in surprise, her back raking painfully against the stone wall. Dangling before her face was a large eyeball, its iris a purpled-black. It swiveled on the fish hook, as it looked around for any sign of sparkling treasure. The Queen swatted at it, praying Barnacle would not see her. She pulled the hood down farther over her jeweled crown and jammed her ringed fingers inside her gown. Just as the eye was turning in her direction, she panicked and fled, crouched over and keeping to the shadows. The eye looked this way and that. After a few moments of detecting no sign of sparkling trinkets, it bounced up and down twice on the hook to alert the pirate to reel it up.

With great disappointment, the ghost reeled in the eye, known throughout the pirate community as the Dead Man's Eye. It had belonged to the most famous pirate constellation in the Universe, Two Hooks Mason. Two Hooks had lost both hands while battling an ancient sea monster named Serpens. The giant three-headed serpent had snapped off both of Two Hook's hands, as the pirate hoisted aboard the vast treasure the monster had been guarding in a hidden grotto. The pirate had fashioned two hands out of whaling hooks. But it was his eye that had made him a legend. Two Hook's right eye could spot a hidden treasure buried beneath layers of sand, hidden in the Milky Way, or laying belly up in the murky waters of Apparition Bay. Due to this, he had more treasure hidden away than all the other looters combined. When Two Hooks was finally killed by a sea monster named Cetus, the famous treasure-hunting eye was up for bid. Pirates, sea captains, and buccaneers from several Galaxies came to bid on the Dead Man's Eye; its legend guaranteed to net them treasure throughout the Milky Way.

Barnacle, being the only ghost in attendance at the eye's bidding, simply slipped into the shadows behind the barrel where the famous eye was being kept. He reached through the boards and locks with his transparent hand, flipped the lock's safety latch from inside, and removed Two Hooks' eye. He was gone with his prize before the bidding was even over.

Now as he floated above the willows of the castle courtyard, he sighed over the failed attempt at securing a rare bauble. The pirate ghost tossed the fishing pole, with the famous eye attached to its hook, back into the galley. "Prob'ly jest some shiny rock or t'other," he muttered, as he walked to the helm and adjusted his eye patch.

He looked up at the sky's familiar landmarks and rolled the wheel over hard to the starboard. The vessel picked up speed as the ghost steered the ship erratically through the sky, taking half of the garden's treetops with him. The poor fish tethered to the ship's stern bobbed in and out of the breaking limbs as if being tossed about on a sea of foliage. Finally, the ship veered off to the east, and the pirate's rank smell dissipated with the evening breeze, leaving only a faint clanging noise echoing behind him.

The Queen stopped to catch her breath. She looked back at the repulsive wad of spit that lay shimmering in the moonlight. Listening carefully, she heard only the faint strains of music coming from the front courtyard. She hurried on, keeping to the shadows, as she glanced up nervously at the full moon above her. Corvus's beating wings thrummed the air softly overhead. Finally, she reached the tall wrought-iron gate that guarded the rear entrance of the castle grounds where she knew Orion's hounds were standing guard. As the Queen stepped through the gate, she noticed one of the dogs was missing, and the other appeared half-asleep and bored. At the sound of the gate's creaking hinges, the canine sprang to life, jaws snapping as the Queen stepped through the opening.

"Stand down!" she demanded.

The dog immediately sat, his ears pointed at attention.

"No one follows me...do you hear?" she snapped. "NO ONE! Corvus is accompanying me, but no other soul is to come down the forest path. AM I CLEAR?"

The dog snapped his mouth closed and sat up straight, his collar tag glinting in the moonlight. The name Canis Minor was etched onto the gold tag.

"Where is Canis Major?" the Queen asked, looking about. Canis Major was the larger of the two dogs. Unbeknownst to the Queen, he was still in the Human World after entering there through Dillon Finnel's painting.

Canis Minor blinked in the moonlight, and eyed the hovering black crow with contempt—drool dripping from his fangs.

"Never mind!" she spat. With that the Queen looked around her carefully, and seeing no one, disappeared into the protective cover of the woods bordering the Kingdom.

The forest surrounding the Star Castle was vast, its paths treacherous, often leading to hidden hazards that had been set up to protect the castle from intruders. The Queen knew the path leading to the cave by heart. As she turned yet another bend in the trees, she thought of the Lamberhook Forest in the Spectre Lands. The dark, forbidden realm lay at the other end of the well's portal...a powerful well that sat waiting in the depths of the cave ahead.

Cassiopeia stopped and looked up through a break in the trees. The 9 planets had begun to align in a vertical pattern, one atop the other, a sign that the time of the Dark Moon was near. When the last planet was in place, their alignment resembling a celestial totem pole, the five wells would alter their locations, and their secret symbols would change.

As the Queen paused to watch the surreal happenings in the night sky, she thought she heard a sound breaking the still quiet of the forest. The large black crow swooped down and rested on a tree branch near her. He too cocked his head and listened to the whisperings of the forest. Something was moving through the brush. The Queen heard it whenever she suddenly stopped. It was following her, she was sure. The soft murmurings of the forest hummed in her ears, but the noises of something scampering through the underbrush had ceased.

"Keep your eyes peeled, Corvus" she said to the crow. "We are not alone!"

The Queen hurried on. The full moon would begin to wane soon, and she would have to wait until the next one. Another month was too long to put off her plans.

Rounding an outcropping of stones, she suddenly stopped. Up ahead, at the end of a small rutted path sat a giant boulder, its shape pressed into the side of a craggy mountain. Cassiopeia crossed to it slowly, once again looking about her for spying eyes. When the night remained still, she reached into the velvet bag, and removed the crown of the fallen King, Scarflon, whom she had banished to the Spectre Lands during the last full moon.

"If a full moon wasn't needed to banish royalty, this would be a lot easier," she hissed to herself.

The Queen approached the large rock. There were four small, irregularly shaped holes in the boulder's face. Turning the crown carefully in her hands, the Queen aligned the four gems of emerald, diamond, ruby, and sapphire with the recesses in the rock. Gently she pressed Scarflon's crown into the holes.

A rumbling noise sounded from deep within the mountain, and the rock began to vibrate. She removed the crown and replaced it into the bag. The massive boulder shuddered; it began rolling to one side, exposing a dark tunnel behind it. Once the space was large enough for her to fit through, Cassiopeia slipped inside the darkness, with Corvus close behind her.

Chapter Twenty-Five

A MAGIC MAP

The cave was cloistered and dank. Cassiopeia felt her way along the jagged walls, her long gown catching in the small stones of the passageway. Though the tunnel was dark, it meant nothing to a constellation who lived in the black night sky. The Queen could see everything around her with crystal clarity. It was only when she was trapped inside the body of Morble, that her constellation's powers abandoned her.

Cassiopeia hurried along. The tunnel twisted and turned, the path sometimes dipping down into a numbing coldness, only to rise again at the next turn. Finally, up ahead, the Queen saw the welcoming sight of the magic stone wall; moonlight from a small opening in the cave's ceiling highlighting it in a warm glow. To any traveling this corridor, the wall would have signaled a dead end with no way out but to turn around and retrace one's steps to the cave's opening. But to the Royals wearing the crowns of the Galaxy, it was merely a secret riddle to be solved.

The Queen removed Scarflon's crown from the velvet bag. She pressed it into the four recesses in the stone wall's face, exactly as she had done with the boulder outside. But this time, instead of the stone making way for her, it merely began to shimmer. Within moments, faint lettering appeared on the craggy surface, as though written by an unseen hand. The puzzle changed each time someone approached the sacred wall. Along with the writing, appeared the images of the 12 Zodiac Signs: Capricorn, Aquarius, Pisces, Aries, Taurus, Gemini, Cancer, Leo, Virgo, Libra, Scorpio, and Sagittarius.

The cryptic writing appearing this time was a riddle which read:

Of the Royal Stars, they number "four"
It fills the sky with bloody gore

Cassiopeia smiled. The riddle would be a hard one to solve for those who did not know the constellations as well as she did. After all, she was one of the most ancient stars in the Galaxy. She knew the first line of the riddle referred to the Royal Stars of Persia. There were "four" of them and they reigned in the sky from as far back as 3000 BC. Antares was one of the four Royal stars, and was reddish in color. It was often given the nicknames of "the Ruddy Star", "the Fire Star", and "the Unlucky Star". To those looking up at it from below, it appeared blood-red in color and stained the velvet blackness of night.

She reached into her long flowing robes and retrieved a small bottle of Lunar Potion. Carefully she applied two drops of the magic potion to the wall atop the image of Scorpio, the Scorpion—the Zodiac constellation in which the bright red star of Antares lived. Moonlight washed over the liquid drops. The stone wall shuddered and then swung open, allowing her access.

Corvus flew in ahead of her and perched on the rocky ledge he knew so well. He had watched as King Scarflon and the Crone had worked their dark magic in this room. He had also watched the Queen of the Glimmer Lands take over the Well Room to continue Scarflon's evil, sending many constellations that disliked her into the well, and to the waiting darkness of the Spectre Lands at the other end.

Cassiopeia entered the small room, dazzling moonlight pouring in through an opening in the cave's roof. The light fell onto a stone table in the middle of the chamber, and a large round object draped in black fabric sitting near the corner of the room. The Queen crossed to the west wall where a large engraving of Orion was carved into the craggy face. She tapped three special "stars" in the constellation's image with her fingernail. A section of the etching swung out, revealing a hidden compartment. Inside rested a box holding the most powerful object in the Universe. A tarnished bronze lock in the shape of an eye held the lid securely fastened.

The Queen once again retrieved the small bottle of Lunar Potion. She dropped two drops carefully into the center of the metal eye, and held the box beneath the moonlight pouring in from overhead. The familiar 'click' sounded, as the lock relinquished its hold. She flipped open the lid and carefully removed the Dark Orb, from where she had replaced it, upon returning to the Glimmer Lands from the Human World. Without Scarflon, or his crown to open the secret passages, she knew the Crone could not enter the cave. It was the safest place she could find to hide the powerful Orb. The Queen had also placed the Crone's eye into the Dark Orb's opening before hiding it away. The round silver ball shimmered in the moonlight, while the Crone's eye waited to release its evil.

Cassiopeia carried the Orb to the center of the room. She flicked open the stopper to the bottle of Lunar Potion. Drawing in her breath, she gently added two drops of its powerful liquid to the Crone's eye anchored in the silver Orb.

Now, as the Queen held the ball tightly in her palm, the rays of the full moon overhead hit the black pupil of the red crystal eye. A blinding light shot out from it, and then dimmed, to illuminate the room in a red glow. A shimmering image began to appear from the crimson light. As the Queen watched excitedly, an ancient map spread out in a hologram through the still air. It filled the small Well Room, hovering in iridescent green, and then settled lightly onto the stone table. Cassiopeia smiled. The great map and its secrets were now hers!

Around the perimeter of the map, ancient images of the constellations belonging to the Glimmer Lands could be seen, both those present, and past. Each time the map was used, it showed the inhabitants of the dimension where it was residing. The Spectre

Lands' evil inhabitants lined the ancient map if opened within the 2nd Dimension. If released in the 3rd Dimension called the Treblin, the occupants of the Toad Kingdom would be shown around the edge, instead of the Glimmer Lands' constellations. Due to the sheer abundance of humans in the 4th Dimension, only those practicing magic in that realm were shown if the map were opened there.

Cassiopeia looked at the blood-red stain that marked each constellation on the map that had been cast out into the well from the Glimmer Lands. She noticed with satisfaction that a crimson mark now rested over the image of Scarflon, the Twin King.

It had been so easy to trick Scarflon, she thought cruelly. She had spied on him, along with the Crone (who was teaching him the ways of the Dark Arts), for several full moon nights from her hiding place in the Well Room's cragged walls. Cassiopeia had memorized the rituals that opened the map from within the Orb and cast constellations into the well. At first, the sight of the Crone removing one of her powerful eyes—and adding it to the Orb—had repulsed her, but she realized the Orb's map would not work without it. The combination of the Orb and the eye created the most powerful talisman in the Universe.

Knowing Scarflon and the Crone had been conspiring to get rid of her, and that they would be using the well again during the next full moon, Cassiopeia had come up with a plan. She had simply sent Corvus with a phony note for Scarflon, in the Crone's forged handwriting on the day of the full moon. The crow had dropped it through the King's bedroom window.

The note read:

SCARFLON-

MEET ME AT REFLECTION BAY TONIGHT, NEAR THE STONE LION BENCH.

I HAVE A NEW OBJECT FROM THE DARK ARTS TO SHOW YOU! CRONE

The Queen had sent Corvus to the Crone's castle in the Spectre Lands several days earlier. The crow was instructed to drop a note (in Scarflon's copied handwriting), unseen, through the window of the castle's Great Hall. The note read:

Crone- I am sending you this note through one of your Siglets.
The Queen has become unbearable. I must rid the Glimmer Lands of her. This is something I must do alone. Your eye is still with the Dark Orb in the cave. I will banish her through the well on the full moon. When she reaches the Spectre Lands, do with her as you wish! Scarflon-

It had all worked like a charm! Scarflon waited for the Crone at Reflection Bay, not realizing he had been tricked; the Crone remained in her castle in the Spectre Lands, not realizing she had been duped by a phony note as well. All the Queen had to do was show up to the empty cave on the next full moon night, and use her husband's crown to enter the secret passages. She retrieved the Dark Orb from its hidden chamber, with the Crone's eye still in place. Then, all she had to do was use the map against Scarflon, in the exact way she was about to rid herself of his twin brother.

The Queen slipped the large velvet bag from her cape pocket and placed it on the floor. She opened its drawstring in readiness for the objects she would hurriedly place inside. Crossing to the far corner of the room, she stopped and looked down at a large object covered with a black draping. Taking a deep breath, she pulled away the cloth and let it puddle to the ground. A foul smell like that of stagnant, putrid pond water escaped the bowels of a stone well that now stood in the bright light of the moon overhead. A sigh welled up from its depths. The Queen wondered if it was breathing in the night breeze of the Glimmer Lands, or exhaling the dead air of the

Spectre Lands.

Cassiopeia ran a long, red fingernail over the ancient well's stone rim. It was covered in symbols. Noting that the moon was shifting positions, the Queen hurried now before its light had moved along the cliff face, leaving the cave's opening in darkness. Without the full moon's illumination, nothing would happen tonight.

The Crone's red eye pulsed with light, sending its crimson glow into the cave's depths. Quickly the Queen placed the powerful ball into the center of the map and peered over it. She turned the Orb slowly around, watching as the light from the powerful eye spread out in blood red over the map's images of the constellations. The beam swept past the drawing of the constellation of Aries, moving on as Cassiopeia continued to turn the Orb clockwise in the center of the map. Pisces, Aquarius, Capricorn….it continued slowly on; passing the images like the Grim Reaper in search of his next victim. Andromeda, Leo, Draco the Dragon. There was a red drop of blood in the center of the drawing of Draco, indicating the Dragon now dwelled in the Spectre Lands. The Crone had captured the flying monster to watch over her domain in her dark kingdom some time ago. Cassiopeia guessed the dragon had been searching for the Dark Orb and the Crone's eye earlier, as it had circled her castle.

Finally, the Queen stopped the Orb's turning. Framed in the Crone's eye's red beam was the image of the constellation of Cepheus—King of the Glimmer Lands!

The Queen's mouth twisted cruelly as she focused the Orb's light onto the King's drawing. It spotlighted the image of Cepheus like a bloody finger pointing to its next victim. Seconds passed, and suddenly the Orb glowed brighter, a humming noise coming from within it. A purple haze began swirling around it, going faster and growing larger—like a tornado enveloping the room. It rose into the air, twirling at a high rate of speed; the force from its vortex whipping the Queen's cape about her in a frenzy. She clung to the Orb, holding it in place as the funnel rose higher. It lifted out through the cave's ceiling opening, and into the night.

Corvus took cover in a small alcove of rocks, high above the map. He flung a wing over his face to shield himself from the flying dirt erupting from the cave floor.

The purple vortex rose higher into the night sky, sweeping over the forest's treetops and toward the castle grounds. It thundered over the iron gate of the garden, sending the frightened guard dog into the forest for cover. Climbing higher the thundering funnel skirted the castle's tall spires, sweeping up and over them, and into the courtyard at the front doors of the main entrance. Constellations were singing and dancing about a spewing fountain. As the cyclone gushed down over them, they screamed in terror and ran.

Cepheus looked up in horror as the giant vortex came toward him in a rush of wind. The King began to run, the thundering sound of a tornado ringing in his ears. Up ahead was the door to the castle kitchen and he sprinted toward it. The funnel was closing in on him. A few more feet and he would be safe! Just as he reached the small kitchen garden that lay outside the wooden door, the vortex roared down upon him. He screamed, and grabbed for a stone garden bench, but it was of no use against the giant force. His fingers lost their grip on the granite seat. He was sucked, feet first, into the swirling mass as though it were a Black Hole. His screams became more muffled, as he was swallowed into its abyss.

As fast as it had come, the vortex lifted and began its backward motion toward the cave. It retreated over the forest's treetops, finally disappearing back through the opening in the cave's roof.

Orion's hound, Canis Minor, watched in terror, his haunches quivering in the darkness of the trees. A small sound of something scurrying through the bushes caught the attention of the dog, and his ears pricked up. His animal instincts returned. He barred his pointed white teeth and growled deeply, his hackles rising along his back. The canine bolted into the underbrush, snapping and snarling.

A sudden flash of white exploded from the bushes, as a small rabbit darted through the greenery and down the path. The big dog was right behind it, barking, and sending dirt and pebbles flying with its scrambling paws. He chased the small rabbit, (known in the constellations as Lepus, the Hare) through the pathways, tearing through bushes until both animals exploded from the depths of the forest. Without pausing, the rabbit made a beeline for the cave entrance, its massive rock still rolled to one side. It scampered into the darkness of the tunnel inside.

In the Well Room the purple vortex hovered above the shimmering Orb, the red eye throwing crimson highlights into the shadowed recesses of the cave. The Queen held tight to the Orb. She lifted it in front of the swirling funnel and the haze parted, showing the frozen form of the Glimmer Land's King. He rotated before her, his eyes frozen, his mouth still hanging open from fright.

"Poor Cepheus," she said insincerely. "Look what you have been reduced to. All that goodness, for *what?* I suppose you can cut cards with Scarflon to decide who will rule the Spectre Lands when you get there, if he is still alive. Of course, the Crone may have something to say about it." She laughed manically and watched as the King's constellation revolved in front of her.

The red glow of the Crone's crystal eye cloaked the suspended figure of the Star King. The beam grew brighter, the Orb vibrating in the Queen's hand. As the ray of crimson light reached its pinnacle of brightness, a star suddenly fell from the King's constellation, and was sucked into the Crone's eye. With that, Cepheus' mortal form dissolved into a cluster of stars in the shape of the King. His royal crown fell, hitting the stone floor. It rolled in a circle until it stopped, clattering onto its side—just as Scarflon's had fallen a year ago. Its precious jewels glinted in the moonlight.

Cassiopeia moved with the Orb across the room. Cepheus's shape followed the crimson light to the well. The Queen paused, staring momentarily at the star cluster that was her husband. Carefully she dripped two drops of the Lunar Potion onto the well's symbols of the twisted Lamberhook tree, and that of Serpens, the Serpent. These secret symbols would send Cepheus to the dark realm of the Spectre Lands, just as it had done with his brother.

Moonlight hit the shimmering drops of potion, puddled into the secret symbols. Light exploded from the well's depths, along with a blast of foul odor that filled the room. Cassiopeia twisted her nose in repulsion.

"I do hope you are happy in your new home, husband dear," she said callously.

With a face showing no emotion, she passed her hand over the Orb, blocking the Crone's powerful gaze. As Cassiopeia watched heartlessly, the funnel dropped the King into the waiting depths of the well.

Corvus the Crow stared, his eyes large in the red glow. His body shook. He doubted he would ever get used to the ritual that removed beings from this world and hurled them into the next. But she had done it! She had sent the other Twin King through the well.

Corvus knew the Queen's plan was to travel into another of the four remaining dimensions to begin her evil control of the people or creatures there. With the Lunar Potion, the Crone's eye, the Dark Orb and the map, she would be invincible. And now the one being who would have tried to stop her was going to a place from which few escaped. The passage through the well into the Spectre Lands would distort the King's once proud form, until he became mangled and twisted, unrecognizable. He would be given a new name, and no one would mark his history as the great King of the Glimmer Lands.

Quickly Cassiopeia returned to the map. She trickled two drops of the Lunar Potion upon the shimmering map's drawn image of a well that sat in the section called the Treblin. In parenthesis beneath this name was written, The Toad Kingdom. The moonlight hit the drops of potion. A luminescent image of a toad magically appeared on the map. Next to it was the symbol for the Zodiac sign that would open the well's portal to the Treblin: Lacerta, the Lizard.

"Corvus!" the Queen screamed. "Don't just sit there like road kill! Take the Lunar Potion. I'll get the Orb and Cepheus's crown. Hurry...while I pack this stuff!"

Cassiopeia picked up the King's crown. She slipped it into the red velvet bag she had waiting on the cave floor. It rested in the bottom of the satchel next to the crown of Scarflon. Lastly, she gently lowered the still shimmering Dark Orb, with the Crone's eye encased in its center, into the bag. The magic map disappeared. Rushing over to the opening in the wall behind Orion's image, she grabbed a blue bag containing the final pod from Luthor's Ghost.

She had used the other to create more Lunar Potion.

"I will need this if the Lunar Potion runs out...," she whispered excitedly to herself, "...and to capture Mudlin."

Clutching both bags, she crossed to the well where the Crow was standing on its rim. He was holding the vial of Lunar Potion in one claw, and pulling at its glass stopper with his beak. The lid would not open as his talons were shaking nervously. The Queen was looking up at the cave opening, as the moon began to slip away.

"Hurry, you idiot!" she screamed. "Put it on the toad shape and Lacerta! HURRY!"

The moonlight shone into the well's depths, illuminating the crumbling walls, and strange symbols carved into its rim. The Queen peered inside nervously. Traveling through the well was never something one did without trepidation. At least her beauty would not be deformed this time, as she was not traveling to the Spectre Lands. She would scout out the Treblin, where Mudlin, the Toad Sorcerer ruled, and use Luthor's pod to kill him with its green poison. She could then take over his 3rd Dimension. Ruling the Treblin would be a start. With Cepheus and Scarflon gone she was now ruling *this* dimension. That took care of the 1st Dimension. The 3rd and 4th should be easy. *How hard could it be to outsmart a Kingdom of Toads and those half-witted Humans?* Taking over the 2nd Dimension would be harder...the Crone would not be defeated easily. Luthor's poison had no power over her.

"Add the potion to the well!" she screamed at the trembling Crow, who was still fumbling with the bottle's stopper. "Oh give it here!" she demanded, reaching for the bottle.

The Queen grabbed for the bottle, while wrestling to pull the drawstring closed on the satchel. Suddenly, the sound of a Baying hound erupted from the dark tunnel behind her. Before Cassiopeia could recover from her surprise, a small white hare bounded into sight and dashed across the room.

"What in the...?" she screamed, as the hare scampered fiercely about the room, the dog hard on its heels.

"Canis, *NO*....what are you....?"

She was cut off as the dog leapt after the rabbit, knocking the Queen off balance. She screamed as she teetered at the edge of the well. As she fell forward, the satchel fell from her hands, its open mouth spilling the Dark Orb and the Crone's eye into the black depths of the well.

"**NOOOOOOOO!**" she screamed, lunging for the bag. The blue pouch holding Luthor's pod fell from her hand into the well. Frantically, she made a grab for it. She slipped and fell, grasping for the well's rim, but her long gown became tangled around her feet and she pitched forward. With a deafening scream, Cassiopeia tumbled headfirst into the sour blackness of the well, and vanished from sight.

Corvus flew up to his ledge to avoid the snapping jaws of the large dog. Canis was trying to find the rabbit that was hiding in a small alcove in the rocks. The flustered canine now turned its attention to Corvus, spittle flying, as it snapped and jumped at the crow, sitting just out of reach. Canis had lost Lepus, the Hare. The juicy meat of an overfed spy would have to do.

Corvus's heart was hammering. He looked up at the cave opening. Only a sliver of the moon could be seen through the hole. He looked at the shimmering symbols on the well of a twisted Lamberhook tree and Serpens, the Serpent, still illuminated from the Queen's banishment of the King to the Spectre Lands only moments before. *The well would have taken her there*, the Crow thought, shivering. What could he do now? He was new to this "Pick a symbol, any symbol and travel the friendly wells!" His best bet was to try and follow her through the well, and his time was running out…it would soon sit in darkness.

The Crow hesitated in his fear, his thoughts whirled. He would have no friend at the castle, as the Queen was the only one who spoke to him. She was right; he was despised as her spy. Corvus looked down at the dog and made up his mind. He was still holding the vial of Lunar Potion in one claw, as he flew quickly to the well. Hovering above it, he paused. He shuddered when he thought of the fate his Queen had just endured, and now he too would share her demise. They would be deformed and twisted as they passed through the repugnant darkness of the portal. He could try flying there from here, but it would take too long. Trying to find her in that deformed world would be hard enough, let alone with time passing.

The snarling dog lunged at the bird, his snapping jaws locking onto the crow's tail feathers. Corvus slammed against the stone wall. Dazed, the crow circled over the well, flying crookedly as he struggled to hold onto the small bottle of powerful potion. The bright light from the well's portal lit up the room.

As Canis Minor neared the well he was momentarily blinded. He screeched to a halt. Several of Corvus's feathers were protruding from the dog's mouth. The rabbit chose the moment to come out from hiding and head for the tunnel leading from the Well Room. But Canis saw him and blocked his retreat. Snarling and lunging, he chased the rabbit about the room, until the frightened creature took the only way out he could find. He scampered full force toward the well—and leapt in!

Shocked, Corvus watched the rabbit disappear into the blinding light. The bird took a deep breath, circled once more, and finally flew into the well, just as the moon passed away from the cave's opening. The crow disappeared into the deep regions of the stone passage. The portal's light went out, leaving the cave in darkness. Canis barked helplessly at the now empty well. He finally turned and fled from the room. Slowly the door to the hidden recess behind

Orion's image, where the great Orb had sat, swung closed. The secret wall with its riddles slid silently back into place.

Chapter Twenty-Six

THE QUEEN'S NEW HOME

Cassiopeia looked about at the darkness and shivered. Her screams at seeing her disfigured body echoed throughout the cave, finally fading into the stone walls. The pale moonlight shining in through the cave ceiling barely illuminated the small area. The wall near the well she had just crawled from began to shimmer, its hard surface becoming reflective. She stood before what was now a darkened mirror, and watched as the last of her beauty from the Glimmer Lands disappeared. Her long braids now hung in matted strands, catching on the torn folds of her eyelids. She reached up and touched exposed teeth where once there had been full red lips. Only a narrow bone replaced the aquiline nose, and seeping sores littered her grey skin. She held her talon-like fingers in front of her. Her satin slippers were gone, leaving her twisted feet bare for the world to see.

As she stared at her reflection with frightened repugnance, a name began to appear across the shimmering wall. In broken letters it spelled out *Morble*. She was back in the Spectre Lands.

The Queen's gnarled hands trembled as she searched the barren dirt floor in panic; looking desperately for the Dark Orb and the Crone's eye that had fallen into the well just ahead of her. She could not believe she had dropped them, or that she was in the cave in the Spectre Lands. She was supposed to be in the Treblin, if only that idiotic bird had done his part! Suddenly, she remembered her husband.

"Cepheus!" she hissed, looking around the small dark cave in a panic for the King she had just banished. *Where was he? Where was his twin brother Scarflon she had also tossed heartlessly into the well?* There would be enemies all around her here in this deformed world. As she watched the shadows about her, she realized her position was not a good one. The Dark Moon would rise in only ten days, and now she had lost the things she needed to take control of the Dimensions.

With renewed effort, Morble searched the cave. Her red satchel containing the twin crowns was not here, nor was the pouch with Luthor's pod. Just as she was about to give up her search, she spotted something glinting in the far corner of the cave's well room. Eagerly she scrambled over to the area. Morble let out a cry of joy as she plucked the Dark Orb from the barren floor. Holding it happily in her hand, she continued to search for the Crone's eye that should have landed next to it. After several minutes, she realized it was not here.

"It likely called out to the Crone. She or her Siglets have captured it," Morble said aloud, her voice echoing in the empty chamber.

Dropping the Dark Orb into her pocket, she stepped to the cave's exit and looked out onto the barren land. Its foul stench assaulted her senses and clung to her skin…the same skin that had, only moments before, been perfumed with rare fragrances. *Somewhere out there are the Twin Kings*, she thought. Both would be seeking her demise. She would go where she had gone the first time she came here a year ago after banishing Scarflon through the well. She would go to Garglon's home in the Lamberhook Forest and hide there until she could decide what to do. The Banshees would protect her there. Morble knew there were no more white pods left in Garglon's garden. It was the only reason Morble had come here before. She had used the last of her Lunar Potion to exile Scarflon, and needed the pods to create more. She was not aware the Crone had stolen them all…all but one.

"That stupid Garglon believed me when I told her I was a powerful witch and had come to help her defeat the Crone," Morble cackled, remembering the day she met Garglon within the twisted forest. "The only place to grow more of the pods was to go beyond the Crone's reach. The Human World seemed the safest place, not only to grow another Luthor, but to hide the Orb and eye while I got everything ready to further my plans. And it had all worked like a charm, until someone boarded over the well. Enough!" she said aloud. "This is not serving me to stand here with regrets."

After checking to make sure she was alone, the Forest Witch wrapped her deformed arms about her and left the safety of the cave.

Chapter Twenty-Seven

ABRA KADABRA!

"And now you say your son is missing as well?" the policeman asked Mr. Finnel, as he sat with David and Marsha at the small kitchen table in Dillon Finnel's kitchen. The coffee Marsha had brought him sat untouched in the mug near his elbow. Officer Skrove was scribbling notes on a small pad and eyeing the couple with mistrust.

"Yes," David said, his voice rising. "How many times are we going to hash this out? My son's back pack is not in his room, and we can't find him anywhere! I'm sure he went out looking for his grandfather."

Officer Skrove's eyebrow arched slightly at the mention of the missing artist. It was clear he thought Dillon Finnel had "disappeared" due to reasons pertaining to some kind of hocus pocus.

"How old is your son?" the policeman asked, flipping back through his notes.

"Eleven!" David said sharply.

Marsha shot her husband a look to quiet down. Officer Skrove shot him a warning look as well.

"What time does your son usually come home if he's been out?" he asked, a biting tone seeping into his voice.

"Before dark," David said, trying to control his anger. "The kid is petrified of being around that forest out there after nightfall." His voice had risen again.

Just then Markus entered the kitchen.

"Markus, I asked you to stay in your room until we are finished here," his mother said, her voice strained.

"I just want to know if you have seen my flashlight," Markus said, staring at the holstered gun on Officer Skrove's hip.

"No," she sighed. "Besides, isn't that T.J.'s flashlight?"

"Flashlight missing, too?" the policeman asked, his tone bordering on sarcastic. It was evident he did not think the Finnel's were giving him all the information about the missing family members.

David Finnel rose from the table and squared off to the man.

"I have had all the insinuations, accusations, and procrastinations I am going to take," he said, his face red with anger. "Either get some other policemen over here to find out what happened to my father and son, or I will report you!"

Officer Skrove rose from his chair and stood, feet firmly planted, looking up at the man who was several inches taller.

"You Finnels are involved in a lot of unsolved questions in this town," he said acidly. "Two people have lost their eyesight, and there are reports of strange creatures running all over the place! Now you tell me that it is just a coincidence all this happened on the same night your father's weird paintings were unveiled at Goreland Elementary? We have witnesses that saw things flying out of the paintings! If that's not enough, weird things are going on in the sky...planets acting all strange and stacking up funny. Now you settle down and let me do my job, unless you want an interior view of a jail cell! I will go to the woods and have a look around, but I am warning you...if I find one thing that leads to any shenanigans on your part, I will lock the lot of you up! I don't go for people messing around with black magic!"

"I can do magic!" Markus exclaimed.

David squeezed his eyes shut and drew in a deep breath, his hands closing into fists.

"Not now!" Marsha said through clenched teeth. It was the last thing they wanted Officer Skrove to hear, no matter how innocent it was intended.

"Really?" the policeman asked, shooting David a meaningful look. "What kind of magic, son?"

"Well, I am working on one where I make my friend Corey disappear," he said happily. "It's harder than I thought it would be. I put the magic cape over his head, and say the magic words, but so far I've only messed up his hair."

"Did you try the trick with your grandpa and brother?" the policeman asked meaningfully.

"That's enough!" David shouted. "Markus, go to your room!" He turned to face Officer Skrove. "I would appreciate it if you would go and look for my family," he said hotly.

"Can I go with the policeman and look for T.J. and Grandpa?" Markus asked hopefully. "I could hold his gun for him!"

Officer Skrove stared at the angry man for a moment while chewing the inside of his lip. He took his time closing his notepad, and sliding it into his shirt pocket.

"Sorry, young man," he said in measured tones. "Please remain in the house until I get back to you," he said to Mr. Finnel. "That goes for *all* of you," he said glancing at Markus.

He walked through the kitchen and dining room. The Finnels heard the front door open and close.

"So I can't go outside and look for Teej?" Markus asked sulkily.

"Markus, *please*...just go to your room!" his mother said, her shoulders sagging and her voice threatening to break.

"It's not my fault everybody is missing," Markus said under his breath. He clumped up the back stairs.

Markus didn't make it to his room. Instead he paused on the second floor landing and peered into his brother's empty bedroom. He stepped inside and poured some dead bugs into the lizard's bowl, scratching the thing's scaly head as he did so. Just then a thud sounded from the attic overhead.

"Grandpa!" Markus whispered excitedly, as he ran from the room, down the hallway, and bolted up the stairs to the attic studio. The door at the top was standing slightly ajar. There was no light coming from the other side.

Markus reached the door and cautiously pushed on it; it swayed open a few inches. He peered inside and saw only the shadows of furniture and paintings. No Grandpa...no T.J. Then what had made the sound up here he had just heard from his brother's room?

Chapter Twenty-Eight

THE SPECTRE LANDS

The next morning, as they left the cave, T.J. couldn't stop looking around. He had never seen a world like this! There were gigantic planets stacked on top of each other, so close he felt he could throw a stone and mar the face of Jupiter—the lowest of the nine. Here the moon was always shining in the sky, its glow slightly more illuminating than the paler sunlight which tried without success to brighten the gloom. The landscape, even in the morning light, was dark and dreary. To T.J.'s artistic eye, it reminded him of a black pen-and-ink drawing that had been rained upon—all the ebony colors running in distorted, twisted forms, making everything seem evil and menacing.

Mandy noticed him surveying the land around them.

"Everything here is a mirror image of the Glimmer Lands where I'm from," Mandy explained. "What I mean is—they both have a castle, forests, a large body of water and a small town. The big difference is that this land looks as if evil has seeped into the roots of the trees and twisted them. It was once just as lovely when Orpheus ruled the 5 Dimensions, and the constellations were equal in their goal for a just and governed Universe. During the Dark Ages of the Human's timeline, evil began to dominate. Witches and wicked creatures claimed the sky as the Humans below looked up and started to worship things unholy. As these constellations' evil grew, they took over the Spectre Lands with the most powerful constellation in the Dark Arts as their guardian—the Crone. Now...it looks like this."

"Kinda smells, too," T.J. said, wrinkling his nose. "It could use a good shot of *Honeysuckle Breezes*," he said, remembering his mother's favorite air freshener.

Mandy didn't know what that meant, but she smiled anyway. Then without another word, the threesome started off through the ruined landscape.

"Where are we going?" T.J. asked again nervously, after they had been traveling through the back trails of the Spectre Lands for hours, with Mandy leading the way. T.J. had a hard time looking at her. In the sunlight, her deformities were amplified. He couldn't believe this scaly creature had been a vibrant girl the night before.

"I don't exactly know," she said. "We need to find the Lamberhook Forest. If I am right, what we are both looking for could be in there. Keep an eye out for twisted, ugly trees."

"As opposed to the pretty ones around here?" he said sarcastically. His heart was hammering. He felt he had just entered one of the horror movies he refused to watch.

T.J. looked at her as they clambered over a pile of rocks. She was having trouble managing her new legs, and the small horns protruding from her ankles kept catching on weeds and tree roots. He was scared, and his stomach was growling, as the sun began to sink lower in the sky. He could hear Twicket's odd rumbling sounds as well, as the boy carried the troll in his hand.

Several times T.J. had seen eyes peering at them from behind clumps of bushes, or high up in the treetops. Something was always moving behind them, only to disappear when they turned to look. Mandy had noticed this as well.

"What's following us?" the boy finally asked the girl, noticing the look of consternation on her face.

"I don't know," she answered quietly, the blob that was now her chin quivering as she spoke. It reminded T.J. of a turkey's wattle. "But something is not right. Why isn't anything trying to stop us? Why are they leaving us alone?"

Twicket eyed her for a moment, and said nothing.

T.J. mulled it over. An idea hit him suddenly and he moaned.

"I bet it's because they know what we're looking for," he said dismally. "That Orb thing. Maybe they are looking for it as well and are just letting us do our thing so we can find it for them, and then...." He broke off.

"And then we won't be needed," Mandy finished for him.

Mandy had stopped by a smelly swamp to get Twicket some fish eggs for lunch. The smell of the vile water nearly caused T.J. to lose the granola bar he had fished from his backpack earlier. He had offered one of the five he packed to Mandy before wolfing it down, but she hadn't wanted any.

"You're kinda quiet," T.J. said to Twicket. He had been surprised to see the troll awake in the daytime, until Twicket reminded him the moon was always out in the Spectre Lands. Yet, the little walking cane had only uttered a few sentences all morning. His large blue eyes had swiveled this way and that, as they scanned the dreary landscape of forests and rivers.

Suddenly, a vaporous form rose from the ground directly in front of them. It shimmered in an iridescent blue, wavering like a candle flame. As the three travelers watched in shock, the mist took the form of an old man, his form bent, hair cascading to the ground. He was holding out his wrinkled hands. In the outstretched palms, he held two glowing stones: one green, and the other black.

"Choose," the undulating shape said in a cracked voice, so low T.J. could barely hear him.

"What?" T.J. asked, staring at the strange little man and the rocks he was offering.

"Choose."

T.J. looked at Mandy, and she shrugged. T.J. took a deep breath and pointed to the green stone.

"You have chosen wisely," the flickering man said. He held the green stone up to where T.J. could see it better. The surface of the smooth rock began to shimmer. A small window opened in its face and lettering began to appear. It reminded T.J. of the old 8 Ball he had where you asked it a question and turned it over to see messages appear in the inky blue liquid.

"It's spelling something," T.J. whispered excitedly.

"Is it directions to local restaurant?" Twicket asked hopefully.

To T.J.'s astonishment, the message appearing in the shimmering green surface read, *"The Well Bucket is the Answer."*

"What?" the boy asked in surprise. As he looked at the writing again, it slowly sank back into the small window and disappeared.

The wavering blue man curled his smoke-like fingers around the stone, and slowly sank back into the earth.

"Holy Faholys! What was that thing?" he asked Mandy. "What does the message mean? Was there a bucket in the cave back there?"

"Do you always ask three questions at once?" she asked, sighing. "I didn't see a bucket. I think that old man is an Oracle. They predict the future. I wonder what the message means."

Something moved through the brush a few feet away from them, and Mandy froze. T.J. halted as well, his heart racing.

"What is it?" he whispered nervously.

Mandy didn't answer him. She stared fixedly at the quivering leaves of a brackenberry bush a stone's throw away. Two long bony fingers were parting the foliage to peer out at the trespassers.

"Don't move," Mandy whispered.

T.J. saw two small, purple eyes staring at them from the parted branches. He could hear a strange sound like something gargling. He clutched Twicket tighter, and pulled him up against his chest in case he needed to start swinging the cane. The troll whimpered in protest.

The purple eyes blinked a few times and waited. Just then a giant black beetle hurried from the bushes, darting across the ground towards a hole beside a large rock. Skeletal fingers from the bushes streaked out and grabbed the bug, snapping its back with a sickening cracking sound. It was instantly pulled into the darkness of the bush. Sounds of crunching could be heard. T.J. thought he was going to throw up. The fingers of the thing's other hand parting the brush released their grasp and disappeared into the foliage.

The three new arrivals waited several moments. Sounds of the creature moving away through the bushes could be heard, along with an occasional gurgling sound.

"What was that?" T.J. finally asked in a hushed voice.

"There are so many horrible things here that I don't know half of them," Mandy said. "They may have once belonged in the Glimmer Lands, or they could have been evil constellations from the beginning of time. We've been fortunate today as most of the creatures here tend to wait for darkness to come out. That's why we need to hurry and find the Lamberhook Forest before nightfall...well, you know...before the sun goes down."

"Is this Lamberhook Forest the same forest old wart head's cane was made from?" he said, nodding toward the troll. When Twicket didn't bother with a retort, T.J. wondered what was going on with the troll. He had Twicket in his right hand and used the cane to poke around in front of him in search of snakes or other things. The only time the troll spoke was to protest each time his shiny cane sunk into the foul-smelling earth.

"Yes," Mandy said, laughing at T.J's nickname for Twicket. It was the first time she had smiled since leaving the cave. "If his cane is made of Lamberhook wood, then it was carved from a tree in that forest. The Spectre Lands are the only place you can find those trees. And stop staring at my leg."

T.J. looked away self-consciously.

"And you no call Twicket names!" the troll joined in. "Me show you what happens to ugly boys who call me "wart head"," Twicket said irritably. "Me hungry."

"Well, look who's back! And, after you sneezed on me two times again this morning," T.J. said hotly, "you can find your own dang food! What will it take to get you to stop this annoying Two-Honker-Slime-Blasting thing every time you see a strong light?"

"Me no can help it," Twicket said, indignantly.

"So why the silent treatment earlier?" T.J. asked the troll. "You scared?"

"Twicket feel funny here," the troll said quietly. "Me feel things. Seem not real…but very real too!"

T.J. eyed him for a minute and sighed. He was tired. It felt like they had been walking forever. He looked about at the strange landscape that was growing darker by the minute. It was worse than any nightmare he had seen drawn in a spooky book. He thought of Markus and how happy he would be here. The kid would probably take pictures, collect rocks, and find a deformed pet to take home! He could only hope his grandfather was near, and that this would soon be over. He could feel the eyes of the creatures here watching them. As they walked along, he thought about the shimmering blue man with the colored stones. The words the *"Well Bucket is the Answer"* kept going through his mind.

Chapter Twenty-Nine

WHEEDLE

At the same moment T.J., Mandy and Twicket were exiting the well into the Spectre Lands', a strange reptilian-like creature named Wheedle was pulling a rickety cart through the back roads of the Spectre Lands. A small lantern dangled from a pole attached to the cart's bench shedding a soft glow onto the twisted shapes of the Lamberhook Forest. Her slanted eyes swiveled to peer into nooks and bogs as the peddler searched for discarded treasures left behind by the creatures and Well Riders that now inhabited the dark kingdom. Her small cart bulged with odd items that could be traded for things that made her life here easier.

A tattered pirate ship sat up ahead in a clearing, and Wheedle smiled. Barnacle was always good for some rumors, and a trade. She spotted the pirate ghost just exiting a stand of Lamberhook trees. He saw the peddler at the same time and ambled over to her. They found a place to sit.

"Did you hear ole Morble is back?" Barnacle asked Wheedle as he bartered with her for a broken compass from her cart. "She fell into da Glimmer Lands' well about a week ago."

They were seated on a log, watching the dark trees of the Lamberhook Forest, as the lantern from Wheedle's cart shed a soft glow over the strange pair.

"Didn't hear it, but I could tell," Wheedle said dejectedly. "Some of the Well Riders are being snatched up faster than I can loot their belongings." She looked over the whale tooth Barnacle was offering. "Same as when Morble was here last time."

"Don't know why ole Garglon took her in before," Barnacle said, always happy for a good bit of gossip. "She must not'a knowed who she was dealin' with. What'd she get fer her troubles? Missin', that's what she got…missin'! Right after Ole Morble learned all Garglon's tricks about those plants of hers, somehow Garglon disappears after she and Morble went to the Human World fer awhile to escape the Crone."

"Don't care what happened to Garglon," Wheedle hissed. "One less person to steal the Well Rider's things. Just wish Morble'd go back to the Glimmer Lands…but she can keep the ugly face!"

Wheedle and Barnacle laughed long and hard at that.

"Who told you she fell into the well?" Wheedle asked, suddenly watching the pirate closely.

"Corvus's beak can be loosened for a fish now 'n then, 'specially if he's hungry," Barnacle said conspiratorially. "That bird sees a lot of what goes on. He was there…in the Well Room in the Glimmer Lands 'n saw the whole thing! Said when she fell in she lost the Dark Orb and some other stuff."

"Didn't know she had the Orb," Wheedle said, mulling the new information over. "She got the Crone's eye too?"

She noticed Barnacle shift slightly on the log. A few seconds passed before he answered.

"Danged if I know," he said simply. He changed the subject back to a safer topic. "If she's capturing things she must be thinkin' a Well Rider found de Orb," the ghost said.

"She must," Wheedle agreed, staring off into the distance. The ghost was keeping something from her. "It's no secret the Crone is looking for it," she continued. "Only reason for Morble to trap the Riders in the trees is to take what they're carrying. Well, the Dark Moon is in two more days. We're all looking for that Orb!"

"I don't like hearin' them Banshee's wailin' away at night," Barnacle said, shuddering slightly. "I guess the Queen…I mean Morble… found her some new friends."

"Yeah...I heard 'em last night...still singin' the song the humans thought was a warning that someone was gonna die. Started in some place called Ireland in the Human World," Wheedle said, handing the compass over to Barnacle. It was of no use to her and the whale tooth would make a good digging tool.

"Poor buggers who end up trapped in those accursed trees," Barnacle said, flipping the broken compass needle in an effort to make it work. The compass had strange markings around its circumference that he had never seen before. "Oh well, got nothin' to do with me," he said. "Let ole Morble have at 'em."

The Lamberhook trees had been grown long ago with the aid of Lunar Potion added to their roots, causing their trunks and branches to become animated beneath the power of moonlight. The trees' wood was originally cultivated for the Dark Arts to be used in creating wands and flying broomsticks. Long ago evil witches and warlords had discovered its use as a prison as well. A magic flute, which had disappeared years ago, had originally been used to unleash the power of the trees and make their trunks open wide. Garglon discovered one full moon night that the Banshee's plaintive notes opened the trunks as well. To her delight she now had ready-made tombs for the people and creatures she no longer needed. Now, Morble had discovered the same use for the twisted trees.

The bartering and gossip completed, Wheedle watched as the pirate sailed off into the darkness. *What is he not telling me?* she wondered. *And what was he doing just coming out of the forest when I saw him?*

She picked up the weathered handles of her cart and started off. Moonlight fell in quilt-like patches on the dusty path. Wheedle's feet left three-toed impressions in the powdery dirt, followed by wobbly lines made by the loose wheels of the cart she was pulling. Her green-and-blue skin was pulled tightly over knobby knees and spindly arms. The peddler's pointed face was a cross between that of a fish and a lizard. The small, angled eyes housed orange irises with glittering gold specks while her pinched nostrils flared to detect scents in the air other than those of rotted leaves and damp earth. Wheedle walked upright and wore a thin, tattered apron.

Wheedle finally stopped and hobbled to the back of the cart. Moving aside several tattered books the humans had left behind, she came to what she was looking for: three small leather bags tied at their necks with knotted rope. She plucked one of the bags from the cart and carried it to the front of the wagon where the moonlight pierced the treetops. Untying the string with arthritic fingers she poured the small pouch's contents into her open palm. Seven colored stones fell into her scaly hand, moonlight dancing off their jewel-like surfaces. Looking about her for spying eyes, Wheedle finally cast the small stones to the ground.

"Find treasure!" she hissed at the stones, which in another dimension were known as Glimrocks. They came from the Glimmer Lands, and had the power to detect things of great worth.

The stones hesitated in the pale stream of moonlight and then began to tremble. First one moved, and then another, until they were tumbling about in an effort to form some kind of pattern. Finally, they arranged themselves into an arrow pointing off to the right of the path.

At first, Wheedle saw nothing but a dirt clod, but as she hobbled closer to the spot the Glimrocks were pointing to, she spotted something oblong imbedded in the moldy swamp grass near the path. She was close to the bog now, and patches of mud-laden grass were more abundant. Hobbling over to the strange object, she prodded one corner of it with a bent, tapered finger and unearthed what appeared to be a blue, cloth bag.

Wheedle held it up to the moonlight and turned it in her hand, brushing dirt clods from its fabric as she did so. It was nothing special, but it was large enough to hold treasure. She eagerly opened it, and peered inside. The peddler was disappointed at first to see only a common-looking white plant pod. She poked it gently. It began to infuse with some kind of green light. Wheedle quickly closed the bag. Though she had never seen one up close, the thing looked like the poisonous pods Garglon used to grow. If it was...she might also be holding the means to create Lunar Potion! *Who had put the thing in a bag, though?* she wondered.

She would hang onto it and find a safe place to hide it. The blue fabric sack needed a little cleaning, but it was definitely useable, and now she may have a source of the powerful liquid that would open the well's portal! She placed the bag gently into the back of the cart and wiped her hands on her ragged apron. Gathering the Glimrocks into their leather pouch, she replaced them into the cart next to the other two bags of stones, each containing seven magic rocks.

Across the field in front of her lay the vast mountain range where the Crone's castle was hidden. Wheedle preferred to keep to the protective edge of the forest, especially at night. Walking across the open field of Drigmot's Passage would leave her vulnerable to anything flying overhead.

As if to underscore her thoughts, a rhythmic, flapping sound came from the forest treetops, and Wheedle hurriedly blew out the lantern's flame. Her glittering orange eyes looked up to watch the black sky overhead. Silence. She took a careful step forward and heard it again; it was definitely the sound of wings thrumming the still air, coming steadily closer. The peddler's heart thudded against her brittle ribcage. Carefully she backed the cart up under the protective canopy of a towering Lamberhook tree. She pressed herself into its deep shadow and listened to the skies.

Moments passed as she waited in tense silence. A gliding shadow fell across the moonlit path a few feet away: a black form made up of wings and a small head. It swept across the silver grass and back again, hovering over the spot Wheedle had been only moments before. Finally, after circling several times, the flying shape moved off until it melted into the other shadows of the Spectre Lands.

With a ragged sigh Wheedle leaned against the solid tree trunk, pressing her thin hands against its black wood. A piece of bark crumbled beneath her meager weight and skittered to the ground.

She glanced at it casually, decided it wouldn't be of any use to her and pushed away from the tree. Another piece of bark, larger this time, crumbled from the spot and fell down to land beside the first. Wheedle turned to look at the tree, afraid the whole thing might be coming down.

It was hard to see in the dark shadows of the forest, however she could make out a large crevice in the Lamberhook tree's face; a deep gouge of broken wood. Wheedle reached up and ran a finger inside the trench, forcing small bits of splintered wood from its mouth. Her hand felt something smooth that gave beneath her touch. Curling her fingers around the thing, she wriggled it back and forth until the tree released its hold on the object. Carefully she pulled a red glowing crystal from the crevice.

Wheedle panted with anticipation. The thing looked like glass, and yet it felt much lighter than what she would have guessed from its size. It fit exactly into the palm of her hand, shedding a red glow on her tight, scaly skin. She noticed it had a small black center, making it look very much like an eye.

Suddenly her pulse quickened. She now knew exactly what she was holding! It was the eye belonging to the Crone! Somehow, the powerful red crystal had ended up here in a Lamberhook tree! How? Had someone hidden it there until they could return for it?

Her eyes couldn't look at the red glowing eye for more than a quick glimpse at a time; its brightness was too strong for someone who lived most of their days in the darkness of the forest trails. Besides, she had no intention of losing her vision to the thing. Everyone knew the Crone's eye could reach into its victim's mind and suck out their memories, along with their eyesight. It could also strip the power from the constellations. Combining its evil forces with the Dark Orb was only one of its purposes. The Crone must be franticly looking for it.

Wheedle thought of putting it back into the tree, and then paused. She was holding in her hand a very important bargaining chip! This crystal eye was something both the Crone and Morble would sell their souls to retrieve. A grin twisted across the scaly face, and her nostrils flared. Wheedle, a lowly peddler, a creature of whom no one gave notice, now held one of the most powerful objects in the Universe! *But where to hide it?* Whoever hid it inside the tree was sure to come looking for it. She had to find a different hiding place.

Wheedle suddenly thought of the Bottle of Whispers she kept in an old fabric bag in the front of the cart, hidden beneath her sleeping blanket. The original stopper had been broken a few weeks ago when her bungling partner, Frinkle, had dropped it while trying to steal it. He knew better than to offer the bottle for trade to anyone. Frinkle was always trying to find something of value in her cart, for what, Wheedle did not know. He knew the bottle was Wheedle's prize possession and she would never trade it. In her struggle to grab it from the little man, it had fallen, landing on a flat rock and breaking the stopper.

At least the antique purple bottle was intact; its gold scrollwork dirty, but lovely to look at. Wheedle had so few things that were lovely. But it was the bottle's contents she treasured even more: her whispers. Not just any whispers! Whispers she hissed into the open bottle, telling of her secret hiding places throughout the Spectre Lands. Whenever Wheedle could not remember where she had hidden one of her treasures, she would whisper its name into the bottle, and the bottle would whisper back its location.

She fished about in the cart, shoving her ratty blanket to one side, until she pulled out the faded burlap bag holding her precious bottle. She had collected so many things from the Well Riders over the years. Now that Morble was capturing the travelers, Wheedle's pickings would be few.

Wheedle loosened the strings to the bag and pulled the small Bottle of Whispers from its casing. She carefully removed the bit of dried cork she had wedged into its mouth to keep the whispers safely inside until she could find a suitable stopper. The red glow from the crystal eye she had freed from the Lamberhook tree shone through the dusky, purple glass as she tried to wedge it into the bottle's opening. It took a few twists, but it finally locked into place. Wheedle held the bottle up happily. It shone like the red star of Antares! It was perfect! Wheedle felt her mind spinning; a strange dizziness made her feel as if she were swimming down into a dark tunnel of water. *It was the eye! She must be careful with the crystal's powerful light!* she vowed.

The sound of beating wings suddenly sounded overhead. With a cry of alarm, Wheedle stuffed the bottle with its magnificent top back into its bag and hid it beneath the folds of the blanket. A rush of wind fanned her sweating face, as the winged creature dove at her cart.

"Get away from me, Corvus!" she croaked, her voice brittle and deep. The large bird had not been seen for several weeks, and Wheedle had hoped he had gone on to another dimension, or was dead. From the looks of him, he may as well *be* dead. The well's passage had torn him apart.

Morble stooped and picked up a small rock. Taking aim, she hurled it at the black creature, but it glanced off a wing, and fell harmlessly to the grass. Grabbing the worn handles of her cart, Wheedle hurried into the protective shelter of the thick tree trunks of the forest, while Corvus's angry cries fell like spatters of fire from overhead.

Wheedle moved quickly through the outer edge of the twisted Lamberhook Forest until she came to a small river, its current slow, and the water shallow. The Moaning River was a place she dreaded. The soft wailing noise the water made as it moved slowly through the rocks always made her shiver. She had heard that the souls of ancient Well Riders from the Human World were just beneath the murky surface. The Crone had stripped them of their sight and drowned them beneath the slow-moving water. Now Morble was back, and Wheedle supposed she and the Crone would battle for the Riders, just as Garglon had done before her. That meant most of the travelers would find their fate inside tree trunks, or buried beneath the river's surface.

Keeping a tight grip on the weathered handles of her cart, Wheedle sloshed through the sluggish water, her feet slipping at times on the slimy river rocks. Several times the rickety wheels of the cart became lodged between some of the hidden river stones, and she had to rock them free. At times the water's wailing became louder, as her efforts to cross disturbed the river bed below. Slimy, kelp-like tentacles writhed around her ankles, threatening to pull her under. Faces, their mouths gaping, floated to the surface. She kicked at them as she tugged harder on her cart. Finally emerging on the other side, she paused to catch her breath, looking back to see the tortured heads sink once again below the surface of the brackish water.

She hurried across the open space of Drigmot's Passage, watching the skies fearfully for Corvus's return. The Passage was more of an open field linking most of the Spectre Land's regions, though it did sport some treacherous trails. She finally entered the welcoming shelter of Haver's Forest.

She slept that night in the protective shelter of the forest's trees, after walking through most of its silent interior. The trees here were of a normal shape, not the writhing, grotesque forms of those in the Lamberhook Forest. There were no Well Riders trapped inside their trunks. Wheedle sat down on the hard-packed ground, leaning her tired back against a large elm. She placed the bag containing the Bottle of Whispers next to her, and wrapped the ratty blanket around it and her thin body. The Crone's eye was getting brighter the closer they came to the evil thing's castle. *The eye knows the Crone is near*, she thought, shuddering. She would have to be very careful to keep its light from shining through the blanket. The peddler finally fell asleep with the stench of Haver's Swamp (which waited on the other side of the forest), filling her nostrils.

Wheedle awakened throughout the night with a start whenever she sensed the sound of wings overhead, or heard a small animal scurrying through the undergrowth. The tattered blanket from the cart was warm and familiar, although it smelled of wood smoke and mildewed fabric. Her precious Bottle of Whispers was tucked snugly up against her side beneath the cover; the stopper's light casting a pale red glow beneath the worn threads.

Chapter Thirty

TREASURES AND SPIES

Wheedle awoke to the sounds of tiny creatures scampering in the trees overhead—-and to see her strange partner, Frinkle, standing in the sun-speckled forest, watching her closely. Frinkle had a habit of disappearing whenever he felt like it. Sometimes Wheedle didn't see him for days, and then suddenly, there he was, like now.

"What you doin' in the forest, Wheedle?" he asked suspiciously. "Did the hut get flooded again?"

"No, the hut did not get flooded again," she said irritably, wincing as she straightened her back from where it had been wedged into the crevice of a large elm all night.

Wheedle was still adjusting to the small luxury of remaining in mortal form during the daylight. In the Glimmer Lands she had always been reduced to just an outline of twinkling stars beneath the light of the sun, only to become mortal when bathed in moonlight. But here in the Spectre Lands, all the constellations retained their breathing forms after they had been here for two days; the trip through the well's portal stripping away their star power and reducing them to lost, deformed souls. The fact that the moon was always out in the Spectre Lands also played a part.

She carefully kept the bag with the Bottle of Whispers covered with the blanket as she rose stiffly to a standing position. With creaking knees she carried her treasure to the waiting cart and placed it safely beneath the seat.

"Where have you been all this time?" she asked, finally giving the squat little man her full attention. Frinkle was less than four feet tall, with crazy sea foam green hair that stuck up in spikes. His face was square and flat, with freckles dotting his cheeks like a connect-the-dots game. Wheedle always thought they looked as if his brilliant orange eyes had blinked and scattered russet-colored spots across his face. His mouth was always twisted to one side, looking very much like someone had shoved it there.

"Out lookin'," he replied in his squeaky voice; his was as high and irritating as Wheedle's was deep and raspy.

"That's what you always say," Wheedle said grumpily.

"That's what I'm always doin'," he replied, yawning broadly. "Any new stuff?"

Wheedle glanced nervously at the spot where her bottle lay hidden beneath the blanket. Frinkle followed her gaze.

"No," Wheedle said, evasively. "I would like to go home and eat something. It was a long night."

As Wheedle limped to the front of the wagon and took hold of the handles, Frinkle peeked quickly beneath the peddler's blanket and into the fabric bag. *Is that all she's hiding?* He thought to himself. *That dumb old bottle of hers. Hey, but what's that cool lookin' red thing plugged into its top? That was definitely new! His new friend had told him to be lookin' for somethin' that looked like a red eyeball!*

Before he could study it further, Wheedle gave the cart a good tug and started off down the packed trail of Haver's Forest. Frinkle hurried up next to her, scrambling in his usual crab-like way. His feet turned in so much the toes of each foot almost touched when he walked.

"So, nothing else of interest last night?" he asked, eyeing Wheedle closely. "No other treasures you happened upon...no little goodies?"

Wheedle cast a suspicious glance at his twisted face. "No...I told you...nothing. Come on...I'm hungry."

"You sure? Nothing else to tell me?" he asked, his eyes squinting at her.

For a quick second Wheedle wondered if the strange object topping her bottle was shining through the blanket. Is that what Frinkle was referring to? She stopped the cart and pretended to tie down a loose bundle in the back, peeking quickly beneath the blanket and into the bag. The red eye looked out at her, its glow threatening to give away her hiding place. Wheedle quickly tucked the blanket tightly around it and covered it with a large, dented copper pot.

The peddler returned to the head of the cart and started off again, her mind whirling as she tried to think of a better hiding place for her bottle and its new stopper.

The sunlight, meager as it was, blinded her momentarily, as she and Frinkle emerged from the cool shadows of the forest. Squinting ahead, she saw the familiar signs of the swamp area.

Frinkle sniffed indignantly at the smell of stagnant water which floated by him on the morning air. He hated the swamp. He deserved better than the horrid mud hut Wheedle called home. As soon as he impressed his new-found friend with some wonderful treasure, he could leave old Wheedle behind. The new friend would have a soft bed for him, and a table with plates and real food—not the swamp beetles and boiled tree roots Wheedle favored. All Frinkle needed was one thing to catch his powerful friend's eye…something amazing!

The swamp's stench cloaked the air outside the simple mud hut where the peddler lived. Wheedle pulled the cart into a secret hole inside a massive wildberry bush sitting next to the two boards that made up her front door. Making sure her cart could not be seen from the outside, she walked over to the door of her hut and wearily pushed it open. After she got rid of Frinkle, she would find a new hiding place for the bottle, but for now, it should be safe in the cart, hidden in the bushes, she thought tiredly.

"Want some breakfast Frinkle?" she asked, as she crossed over to the wooden bowl of swamp grass on the small counter to the right of the door.

"Temptin' as that is, think I'll pass," he said in disgust. "Want me to unload the cart?"

"No!" Wheedle cried, whirling around to find him squinting at her. "I'll do it later...not much to unload really."

Frinkle stared at her for a moment, twisting his mouth even more to one side.

"Okey smokey," he said finally. "Guess I'll just go see if anythin' o' interest came through the well last night, seein' it wuz a full moon and all. I thought I seen somethin'...maybe 'nother Well Rider came here."

"*Saw* something..." Wheedle corrected him tiredly.

Frinkle shrugged, shoving the thin wooden slats of the door open. He glanced back over his shoulder to see Wheedle pulling an old pot out of the wooden crate in the corner. *Yep!* He thought. *Gonna boil water for tree roots! I gotta get a new life!* The door swung shut behind him.

Wheedle finished her meager breakfast and looked tiredly around the dusky room. She noticed her small cot, which looked inviting from its place against the mud wall beneath the hut's only window. Frinkle's tiny straw bed lay in a jumbled heap by the sooty fireplace where tree limbs thrust their brittle fingers through the walls of the hut. Wheedle had turned the roots into shelves to hold her favorite things she had found over the years; simple treasures of wood, glass, and stone.

"All these days," she said sadly to no one. "All these days of living like a hermit. I do miss my old life in the Glimmer Lands."

She stood looking at Frinkle's unmade bed and remembered the evening he knocked on her wooden door asking for a place to stay for the night, complaining things were chasing him. Wheedle had never seen the strange little man before and wondered if he were a Well Rider, or perhaps another constellation that had been cast out, or fallen. With everything coming to the Spectre Lands becoming deformed and their names changed, Wheedle had no idea that first evening who the comical creature at her door was. Still, she had offered him a bed for the night. He had managed to stay on, helping her look for treasures throughout the Spectre Lands. At first she had welcomed the company, but lately he had become more annoying, and was forever disappearing, or going through her cart when she wasn't looking. *What in the world was Frinkle looking for?* she wondered.

Wheedle shuffled out the door into the dismal sunshine. The air smelled of baked mud and rotten eggs. The peddler cast a glance at the tall grasses which grew only a few feet away, surrounding Haver's Swamp. A large frog erupted from their shelter and plopped loudly into the thick water. Wriggling in elongated S-shapes, a water snake slithered from the grass and entered the water where the frog had just disappeared beneath the surface.

She cast an eye toward the sky and noted Uranus had moved. The planet was now closer to aligning with the others which hung in a stacked pattern in the sky. Even the sun's light could not completely shut out the soft glow of the moon that was forever holding court over the vile landscape. The giant planets seemed to be within inches of touching the soil of the Spectre Lands. She sighed. Time was running out. In only two days' time the Dark Moon would rise over the Spectre Lands, and the wells would change once more. Wheedle would be stuck here for another 100 years!

But I have the Crone's eye! she thought happily, a sudden thrill of hope surging through her. *I might find a way out of here after all!*

The peddler walked to the wildberry bush and pushed aside the branches that hid her cart's secret hiding place. Entering the seclusion of the prickly branches, she approached the small cart and reached beneath the wooden seat. Carefully she pulled her tattered blanket out into the light. Wheedle could feel the bottle's weight through the thin threads. The peddler carefully unwrapped it and opened the bag. She screamed out in dismay, her ragged cry scaring a Fluging Bat from its nest nearby. The object weighting the blanket was not her precious Bottle of Whispers.

Lying in the tattered threads was a rectangular-shaped stone…a common rock!

"FRINKL-L-L-L-L-E!" she screamed.

Chapter Thirty-One

FRINKLE'S QUEST

Frinkle plodded along through the shadows of Haver's Forest. He would take his secret shortcut to his new friend's place. He looked again at the purple bottle with the glowing red stopper he carried in his plump little hands. He never did understand Wheedle's fascination with this dirty old bottle. So it had her whispers in it. So what? None of her treasures were worth anything. He couldn't understand why she bothered hiding them and then whispering their location into a dumb old bottle. The thing she crammed into its neck was kinda cool though. Maybe his friend would think so too. It looked just like what he told Frinkle to find! The little man wished it would stop glowing. It made him nervous, and when he looked at it, and he got kinda dizzy and scared.

Something crashed in the treetops overhead, and Frinkle stopped, hiding the bottle quickly in the deep pocket of his only vest; the fabric glowed an eerie red. Another sound of something ripping through the branches came from behind. Whirling around, he caught a glimpse of pink wings in the tree to his left.

"Oh great!" he muttered. "Siglets!"

Before he could decide which way to run, several green bodies, with pink wings and red tufts of hair, dropped to the ground around him. Their short stinger tails quivered in excitement as they looked Frinkle over with their glittering blue eyes.

"What do you guys want?" Frinkle asked, looking over their heads for a means of escape. "Wheedle has all the stuff in her cart. I don't gots nothin'…honest!"

Two of the Siglets edged closer to the little man and sniffed at his dirty clothes. One poked a finger into his torn pants pocket.

"Back off!" Frinkle yelled. "I told you. I don't gots anythin'. Go bug somebody else!" The little man had a hand pressed over the incriminating red glow shining through his vest pocket, hoping to keep it hidden.

The Siglets looked at each other, considering their options. Then, without warning, they sprang at Wheedle's assistant, stinging him with their pointed tails. They rolled him in the dirt and twigs until his spiked green hair was filled with debris. His lip split open, and he cried out in pain. As one of the flying creatures tore at his clothes, another Siglet caught sight of the red glowing bottle, and plucked it from the protesting little man.

"Hey! That's mine!" Frinkle yelled, snatching at the bottle the Siglet held just out of the short little man's reach.

The green creature studied the bottle, turning it around and around in its taloned fingers. Eyeing the red crystal stopper, it pulled at it until it came free from the bottle. Frinkle dove for the stopper, but the Siglet tossed the Crone's red eye to another of the winged creatures, who held it tightly and lifted off the ground, hovering too high above Frinkle's head for him to reach. The other Siglet pressed an eye to the purple bottle's opening in an effort to see inside. Suddenly whispers began escaping through the container's mouth, lacing the air with Wheedle's raspy voice.

The winged creature dropped the bottle in astonishment and backed away. With high-pitched squeals, the Siglets ran doggedly down the path, flapping their short wings, until they all lifted into the clearing in the treetops and disappeared from sight—Wheedle's precious stopper with them.

Frinkle sat up with a moan. Red welts were already forming on his arms and hands from the creature's stings. He brushed bits of forest from his hair and irritably fished small rocks from his already torn pockets. Blood trickled down his chin from his cut lip. The sound of Wheedle's whispering voice reached his ears, and he turned to see her Bottle of Whispers lying on its side near him. He scrambled over and picked it up. The peddler's hushed voice floated out of the bottle's opening:

"White pod buried in a blue bag in hollow by yellow ragweed bed," the voice said. As Frinkle listened, it went on: "Secret patch of Monkhood Mushrooms discovered by Karplin's Marsh with nest of black flies."

As the whispered locations of Wheedle's precious treasures continued to leak out of the bottle, Frinkle became nervous. She was going to kill him! He stuck his chubby finger into the bottle's opening and kept it there. Wheedle's voice stopped and all was silent. Breathing a sigh of relief, Frinkle dusted off his clothes and started off again. Without the red glowing crystal, the dusty old bottle wasn't worth much to anyone other than Wheedle. He would have to find something else with which to tempt his powerful new friend.

Frinkle thought over his dilemma. He would have to find some kind of stopper for the bottle that looked like the one the Siglets had stolen, and then somehow get the thing back into the peddler's cart before she missed it. Then he would try to find something else to gain favor with his friend.

Fuming, the little man took his shortcut past the three boulders resembling hog heads, irritated by the itch surrounding each of the Siglet's stings. The red, raised bumps burned, and he longed to find a patch of mud with which to coat them. Wheedle had taught him that mud would take away the pain of Siglet stings; but Wheedle always used the *smelly* mud from the swamp. Thinking of Wheedle, he cringed. What if she already knew the bottle was missing? Well, if Wheedle kicked him out, then his friend would just have to take him in.

Frinkle had met the strange "friend" one day while looking for Well Rider treasure by Apparition Bay. The Cove behind the Bay was not a place the little man liked to venture near, so he kept to the marshes and forest's edge. He had been watching the dark waters of the Bay in case anything ugly surfaced, when he saw movement in the old ship's hull half-hidden in the bushes. Frinkle walked carefully over to the weathered boards of the remaining half of an old boat, and heard someone from inside call out to him.

"Come closer," the voice said. "I have something for you."

Frinkle hesitated, and then edged closer to the dark interior of the ship.

"What you gots for me?" he asked, stopping far enough away from the boat's opening so that something could not reach out and grab him.

"I want to be your friend, Frinkle," the voice said. "I cannot venture out so you will have to find the things I need. Do this, and I will give you power, a wonderful home, and treasure beyond your wildest dreams! I am a very powerful man, Frinkle. Do not disappoint me!"

Frinkle stood now on the hilltop looking down into the valley below. His stomach rumbled, and his entire body hurt. He could feel caked blood on his chin. There was danger everywhere in the Spectre Lands, and he was tired of always being on the look-out for some creature wanting his demise. Now the precious red thing that might have tempted his friend was gone.

Frinkle looked around nervously and decided to take an overgrown path leading away from Haver's Wood. A slight rustling noise in the bushes to his left startled him. He sprung back, expecting to be besieged with yet another Siglet attack. Instead, two soft, furry ears rose from the wildberry bush he was eyeing. With a sigh of relief, Frinkle realized it was just a rabbit.

"That dumb rabbit could be lunch," he muttered to himself.

Frinkle crept softly over to where the two ears were quivering gently, as the small animal nibbled on the black fruit. Being careful to keep one finger firmly planted in the Bottle of Whisper's opening, Frinkle edged ever closer to the wildberry bush—and *sprang!*

A cry ripped through the bushes, but it was not from the animal.

Frinkle had grabbed the long, narrow ears of a Rictor; a horned turtle with clawed feet. The horn, sprouting from its blunt snout, was now embedded in Frinkle's knee. Screaming with pain, the little man shot from the bushes and crawled to the nearest rock to examine his wound, nearly dropping Wheedle's bottle in the process.

"This whole day stinks!" he yelled into the forest, frightening a few small, black fairies into flight. Frinkle leaned over and spit on the ragged cut, already beginning to swell on his left knee. The Rictor was pushing its way through the foliage in search of a quieter breakfast, its long ears gliding above the bushes like a floating 'V'.

Frinkle pushed off from the rock, wincing from the pain in his knee. With a huge sigh, he looked around at the forest and his options: the trail leading down to the open valley and Apparition Bay (where his new friend lived); the path leading back to Wheedle's house; and the small footpath winding off to his right through the bushes where the Rictor had headed. After a few moments of indecision, Frinkle finally chose the path through the forest he had just traveled. One run-in with a Rictor was enough, and without the red glowing thing, he had nothing now to offer his friend; he'd just have to be careful to avoid the Siglets, if they were still around. He hoped nothing had heard him cry out.

Limping painfully along, Frinkle scratched his stings and mumbled at tree roots that got in his way. He looked at the purple bottle with his finger stuck inside it. How was he going to find a crystal topper to replace the one that was stolen? Frinkle had never seen the Crone, indeed he had no idea about her crystal eye, or the power it held. He listened to gossip when he came across it, but for the most part, the little man preferred to live his days as ignorant as possible of the world called the Spectre Lands. All he cared about now was his new friend and the promise he had made Frinkle if he brought the objects the friend was looking for. He hadn't yet found all of them, but he hoped he could tempt his friend with some of Wheedle's treasures.

He sighed and followed a path heading toward the rotten smell of the swamp.

Chapter Thirty-Two

CRYSTAL, CRYSTAL, WHO'S GOT THE CRYSTAL?

Six Siglets flying above the ruined landscape of the Spectre Lands dipped in and out of the forest treetops with the Crone's eye clutched in the talons of the creature bringing up the rear. His face still bore the burn scars Morble's torch had inflicted upon him.

A black shadow fell in behind the Siglets, as they floated over the open fields of Drigmot's Passage near the Crone's deteriorating castle. Its large flapping wings thrummed the air quietly, closing in on the Siglet carrying the powerful eye. The red crystal glistened in the afternoon sun, speckling the creature's claws with its crimson glow.

The Siglet thought of the Crone's ecstatic reaction to have her precious eye back. It was sure to bring him favor. Her anger when the Siglets had found only some fake red stone when they raided the Finnel home in the Human World still made the creature tremble. He was lucky to still be in one piece. He remembered watching her fling the phony ruby out of the window in the castle's Great Hall as she screamed, "Idiots! Does this look like my powerful eye? How dare you bring me this piece of human junk?" The silver ball they brought from the human home met the same fate—sailing through the air and narrowly missing the Siglet's head who had proffered it to her.

"MORONS!" she had screamed again, the stone castle walls echoing her words in mocking repetition. "That is NOT THE DARK ORB! It's a silver piece of JUNK, you flying imbeciles!"

Both the red ruby, and the silver ball, had landed in the tall grass at the base of the castle's mountain.

The Siglets flew now through the still air, hoping their new find would redeem themselves to the Crone. *This will make her happy*, the Siglet carrying the precious eye now thought, as he flew behind his fellow creatures. *This had to be it!*

The Siglets swooped down low over the Black River that encircled the Crone's castle before it meandered off into the rocks and trees. Even in the sunlight, its dark, swirling waters hid the river's depth. Moss-covered, muddy banks flanked the swiftly-moving current; an occasional dark head leaving ripples as it surfaced for air. Unlike The Moaning River, this body of water was filled with deadly creatures to insure no one traversed it as a means of reaching the Crone's castle.

As the group of flying Siglets tilted into the afternoon breeze, and turned toward the tall window in the castle's tower, a large black bird finally overtook the slowest unsuspecting Siglet at the rear. With an angry cry, Corvus the Crow dove, crashing into the green-bodied creature. The crystal eye slipped from the thing's grasp and fell into a tall pine, bouncing through its branches, until it dropped finally into the ebony depths of the Black River. Corvus and the Siglet both dove after it, only to be thwarted by the prickly needles of the towering pine tree. Corvus flew lower, trying unsuccessfully to fit his massive wingspan in-between the clustering of trees flanking the river at the point the eye had disappeared. As he brushed past the trees, many of their pine needles spiraled down into the river below, and floated off on the currents of black water; unseen creatures from beneath the surface snapping at the intruders littering their domain.

Several times Corvus cried out in frustration as he tried unsuccessfully to find a way to the river where the eye had fallen into the current. The Siglet was right behind him, darting between trees and trying to see any kind of a crimson glow beneath the dark surface.

Corvus finally admitted defeat and disappeared over the forest treetops. The injured Siglet was not as quick to give up. He flew around a stand of trees and landed on some parched ground. He limped to the river and looked into its swirling waters with his badly burned eyes, hobbling back and forth along the bank looking for a red glow in its black currents. It was gone. The Crone's eye was somewhere in the rushing water, perhaps even farther downstream. Finally he flew off to join the others hovering near the castle, waiting to make their entrance into the fortress through the tower window. They were not happy to hear from the reporting Siglet that the red crystal they were bringing to the castle's owner was lost.

As the Siglets angled toward the South Tower window, they glanced with fear at the massive dragon lying on the battlement of the North Tower, its huge tail wrapped about the pointed roof. They saw Draco eyeing them with hooded green eyes, his breath making a rhythmic rushing sound as it went in and out. There was a smell of burnt skin about him, and though he was one of the Crone's spies—and should be on their side—the Siglets did not trust that he would not flash out at them with his forked tongue and devour them whole. Hurriedly they flew into the open tower window and away from the intense heat emanating from his parted mouth.

Over in Haver's Swamp, Wheedle was pacing about her hut, waiting for nightfall, while cursing Frinkle's name. She wondered what he had done with her bottle. If he had given it away, there was going to be a fight like none the little man had seen! Her orange eyes, glowing even brighter in her rage, watched the afternoon turn into evening from her hut window. *Sunlight always seemed to be wasted in the Spectre Lands,* the peddler thought. There was no gaiety here, no picnics, or lazy fun-filled afternoons like she had known in the Glimmer Lands. While waiting for the cloak of darkness to hide her from Corvus, and other creatures here, she keenly felt the wasted days. *I may as well be a vampire,* she thought dismally. *I have become a creature of the night!*

As the hours passed, and the night was finally upon her, she left the safety of her hut to go looking for her wayward apprentice. Wheedle walked out to her hidden cart, keeping one eye on the sky overhead. She reached into a small wooden crate filled with odds and ends she had taken from the human Well Riders she kept in the back of the cart. Her favorite item was a small box of matches. How delighted she had been when she first read the directions on the box and discovered that by striking them you could produce fire! She used them sparingly, only rarely cooking in the open fireplace in her hut. The chimney smoke always alerted the Spectre Land creatures that she was at home.

Wheedle plucked a match from the box and struck it against the rough strip attached to its side. Up leapt a small flame. She quickly lifted the metal hinge of the lantern hanging from a pole on her cart and stuck the burning match to the wick which glowed softly in the evening dusk. Looking again at the ensuing night sky, Wheedle picked up the weathered wooden handles and backed the cart toward the path that led into Haver's Forest, where the treetop canopy would protect her from things with wings.

The swamp smell permeated the air. The sun had baked its mud and freed the gases which swirled overhead in an invisible odor of rot. She reminded herself she needed to look for newt eggs when she got back; they were especially good if they had baked all day near the swamp in the miry bog. It was also this time of year that the glowing mushrooms could be harvested. She had seen their iridescent green light one night as she passed the bog by the Lamberhook Forest. It looked to be a good crop of them. Wheedle pressed her thin lips together. *Newt eggs, glowing mushrooms…how sad…she had finally adjusted to eating the Spectre Lands fare, when she had once dined on sumptuous feasts in the Glimmer Lands,* she thought tiredly. It had all changed the night she was betrayed by the one who should have loved her above all else.

Somewhere in the distance she thought she heard Corvus's angry cries. She paused, listening to determine if he was flying closer, or moving farther away. The bird's cries grew fainter and Wheedle breathed a sigh of relief. She knew Corvus had been the Queen's spy when Wheedle lived in the Glimmer Lands. She supposed he was still her spy here.

Wheedle slid a forked tongue along her dry lips and remembered the times Corvus had dove at her cart. Everyone knew Wheedle collected everything she could find in the Spectre Lands in a vain hope of discovering something she could trade for a return ticket home through the well. Her small cart was a veritable garage sale of trinkets and junk. *The Crow must think she has something of importance belonging to the Queen, which was true, until that green-headed little sneak made off with it this morning,* Wheedle thought angrily.

The Crone's red eye was powerful, and Wheedle knew from her secret visits to the Glimmer Lands' cave, it was used in the Dark Arts. Cassiopeia…or rather Morble, was probably cooking up something, which explained Corvus' frequent visits. With the Dark Moon only two days away, it no doubt had something to do with the changing of the wells. Morble would pay dearly for the crystal, as would the Crone! If she could barter for the map and the Orb, she might obtain her freedom and return home. She had to get that eye back!

The lizard-like peddler jerked her creaking cart and pulled it through the woods. Wheedle breathed easier once she felt the shelter of the trees overhead. Corvus could not get to her here, nor could Draco when the dragon made his nightly survey of the Lands. She would look for treasures while trying to track down Frinkle. She hoped with all her heart that her precious Bottle of Whispers was safe.

Chapter Thirty-Three

LET'S MAKE A DEAL!

"Shh," Mandy said suddenly, putting her hand up to warn T.J. to stop. "Something is up ahead. There's a light in the trees!"

They had been wandering the strange land for hours. T.J. was exhausted and starving. Twicket complained non-stop about his hunger issues, and wanting to go home to Mudlin, the Toad Sorcerer.

Wheedle, who was walking through Haver's Wood only a few feet away, suddenly stopped and listened, the small opening on each side of her head widening, as she strained to detect the location of the noise she had just heard. There it was again—the unmistakable sound of footfalls on the hard-packed path. She thought about extinguishing the lantern, but decided against it, hating to waste the match. Perhaps it was Frinkle. Of course it could be anything. There were deformed constellations everywhere. She paused, peering through the trees in an effort to see who was coming toward her.

A twig snapped. She looked in the direction of the sound and saw a human boy and some creature with wild orange hair making their way along the path! They were new to her—obviously Well Riders. She wondered if she should hide, or wait to see if they had anything of value on their persons. Once the Crone or Morble got hold of them, they would be done for anyway.

The thing with orange hair, who was walking ahead of the boy, caught sight of the peddler and smiled. She looked harmless enough, Wheedle thought...ugly, but harmless. Perhaps there will be some good bartering today!

Wheedle waited as the two approached. The boy was carrying a strange-looking stick that the peddler eyed closely.

"What are you in need of?" Wheedle asked, before the pair came to a complete stop next to her cart. "I have many wonderful treasures in my wagon," she said, grinning uncomfortably. Smiling was not a familiar thing for the lizard and it showed.

"Information," Mandy said lightly, peering into the back of the cart. T.J. stood staring at the strange creature before him. Its head looked as if a fish and a lizard had battled for domain and finally decided to call it a draw. The thing was eyeing him and Twicket, with its large amber eyes.

Wheedle turned her attention to the creature with orange hair who was poking about in the wagon.

"Here, here," the peddler snapped. "I do all the exploring of my cart! Get your hands off! Well Riders think they can do whatever they want...not with *my* cart!"

Mandy backed away, still smiling. "You have quite a lot of stuff in there," she said amiably. "Do you do much business with the creatures here?"

"Some," Wheedle said, eyeing the thing suspiciously. It was wearing a tattered dress. The peddler guessed it was female. "A few have useful things from time to time. I don't remember seeing you around here...you or your friends," Wheedle said, her eyes becoming hooded. "New, are you?"

"You could say that," Mandy said pleasantly. "Now, do you by any chance know of some humans, like this boy, who would have come here recently? An older man?"

"Whatcha offering?" Wheedle said, slipping smoothly into her best bartering banter. She knew nothing of the man the "girl" was inquiring after, and if he had come this way, the odds were he was now embedded in a Lamberhook tree.

Mandy hesitated and looked at T.J. "Do you have anything in that bag of yours we could trade for some information?" she whispered to the boy.

T.J. thought about the assortment of things he had quickly gathered and put into his backpack. "Like what?" he finally asked, bewildered.

As the two discussed their options, Wheedle stepped closer to Twicket and studied the troll's head. Twicket eyed the peddler with distrust, his large blue eyes following her every move.

"I'll trade you the information for the ugly stick," Wheedle announced bluntly, fully intending to make up a lie as to the location of the missing man.

"Who you callin' ugly, you fish head!" Twicket declared. "Me see better faces on dead frogs!"

"Twicket is not for sale," T.J. said, smothering a smile. "Let me see what I have in my..."

"The ugly stick, or no deal," Wheedle said, folding her spindly arms to announce a compromise was not an option. Her scaly elbows stuck out like bones from a turkey carcass.

"Believe me, you don't want this...uh...ugly stick," T.J. said convincingly. "He shoots green slime out his nose twice a day...morning and evening, *and* he's obnoxious."

Wheedle looked unconvinced and stood her ground. "You want to find your friend, or not?" she said.

"T.J.! Me no want to go with lizard face!" Twicket cried. "Maybe she eat poor little trolls!"

Wheedle laughed, a dry deep chuckle that came from a rarely used place far within her. "I don't want to eat you," she said with amusement, "but I have a feeling I could do some good trading with *you* in the bargain." She studied the troll's face while deciding on its value. If Frinkle had traded her Bottle of Whispers, along with the red crystal stopper, she was going to need something extraordinary to barter with. The strange markings on Twicket's cane had not escaped her notice.

T.J. stood trying to think of something he could offer this strange creature. His eyes fell on the old broken lantern that hung from a wooden pole nailed to the bench seat of the peddler's cart. A soft glow from a lit candle shone through the dirty glass.

"What if," he said, taking on an air of mystery, "I could give you something that would be the only one of its kind in the Spectre Lands? Something that would make you the envy of every creature here? Something that would make traveling the dark roads of the forests easier?" The boy looked at her with a satisfied smile on his face.

Wheedle tilted her pointed head, and studied him for a moment. *She is wavering*, T.J. thought happily.

"Let's see it," Wheedle demanded, her arms still folded tightly.

"First tell me where my grandfather is," T.J. volleyed. He turned Twicket's face away as if to make his point.

"Me no can see lizard head!" the troll cried, as he now faced a tree trunk. "Me seen trees before!"

T.J. sighed and turned the cane in his hand so Twicket could watch what was going on.

"Tank you," the troll said simply.

Wheedle hesitated a moment, then turned toward the cart. She hobbled to the rear, and keeping her back between Mandy and her view of the cart's contents, fished around in the clutter until she seized upon a small brown leather bag. She pulled the pouch from under a stack of books belonging to Well Riders and turned to face the children.

"I have some lovely Glimrocks here," she said, dangling the leather pouch in front of them. "Very helpful when navigating the Spectre Lands when you are new here," she said, holding the bag up where T.J. could see it. If she could interest them in something of which she had several others, she could get out of the lie, and still get whatever the boy had in his bag.

"We would like to see the stones, please," Mandy said softly, not wanting to ruin the deal.

Wheedle eyed the three customers before her, and finally opened the bag, pouring out seven, brightly colored rocks into her green, scaly palm.

"May we see a demonstration, please?" Mandy asked. "Not to be rude, but they could be common river rocks."

Wheedle's nostrils flared, and the lids over her eyes lowered, as she glared at the female creature menacingly. Her wide mouth opened, exposing small sharp teeth.

"Show me what you're offering first," she said in a low guttural voice, returning the rocks to their bag.

T.J. looked at Mandy with a scowl as if to say, "What has this got to do with finding my grandfather?" Mandy shot him a knowing look that said, "Trust me."

He handed Twicket to Mandy and pulled his backpack from his shoulders. He set it on the forest floor and unzipped one of the flaps. Wheedle eyed the bag jealously—all those wonderful hidden compartments. Finally T.J. lifted something strange from the pack. It was long, silver, and shiny. It had a large round head with glass over it, like a giant eye. Wheedle's eyes widened and she stepped eagerly toward the boy.

"What is it?" she asked in a raspy voice, her excitement showing.

T.J. grinned and turned the giant eye toward the ground. He pushed something on the object's side and suddenly a large golden sphere of light appeared on the forest path. Wheedle jumped back, one hand grabbing the cart's side to steady herself.

"Is it magic?" she asked, breathing hard.

"Of course," T.J. lied. "It's a magic light that you can carry with you everywhere! No need for fire, or lanterns. Now, do we have a deal?"

Wheedle stepped over to the boy hesitantly and looked carefully at the metal object he was holding. T.J. pushed his thumb against a square button, and the light suddenly went out. The peddler's eyes grew larger, and her mouth opened as she panted, her tiny teeth showing. She reached out for it, and T.J. handed it to her. Wheedle turned it over and over in her hands. Finally, she tipped the large round eye toward her face and peered into it. As she did so, her finger hit the switch and light shot out, blinding the creature.

"Ahhhhhhhhh!" she screamed, stumbling back, the flashlight clattering to the forest floor. She stood rubbing her eyes, white spots swimming before her like fireflies.

"Me no would look into the end where the light come out," Twicket said sagely, watching as the peddler blinked over and over. "Fish head not too smart," he muttered to T.J.

The boy picked up the flashlight and checked to make sure it still worked. Wheedle was recovering her sight, and stood before them frowning, suddenly undecided.

"It's ok," T.J. said. "Just don't look into the round part. So, you want it?"

Wheedle paused, her eyes still stinging. "You have a deal," she said finally.

"Not quite," Mandy corrected. "Put the rocks on the ground, please."

Wheedle reopened the bag and poured the rocks into her open hand. She bent stiffly and tossed the seven small stones to the forest floor. She looked at Mandy inquiringly. "Where?" the peddler asked.

Mandy paused, and then said, "Lamberhook Forest."

Wheedle studied the girl with interest. "Do you know of the dangers in the Lamberhook Forest?" the peddler asked, eyeing her closely.

"Yes," Mandy said nonchalantly. "At least I have heard rumors."

Wheedle's face twisted with amusement.

"Oh....you have heard *rumors?*" the peddler said, sarcastically. "Well then I guess you know it all!"

Wheedle eyed the creature with the wild hair for a moment. She glanced at the gold bracelet that still encircled Mandy's deformed wrist. The peddler's nostrils flared as though she were sniffing the creature. Her round orange eyes wavered, and a small hiss escaped her lips. After a few moments, she bent over the rocks.

"Lamberhook Forest," she commanded hoarsely.

As the group watched, the stones suddenly began tumbling over each other in a haphazard way. They scurried about the forest floor, going around and around in circles, before finally falling into formation. One by one the rocks lined up until they had formed an arrow. It was pointing down a pathway branching off to T.J.'s left.

"Holy Faholys!" T.J. said in surprise. "That is so way cool!"

"Ask rocks to point to beetles," Twicket said eagerly. "Me be hungry!"

"How can you be hungry?" Wheedle croaked, coming closer to him. "You don't have a stomach!"

"How you be talkin'?" Twicket asked stubbornly. "You don't have a brain!"

"All right you two," Mandy said, sighing. Looking at Wheedle she said, "*Now*, you have a deal!"

"I will still trade you information about the old man," the peddler said in a whisper. "Give me the ugly stick, and I will tell you where to find him...the man you seek." Twicket began to retort to the name calling. T.J. put a hand over his mouth, struggling with him. "I saw him over by Haver's Swamp. White hair, glasses, brown shoes." The lizard embellished her description in an effort to bolster her story and win the strangers over.

Mandy smiled and said, "Actually, I think I might know where he is, but thank you anyway, uh....what did you say your name was?"

"Wheedle," the peddler said, looking over the creature with red hair suspiciously. "And your name?" The question was pointed, as if anger was behind it.

"Worken," the girl said simply.

"That your real name, or your name here?" Wheedle asked, her eyes blazing.

T.J. turned to look tiredly at Mandy.

"What are you doing? How is any of this helping me find....," he began, but Mandy gave him a conspiratorial look.

"Thank you for the Glimrocks," she said to Wheedle, ignoring the creature's question about her name. "Oh, I do have one other question for you. It isn't very important, just curious since you know this area soooo well," Mandy said, hoping to flatter the reptile before her. "Have you by any chance seen a small silver ball?"

Wheedle's orange eyes glowed in the forest's shadows.

"Small silver ball?" she croaked, her eyes becoming hooded again. "No. I don't believe I have."

"Well, no matter," Mandy said lightly. "We better be on our way."

She didn't catch the cruel grin that slid across Wheedle's pinched face. The two would be dead inside the Lamberhook trees before the morning, the peddler thought. Then she would simply take the troll head stick, knowing Morble was only interested in finding the Dark Orb and the eye. *And the creature's silly question about a silver ball,* Morble thought hotly. Did she really think Wheedle was so stupid! It was the Dark Orb she was speaking of. Her eyes flashed with anger, as she studied the red-haired creature before her.

Wheedle walked back to her cart, and grinned to herself. She had her magic light the boy had traded her, and she would soon have the ugly stick. All it cost her was a bag of rocks, of which she had others. The trade had cost her nothing!

Mandy gathered up the Glimrocks, as Wheedle handed her the leather pouch that went with them. The peddler pointed the flashlight at some bushes and pushed the button. The light came on, frightening a small snake that slithered quickly into a hole beneath a tree root. Wheedle pushed the button again, and the light went out. She thumbed it again and light shot out into the trees. She smiled her sharp-toothed grin and carried her new prize to the cart. This she would *really* have to hide from Frinkle!

"Keep the ugly stick," she said. "This is a good trade."

Suddenly a thought came to her and she turned to the children who were preparing to leave. The flashlight's bright beam caught Twicket full in the face.

"How did you get through the well from the 4th Dimension of the humans without becoming deformed?" she demanded, eyeing T.J. closely. "What other magic do you have in that bag?" Her thin mouth pulled back into a feral sneer, as she stepped closer.

Twicket's face was contorting in spasms, as he tried hard to resist the flashlight's glare. His nose twitched uncontrollably.

"Ahhhh," he moaned.

"Tell me what else in that bag!" Wheedle threatened, enjoying the fear she saw crossing the boy's face.

"AHHHH….," Twicket said again, louder. He felt the sneeze building beneath the bright light.

"Twicket…*what?*" Mandy began, but was interrupted when the troll let it blow!

"CHOOOOOOO!!!!!"

Green slime shot out of his nose, plastering the startled face of the peddler before him. Wheedle fell back in surprise, green mucous coating her eyes and face.

"My eyes!!!" she screamed, dropping the flashlight. "I can't see! I can't see!"

She clawed at her eyes to clear away the slime. Just as she managed to open them into slits, Twicket hit his second sneeze.

"AH, AH, AHHHHHHHHH, CHHOOOOOOOOO!"

The second round knocked Wheedle to the ground, where she writhed screaming beneath the avalanche of mucous.

Mandy grabbed the flashlight and motioned for T.J. to run. They took off through the woods, looking back to see the bent shape of the peddler still rolling on the forest floor as she struggled to clear her face.

Chapter Thirty-Four

GLIMROCKS

When Mandy was sure they were far enough away, she stopped, panting. T.J. was bent over, his hands on his knees, trying to catch his breath. He leaned Twicket against a rock, as he turned a reddened face to Mandy.

"What the heck were you doing back there?" he accused. "We've got nothing but a bag of rocks. We still don't know where Grandpa is!"

Mandy took a few deep breaths, and when her breathing leveled out, stared at the boy with her hands placed firmly on her hips. The gills in the bulbous mound on her chin opened and closed repeatedly, drawing in the air.

"She didn't know where he was," she said, still breathing hard. "She was lying!"

"Oh really! And you know this because WHY?" T.J. demanded.

"Good grief, T.J.," Mandy said irritably. "Didn't you hear her description of your grandfather? She said he was wearing glasses. Does your grandpa wear glasses…or brown shoes for that matter? I've only seen him in white sneakers."

"She said he was wearing glasses? I missed that. I think I was trying to keep Twicket quiet. And yeah, he never wears anything but tennis shoes. Hey! How do you know what he looks like?" T.J. asked in surprise. "When did you see him?"

"I told you, I came from one of his paintings," Mandy said. "There were several nights when the moon was shining in that I watched him in his studio before I finally came from the canvas.

That doesn't matter now. We need to concentrate on finding him, and all the things we need to get out of here. As for the rocks, Glimrocks don't just show you how to get around," she said, looking pleased with herself. "They are called Glimrocks because they are from the Glimmer Lands. They know more than to just point at pathways when you tell them to find something."

She paused, waiting for T.J. to get her meaning. When he still stared at her in confusion, she sighed.

"If we tell them to find certain objects, they should point the way," she said, her eyes sparkling. "They find things of value. That's why I was content to trade Wheedle for them. I knew she was lying, and I knew the rocks would show us where your grandfather is. And, they do come in handy when you are lost."

"Me thinkin' girl smart one in bunch," Twicket said from his place against the rock.

"Me thinkin' you might want a closer look at the swamp we passed back there," T.J. threatened, as he picked up the troll.

"Ok, ok," Twicket said, a frightened look on his face. "Don't forget, it Twicket that blow snot on ugly fish back there!"

T.J. couldn't help laughing. "Yeah, you did good that time. And, we got the flashlight back. Ok, Mandy...now what? How do the rocks help find Grandpa?"

"Wheedle was probably using the rocks to find treasure around here," the girl said. "Can you think of anything your grandfather might have had on him that would be considered valuable? Keep in mind, valuable in this place could be a belt buckle."

T.J. ran a tongue over his cut lip and thought. In his mind he studied his grandfather's image as he had seen him last.

"He never wore belts," T.J. said, almost to himself. "Clothes don't count?"

"I doubt it," she said. "Anything? Like a watch, or a ring?"

"His wedding ring," T.J. said sadly. "It's the only piece of jewelry he ever wears."

Images of his grandmother's funeral came rushing back. He

saw his grandfather lean over the casket and kiss his departed love on the forehead. As T.J. sat next to the elderly gentleman during the eulogy, he had watched as Dillon caressed the small gold band on his left finger over and over, as if it were a magic talisman that could bring her back.

"A ring," T.J. repeated. "A small gold band."

Mandy was watching the boy's face, noticing the pain that had flickered there for a few moments.

"That should work," she said. "Let's hope so anyway."

"Mudlin have fancy clasp on him's robe!" Twicket offered hopefully. "We look for Mudlin too, ok?" His little face looked at Mandy hopefully.

"I am not sure Mudlin is here in the Spectre Lands, but sure, Twicket....we can try," she said kindly.

Mandy glanced at the shifting moon, and the shadows crawling from the tree roots across the paths ahead. Her mind kept going back to the peddler. There was something about the eyes...something familiar. She couldn't shake the feeling, and it made her tense.

T.J. suddenly jumped, as something he thought was a tree stepped out onto the path before them. It was a strange-looking shape that would change color and form depending on what was standing before it. A moment ago it had mimicked a tree's rough wood...now it was the shape, and grey color of a giant boulder sitting next to the path. It moved again, crossing to Mandy, and morphed into the girl's shape with bright orange-red hair and purple scales.

"What the heck?" T.J. said, as he watched the form become a stand of willow reeds and finally, as it floated over to the boy, a shape that looked like T.J.'s twin.

Mandy studied the strange amorphous mass closely, as it wavered in and out of colors trying to capture T.J.'s green shirt and blue jeans.

"This thing is freaking me out!" the boy said, nervously, as he

Began backing away. "What do you think it is?" he asked.

"I'm not sure," Mandy said quietly, "but it could be Chameleon from the Glimmer Lands. You people in the Human World named a lizard after her. She tends to blend in with her surroundings making it hard for a predator to see her."

The shape shifted out of T.J.'s form and melted into the ground, turning the same dark, muddy color. It disappeared from view.

"How do you know you're not stepping on it?" T.J. asked. "That is just freaky stuff!"

"I think our best bet right now is to find a place to stay for the night," Mandy said, ignoring his last comment. "There are things you don't want to run into after dark around here."

T.J. swallowed. "Can't we just grab Grandpa, hop in the well, and go home before it gets any darker?" he asked hopefully.

Mandy's eyes narrowed. "It is not just your grandfather we are looking for," she said in a stern tone. "You promised you would help me with my mission as well. Besides, we don't know the well's symbols for the Human World."

T.J. sighed, looking defeated. "Ok...it's your turf. You call the shots."

"It isn't *my* 'turf'," she said. "But my...friends are here, and I have to try to help them. Let's throw the rocks down again and ask for the way to the castle," she said finally.

"*The castle?*" T.J. cried.

"*The castle?*" Twicket joined in, trembling.

"Unless you want to spend the night in the woods, it's the only real shelter I know of around here, well....except for the small town by Apparition Bay, but believe me, you don't want to go there!" Mandy said, as she untied the leather bag holding the Glimrocks and tossed them to the ground. "Look, the castle is a big place. We can find somewhere to hide!" She did not tell T.J. and Twicket her real reason for wanting to go there.

"The Crone's castle," she said, and watched as the stones tumbled over themselves, until they finally formed an arrow pointing off through a tangle of trees.

Chapter Thirty-Five

CREATURES FROM ANOTHER WORLD

T.J. and Mandy followed the Glimrocks through Haver's Wood. Each time they came to where the path split off in different directions they would throw the rocks down and repeat "Crone's Castle"; and each time T.J. would get a knot in his stomach at the thought of it.

"Me hungry," Twicket announced for the fourth time in five minutes.

T.J. was holding him, sometimes using the troll's cane to push bushes out from the path, as they made their way through the rough terrain of the forest.

"No be using Twicket for pokin' and pushin'!" the indignant troll yelled, as a bramble bush poked him in the eye.

"How much farther do you think it is?" T.J. asked, feeling the fatigue from a long day setting in. He was tired of walking through dark forests. "Can we just sit for a couple of minutes?"

Before Mandy could answer him, he plopped onto a flat-faced boulder. Unzipping his back pack he dug around inside until he found the slick foil wrappers of the granola bars. This time Mandy accepted one. The look on her face as she bit into it signaled it was not something she would normally be fond of. After finishing half of it, she fed the rest to Twicket.

The next several minutes were filled with the sounds of Twicket munching on the bar's peanuts. The noise underlined the hunger T.J.

was still feeling. Granola bars only went so far. He stood and looked about him at the forlorn landscape with its twisted trees and blackened shrubbery.

"I don't suppose there are any edible berries around here," he said, not daring for an answer in the affirmative. Mandy merely gave him a hopeless look.

Twicket spotted something moving across the path several yards ahead of them. T.J. saw it at the same time and quit talking. He clamped a hand over Twicket's large mouth, just as the troll was about to comment. The three of them froze, hoping whatever it was had not seen them. T.J.'s first hope of it being his grandfather quickly disappeared as the fleeing creature appeared to be crawling on several legs with a frightening hissing sound coming from it.

Twicket let out a small squeal from behind T.J.'s trembling hand. The boy shook the troll to emphasize that he needed to make no sound.

The creature crawled a few more feet away from the threesome and then stopped. The moonlight filtered sporadically through the dense forest treetops so that the large form was mostly hidden in the shadows in the pathway ahead. It turned to the left and seemed to be looking for something. Turning a little more, the hissing sound became louder, as it sensed the children who stood rooted to the path, their breath threatening to burst from their lungs. It finally swung around completely until it was facing them, its eyes glittering in the dark.

T.J. lost his nerve and began backing up. The thing hissed louder. The boy was now sure it had seen them. Twicket was whimpering loudly, and T.J. could feel the troll's spit coating the palm of his hand, which was clasped tightly over his mouth. Mandy did not move.

Moments passed as the creature came a few more steps toward them, until it was partly beneath a ray of moonlight penetrating the canopy of interlaced leaves. T.J. inhaled sharply, as he saw the large bony head with the pointed nose and open jaws. On each side of the lobster-like face were two large pinchers whose claws were snapping angrily at the air. Its eight legs were twisted into grotesque shapes, several of which seemed to be torn and hanging at odd angles.

"What is it?" he whispered to Mandy in a panic.

At the sound of T.J.'s voice, the thing surged toward them a few feet and stopped again, hissing and snapping. The rest of its body came into view in the dim light from overhead, and Twicket, no longer able to keep quiet, yelped. The body of the creature was a series of articulated sections that moved independent of each other, like train cars backed in tightly behind one another. These body parts were torn and broken as well. Bushes were being ripped apart as the thing's gigantic, curved tail whipped from side to side. The tail was also in sections, and reminded T.J. of the toy wooden snakes you could buy that wiggled back and forth on connecting hooks. However it was the small pointed object sitting atop the curved tail that caused his fear to double. A massive stinger vibrated in the moonlight as the tail beneath it thrashed the foliage into pieces.

"Scorpio, the Scorpion, I think. At least he was before he came here," Mandy said, in hushed tones. "We may be in trouble."

For the first time, T.J. noticed that there were not *two* eyes glinting in the moonlight, but several. One after another, four sets of eyes sitting on each side of the scorpion's head would open, and then close. He thought two of them looked bloodied. He felt his knees going weak. This thing was enormous. It looked nothing like the small desert scorpions most mortals think of. He could only imagine how much poison the stinger held.

"What is that bright red thing shining on its back?" T.J. asked, as he continued to back down the path, tripping over tree roots as he went. He was afraid if he turned and ran the thing would lunge after them. As it was, it seemed to be considering them...for dinner probably, but considering them nonetheless.

"Antares," Mandy whispered, her heart beating fast. "It's one of the brightest stars in the heavens. Some called it "the rud-.....," she was cut off by T.J. hastily butting in.

"I know what Antares is," he whispered impatiently. "I know my stars! It was called "the ruddy" because of its red hue. It was also called the "Fire Star", and it's found in the constellation of Scorpio. Are you trying to tell me that hideous *thing* is the *constellation* of Scorpio? He looks like someone put him in a blender."

"This is the Spectre Lands!" she derided the boy. "None of us are what we were before we came through the well," she said shortly, once again feeling the sadness over her own distorted body.

Each time the children spoke the creature hissed louder, its claws snapping at them, as its legs moved the mammoth body a little closer. T.J. wondered why it didn't just attack them and get it over with.

"Throw shoe at it!" Twicket said, finally finding his voice. "You got giant feet!"

"Oh yeah, that will do it," T.J. whispered, but noticed that the creature had backed up a step when Twicket spoke.

"That's odd," T.J. said to the troll.

"Odd? You odd!" the troll shot back, as the scorpion snapped at them from only a few feet away. "Me so scared me would wet meself if me had plumbing!"

To T.J.'s surprise, the scorpion took another hesitant step back, its broken legs fumbling over rocks and tree roots. The boy looked at the troll with new interest.

"Have you been here before?" the boy asked. "Did you sneeze on that thing once?"

"Me think me be here once with Mudlin," Twicket said. "We discuss Twicket's travel log 'nother time!" the troll said nervously.

Mandy looked at T.J., her face screwed up in confusion.

"He seems to be afraid of Twicket," T.J. whispered.

The giant scorpion was thrashing its tail wildly, the clacking noise of its pinchers echoing throughout the forest. It seemed agitated, as if it didn't know what to do next.

"Watch," T.J. said to Mandy. "Twicket, tell it to back up."

"You *nuts?*" Twicket yelped. "Me no sayin' *back up* to snappy face!"

Scorpio suddenly scampered back, its huge tail breaking a low-hanging branch as it went. It was hissing frantically, and clawing the air with its clacking claws.

"What in the world?" Mandy said, turning to look at the troll. "Why is he afraid of you?"

Twicket was staring at the retreating monster with its tail flashing in the moonlight. A memory shot suddenly through his mind. Mudlin was standing near a well chanting something while holding the troll in his hand. The Toad Sorcerer had been looking at Twicket's cane closely and reciting words the little troll did not understand. The distorted land around them had smelled of rot and ruin.

Suddenly something had made a noise in the bushes behind them. Twicket remembered Mudlin had turned toward the sound, but the troll had been unable to see anything as he had been facing the wrong way. Mudlin held Twicket high while shouting out words that were foreign to the troll. A vibration shook the air, including the troll-head walking cane. He recalled a cry coming from the brush. When Mudlin turned around, Twicket caught only a glimpse of a large tail with a stinger atop it, disappearing into the dense woods.

Now the giant scorpion hissed at them once more. Finally, it turned away, scrambling down the path until the last red glow of Antares was lost in the blackness.

"Ok, that was just weird," T.J. said, eyeing the troll. "Seriously...what did you do to it? It had to be more than hitting it with green snot in a former life?"

Mandy laughed, relief flooding over her, as the final sounds of the thrashing creature faded away.

T.J. stared at the innocent looking troll and realized there would be no answer forthcoming. Twicket was lost in thought, as he had been earlier. He was remembering things here…of being here with Mudlin…and….

"Ok, now what?" T.J. said, looking around him at the shadows that were undulating in the fickle moonlight. "Is that castle much farther? And if it has a stable, I vote we stay there instead of inside."

"If Crone has stable, it prob'ly filled with dragons," Twicket said.

"Thanks, Twicket!" T.J. barked. "You're a real pal!"

"Yeah…me know. Back in Treblin, me known as troll most likely to make you day!" The troll's ears quivered as his grin spread across his face.

"I'll make your day!" T.J. warned.

Mandy sighed and threw down the Glimrocks, giving the order for the castle's location. They were soon on their way through the twisted trails of Haver's Wood. As they rounded a large rock formation that looked very much like hog heads, Mandy raised a hand, signaling for them to stop. She could see a strange green light up ahead in the distance. T.J. had just glimpsed it as well. It was a soft glowing field of green.

They walked toward it quietly, being careful not to step on dry twigs or stumble over rocks. Twicket's large blue eyes kept swiveling to look for creatures that might be watching them from the bushes and tree limbs. As they cleared an expanse of bushes, Mandy became uncomfortable. The green light was closer, its iridescent glow staining the foliage around it. But it was not the light bothering her. The trees were different here. She had been noticing for the last several yards that the pines, elms, and oaks gave way to twisted trees with shimmering black wood and grotesque shapes.

T.J. noticed she had slowed down and turned to look at her.

"What's up?" he asked.

"These are Lamberhook trees," Mandy whispered, as if the trees were listening. "We are coming into the Lamberhook Forest boundaries."

Twicket looked at the trees from whence he'd been created and smiled.

"Me feel like me home," he said, a longing wistfulness in his voice.

"This is not a happy place," Mandy said in hushed tones. "I've heard about these woods in the Spectre Lands," she said. "There's much more living inside these tree trunks than termites."

She shuddered. Quickly, she undid the leather bag holding the Glimrocks.

"Show me a different path to the Crone's Castle," she whispered urgently to the rocks. She tossed them to the forest floor and waited. They scampered and rolled, tumbling about until they formed an arrow pointing down the same path as before.

"*No*," Mandy insisted. "A *different* way...*away* from the Lamberhook Forest!"

"I thought we spent all day trying to find this place!" T.J. said, sounding a bit grumpy. He just wanted to sit down, eat something, find his grandpa and get the heck outta Dodge!

"Not once the sun has set...not with the moonlight at its brightest," Mandy said ominously, and picked up the stones again. She tossed them down, and again they pointed down the path toward the green glowing light and tangle of misshapen trees.

"Suddenly a GPS system sounds really good," T.J. muttered.

"What GPS?" Twicket asked.

"It means 'Gotta Plan Something'," T.J. said sarcastically. "Any ideas, Mandy?"

"Unless you want to beat your way through the bog, wildberry and bramble bushes, I guess we have to follow this path on down, or turn around and go all the way back to where we met Wheedle. If your grandpa is in here, we might get a miracle and find him."

Before T.J. could state a preference, Mandy started off toward the green light. T.J. hesitated, looking around at the twisted trees and darkness that lay behind them. He tried to swallow, but in his fright he found his mouth was too dry. Clutching Twicket tightly, he quickly chased behind Mandy, stopping only to adjust his backpack when the straps were biting into his shoulders.

"You got sweaty hands," Twicket complained.

"You've got bad breath," T.J. countered.

"Turn off the flashlight," Mandy whispered over her shoulder. "We don't want to give whatever lives in there any indication that we are here."

T.J. grimaced and slid his thumb along the switch. The light went out, leaving only moonlight and a green glowing patch of ground to illuminate the Spectre Lands. *Harmon's Wood would be nothing after this little episode*, he thought.

After walking a short distance, they could smell the fetid odor of bog water. The path had begun a decline toward the iridescent light; the hard-packed earth becoming spongy and squishy.

"Watch your step," Mandy said. "I think we are coming up on mire."

T.J. could feel his feet sink with each step. Nervously he picked his way along, using Twicket to test the ground before him.

"You getting me cane all muddy!" the troll yelled.

"Shhhhhhh!" Mandy whispered back to them.

"Can't we walk on the other side of the trail?" T.J. asked as his tennis shoe sunk into the soil.

"Karplin's Marsh is on the other side," Mandy whispered impatiently. "If you like giant, biting black flies, go ahead...I'll stick with this route."

They finally pushed through a stand of tall willows, and the green light spilled out into the darkness.

"They are Monkhood Mushrooms!" she exclaimed. "I have never seen so many in one place!"

"Are they poisonous?" T.J. asked, thinking anything growing in this brackish muck couldn't be good for you.

"They are to humans," she said mildly, bending over them. "They are phosphorescent, that's why they glow. They are supposed to grow all over the place here, but usually in small batches of five or ten. We learned about this area of the Spectre Lands back home."

As she bent to pick a few of the phosphorescent fungi, a dozen tiny creatures, glowing in an eerie green, scampered from their homes in the clusters of mushrooms, and darted into the bushes. Trails of tiny green lights could be seen running through the underbrush.

"What the heck?" T.J. gasped, bending over to try to see into the bushes. "What were those?"

"My guess is they were originally the Fireflies of Asparia. It is a very old cluster of stars from long ago which lit up the night sky, usually in the autumn months of your world."

A sloshing sound could be heard off to their left in the distance.

"Now what?" T.J. whined.

"Actually, that is a good sound," Mandy said. "I think it's the Black River, which means we are close to the castle. Unfortunately, we will have to cut through a portion of the Lamberhook Forest to get there, but maybe if we hurry, nothing will know we are here."

"I thought we were already in the Lamberhook Forest," T.J. said.

"Look at the other side of this mire," Mandy said. "See up ahead? Nothing but Lamberhook trees. We have just been walking on the edge of the forest. If it weren't for this bog, we could cut through here, but believe me, you don't want to take a chance with this sludge. It will swallow you whole," she said, a frightened look on her face.

"Sounds fun," T.J. said caustically. "Why are the Lamberhook trees so ugly?" T.J. asked, staring uneasily at the towering grotesque shapes. He pulled his foot from the spongy ground with a loud sucking noise.

Mandy paused, wondering if she should tell T.J. the history of the trees. Her fear since they arrived in the Spectre Lands was that T.J.'s grandfather was quite probably inside one of the deformed trunks, a prisoner of wood and bugs, put there by the Banshees. If he was, then the artist was probably forever lost to T.J.

"It's the Spectre Lands," she said instead. "Everything here is ugly."

"I see you point," Twicket said, looking deliberately at the boy, a wide grin creasing his rubbery face.

T.J. was about to retort when a clanging sound echoed over the treetops. He looked up in surprise to see a large pirate ship sailing over the Lamberhook Forest, something tied to a thin slip of rope, trailing behind it.

"You have got to be kidding me!" T.J. cried, as the vessel banked to the south and disappeared behind the pines of Haver's Wood. "This place is completely NUTS!"

Mandy smiled. "That's Barnacle," she said. "He sails between here and the Glimmer Lands all the time. He probably knows more about what's going on in the two kingdoms than anyone, well, with the exception of Corvus."

"Corvus? The constellation of the Crow?" T.J. asked.

"He's the Queen's spy," Mandy said. "I'll tell you later. We better get going."

"Why don't we just flag down ole Barnacle, and ask him if he knows where this Orb thing is, since you say he knows so much. Maybe he's seen Grandpa!"

"He may know a lot, but he's not to be trusted," Mandy said quietly. "He would sell you out to the highest bidder any day, and he is a notorious gossip! Believe me, if Barnacle knew where the Dark Orb was, he would already have it, and be finding ways to make money off of it, or barter it for power. He is, after-all, a pirate. If he did see your grandpa, he would want something for the information, and he's as big a liar as Wheedle, probably bigger."

The threesome moved on. After slogging along the edges of the putrid bog, they finally placed their feet on solid ground, as the trail through the Lamberhook Forest stretched out before them.

"I'm not going in there without a flashlight," T.J. declared, his nerves screaming.

"No flashlight," Mandy said, firmly.

"How are we supposed to see in there then?" T.J. asked hoarsely. His knees were trembling, and Twicket was shaking due to the boy's quivering hand.

Mandy paused. She wasn't thrilled about feeling their way through the woods either. Even though she was a star and could see in the darkness, the Forest was a whole different thing. The two of them stared into the trees, where the only thing breaking the dark interior was a very faint green glow, buried somewhere in the trees.

"What is that?" T.J. asked.

"More Monkhead Mushrooms," she said. "I told you, they are everywhere around here. I suppose we could try carrying some in our hands to see with, but it would be hard to direct the light down a path. At least if anything saw them they might not think much of it since they grow here. If only there was a way to use them like a torch."

T.J. thought for a moment, and then turned to stare at Twicket.

"What?" asked the troll.

"Me tummy no feel so good," the little cane complained a few minutes later.

"Shut up and close your mouth," T.J. said. "You're diffusing the light!"

Twicket shut his mouth, and green phosphorescent light shot out of his bulging eyes. T.J. was holding him out in front of them like a spotlight.

"How many mushrooms did you feed him?" Mandy asked with concern.

"You said they were only poisonous to humans," T.J. said

grinning. "Bet he won't be hungry for a while. I put a bunch more in the backpack in case he needs to be refilled."

"Me no be used like flashlight!" Twicket wailed, an eerie green light exploding from his mouth. T.J. clamped his hand over the troll's mouth again, and Twicket's eyes turned into high beams.

The children walked through the twisting paths of the Lamberhook Forest, Twicket's green gaze leading their way. T.J. gently turned him side to side, spilling the green light into bushes and down darkened pathways. It was frighteningly quiet here. There was no sound of birds, or small forest creatures, not even the sound of a centipede turning a leaf as it crawled along.

"I would have pictured bats," T.J. said, trying to sound braver than he felt. The trees' shapes were getting to him. Some looked as though their misshapen trunks were forming faces in the smooth black wood. Tree knots became noses, and holes were gaping mouths. They looked as if they were in agony; reaching their long, twisted branches to the sky in an appeal for help.

Something scurried through the bushes off to T.J.'s right. A bush to his left trembled as something moved through its branches.

"Do you hear that?" he asked nervously. He glimpsed something scurry across the path ahead of them, its small green head caught in Twicket's stream of light. "What is that thing?" he yelped. "It looks like a cabbage head…with feet!"

"Shh," Mandy cautioned nervously. "I think they are some of Garglon's plants. I've heard they walk about at night in the Forest."

"They're *what?*" T.J. hissed. Mandy merely waved him on.

The group hurried on, watching the bushes carefully. They stopped as they came to a place where the trail split into two paths.

"Since the left path slopes down, I'm guessing that's the one leading out of here to the river," T.J. said, waiting for Mandy's approval. He saw her reach for the bag of Glimrocks.

"Let's make sure," she said, opening the bag.

Suddenly, a wavering blue light emerged from the ground before them at the place where the path split. It slowly took the form of the old man with flowing hair. The iridescent light shed a blue glow around the candle-like figure.

"Choose," the flickering blue man said to T.J., as he held out two stones; a blue one in his left hand, and an orange one in his right.

"Again?" T.J. asked, surprised to see the undulating figure. "Is it a clue to the well bucket?"

"Choose."

"Uh...I guess the blue one," T.J. said uncertainly.

"You have chosen poorly," the vaporous man said, and disappeared into the ground.

T.J.'s heart was hammering. "What does that mean?" he said terror-stricken. "Is something bad going to happen?"

They nervously stood in the darkness of the Lamberhook Forest and listened...for what, they were unsure, but the little's man ominous words left them rattled. It was deadly quiet. Twicket's green glow washed across the twisted trunks like an eerie spotlight.

"Listen!" Mandy whispered excitedly. "Hear that? It's the Black River! I think we're almost out of here!"

"Yeah, but which path? I picked the stone in his left hand. Maybe that means the trail to the left is the wrong choice," T.J. said, looking down the left path that sloped downhill, and the other that twisted off at a slight incline to the right. He was nervously shining Twicket's eyes into the tangled bushes and deformed trees, still expecting something evil to assault them. He took two tentative steps down the path to his left as he waited for Mandy to toss down the Glimrocks. He suddenly turned around.

"Mandy, listen, as long as we've come this far, let's just hurry and throw down the rocks, and tell them to find Grandpa's gold ring! He might be close by!"

Before the final syllable left his mouth, two tall slender figures floated from behind a mammoth tree trunk standing off to their left. Mandy screamed and fell back. T.J. yelped, brandishing Twicket before him like a sword.

"No be pushing Twicket at ugly girls!" the troll screamed, green light pouring from his mouth.

The two hags floated onto the pathway, blocking the final steps that would have led the children out of the forest. Long dresses of seaweed hung from their bony shoulders, the long sleeves wrapping around their skeletal wrists in dripping kelp. Their faces were worse than the Crone's, T.J. thought, with ruined flesh hanging like tentacles from their noses, partially hiding their gaping mouths. Green slime dripped from open wounds on their cheeks and foreheads. Their hair looked like wet, writhing snakes. The iridescent glow from Twicket's head glinted off their green-and-gold eyes, and turned their skin a ghastly puke color. T.J. felt his knees turn to rubber.

"Run!" Mandy screamed, realizing there was no longer a need to whisper.

"Run?" T.J. screamed back. "Run WHERE?" He spun around wildly looking for a place to make their escape. He accidentally dropped Twicket, who yelped when his nose hit a rock. Mandy grabbed the troll cane and turned to face the two sirens.

The Banshees' mouths were opening wider, exposing dripping kelp in the form of teeth. Suddenly a high-pitched, keening wail rose from the mouths of each of the floating shapes. The forest seemed filled with the rhythmic cry. T.J. felt himself getting dizzy.

"Don't listen!" Mandy screamed.

But T.J. could not tear his gaze away from the green iridescent eyes, their gold streaks pulsating with the Banshee's song. He felt himself floating away in his mind. Things were becoming darker, as though he was being pulled down to the depths of a dark green-and-blue ocean; seaweed wrapping around his helpless form. All around him was a green glow. He was unaware a Lamberhook tree near him was twisting in the moonlight, its trunk beginning to gape open like a wound.

The wail reached a crescendo, as Mandy reached to cover the boy's ears, nearly dropping Twicket as she did so. The Banshees' eyes shot out a climatic stream of bright gold light.

Twicket felt the beam from their eyes hit him full in the face. He blinked several times and tried to look away. His nose twitched, his eyes bulged.

"AHHH!" he said, trying to hold it in.

Mandy heard him and realized what was happening. She held the troll so he was facing the two floating spirits.

"Me no can ..... help ....it!" Twicket cried.

"Let 'er rip!" Mandy cried.

"AAAAHHHHHHH CHHHHOOOOOOOOO!"

The green mucous hit the first Banshee with such ferocity that she fell back, sputtering and coughing. Her wail abruptly ended as her mouth was filled with the green gelatinous mass.

Before the other hag could understand what had just happened, Twicket reloaded.

"AHHHH....AHHHHH....AHHHHHHHHHHH CHOOOOO!"

The blast of slime was filled with small chunks of Monkhood Mushrooms. The second Banshee went down like a torpedoed submarine. They lie on the ground, clawing green mucous from their faces, their hypnotic eyes muted beneath a layer of foul slime.

T.J. stood rooted to the spot like a zombie. Mandy grabbed his arm and pulled him away, the boy's stumbling feet tripping over every obstacle in the path. She could hear the hag's pitiful moans behind her, and their cries of anger.

"Come on!" she urged the boy, who was finally showing some signs of life.

Mandy pulled him along, watching over her shoulder for the hideous creatures. She could hear them thrashing through the bushes, as they tried to blindly follow the threesome. T.J. was still walking as though in a trance, and his dead weight was slowing them down. The edge of the Lamberhook Forest was only a few steps away.

A branch cracked behind them and Mandy heard the hissing gasps of the two Banshees, as they closed in. Each time they tried to sing, they gagged on Twicket's mucous, still filling their throats. Mandy looked over her shoulder and saw one of the hags rise from a stand of bushes, her gnarled fingers reaching for T.J.'s backpack. Mandy gave T.J. a hard push. He fell over a large rock and rolled down a short hill. He finally came to rest near the valley beneath the forest. Mandy hurried down the slope and fell onto the parched ground next to him, Twicket still held tightly in her hand. The Banshees screams rose in garbled tones of rage from the black trees behind them. She turned to see the two floating shapes screaming at them from the forest's edge, afraid to go any farther.

Still panting, Mandy looked to the mountaintop on the other side of the river. Seated beneath the moon's silver glow was the crumbling castle of the Crone—holding court from a rocky cliff face high above the Spectre Lands.

Chapter Thirty-Six

A VANISHING ACT

Markus stood in his grandpa's sanctuary and tried to see in the darkness. He looked around for the cause of the sound he had heard moments before while standing in T.J.'s room. The studio smelled of oil paints and mineral spirits. Markus had only been in this room a few times. He did not share T.J.'s love of art and science. One of the last times he had been here, a Siglet had attacked the window.

"Grandpa?" he called out in the shadows. He fumbled in the dark, but could not find the switch. "Dangit, it's dark in here," he whined.

As his eyes adjusted to the blackness, he could see the window curtain across from him. He walked over to it, banging his leg against Dillon's chair, and finally whipped the curtains open that T.J. had been careful to keep closed. Moonlight flooded the room. Finding the light switch, he flipped it on. *Where has he gone?* Markus wondered. He turned to see the giant painting of Da Vinci's *St. John* shimmering in the moonlight. There was a young man in the painting smiling out at him. He sat with one leg resting across the other, an animal fur about his loin. He was holding a staff in one hand and pointing toward a cave with the other. Markus followed the pointing finger with his eyes and was amazed to see a well sitting back inside the cave's mouth.

Forgetting his search for his grandfather momentarily, he stepped over to the painting and stared open-eyed at the well. Golden light pouring in from the moon outside the studio window bathed the masterpiece in a shimmering glow.

"Cool," Markus breathed. He reached out a timid hand to touch it. As he did so, the well in the painting began to glow; an eerie white beam seemed to be coming up from within it, illuminating the cave walls with a wash of shimmering light. As the boy watched, his mouth hanging open in surprise and anticipation, the light grew stronger, and he saw a transparent pair of hands reach out from within, and grab hold of the well's rim. All at once an elderly ghost with a long flowing beard hefted himself up and over the stone edge of the well, and stepped down to the ground. To Markus' astonishment he was wearing his grandfather's Boston Red Sox jacket!

"Oh my," the elderly gentleman said, as he placed a hand to his back, and stretched. "I really must find another way to travel."

He stepped down from the painting and crossed slowly to Markus.

"Close your mouth, son," he said mildly. He looked around the studio. "Dillon still missing? Well, enough is enough. It is time to go and find him. I have a feeling I know where he is."

He looked at Markus, who was still standing in shock.

"Well, come along boy," Leonardo Da Vinci's ghost said. "I may need some help. Are you any good at navigating forests?"

Markus blinked but could not find his voice. He had heard about the ghost but had yet to see him.

"Wonderful, I will be traveling with a ventriloquist's dummy...I'll be doing all the talking. Let's go," the man said, placing a hand on the boy's back, propelling him toward the studio door. "Hurry it up, boy...there is no time to lose!"

"Where are we going?" Markus asked, finally finding his voice.

"To find your grandfather. I would use the well in my painting but it won't take us where we need to go. We shall have to go the old way," the artist muttered.

"I don't get what you're sayin'. And, why are you wearin' Grandpa's ball jacket?" Markus said, as the famous artist went before him down the attic steps. The boy's eyes opened wide as he watched the Boston Red Sox jacket bob along down the stairs, with only a transparent head, hands and legs peering out from it.

"Dillon let me borrow the jacket," the ghost said hastily. "I like the swooshing sounds it makes." The ghost swung his arms as he walked, demonstrating the noise the satin material made.

"Crimination!" Markus breathed. "Wait 'till Corey Greenman hears about this!"

The ghost and the boy walked to the stairway leading down to the first floor, and listened for sounds of anyone moving about.

"Now be real quiet, unless you want to explain to your father about the strange man in the ball jacket," the great artist warned.

Markus didn't feel he could explain it, so he kept quiet. He followed Leonardo down the stairs where he could hear his mother doing dishes in the kitchen. When they reached the front door, Markus opened it as quietly as he could. The hinges squeaked slightly, and he hurried through it with the artist, closing it gently behind him.

Leonardo was rounding the corner of the house heading for the back yard. Markus ran to keep up with him. The moonlight washed over them, its light filtering through the ghost before him. Only the baseball jacket Da Vinci was wearing appeared real, as it floated across the yard. Markus felt as if he were dreaming.

Leonardo stopped at the edge of Harmon's Wood and looked back at the boy.

"You will need to keep your wits about you, lad," the ghost said. "Can you do that?"

Markus nodded hesitantly, wondering what was going to be required of him. All he cared about right now was that he was keeping company with a dude that had just crawled out of a well in a painting, and he was going on an adventure!

Leonardo led the way into the forest; the swishing sound of the baseball jacket blending in with their footfalls. They walked on and on, and just as Markus wondered if they were ever going to get to the adventure part, they came to the cave.

"In there?" Markus asked, as the ghost came to a halt before the cave's opening. "Uh...the Well of Ghosts? I don't think so. Been there, done that, don't even *want* the T-shirt," he said, backing away.

Moonlight was shining down onto the ancient well only a few paces ahead of them. Leonardo walked over to it and motioned for the boy to follow him.

"Let's get going," the artist said, in a tone that brooked no refusal. "I may need the help of a mortal."

"Wait a minute," Markus said, terror pounding at his ribcage. "Grandpa's in the *well?*" He noticed the rest of the boards were now missing, leaving a black, cavernous hole.

"Other end of the well, boy...other end. No time to lose," Leonardo said, and pulled Markus over to the crumbling cavern.

Leonardo climbed up onto the well's rim and sat, swinging his ghostly legs over, until they dangled above the dark opening. The moonlight shone around him, and onto the strange symbols cut into the well's stone. He pulled a small blue bottle from the pocket of the Red Sox jacket and undid the stopper. Carefully he tilted the bottle until two small drops fell onto the well's symbols of the twisted tree, and the Zodiac sign of Serpens, the Serpent. The symbols glowed with an eerie light.

"Hey! You went in my room!" Markus yelled, recognizing the small bottle he had secreted the magic potion in. The dirty soda bottle had seemed unbefitting such an amazing liquid. He had filled a small empty perfume bottle he'd taken from his mother's room, and hidden it beneath a loose floorboard in his bedroom. Markus had noticed some of the potion was missing the day before.

"You do not know what you are tampering with, young man," the ghost said, anxious to be on his way. "I saw what you did with it in your magic show. I also saw what the strange hag in the forest here did with it just before she jumped into this well. I watched, as she dropped liquid that shimmered just like the stuff in this bottle, onto two symbols on this well's rim. Being a ghost has its advantages when spying on people. Besides, you forget I tutored

Dillon on the paintings that ended up at the school fair. I believe that potion, and the paintings of the ancient evil constellations, have something to do with where your grandfather is. The hag I saw go into the well looked just like the painting I helped him with called *The Crone*. I believe your grandpa is at the other end of this well."

Markus stood next to the well and hesitated. Things were getting out of control.

"Just do what I do and you will be fine," Da Vinci said reassuringly to the boy. He replaced the small blue bottle carefully into the baseball jacket pocket.

A few seconds later a glow swam up from the well's interior, growing brighter and brighter, until an intense beam of light shot from the mouth, illuminating the cave like fireworks.

"Ewww!" Markus said, blinking in the strong light. "Does it always smell that bad?"

"Get over here, boy," Leonardo called hurriedly. "You are in for the thrill of your young life! We are going to visit another dimension!"

"Lemme grab my magic pack...we might need it!" Markus said, as he turned and darted from the cave. "Be right back!"

"We don't have time for that!" the artist cried, looking up through the cave's opening at the waning moon. "I can't wait any longer," Da Vinci said, and disappeared into the white light of the well.

"Wait!" Markus called, turning inside the cave's entrance, just as the moon slid behind the trees. The cave room went dark, as the light from inside the well faded away. Markus ran over and peered into the darkening abyss, and felt his heart sink. He had missed the adventure!

"Hey!" he yelled into the black void, "Come back here!" He watched as the well's carved symbol of a twisted tree, and a strange serpent-like image, stopped glowing.

Little did he know his big brother had entered the well, and was now traveling through the back roads of another dimension. Or that

T.J. was, even now, heading for the castle of the evil ruler of the Spectre Lands.

Chapter Thirty-Seven

THE BLACK RIVER

Twicket's eyes were still sending out a green luminescent light, as Mandy and T.J. picked their way down the grassy slope, leaving the Lamberhook Forest farther, and farther behind. T.J. kept looking back, expecting to see the Banshees coming after them.

"They won't leave the forest," Mandy said, noticing the boy's actions.

"What were they doing back there?" T.J. asked. "I mean, what's with the whole American Idol Voodoo try-outs thing?"

"Me tummy still no feeling so good," Twicket moaned, green light escaping from his lips.

"They wanted to add you to their garden," Mandy said, as they clambered over a pile of rocks. "In a few more minutes you would have been part of a Lamberhook tree."

T.J. stared at her, speechless. Finally he blurted out, "Why just me? How come you weren't in any danger?"

"Their song doesn't work on constellations," the girl said simply.

"They put people inside the trees?" T.J. asked incredulously.

Mandy didn't answer him. She was looking at the planets stacked one above the other in the darkness. This alignment would not come again for 100 years, and it was amazing to see! T.J. followed her gaze and stood transfixed as well. He had never seen anything like it in his life. The moon was enormous! He thought of how his grandfather would love to see this amazing sight, and sadness washed over him.

"Wait," T.J. said, as he looked at the glowing lunar face. "We had a full moon last night when we did the whole well trip. Why is it full again tonight? Is this another Phantom Moon anomaly?"

"Time doesn't matter when you go through the well's portal," Mandy said quickly. "What happens in your world doesn't necessarily align with what goes on here, or any other dimension. Look we can go over all this later," she said restlessly. "Let's get going."

T.J. felt something tugging on his pants leg and stopped. He looked down to see a strange purple plant with long, filmy tendrils snagged on the denim fabric of his jeans. Reaching down he tried to release its grip. The long, finger-like extensions of the plant felt sticky, and he had a hard time removing their grasp.

"Ew," he said, wiping the syrupy residue from their tendrils onto his pants. "What is that?"

"It's an insect-catching plant," Mandy said, wrinkling her nose at it. "I think it was part of Garglon's garden inside the Lamberhook Forest, but when the evil witch disappeared a year ago, the plants were captured, most ending up in the Crone's castle. Some of them escaped and are scattered about, like the ones we saw in the Lamberhook Forest. Just be careful what you touch."

"Garglon? You mentioned her before. I'm guessing I don't want to know," T.J. said, as he stared at the spooky plant.

"What you probably don't want to know is she disappeared after going into *your* world," Mandy said. "I told you things from this dimension have been finding their way into yours for some time now. It's one of the reasons we have to find the Orb and stop all of this!"

T.J. thought about all the times he had heard strange noises coming from the forest at night as he lay in bed. Had he been listening to other creatures coming into Harmon's Wood from other worlds?

"Wait," T.J. said suddenly. "What do you mean 'some of the plants escaped?' How does a plant escape?"

"Garglon's plants are not like the plants in your world, or mine for that matter. Like I told you, they can move about. It's a bizarre thing to watch."

"Yeah...been there, seen that!" T.J. said, shivering at the memory.

The sound of the Black River grew louder, as the group continued on, T.J. watching the plant life with renewed interest. The rocky cliffs and trees ahead of them now hid the castle as they hurried through the Ribhound Valley of the Spectre Lands. Drigmot's Passage had been uneventful. It made Mandy nervous as she couldn't help thinking they were being watched. Though she couldn't see the castle from this vantage point, Mandy knew it sat just atop the formidable mountain ahead, its tower windows overseeing everything.

"Why do they want you in the trees?" T.J. asked again, looking back at the twisted shapes of the Lamberhook Forest off in the distance. The moonlight reflected off their black shiny surface, making them appear to undulate and move.

"Me think me may throw up now," Twicket moaned again.

"Let's not worry about the trees right now," Mandy said simply. "You owe Twicket for doing his nozzle thing. He saved your life back there."

T.J.'s mind was spinning.

"But why do they want to capture you and put you in trees?" he persisted, ignoring the part about Twicket saving his life.

T.J. stopped walking and stared at her. The green light from Twicket's eyes made her look ghostly in the darkness.

"Wait a minute!" he said, a sinking feeling coming over him. "Is that why you said the Lamberhook Forest was the first place to look?"

He was not ready to hear what the girl was probably thinking about his grandfather. Gathering his courage, he asked, "Just tell me this," he said, swallowing the fear. "The…uh…Well Riders…if they are in the trees…are they…dead?" He was trying desperately to stop the image of his grandpa imprisoned in a tree.

Mandy stopped and turned to look back at him. Twicket's green light seemed paler, and she guessed the mushrooms were wearing off. The little troll cane was swallowing over and over, and did not look well.

"I don't know. He may not be in a tree. Please, let's concentrate on what we need now. We are looking for a silver ball, a red crystal eye belonging to your favorite Crone, and…a miracle."

"Thanks," T.J. said sarcastically, staring miserably at the black ground.

Before Mandy could reassure him, a gurgling noise came from deep within Twicket. T.J. looked down at the little bald head who was reeling slightly.

"Are you going to throw up?" the boy asked nervously, getting ready to toss the cane down before he erupted.

"Bllluuurrrpppppp!" The troll threw up green chunks of Monkhood Mushrooms, covering the boy's shoes.

"Oh for Pete's Sake!" T.J. cried, tossing Twicket into the grass. "Is that all you do, shoot green stuff out of that face of yours?"

Mandy picked up the poor troll who was no longer glowing with green light.

"You ok?" she asked kindly.

"Me feel much better," Twicket said brightly. "Me hungry."

T.J. was scraping his shoes against the tall grass in an effort to get the green bile off of them.

"You carry him!" he barked at Mandy.

She laughed. "Come on," she said, holding onto Twicket. "It's still dangerous to be out here."

With that, she turned and walked off, watching the Black River carefully. The giant shapes of the planets hung above them, their alignment reminding Mandy that the Dark Moon was in two nights. She felt panic rise up inside herself. How could she possibly get everything into place in time, even if she did find all the items needed? She hadn't told T.J. her real reason for going to the castle.

The moon sat like a giant glowing sphere at the edge of the Ribhound Valley. From where the children stood, it appeared to be touching the ground, half of it hidden beneath the horizon. T.J. looked at it, marveling at its enormity. The planets of Saturn, Uranus, Jupiter, Mercury, Mars, Neptune, Venus, Earth and Pluto were stacked one above the other like massive marbles rolled into place.

"I guess they let Pluto play with the big boys here," T.J. said. "It's weird to see the earth. Makes me feel like an alien." He stared at the surreal scene for a few moments, and then said, "So if you already have a moon hangin' up there, where is this Dark Moon coming from?" he asked.

"You don't like not knowing all the answers, do you?" Mandy asked him impatiently.

"It's the scientist in me," T.J. said proudly.

"It the obnoxious in you," Twicket muttered.

They climbed over a long ledge of rocks, their feet sliding along the slippery surface as the waters of the Black River lapped at their edges. The thick moss lining the river bank smelled of fungus and clammy soil. T.J. paused and looked up and down the length of the ebony-black water.

"Let me guess...no bridge across these happy waters?" he asked drolly. "How do we know how deep it is if we can't see the bottom?" he asked. "And more importantly, how do you know what's under there?"

Mandy stood looking at the rocks protruding here and there from the ebony current. There didn't appear to be a good place to cross.

"We need something to probe the water to see how deep it is here," she said.

T.J. looked at the troll's cane the girl was holding. Twicket caught his stare and yelled out.

"No! You no be sticking poor Twicket in dark water! There be scary things waitin' to eat me poor little cane!!!"

Mandy twisted her lips to one side, considering.

"He could be right," she said, peering again at the water. "We are near the Crone's castle. There's no telling what's in there to keep visitors away."

"Oh give him here," T.J. said, wanting to be out of the open valley, and under the cover of the cliffs, waiting on the other side of the river.

T.J. snatched the screaming troll from Mandy and leaned out over the swiftly moving current. With Twicket threatening all manner of revenge, T.J. carefully poked the troll's cane into the river. It sank up to the middle of his cane, as the black water sloshed around the staff.

"That's not bad...maybe two feet deep right here," T.J. said, just as the troll shrieked.

"Something slimy on Twicket's bottom!! Pull me out! Pull me out!" the troll screamed.

T.J. pulled the cane from the water. There was indeed something slick and slimy clinging to the troll's wooden staff.

"Ewwww!" Mandy cried. "What is it?"

T.J. held the troll's cane up to the moonlight.

"Looks something like leeches, except these things have teeth!" he said, screwing up his face. "Yuk!"

"Yuk? Me tell you YUK! Get 'em off Twicket!" the troll pleaded.

T.J. stuck the cane between the rocks lining the riverbank and scraped off the black slimy creatures. Their suckers let out a slurping sound, as they released the wooden cane. They crawled along the river rock, leaving a slimy trail behind them, until they finally plopped back into the water, and disappeared from view.

"Be glad your cane is made of wood," T.J. said. "Typically leeches suck your blood!"

"Well that settles it," Mandy said. "I'm not wading through that water! Scaly legs or no scaly legs, I don't want those things on me!"

T.J. looked around for a solution. The river was not extremely wide—maybe fifty feet at the most where they were standing. He watched the water eddying around the rocks that popped above the inky current. The only problem was that none of them were close enough to each other to form a stepping-stone path across the river. The boy stared at the giant boulders in the dark currents. As he looked at the moonlight bathing their shiny surfaces, a thought popped into his head. He reached into his backpack and pulled out the small bottle of Lunar Potion.

"What are you doing?" Mandy said nervously. "Don't drop that! That's all I took from your brother's bottle. There isn't anymore!"

"Trust me for a change," T.J. said. "Grab a good solid stick and pick a rock."

"What?" the girl cried. "What are you planning to do? We can't waste the potion!"

"You want to get to the castle or not?" the boy asked her.

"Yes, but...," she began, looking nervously at the powerful potion in T.J.'s hand.

T.J. walked a few feet over to a stand of pine trees and snapped off a dead branch. "Here!" He tossed her the sturdy limb that was about four feet long. "I'll use Twicket. Let's go."

"*Use Twicket for what?* Go where?" the troll cried out. "Why me no get no say in what happens to poor Twicket?"

T.J. carefully stepped out onto a large boulder closest to the shoreline. He steadied himself, and then sat down cautiously on its slick surface, careful not to get his feet in the dark water. He could envision skeletal hands coming out of the frothing foam to grab his ankles and pull him under. He swallowed, and opened the small stopper of the Lunar Potion bottle.

"Hurry," he called to Mandy, who was hesitating on the river bank. "Find a big rock you can sit down on. Here...take this one by me!"

Mandy stared at him for a moment, and then hesitantly stepped out onto the large flat boulder, near the one where T.J. was seated. Struggling to keep her horned feet from the water, she finally managed to sit down. The boy reached over carefully and dropped a few drops of the Lunar Potion onto her rock's surface.

"I hope this works," he said, as he dropped the shimmering liquid onto his own rock.

Moonlight played down on the wet surfaces of the boulders. At first nothing happened, and then Mandy could feel the solid stone begin to quiver beneath her. The drops of Lunar Potion exploded with light beneath the moon's powerful glow.

"Oh my gosh!" she yelled. She grabbed her stick in both hands and waited to see what happened next.

T.J.'s boulder suddenly shuddered and began rocking in the waves, like a loose tooth trying to free itself.

"Whoaaaaaa!" the boy yelled. He pushed Twicket's cane into the mud behind him, and shoved off from the river bank.

Mandy watched him and did the same, as the two large stones began pushing their way through the swirling water. The boulders were shimmering in a pure white light of energy, as the moonlight brought them to life under the Lunar Potion's power.

"Me no want to be in water!" Twicket was screaming, as T.J. used him like an oar to propel the rock through the current. It was unsteady going, as each rock seemed to have a mind of its own. The boulders would weave here and there, turn back, go upstream, and then downstream. Twice the massive rocks lifted into the air, only to come crashing down into the inky water again. T.J. was finding it difficult to stay on, let alone get his boulder to stay on a straight course, and simply take him to the other side of the river. Mandy was having the same problem, and was almost bucked off twice.

"Leechy things on Twicket!" the troll cried out.

T.J. scraped the disgusting things from the troll's cane and tried again to tame his rock.

"Something coming!" the troll suddenly screamed, looking upstream at a giant wavelike action in the water. It wove back and forth through the current, with only the ripples around it giving it away. A large tail surfaced and went back beneath the surface.

"T.J.!" Mandy cried. "We have to get out of here! How do you make these rocks follow orders?"

T.J. was watching the approaching motion with horror. Whatever it was had to be huge! *If the tail was that big, then what must the head look like?* the boy wondered, fear gripping him like a vise. Suddenly the Marek brothers seemed like a picnic. He strained to make out a form in the fast-moving current.

Quickly, he again pushed Twicket's cane into the water and shoved off from the nearest rock, finally propelling his boulder in the right direction. The shore was only a few feet away. As he dipped the troll into the water again, something snatched the cane from his hand. It pulled the walking stick beneath the surface.

"Twicket!" T.J. cried, searching the water frantically.

Suddenly a giant head sprung from the black current, snapping at the boy. It was the largest snake T.J. had ever seen. It still held Twicket in its jaws. The poor troll was screaming for his life!

"It's Hydra!" Mandy cried out in terror. "It's the water snake! She was a constellation in the Glimmer Lands!"

"*She?* That giant thing is a *she?*" T.J. croaked. "I thought Hydra was a guy snake!"

"That's Hydrus...he's much smaller," Mandy called. "Do something, T.J. You can't let her eat Twicket!"

The beast dove beneath the surface again, and T.J. heard Twicket gurgling beneath the water. He knew he had to do something. Grabbing the nearest river rock he could find, he raised it over his head, and waited for the serpent to surface again. Only the swirling current could be seen. Moments passed, and T.J. was sure the troll was gone forever.

Finally, the snake surfaced several feet away, too far for the boy to bring the rock down directly upon its head. Twicket was frozen with terror, his blue eyes fixed, and water pouring from his open mouth.

Without pausing to think, T.J. hefted the large rock in both hands. He heard his father's voice in his head saying, "Just shoot the dang thing!" T.J. flung the rock at the snake with every ounce of courage he had. The rock hit the giant head cleanly in the center. A *CRACK* sound was heard as the creature's skull split, spilling Twicket from its mouth. As the troll was carried downstream in the current, T.J. lunged across his boulder, and caught Twicket's cane just before he disappeared under a black, swirling eddy.

The boy held the troll tightly, and pushed off the remaining rocks until, after several tries, he finally navigated his boat of stone to the opposite shore. T.J. hopped off and laid Twicket in the grass. The little troll's eyes were open, and he was babbling incoherently.

"Ma almo die," he garbled.

Mandy finally managed to get her rock across, and jumped gratefully to the muddy bank, her horned ankles leaving marks in the mire. She dropped in exhaustion next to T.J. who was leaning over the troll trying to understand him.

"Ma chok," Twicket said in garbled words. "Ma moff...get ow ma moff!"

"I think he said he's choking, and to get something out of his mouth!" Mandy said.

T.J. pulled the troll's mouth apart and was shocked to see a red glowing rock inside. He gently plucked it out with two fingers and held it up in the moonlight. The red glare from the object became brighter.

"That's the Crone's eye!" Mandy cried out. "How in the world did that get into his mouth?" She grabbed the crystal from T.J. "This is unbelievable!" the girl kept saying over, and over again, as she turned the evil crystal in her hands.

Mandy had an odd feeling come over her as she stared at the red beam of light which was getting brighter by the second. She closed her fist around the crystal to shut out its glow.

"Here, put this somewhere deep in your bag where its light can't be seen," the girl said nervously, handing the Crone's eye to T.J. He held the revolting eye with two fingers and placed it deep into a zippered pocket of his backpack, sealing it shut.

"Do you realize what we have here?" she asked excitedly. "We now have the Crone's eye *and* the Lunar Potion. We only have to find the Dark Orb! I think we have a real shot at doing this, T.J.!" she said happily. Despite her hideous appearance, T.J. suddenly saw the beautiful girl he remembered looking back at him through her happy eyes. He smiled.

"Uh oh! There goes our ride," the girl said, watching in amazement, as the two large, and glowing boulders took off down the stream, leaping about like children freed from school for summer vacation.

"You ok, Twicket?" the boy asked the troll, who still looked dazed. Water kept gurgling up and spilling out of his mouth. T.J. ripped several more leeches from the troll's cane and slung them into the river.

"Me think me eat most of river bottom," the troll finally complained.

"Well, thanks to you, we have the Crone's eye," Mandy said happily. "I wonder how it ended up in the river?"

"Let's get out of here," T.J. said. He picked Twicket up.

"Next time you rock riding, you get you own stick," Twicket said grumpily.

"Why didn't you just slime the thing?" T.J. asked, sarcastically.

"Why you not throw you big shoe at it? It gigantic!"

"That way," Mandy said quickly, to cut short an argument. She pointed to a small trail that disappeared through some trees bordering the base of the mountain.

"We've got the eye and the potion," T.J. pointed out. "Can we skip the castle tour?"

"We still need the Dark Orb," Mandy reminded him. "And, do you really want to spend the night out here...with creepies and crawlies?"

"I'll take Trails of Death for $200, Alex," T.J. muttered, trying to sound braver than he felt as they entered the stand of trees. Behind them, a giant severed snake's head, its skull cracked, and its eyes lifeless, washed up onto the river bank.

Chapter Thirty-Eight

HIDDEN IN THE WOODS

Corvus flew through the shadows of the Spectre Lands in search of his Queen. His small brain was awhirl with images of what her joy would be at seeing the Lunar Potion returned to her. He had managed to hold onto it when he tumbled through the well. He could also report as to the whereabouts of the Crone's eye. He had marked where the eye had fallen into the Black River after he had attacked the Siglet carrying it. Once he found Queen Cassiopeia, they could go to retrieve it from the black waters. Hopefully, they would rule the 5 Dimensions together, just as they had planned. All they needed now was to find the Dark Orb.

Corvus was anxious to rid himself of the deformities he'd incurred from his travel through the well to this forsaken land. His feathers were missing in several places, leaving only scorched skin. His beak was broken, part of it hanging at an odd angle, and strange lumps, looking very much like bug cocoons, covered his claws. The name Darmos had appeared on the mirror in the cave when he exited the well and looked at his repulsive reflection. He chose to ignore the Crone's new name for him; he didn't plan on being here for long. He was one of the lucky ones who could fly home.

Something was moving through the forest surrounding the Crone's castle below him. The crow circled again, looking for an opening in the thick trees. There! He could definitely see two figures carefully threading their way through the tall pines. Corvus dipped lower for a better view and was surprised to see a human boy carrying a strange stick. Walking next to the human he could see a creature with purple scales and bright orange hair.

Corvus circled again and again, his thoughts racing. The only way for the human to be here was for him to have opened the well's portal with Lunar Potion. *Where did a human child get hold of the potion?* the bird wondered. *If he has Lunar Potion, perhaps the boy has the Dark Orb, as well. Showing up with the Orb and the Lunar Potion would garner him the Queen's unwavering favor! He would be in a very powerful position,* the crow reasoned. He glanced down at the human boy again. *What was that strange-looking stick with a green head on it?* Corvus also noticed the human had made the passage through the well without becoming deformed. The pair had also managed to survive crossing the Black River. *Something strange is going on here,* the bird thought.

Finally the crow made up his mind. He would first find the Queen. It was possible she already had the Dark Orb that had fallen into the well just ahead of her into the Spectre Lands. If not, she would know how to take care of the human boy if he did have the powerful ball. Corvus glanced down once more upon the two shapes moving through the woods toward the Crone's castle.

The crow flew off, his keen eyesight searching the twisted world beneath him for any signs of his Queen. He had no idea what she might look like after falling through the well. He shuddered, hoping he would recognize her.

Corvus beat his wings against the night air, the enormous planets aligning at his back. Time was short; in two nights the Dark Moon would rise! If his Queen had the Dark Orb there was a chance they could have everything in place before the wells changed, along with their secret symbols. But they would still need the Crone's eye. He needed to find the Queen to ask what needed to be done next!

A high, keening wail wafted through the night air, its plaintive song swirling in eddies of notes, rising and falling. It was the Banshees. Flying high above the Lamberhook Forest, Corvus wondered how many lost souls were now embedded in the grotesque trees, their arms and legs becoming branches and roots. The

Banshees cry grew louder and he found himself grateful their song had no effect on constellations.

Up ahead, curling like a wispy snake, he spotted a tendril of smoke crawling over a stand of Lamberhook trees, its image ghost-like in the darkness. Corvus made a beeline for it. He could smell the putrid odor of burning plants as he grew closer to the dissipating finger of smoke. It was climbing from a small clearing below, where he could see a garden lined out in three perfect rows. A small trail led to a large grouping of Lamberhook trees. The trees seemed to meld into each other, making a gigantic, morphed hut composed of shiny black trunks and twisted limbs. He could see a small door and several oval windows carved into the makeshift house.

Corvus flew down and sat on a tree branch overlooking the garden. The Banshees' song had stopped, their dreadful mission accomplished for the night. He cocked his head, listening intently for signs of life coming from the tree hut. He knew this place. He knew this garden. It belonged to Garglon, a witch second in power only to the Crone.

Corvus now looked down upon the fragmented rows of misshapen plants. There were not many left after the Crone had decimated the garden. Their hideous faces were highlighted in the moonlight, as they moved about the garden, whispering to one another.

The crow turned his attention to the hut just off to his left. A round yellow glow of light was coming from an opening high up on the left-hand side of the grouping of tangled trees. Soundlessly he flew to it and lit on the rim of the tree's window. He could feel the warmth of a fire emanating from within, and saw smoke rising up until it exited another opening in the trees higher up. He leaned forward and peered into the orange glow of the room beneath him.

In the golden light of the tree's interior he saw crude shelves crammed with hollowed out wooden tree roots acting as bowls, holding all manner of herbs and powdered plants. A table made of tree limbs sat against one wall. Hunched over the table, her back to him, was a misshapen woman, her hair matted with leaves and bits of bark. She was muttering to herself and running her hands over a paper scroll lying on the crude table. The bent form was tossing something onto the table...something that rolled. Corvus could see her bony elbows protruding from her torn garments. Her calves and bare feet could be seen below the ratty gown she was wearing; her toes long and gnarled with broken, dirty nails. Obviously Garglon had returned.

Corvus watched her intently, his small black eyes glittering in the glow of a fire. He could smell the odor of burning leaves, and something he had never smelled before emanating from inside a black pot hanging over an open flame in the center of the hut's interior. It made his head dizzy.

The creature below him continued to mutter, at times her croaking voice raised in anger.

"It must be here," she muttered over and over again. "It fell into the well! I saw the symbols on the well's rim glowing! It was the Lamberhook tree and the symbol for the Serpent! I saw it! The Crone's eye had to have fallen here. But that crow! That stupid crow has the Lunar Potion! When I find him, I will cut him into bits and feed him to the garden outside! The Dark Moon is in two nights! I must have my beauty back! I *will* rule the 5 Dimensions!"

She turned away from the table, and the orange glow of the fire illuminated the distorted features of her face. Her eyes were sunken pools of black with only a glimpse of a green iris peering out. Most of her nose was missing, leaving only a cavity with two holes and a ridge of cartilage. Her small mouth was twisted to one side, and her bottom lip was missing, exposing a row of uneven teeth. Beneath the strands of tangled blond hair only one ear was apparent; an emerald earring still clinging to the shredded lobe. The tattered gown that once held shimmering threads of gold and a jewel-encrusted collar, now hung in tatters, faded and stained.

Corvus looked down in horror at the remains of what was once his Queen. His small heart hammered against his ribcage, as he watched her limp across the room to a large rain barrel. She gripped its rim with her crippled hands and leaned over the circle of water. The Queen looked down sadly into the reflection of her disfigured face. The muscles beneath the skin contorted with pain. Her shoulders shuddered with sobs. She gripped the wooden rim tighter and exclaimed:

"It was within reach...*all of it!* The power...absolute power! To be ruined by a bird and a wretched dog!" she sobbed. She slapped at the water with her withered hand, sending it sloshing over the sides.

Corvus trembled as he listened to the Queen's hatred of him. She would never let him join her now. He would have to change his plans.

Two tall shadows fell across an oblong opening near the table that overlooked the garden. The Queen quickly looked out and then hobbled to a small wooden door set deeply into the black tree trunks. She lifted a wooden latch and walked out into the moonlight, leaving the door open. Corvus could see only her hunched back and what appeared to be the bottom of one of the Banshee's floating forms; its long green, luminescent legs, fringed with dripping kelp and seaweed, hovering several inches above the ground.

A ray of moonlight fell into the room through the open doorway. It illuminated a weathered map spread out across the crude table where the Queen had been standing. The scroll showed the trails and hiding places of the Spectre Lands. Lying atop the map were three small stones in the shape of skulls. Witches would toss the Skull Stones onto maps when searching for something, much like the Glimrocks from the Glimmer Lands were used in that realm. If the desired location was found, the eyes on the Skull Stones would open, their light pointing the way along the map. But today the stones had repeatedly pointed to the image of the castle on the parchment scroll. Fearing they were merely showing her the way to the Crone and her *other* eye, Morble had erupted. She would have a hard time ridding the evil ruler of her eye, especially if she was sequestered in her fortress of stone.

The moonlight glinted off a shard of glass lying on the table. A beam of light ricocheted off the sliver and shot up to a small silver ball, half-hidden on a shelf high above the map table. The crow's eyes bulged. She did indeed have the Dark Orb!

"Did you find anything?" the Queen demanded of the two floating forms before her. "Has anything else come through the well?"

The answer was apparently in the negative, as the Queen erupted.

"Then go beyond the forest if you must! You have failed me in finding the eye, and I am stuck here without that potion. Find a way to get into the Crone's castle, and either get me the potion she hides there, or bring me one of Luthor's pods she is growing. We can at least go home to the Glimmer Lands since I know the symbols, but I need the Potion! Do you want to stay here for the next 100 years? Then GO! Find the things I ask, or you will live your days in these hideous woods!"

She returned to the interior of the hut, slamming the wooden door behind her. The firelight cast her hunched shadow against the wall, and reflected off a dark flying shape making its way back up to the window.

"I will have the power!" she screamed. "I did not go through all of this pain and trouble to have my destiny be a life lived in this hellish tree! I will not go through eternity with two cast-out Banshees! I am Cassiopeia! I am the Queen of the Glimmer Lands! I *will* rule the 5 Dimensions!"

Her raspy cry filled the hut and rose into the treetops of the Lamberhook Forest, where Corvus was flying swiftly away through their boughs, the Dark Orb clutched fiercely in his talons. He knew now he was on his own. He also knew exactly where to hide the Orb—the same place he had hidden the vial of Lunar Potion. It was a perfect hiding place—a place where no land-dwelling creatures would find it.

Chapter Thirty-Nine

LOST AND FOUND

The light from the window of the mud hut cast a golden glow upon the wildberry bush outside Wheedle's window. Frinkle had been watching from the forest a few feet away, hoping the peddler would turn in for the evening. The disgusting smell of boiled tree roots floated out to him. Between the odor of Wheedle's cooking, and the cloying stink of the swamp, he thought he might just throw-up, even though he hadn't eaten anything all day.

He wasn't at all sure his plan would work. But dang, if the object he found near the Crone's castle didn't look a lot like the red crystal that had been used as the stopper for Wheedle's Bottle of Whispers!

Frinkle had changed his mind about heading back to the peddler's hut after the Siglet's stole her precious bottle stopper from him. He was in no mood to have her scream at him! So he decided to try and convince his new friend to give him another chance to find the thing he kept hounding Frinkle to come up with. Each time Wheedle had come back from collecting trinkets from the Well Riders, Frinkle had looked through her cart. But he had never found the round silver ball his friend so passionately sought. He had promised Frinkle power and a new home if he found it, *and* a red crystal for him, knowing Wheedle's assistant was his best bet of getting his hands on anything that came through the well.

But now...*now* Frinkle had found it! It had been lying beneath the tower window on the north side of the castle, as he made his way toward his friend's home.

Frinkle had left looking around the castle as his last resort. The towering mass of stone scared the beejeebies out of him; not to mention that dragon who was always hanging around, the Siglets, *and* then there was navigating across the Black River to get there.

He had pulled his little hollowed-out tree trunk from his hiding place inside a thick stand of nickelbeard bushes near the river. Crusty, dead bodies of dried-up leeches clung to its bottom. He had fashioned the crude little boat to carry him across the Black River. Once in the water, Frinkle always laid low inside the small vessel. As the current carried it through the black waters, he made loud snorting sounds, mimicking one of the river creatures he had heard before. It always seemed to work. Anything from under the inky current must have thought he was one of them.

The little man pushed against rocks with a stick, protruding from a small hole above the water line on the side of the boat, to help him navigate across. Something *had* poked its head above the black current and sniffed at the small vessel. Frinkle was lying flat, holding his breath. He could hear the thing snuffling, and snorting, as it ran a snout along the rough hull. Frinkle screwed up his face and grunted loudly, "*Snort...snort, snort, snort!*" Finally, he heard the creature splash beneath the surface and swim off.

Frinkle thought back to his discovery of the amazing object outside the Crone's castle. It was the thing lying next to the object that had first caught Frinkle's attention. A flash of moonlight had reflected off a glittering chain he had seen in a tall stand of weeds. Attached to the chain was a beautiful round, red stone! The stone didn't have a black dot in its center like the one his friend told him to look for. But, Frinkle thought it just might be good enough for Wheedle. In fact he could hardly believe his luck in finding the little thing. It didn't glow like Wheedle's stopper, but it was pretty! And lying next to it, he had found a round object with a silver surface! The words of his new friend were ringing in his head, as he stooped to pick up the shiny silver ball.

"Find it!" the creature had screamed at Frinkle, from the shadows of the broken ship in Apparition Bay. "I don't want your useless trinkets! Bring me the Dark Orb! It must be here! It is a silver ball about this big!"

The friend had shown Frinkle the dimensions by holding his hands apart about the size of a Friggit Frog. Frinkle remembered cringing when he looked at his friend's hands. They were twisted, and where the flesh was rotting away in places you could see bone. They didn't smell very good either, but after Wheedle's swamp, a bad odor was a subjective thing. Frinkle also noticed a small marking on the friend's right wrist...it was the symbol of a crown.

"This has to be it!" Frinkle whispered excitedly to himself. He turned the silver ball over and over in his hands. Fate had smiled upon him! A red crystal to replace Wheedle's stopper, and now the Dark Orb his friend desired so much! Wheedle wouldn't kill him, and he would be rewarded by his friend. Life was looking good!

"Ok....," Frinkle had said to himself. "I got's to put this here red thing back in her bottle 'fore she finds it's missing. Then I go see my friend!" His mood had greatly improved as he headed for Wheedle's hut.

The light finally went out inside Wheedle's crude structure, made of mud and a hollow tree trunk, leaving the moonlight as Frinkle's only night light. The croaking sound of the massive toads living near the swamp was deafening, as the little man tiptoed across the open area, and headed straight for the bush where Wheedle always hid her cart. He slipped silently into the opening in the foliage and ran his small hands over the side of the crude wagon to get his bearings in the darkness of the wildberry cave. His fingers could feel pots, books, something that squished when he touched it, what felt like old clothes, a broken spoon, and an old clock that was missing a hand. Frinkle knew every item in the peddler's traveling store. What he needed was the sack in which Wheedle kept the Bottle of Whispers.

Being careful not to make anything clank or clatter, Frinkle finally felt his way under the cart's wooden bench. There it was! He could feel the rough burlap of the sack where Wheedle kept the thing! Gently he pulled the bag out from its hiding place and carried it out into the moonlight. Being careful to stay out of sight of the hut's window that looked out onto Haver's Swamp, Frinkle opened the sack and pulled out the rock he left there earlier. He reached into his vest pocket and took out the Bottle of Whispers, a clump of mud stuffed into its opening. It was all he could find to plug it to keep Wheedle's whispers from escaping.

He plucked the dried mud from the opening and cast it away. He had already removed the fancy red stone from its casing while he walked the long way to Wheedle's hut from the Black River near the castle. He kept the chain and setting that had held it in place. One thing Wheedle had taught him was to never discard anything. You never knew when it could come in handy.

Grunting under the effort to get the dang thing to fit into the bottle's mouth, Frinkle finally twisted the red gem into place, just as a whisper was gurgling up from inside. He held it up to the moonlight. It was not nearly as special as the other object, but he thought it might just work! He placed the bottle back into the burlap sack. Keeping Wheedle's good graces was important for now...just in case his new friend wasn't happy with anything Frinkle brought to him. After all, the little man needed a place to sleep, away from the creatures of the Spectre Lands, even if it was Wheedle's smelly hut.

A twig snapped in the forest behind him. Frinkle whirled around, his heart hammering.

Siglets? Creatures with teeth? Creatures without teeth? Thoughts exploded in his frightened mind. A few brief moments felt like several eternities. It was never a good idea to be wandering around in the Spectre Lands at night. He thought he saw two golden eyes peering at him from beneath a bush, located just a little farther inside the forest's edge.

Frinkle backed up slowly, cradling the sack holding Wheedle's precious bottle. His heel felt the sting of a wildberry limb poking into it, and he knew he had reached the bush where the cart was hidden. He ducked his head and backed into the opening, keeping his eyes focused on the area where he thought he had seen something watching him. Once inside the large bush, he hurriedly returned the bottle to its hiding place beneath the seat. He was breathing hard. Now what should he do? Wait here? Go inside the hut and go to sleep? There was no way he was going to try to travel and find his new friend in the nighttime.

To underscore his thoughts he saw the enormous shadow of Draco fall across the swamp as the creature circled overhead. The smell of singed flesh wafted down to him.

Sighing heavily, Frinkle pulled Wheedle's ratty old blanket out of the cart and made a bed on the ground where he could see from between the wheels of the cart. From here he could look out from the protective cover of the bushes into the night for anything coming this way. His stomach rumbled from hunger.

Putting his fingers inside his vest pocket he checked to make sure the silver ball was still there. His fingers felt the slick, cool surface and he smiled. He also felt the flat face of the thing he had found earlier. Pulling it from his pocket he looked at it again. It didn't light up anymore the way it had when he first found it in the weeds near the Ribhound Valley five days ago. It was small and black and had strange buttons all over it. When he found it, it was making a buzzing noise, and it vibrated in his hand. A small window on it lit up with a man's picture. It read *David* under the man's face. Frinkle thought a beast from the Void had come through the well and dropped it, and was trying to beam him up into darkness.

"It's a Mind Snatcher!" the little man had thought, his eyes bulging. He pushed a green button with a flashing light on it, hoping to turn the thing off. Instead it started ringing, and he then heard a young voice say, "Hello? Grandpa?" Frinkle had listened for a moment, and began pushing all the buttons to get the thing to shut up. When he pushed the red button, the voice went away. The *David* face showed up a few times, and Frinkle pushed the red button to make it go away. Shortly after that the strange device didn't light up again. He had kept it to give to Wheedle in case she was still mad at him. She was always mad at him. Maybe if he gave it to her, the Void people would beam *Wheedle* up!

Frinkle placed the black Mind Snatcher back inside his pocket. He cradled the broken spoon he had grabbed from the cart up against himself, for use as his only weapon, and finally felt sleep overtake his tired body.

Chapter Forty

GONE FISHING!

Barnacle dodged a flock of low-flying Mule Geese as he tacked his pirate ship to the lee side, and sailed through the pale morning sunlight.

"Ugliest birds I e'er did see," the pirate ghost muttered to himself as he watched the nine birds narrowly miss tearing his already tattered main sail. The once beautiful creatures from the Glimmer Lands were now mutated clumps with missing feathers. Their tails resembled that of a mule's, thus changing their name from Cygnus the Swan to Mule Geese here in the Spectre Lands. Their beaks turned upward, as though pointing toward the home they left behind.

Barnacle sailed above the Spectre Lands, always keeping a keen eye out for treasure...especially the powerful Dark Orb. The pirate ghost thought of all the revenge and glory that could be his if he got his hands on that silver ball! He could not believe his luck when he found the Crone's eye just outside the cave with the well. To be correct, Two Hooks Mason's eye had found it, while dangling from its hook in search of treasure for the pirate. Barnacle figured old Morble had dropped it when she came through the well here. It was no secret she was madly looking for it. He wasn't sure if she had the Orb. In the meantime, he would keep looking for the silver ball. *With the Orb and the eye, he would be the most powerful pirate in the Universe! Why, it could probably turn him back into mortal form*, he thought eagerly.

The problem with the eye was that it was always glowing, trying to reach out to the Crone. So, Barnacle had hidden it in a deep hole in a Lamberhook tree in the forest, where no one would see its light and find it. At least, that had been his hope. He was unaware Wheedle had stumbled upon it, used it as a bottle stopper, and it had pinged around the Spectre Lands ever since.

As Barnacle skirted a stand of Lamberhook trees, he could see the rushing current of the Black River up ahead. Even in the sunlight, the water was an inky black.

"Whoever designed dis world shoulda opened a new box of crayons," the pirate muttered, spitting over the side for emphasis. Barnacle sailed along over the parched land, keeping an eye out for the Orb. Up ahead, the morning light glinted off the flecks of quartz embedded in the stones of the Crone's castle, sitting like a disfigured cake topper upon the craggy mountaintop. Barnacle found himself wondering what the Crone did in there all day. He had never seen her leave her fortress in the sunlight, and very rarely at night.

"Got's her minions to do her biddin'," he mumbled. "Let de other guys get der hands dirty doin' yer bizness!"

Barnacle didn't want to risk the Crone seeing his ship so near her castle. The last time he had gotten too close she had sent a flock of Siglets after him. The Siglets weren't as bad as that dang dragon. The pirate figured she thought he was spying for the Glimmer Land's Queen, but he had no use for anyone but himself. He was nobody's spy and nobody's friend!

The ghost steered the ship silently into a tall stand of trees at the edge of the Lamberhook Forest. He had tied down the clanging fry pan earlier, as he set about looking around the castle for lost trinkets—in particular the Dark Orb. He would ride on Volans from here…much easier to hide amongst the trees and rocks on the mountain's face, than with a large ship.

"If that dang Orb ain't with the Crone, den I be a land lubbin' sea bass!" he said excitedly, as he reeled in the tether tied to his faithful fish Volans, and prepared to mount the flying grouper. "But while we be here, let's go check on dat eyeball to make sure it's still safe."

He settled himself into the saddle, kneed the fish, and sailed off through the trees.

Chapter Forty-One

TRESPASSING!

T.J shushed Twicket again for the fifth time, as the three weary travelers circled the base of the Crone's castle looking for an entrance. Unable to find one the night before, T.J., Mandy and Twicket had slept inside the forest flanking the castle. T.J. was not at all happy to be there. Throughout the night, he awoke to whispering sounds, as though the trees were passing along the little group's whereabouts. Something with tiny feet had climbed into his pants leg, and the boy had gone into a spasmodic dance to rid himself of it. A small creature with eight legs and a long snout, had gone sailing through the air, as T.J. flung it from his leg.

"Wussy boy," Twicket sniggered.

"I hate this place!" he said, more loudly than he meant to. He had looked about him at the moving shadows and shivered.

Mandy was leaning upon a large boulder, happy to be off her feet. Navigating with her new horned ankles had been tiring.

"Can we at least turn on the flashlight?" he pleaded.

"Of course not," she said tiredly.

"Can we look for a well bucket, then?" he asked.

"T.J.,…forget about the well bucket! Just because you saw it scribbled on a rock doesn't mean anything."

"You told me yourself the little blue guy was an Oracle…that he predicted the future." T.J. countered. "*'The Well Bucket is the Answer'* must mean something. The fact that it mentions the well should make you take notice."

Mandy watched him in the shadows and said nothing.

"I just feel it's important, that's all," T.J. muttered.

They walked out into another dreary day in the Spectre Lands. Keeping to the shadows of the mountain, they continued circling the base of the crumbling fortress, peering behind every bush and close-fitting tree trunk, looking for an opening.

"You said we were only coming here to have a place to hide during the night," T.J. said, referring to the castle. "Instead, we end up in some spooky woods sleeping on rocks! Well, it's daytime now, and we should be going to look for my grandpa! Why are we messing around with the crazy lady?"

"Could you just trust me for once? Please?" the girl sighed. "Who do you think is the best bet for having the Dark Orb? My guess is that it is in the castle!"

Now that she had the Crone's eye Twicket found in the river, Mandy was relieved to abandon her mission of obtaining the other eye directly from the Crone's face! She had kept that agenda secret. T.J. would have freaked out at the thought of it.

"Me have complaint," Twicket said, suddenly to T.J. "You not nice to trolls. Stop being mean to poor Twicket," the little troll head whimpered. Ever since the walking cane had sneezed twice on T.J. when the sun came out, the boy had been angry with him.

"Being mean to you? Being mean to *you?*" the boy jeered. "Look at my pants! Before I met you they were *blue* jeans, now they look like a bad commercial for camouflage fatigues...nothing but green and brown!"

"Will you two please be quiet?" Mandy whispered hoarsely. "Do you want to get caught out here...right next to the castle? Call me naïve but I'm guessing the tea table here is not set for visitors!"

The three weary travelers continued to circle the base of the mountain where the Crone's castle sat, high above their heads.

"Why are we looking down here?" T.J. whispered. "Doesn't the castle have any doors?"

"I heard there is a secret passage into the castle at the base of the mountain somewhere," Mandy said. "Or would you rather scale that rocky mass above us?"

T.J. looked up at the ongoing line of rocks, briar bushes and vines. His answer was to renew his efforts to find a secret passage.

"Big surprise," T.J. said grumpily, after they had been at it for an hour. "No way in. Not that I want to go in, but I'm starving. Does the Crone eat normal food, or is it all bugs and the bones of Well Riders?"

The only thing the boy had eaten in over a day was a granola bar and a stale bag of raisins from his backpack that had been there since the Boy Scout Jamboree he attended five years ago. He was not in a good mood.

Mandy moved aside another cluster of clinging vines crawling along the mountain wall; a small snake slithered out of the leaves, disappearing into a hole in the crumbling stone. Mandy jumped and managed not to scream. She was about to let go of the vines, when she looked again at the hole the snake had disappeared into. She studied the strange indentations in the rock.

"Does this look odd to you?" she asked T.J., regretting the choice of words the moment she uttered them. "Let me rephrase that…does it look like something might fit into these small holes?" She was running a scaled finger over the indentations.

T.J. leaned closer and looked at the markings.

"Kinda looks like the outline of a face," he said quietly. "See? There's the nose…kind of a twisted mouth right there."

Mandy stared at it, and did indeed see what looked like a crude drawing of a tortured face. The largest of the holes appeared to be one of two eyes. Suddenly she started.

"Get the Crone's eye out of your bag and hand it here!" she said in an excited whisper.

"What? Are you nuts? That thing glows brighter every time we get close to this castle! She'll see it!"

"I'll be quick!" Mandy said, holding her scaled hand out for the red crystal.

T.J. hesitated and looked high up at a tall tower window of the castle that looked down over where they were standing.

"Someone just put me out of my misery," he muttered, as he unzipped the backpack pocket.

"Me would raise me hand to volunteer for that, but me no have hands," Twicket said, his rubbery grin spreading across his face.

T.J. was too nervous to retort. Leaning Twicket against the castle wall, he carefully lifted out the red crystal eye. He had wrapped it in a discarded granola bar wrapper in his backpack the night before. Still in its foil, he handed the eye to Mandy, and stepped back.

Taking a deep breath, the girl carefully unfolded the crinkling wrapper, cringing at the noise it made. T.J. kept glancing up at the tower window, sweat beading up on his forehead. Something overhead smelled like burning skin. Images of humans roasting over an open spit assailed his already nervous mind.

Suddenly a bright glare of red light shot out of the wrapper, covering the castle's stone in a crimson wash of color.

"Put it back...put it back!" T.J. hissed, trying to grab it from Mandy, and stuff it back into the foil.

Instead, the girl hurriedly turned it in her hands until the black pupil of the red eye faced outward. She pushed it into the opening in the stone face where an eye would sit in the etching. It fit perfectly! She felt her head swimming from the bright red light, and had trouble focusing.

"Oh crap!" T.J. yelped, as the ground began to shudder beneath their feet. He kept his eyes away from the crystal's beam, but he could feel it pulling him in.

Beneath the crude face etched in the castle wall, four large stones began vibrating. The blocks suddenly swung out, revealing a dark tunnel into the fortress's interior.

Mandy and T.J. squinted in the red glare of the eye to see inside.

"Here!" the girl whispered anxiously. "Hide it, quick!"

T.J. took the Crone's eye from the girl's shaking hand. As he did so, the red light illuminated a section of Mandy's wrist where her gold bracelet had momentarily slipped away. She had a marking in the purple scales that stood out in the bright red glare. It was the symbol of the Gemini Twins!

A fragment of conversation swirled through the boy's mind. It was Mandy talking, back when they were still in Coven Bay saying, "Somewhere on every constellation you will find a marking of their sign," Mandy had said. *She is one of the Gemini Twins!* T. J. thought wildly. She had come out of one of his grandpa's paintings, leaving the other half of the constellation still painted there! But, where was the other Twin? It could be anyone…even a boy. Twins weren't always of the same sex. Was the other twin here in the Spectre Lands? Back in the Glimmer Lands? Maybe the other half of Gemini had come out of the painting looking for Mandy after they came here, and was still back in Harmon's Wood.

The thought had been quick, as the boy hurriedly replaced the eye into the granola bar wrapper, and shoved it back into the pocket of his back pack. His mind was swirling, and not just from the effect of the Crone's eye's power. He was jerked back to the happenings going on now as he saw Mandy plunge into the dark tunnel.

"That's it?" T.J. hissed at her back. "Just go on in? You don't know what's in there!" His heart was exploding at the thought of going into the dark passage where anything could be waiting for them. "You don't know the Orb is in the castle!"

"No flashlight!" he heard her whisper, and then she disappeared into the blackness.

"Great…jussssstttt wonderful!" T.J. muttered, gnawing his lip, noting that the cut there was beginning to heal. Fear knocked on every door in his mind. He looked behind him at the Spectre Lands, and then back at the tunnel. He felt like screaming. Finally, with his heart racing he said, "Ok, troll face—with your underground "me-can-see-in-the-dark" crap—you lead the way. And don't you lead me anywhere stupid!"

"Mama's boy," the troll mumbled, as they headed into the tunnel.

Chapter Forty-Two

FRINKLE'S FRIEND

Morning found Frinkle making his way through the tangled branches of Haver's Forest, following the trail he knew so well. He was still limping from his run-in with the Rictor Turtle, and the Siglet bites only itched more as the days passed. He was so sick of living in this world built from nightmares and deformed creatures. The silver ball he could feel in his pocket was his ticket out of here! He just knew it!

Frinkle stepped carefully across the stones spanning the width of the Moaning River. His small shadow played among the current's ripples, conjuring up sighs from beneath the water. He looked down nervously, expecting to see faces bubbling up to the surface. As the outline of a shallow skull began to appear, he hurried faster. With a sigh of relief, he hopped onto the river bank and disappeared into a stand of Lamberhook trees.

After walking through the mutated forest for several minutes, the smell of damp earth and fungus-infested water floated to him through an opening in the trees. Around the next bend in the trail was Apparition Bay. Wheedle's apprentice crept toward the opening in the twisted trunks and peered out. The sunlight did nothing to dispel the gloom hanging over the dark Bay. He knew just below its surface were many of the Glimmer Lands' constellations that had been turned into hideous beings with unrecognizable names. The Nereids were sea nymphs that had once been the most beautiful creatures in the heavens. He had heard through Wheedle that Cassiopeia had tossed them into the well for saying their beauty outshone hers. Frinkle shuddered to think what they looked like now.

When nothing seemed to be stirring, the little man stepped out onto the marshy ground, which skirted the water's edge, feeling his bare feet sink into the soggy beach with each step. It smelled of dead fish. He finally found solid ground and hurried on toward the secret home where his friend was living.

Something breached the dark surface of the water and dove back beneath the waves of the Bay, large ripples cresting out from beneath its impact. Frinkle stopped and looked at the water, his heart racing. He knew there were sea serpents living in the murky depths, as well as banished whales and other creatures that once made up the large ocean segment of the Galaxies. He had even heard of some strange little men with lanterns who walked on the bottom of the Bay, and it was the lights from those lanterns that twinkled up from the water's depths at night, making the body of water sparkle like a reflection of stars.

Just then, something green shimmered across the water, heading toward him. As it drew closer he was able to make out seven floating hags, their long, misshapen arms dragging in the water behind them. He could see their eyes flashing as their mouths made indiscernible sounds. Their heads were bald. It was the Pleiades Sisters, once beautiful constellations sought after by Orion himself.

The little man began running, his knee stinging. Glancing back over his shoulder, Frinkle hurried ahead until he saw the weathered pole rising into the sky. He knew just beyond was the outskirts of a small town; it was simply referred to as Apparition Cove. Several dark, dilapidated buildings comprised the little hamlet. No one went into the Cove. It was here that many of the original Dark Arts constellations lived. Many a night Frinkle had watched purple and green sparks fly out of the treetops of Apparition Cove, rising into the dark sky to form strange outlines and shapes. He didn't know what it meant, but after each sighting he would hear rumors of another creature gone missing from the Spectre Lands. There was supposed to be some kind of store in the scary village…a store that sold things with strange names for strange purposes.

To someone not knowing what they were looking for, the long pole that Frinkle was now staring at might have resembled a broken tree bent at an odd angle, and resting against a boulder. But Frinkle knew better; the pole was a damaged ship's mast. At the other end of the mast, buried in brush and overgrown weeds, was the remains of an old ship; only a section of its hull clung tenaciously to the ground. The rest of the vessel was at the bottom of Apparition Bay.

The large body of water continued to make sloshing noises, as creatures surfaced and disappeared. He paused staring at the boat's fractured hull. Carefully, not wanting to make any noise, Frinkle stepped up to the hole in the ship's side and peered into the darkness. His nose wrinkled in disgust at the foul smell. He doubted the inside of a dead whale's stomach could smell worse than his friend's chosen hiding place.

Something stirred in the darkness off to the little man's right, and his stomach knotted. He hated looking at his friend. He would prefer the friend stay inside the shadows and just talk to him from there.

A voice welled up from the black interior.

"Have you got it?" a rasping whisper asked.

"Yes!" Frinkle said, his voice shaking. "Told you I would! Look here! It's the silver ball fer sure!"

A rotting hand reached out from the darkness, its decomposing palm open to receive the treasure. Frinkle swallowed hard and took the silver ball from his pocket. With shaking fingers he dropped it into the outstretched hand, trying hard not to touch the skin.

The hand clutched the ball and pulled back into the shadows. Once again, Frinkle caught a glimpse of a marking on the creature's wrist…it was a crown. The rotting hand could only belong to a royal from the Glimmer Lands…but which one? Tense moments passed, with the only sound coming from the sloshing waters of Apparition Bay. Just as the silence was about to overcome Frinkle, a guttural shriek came from the depths of the ship's blackness, rising to a high-pitched scream.

"Incompetent toad!" the voice exploded. "This is not the Dark Orb! It is a ball—a common human ball!" The small silver ball was hurled at the little man's head. Frinkle ducked just in time, as the baseball landed in the dirt next to him.

"That's *all* you *have?*" the shrieking voice continued. "No real Orb? Or the Crone's eye? No vial of Lunar Potion, or a white pod that creates it? You have failed me for the last time!"

Frinkle saw the shadows moving fast toward him. He backed hurriedly away, his heart feeling as if it were about to explode.

"But I hads a red eye! The Siglets took it! They gots it, honest!" Frinkle yelled. "I don't knows nothin' 'bout no thingy of liquid!"

A foot made mostly of bone, with fragments of green flesh clinging to it, stepped from the darkness. That was all Frinkle needed to see—he turned, grabbed the silver ball, and ran as fast as his turned-in toes would let him.

Chapter Forty-Three

IF WALLS COULD TALK

Twicket's eyes peered into the twisting labyrinth of passages winding through the underbelly of the Crone's castle. T.J. was holding onto the troll's cane for dear life, since all he could see was dark upon dark.

"Stop choking Twicket!" the troll squeaked for the third time.

"Where are we going?" T.J. whispered hoarsely. His heart was pounding so loud he could hear it thudding inside his ears. The darkness brought back thoughts of all the horror he had been experiencing every time they were near the well. The black world around him felt like it was sucking away his life.

"Me trying to see Mandy," Twicket repeated. "Too many tunnels. Me no know where she went."

"If we don't get out of here soon, I'm turning on my flashlight, I don't care who or *what* sees us!" T.J. whimpered.

Twicket had repeatedly told him that by taking advantage of his night vision they could move along in the blackness unseen, instead of alerting something with a bright beam of light. T.J. had even tried pulling the remaining Monkhood Mushrooms from the back pack to see if he could at least use a soft green glow to steer by, but as he pulled the slimy batch from his bag, they were no longer glowing.

"No last very long after you pick 'em," Twicket said, when he smelled the mushrooms in the boy's hands. "Too bad you no can use poor Twicket as torch again," the troll said sarcastically.

T.J. became aware of a humming noise that seemed to permeate the air. It was like a high-pitched frequency, but he couldn't place the sound. He tossed the withering mushrooms to the ground and wiped his hand on his pants.

"Do you hear that humming sound?" he asked Twicket, as he banged his shoulder painfully into a stone wall.

"Course me hear it. Trolls hear and see better than dumb humans. Me thinkin' it comin from walls," Twicket said matter-of-factly.

"What do you mean, *comin'* from the walls'?" T.J. asked nervously.

"Me think the walls be alive in here. Me see faces in the stones. Me also think they know we be here." Twicket said, not as confident as before.

T.J. banged into another corner right before Twicket told him to turn left. Each time the boy ran into the stone walls in the darkness, the humming noise escalated.

"Me thinkin' they no like you bumpin' into 'em all the time," the troll said. "Try stay to middle of path, ok?"

"How can I stay to the middle of the path if I can't *see* the middle of the path?" T.J. spat. The thought of living walls was totally unnerving him.

"That you issue, not Twicket's," the troll said indignantly.

Something wet ran a path up T.J.'s left arm, leaving a trail of slobber behind. The boy jumped.

"What was that?" he yelped, wiping the slime from his arm with his other hand, almost dropping Twicket as he did so.

"Tongue," Twicket said simply.

"*Tongue! Who's tongue?*" T.J. cried, crossing his arms tightly around his body.

"Wall's tongue...faces in the stone here," Twicket repeated. "You keep away from the walls, ok?"

Suddenly a whisper came from up ahead. T.J. was never so happy to hear another familiar voice in his life.

"Twicket? Up here," the boy heard Mandy whisper from the darkness. "Be careful, there is something very strange about the walls here."

Twicket sighed. "Me think me only big brain in bunch," the troll said dramatically.

T.J. blinked repeatedly in a failed effort to see something in the distance. Twicket told him to take a few more steps forward and the boy complied.

"Stop," Twicket said abruptly.

T.J. stopped, and felt something brush against his forearm. It was rough and scaly and he jumped.

"Easy, it's just me," Mandy said quietly from the darkness. "I found a set of stairs up ahead. I think we can get out of this maze, but we have to be very careful. I have a feeling every move we make is being reported to the Crone."

"Reported by *what?*" T.J. gasped.

"You ever hear the human expression 'If walls could talk?' Well, I think these can. At least in a language the Crone understands. Just keep your eyes open...well, when you can see again," she said to the boy. "Follow me, Twicket."

"Step, step, step," the troll said in a bored voice to T.J., who was carefully following the instructions. He wanted to reach out and feel a wall to guide him along, but now all he could think of was that he would be feeling a living thing's face. He shuddered and stepped along in the darkness, clutching the walking cane.

"Over here," he heard Mandy whisper.

"Turn right," Twicket intoned.

T.J. stepped slightly to his right, bracing himself for another impact with a vibrating wall. His foot hit something, and he stopped.

"We be at steps now," Twicket said. "Reach with you toes and climb up. There be one, two, fifty-eleven, seventeen, forty-nothin...," the troll counted out.

"*What?*" T.J. hissed. "What are you talking about?"

"There are nine steps," Mandy whispered, and T.J. could hear the amusement in her voice.

"That how we count in Treblin," Twicket said, sniffing indignantly.

T.J. stepped up, and scooted his foot along, until he felt the next step. He then stepped onto that one. He was a nervous wreck wondering if he was going to step over the side of the stairwell and fall to the stone floor below.

"Tell me if I am not in the center, ok?" he begged the troll.

"You think me want you fall when you carrying Twicket?" the troll asked hotly. "Just keep goin', Wussy Boy!"

T.J. swallowed his anger and took another step up. *Only six more to go,* he thought. He counted them off, and when he had reached the ninth step, he stopped and waited for further instruction. He heard a creaking sound and suddenly light poured onto his face. He blinked in the sudden glare, his head dizzy from the abrupt change. As his eyes adjusted, he saw a large wooden door standing open. A hallway on the other side ran several feet before veering off to the right. Mandy was already following it down, as Twicket's two sneezes sounded next to him.

Chapter Forty-Four

WHICH WAY OUT?

"There is nothing more you can offer me," the voice rasped. The sound was that of ragged air rising from a bottomless pit. It faded in and out with no substance.

"I don't know what you want from me!" Dillon Finnel said in a rush.

He was standing in a large room made of crumbling stone. Unlit torches lined the walls and a crooked chandelier made of strange-looking branches hung from the high ceiling. He reached out to the back of one of the weathered, high-backed chairs that flanked an enormous stone fireplace, in an effort to steady himself. He was exhausted. The surface of the chair felt odd and he looked down to see he was holding onto a large femur bone. He jerked his hand away in repulsion.

"You painted the paintings with Lunar Potion," the Crone said, gliding near enough to the artist that he could smell her rank breath, and feel its moisture on his cheek. "Where did you get it?"

"I don't know what you're talking about!" he cried, for the hundredth time. "I have never heard of Lunar Potion. All I know is something happened to my art. First the parrot flew out of a painting, and a well appeared in another one. You grabbed me in my studio. That's all I know...I promise!"

"That's a shame," the Crone purred. "I was hoping several days chained in a dark room would loosen your tongue." She reached out and ran a ragged fingernail along his cheek. Dillon screamed as blood ran from the cut.

"You would be dead by now if your memories had not borne you out," the Crone hissed. "But somehow, the potion got into your paints. That means something from this, or one of the other dimensions, has been to your world recently. I also know the Dark Orb was in the woods behind your home not long ago. You...or your family, know more than you are saying. I have robbed you of *your* memories. If I need to return to your world and do the same to the rest of your family, it is easily arranged—as is total blindness!"

The Crone floated across the Grand Chamber of the castle and peered from the window. She studied the planets aligning and anger raged through her. Dillon watched her, fearing the wrath that was about to be unleashed.

"The Dark Moon comes tomorrow night! All I have worked for will be reversed, and for nothing! *Nothing!* If anyone gets their hands on the Orb, the constellations I have dragged here will all go home! I will be blocked from ever controlling the other dimensions when the well and its symbols change locations." She brushed her tangled grey hair away from the single eye, whose red glare stained the bleached stone walls around her.

"Scarflon!" she continued, her rage building. "I knew he was much too weak to leave in charge of the well and Orb. Letting that stupid Queen banish him and take control!"

She floated over to look at the frail man standing helplessly in the corner of the decayed chamber. He had moved away from the fireplace as he noticed the stones forming its mantel had mouths that were moving silently. Small furry things scurried across the floor.

"All humans are ungrateful bags of flesh," she spat, pressing her hideous face closer to his. "If I had brought you here through the well instead of the painting, you would be a deformed sack of guts— yet do you show your appreciation?" She scratched him again, and the artist cried out, pressing a hand to the fresh cut.

Just then a high-pitched noise began echoing through the cavernous room.

"Do you hear that sound?" she asked, a low, guttural cackle

sounding from deep within her. "The walls are telling me I have visitors in the lower chamber." She paused and listened intently to the sound, as the stone faces of the walls melted in and out of distorted shapes, their mouths moving rhythmically. Their message seemed to please her. Her mouth spread wide with happiness, pressing the folds of wrinkles into matching troughs on each side of her mangled nose.

"It appears a trip to visit your family won't be necessary after all. Would it surprise you to know that even now, your grandson is in my castle?" she cackled cryptically next to his ear. "I've been watching them cross the Ribhound Valley from my window. All I had to do was wait for them to come to me. The bonus is now I know they are also carrying my missing eye!"

"My grandson is *here?* That's impossible," Dillon said, his heart hammering. He stepped away from her, the stench from her breath, and fear for his grandson, causing his stomach to roil.

"One would think," she whispered.

"How did he get here?" Dillon asked, swallowing hard.

"Not the way you did," she sneered. "He came through the well with some creature, and a talking stick. Spies can be useful." She circled the cowering man, enjoying his fear.

"I know the Dark Orb is near," she whispered. "I can *feel* its nearness. And now I am soon to be reunited with my eye! The only way into the tunnel beneath here is to use my eye on the mountain's face. It appears the boy is very resourceful." She grinned again, her face a maze of gouges and scars. The walls continued to whisper to her.

"I have no more time to waste on you," she said, floating to the open window. "While blindness would be a fitting judgment for an artist, I want you to *see* what's about to happen to you."

She signaled with her hand, and watched as a black shadow flew toward her from inside a window on the next tower. As it neared where the Crone was standing, the shadow broke apart in a flurry of black wings. Small red eyes pierced the bleak sky, as dozens of

Flugling Bats streaked toward her. Their small fangs glinted in the pale sunlight. She moved aside as they came in through the window with a rush of wings. Dillon cried out as he saw the flurry of bodies come toward him, following the scent of fresh blood.

"You know what to do," the Crone said mildly to the winged creatures. "Only this time—finish the job. You let Scarflon escape *his* fate. I will not tolerate inefficiency." She smiled cruelly at the artist. "Oh, and do save some of the parts for my *chandelier*," she said to the swarm of flying bodies.

Dillon looked up in terror at the swaying lights above him. He noticed for the first time that the chandelier was not made up of twisted branches as he had first thought; he was looking at skeletal hands, their brittle fingers holding small candles.

"I have to attend to some visitors in the castle," she said, relishing the look of horror on her guest's face. She motioned to the flying creatures.

As the Crone floated from the room, she heard the petrified screams of Dillon Finnel, as the bats descended upon him.

Barnacle floated over the Black River on his pet fish Volans, keeping a look-out for the Crone, or her Siglets. He was in a terrible temper. Someone had found his hiding place in the Lamberhook tree where he had stowed the Crone's eye.

"Can't trust nothin' here," he scowled, and spat a wad of bile out into the air.

The pirate had the fishing pole with the Dead Man's Eye in one hand, and Volan's reins in the other. He guided the large fish past the twisted tree shapes of the Lamberhook Forest. Down below, he saw an outcropping of rocks and tugged the reins in their direction. The fish banked to the right, as Barnacle leaned over to peer into the craggy enclave. As Volans skirted a stand of trees, the pirate ghost reined her in, and she stopped, floating silently in the air. *This is as good a place as any*, Barnacle thought, as he took the fishing pole in both hands and began letting out line. He was now looking for the Dark Orb, *and* the purloined eyeball belonging to the Crone.

The Dead Man's Eye swung erratically through the air, its iris pivoting this way and that, as it looked for treasure. Barnacle guided the pole slowly over the uneven terrain, letting out more line or taking it in, as he propelled the eye through the obstacles of the forest. Volans floated slowly along, burping occasionally, as she usually did when swallowing too much air. Barnacle had grown used to the fish's habits, and ignored the continual stream of foul breath that accompanied each belch.

The pirate ghost had just maneuvered the fishing pole over a patch of tall blankwood reeds when the eye began jumping up and down, nearly pulling the pole from the ghost's hands.

"Whoa thar, Matey!" he said excitedly. "What have ye found thar, Two Hooks?"

The eye continued to swing in excitement in close circles, targeting an area in the center of the tall, poisonous reeds. Barnacle jerked on the fish's reins. Volans sailed lower into the trees, until her belly was just inches away from the crusty heads of the blankwood reeds. Barnacle leaned as far over as he dared and peered into their center. At first he saw nothing but waxy leaves, and black heads encrusted with crystals of poison. He knew if something other than a ghost touched the plants they could kiss their sorry keister goodbye! *Garglon's garden creatures were nothin' to mess with*, he thought.

"Methinks ye blew it this time," he began to tell the eye, and then he saw something red just beneath a cluster of leaves. He leaned closer. There was definitely something soft-looking, and red in color poking from the tall reeds.

Barnacle hurriedly reeled the eye up and removed it from the hook, placing it carefully between the paired fins atop Volan's head.

He then lowered the bare hook back down into the reeds, trying hard not to snag it on the ragged foliage. It took several tries, and several snags, before he managed to hook the piece of red fabric he had seen buried there. As he pulled on the reel, he was surprised to see that the object slowly coming out from under the leaves was quite large. By the time the thing came up through the reeds he could see he had landed what looked like a velvet bag. Judging by the weight pulling on his line, it was a pretty good catch!

The sound of a softly whirring fishing line filled the silence of the woods, as the ghost reeled in his prize. Finally, he leaned over and wrangled it from the hook. Placing the pole in the leather holder attached to Volan's saddle, he quickly looked into the open satchel. Two golden crowns, with glittering jewels, were snagged on the fabric threads in the interior of the velvet bag!

"Gutless sardines!" the pirated yelped. He slapped a transparent hand over his mouth, as he looked about to see if anyone had heard him. When nothing happened, he stuck his hand into the bag, and untangled a bejeweled crown from the satchel's torn interior. The Dead Man's Eye was leaping around on the fish's head in its excitement. Barnacle breathed in and out in exhilaration. He had hit pay dirt!

"We did it, Fish Head!" he whispered excitedly to his floating vessel. "Ohhhh....," he said suddenly, as he realized just what he was holding. "This be the crowns of da Twin Kings! *Headless Herrings!* How'd dey end up here?" He rotated the crown slowly in his hands, as he glanced about his surroundings nervously. The jewels encircling the crown twinkled in the pale light.

"Best get dis back to da ship!" he said anxiously.

He placed the crown gently into the bag alongside the other one and pulled the drawstring closed. Slipping the satchel's loops around the saddle horn, he jerked on Volan's reins, and guided her out of the woods.

The shortest route back to the pirate ship was past the castle, and Barnacle decided to risk it. The longer he was out here in the open, the longer he was exposed to anything flying around in the Spectre Lands. He was not going to risk losing this precious cargo. His only hope was that the Siglets would not see him, and the Crone was otherwise engaged. He would fly low past the castle's foundation to avoid all of the tower's windows.

The ghost skirted the castle, keeping as close as he could to the tree line, and finally saw his ship up ahead, the rusty anchor hanging limply in the air. He lightly spurred Volans' belly to encourage the lazy fish to fly faster. Finally, they reached the tattered ship and Barnacle guided the flying grouper to its stern. He climbed aboard the boat and tied the fish's tether to a mooring hook on the gunwale, just above the peeling letters that read *Vela*. Removing his fishing pole from the grouper's saddle, he stuck Two Hook's eye back on the hook. The moment he did the eye went crazy, jumping up and down in a frenzy.

"Settle down!" Barnacle yelled. "I know, I know…we gots treasure here! You did good…now settle down!"

But the eye continued to dance about on the fishing line, its iris looking up toward the sky with excitement. Barnacle looked up as well and saw nothing but tattered sails, the leaning mast, and his ship's dilapidated crow's nest.

"Ok, Two Hooks, ye've had enough fer one day! We'll go out agin' t'morrow! Sure wish ye could find dat Orb, though."

Barnacle tossed the fishing pole into the galley, and then cradling his prize, followed it into the belly of the ship.

Chapter Forty-Five

THE CRONE'S VENGEANCE

Dillon Finnel was floating. His body dipped up and down, as a rushing sound filled his ears. His first thought was that he was dead, and being borne up to heaven on a cloud. Then the pain exploded through every pore of his body. He tried to open his eyes but they were stuck closed with dried blood. His arms and legs were on fire, as though barbed wire had ripped him to shreds. A sloshing noise penetrated his pain, and he realized he was floating in water, not a cloud. Then the sloshing was replaced by the rising cacophony of moans...dreadful, soulless sounds of things that had known life, but no longer.

Dillon felt something tugging at his tattered shirt sleeve, and he realized he was being pulled beneath the water's surface. This was it, he thought. This was death.

The castle hallways seemed to wind around-and-around, with no beginning and no end. Dozens of large wooden doors with oversized brass keyholes, and rusted knockers, ran along one side of the twisting labyrinth. Mandy and T.J. quickly learned they were all locked, as they tugged on one after the other. As T.J. passed a small window overlooking the Black River, he stopped and gripped the stone window ledge, his eyes bulging. There, right before him, flying only a few feet below the window, was a tattered pirate ghost sailing along on a floating grouper! The fish kept belching every few feet. A long fishing pole was strapped to the fish's saddle, and the ghost seemed to be carrying a red bag of some sort.

"Mandy!" T.J. whispered. "Get over here…you gotta see this!"

Mandy stepped over to the boy and looked out. She was about to laugh, when she noticed the red bag Barnacle was carrying.

"That looks like the Queen's bag!" she said excitedly. "That strange little pirate may have some of her things in there, and if he does, he just might have the Dark Orb!"

"How do you know it's the Queen's bag?" T.J. asked, watching as the pirate steered the fish around a large boulder.

"I've seen it," Mandy said quietly. "A long time ago…in a cave in the Glimmer Lands. You can see the gold crest on its side." Her voice trailed off, as a spasm of pain ran across her scaly face.

"You ok?" the boy asked, a wave of revulsion coming over him as he watched her bilious chin quiver in the sunlight coming in through the window arch. He doubted he would ever get used to looking at her in her current condition.

"What?" she started, and then blinked. "Of course I am."

Barnacle had floated too far away to call out to him without fear of being discovered, so Mandy turned away from the window.

"We still need to check out the castle while we're here," she said, reading T.J.'s mind. "Barnacle may have the Orb in that satchel, or he may not. I have seen the Queen put everything she values in that bag, so it is a hopeful sign. I promise, only a couple of hours here, and if we don't find anything, we'll take the Glimrocks and go look for your grandpa before the afternoon light is gone. We'll see if we can get Barnacle to talk to us, but it's probably a lost cause. If he found something, he isn't going to share!"

"Why not just ask the Glimrocks to find the Dark Orb?" T.J. whispered. He felt the walls were listening to everything they said. He just wanted out of here.

"I doubt that will work," Mandy said dubiously. "I would have already tried it outside if I thought the rocks could find it."

"You said they can find treasure," T.J. insisted. "I call the most powerful thing in the Universe pretty valuable!"

T.J. liked any idea that would speed things up and get them out of the castle. He had been hearing sounds coming from behind the locked doors as they tried to open them. None were sounds he could place, which made him feel even more nervous. Something was cackling behind the one nearest to them.

He handed Twicket to Mandy and unzipped the large compartment of his backpack, being careful not to undo the smaller pocket containing the Crone's eye. He grabbed the leather bag holding the rocks and handed it to the girl. Mandy handed Twicket back to him, and opened the pouch.

"Me like Mandy holding Twicket better," the troll said, "Scaly hands and all!"

"Thanks, Twicket!" Mandy said wryly, as she poured the glittering stones into her disfigured hands. "Find the Dark Orb!" she commanded, and tossed the rocks to the floor.

The stones sat still for a moment, and then slowly began to move. Some went one way, and some went another, as they scurried around in a confused array.

"What's wrong with them?" T.J. asked. "Are they broken?"

"I told you I didn't think it would work," she said.

Mandy scooped up the trembling stones, and repeated her command.

"Find the Dark Orb!" she said, with more authority.

She tossed the stones to the floor and once again they tumbled about, rolling up the hall and back down, twisting and turning in circles. Just then, a large shadow fell across the stone floor as Barnacle's pirate ship sailed past the window and high above the castle battlements, out of reach of the sleeping dragon, who was snoring loudly.

Just as Mandy was about to give up and return the stones to the bag, they suddenly vibrated and hurried together, stacking themselves one on top of the other, until they were standing upright like a totem pole.

"What the heck does that mean?" T.J. asked.

"I have no idea," Mandy said, staring at the stone's strange configuration.

"Maybe it mean we standing in right place for Orb, but maybe it be under us or over us, since rocks no can point up or down," Twicket said.

"Well we know what's under us," T.J. said darkly. "I for one am not going back into that maze of tunnels without my flashlight turned on. What's over us, Mandy?"

"I have no idea. I am so turned around with all these winding hallways. It could be a tower, or a room. We haven't even passed a staircase the whole time we've been walking in this hallway, so I don't know how we would go "up" anyway."

T.J. had been looking at the locked doors lining the hallway. An idea suddenly occurred to him. Perhaps the Crone had prisoners behind the doors. What if one of them was his grandfather? He suddenly scooped up the small tower of rocks, and barked, "Find my grandpa. Find his gold ring!" He tossed them down before Mandy could stop him.

With his heart beating rapidly, T.J. watched as the stones scampered around in circles, much like they had done in the forest. Finally they jumped together and formed an arrow pointing directly at the window overlooking the Black River, and the Lamberhook Forest beyond.

"They pointed outside! He *is* here in the Spectre Lands!" the boy whispered excitedly. But then reality sank in. "The Lamberhook Forest," T.J. muttered to himself. "That's what it means...he's in one of those trees." The boy's face went white. He missed the look of fear that swept across Mandy's distorted face.

"We don't know that for sure," she said, trying to sound more optimistic than she felt.

"Me turn!" Twicket pleaded. "Ask rocks to point to Mudlin clasp on him's robe!"

Mandy started to repeat that she doubted Mudlin was here, but decided to show the troll instead. She picked up the stones and whispered, "Find Mudlin's clasp."

"It got big emerald in it," Twicket offered excitedly.

"Find Mudlin's "emerald" clasp on his robe," Mandy corrected, and tossed the stones to the floor. They lay there motionless. She repeated it again, and again they sat dormant. "I'm sorry, Twicket. Mudlin is not in the Spectre Lands." The troll sighed, frowning.

Mandy picked up the stones and replaced them into the leather bag, which she held onto. She looked sadly at Twicket's depressed face.

"Let's see if we can find a staircase," she said, and started off before T.J. could offer up any objections. Her heart was heavy. She was now sure the rocks he had tossed down asking for his grandfather's ring were pointing to the Lamberhook trees. The odds of T.J. finding his grandpa, and getting him back, were almost impossible. She had to keep them both focused on finding the Dark Orb, saving her own people, and getting the boy back home.

"Maybe there is a staircase behind one of these doors," T.J. said, as he followed along behind Mandy, stopping to pull on their handles. His fear had evaporated. All he could think of was losing his grandfather to a tomb inside a twisted tree trunk. As he pulled on the large brass ring of an immense wooden door to his right, something threw itself at it from the other side, the wood making a splintering sound. T.J. fell back, his heart banging against his chest.

"CRAP!" he yelped. "What was that?"

The door shuddered again, as something hurled itself against the ancient wood.

"I'm outta here!" the boy said, running and grabbing Mandy by her elbow.

As he said this, the walls, which had been humming in a continual low frequency, began to ramp up the noise. The threesome stared with bulging eyes at the stones. The rocks comprising the castle walls began to shimmer and contort in and out of strange shapes. T.J. covered his ears as the low humming turned into a wailing crescendo. It was still not enough to shut out Mandy's sudden scream.

T.J. turned to see what had happened. His heart skipped. Floating rapidly down the hallway toward them, her eye's blood red glare reaching before her like a search light, was the Crone. Her wild grey hair was flying behind her and the threadbare gown she wore barely covered the skeletal shoulder blades protruding through the scarce gray fabric. Her arms and hands looked to T.J. like winter's naked tree branches, gnarled and curled from lack of moisture and sun. Her face was a map of deep scars and gouges; one operating as a wide mouth now hanging open in a fierce scream.

"Run!" Mandy yelled, as she took off.

T.J. turned to run after her, but the Crone's gnarled finger snagged the strap on his backpack, jerking him off balance. He fell back onto his elbows, pain shooting through his funny bone as he hit the stone floor. Twicket flew from his hands and landed a few feet away, emitting a loud "Oomph!" The backpack fell against the wall, as it came loose from the boy's arms.

Crawling backwards like an upside-down crab, T.J. tried to put distance between himself and the creature that was bearing down upon him. It was hard to turn away from the dizzying glare from her eye, and he felt himself getting sick. Just then a red bolt of light shot out of the pouch in his backpack from the zippered pouch which had opened during the attack. It hit the wall across from him, like a ball of red paint.

A sound somewhere between a cry and a hiss came from the Crone's gaping mouth, as she sprang upon the boy's pack. She ripped the zipper the rest of the way open. A red stream of light poured out from the opening.

"Ahhhhhhhhhhh!" the Crone screamed, drool dripping from her lips. "Ahhhhh!"

She pulled the eye carefully from the remains of the foil granola wrapper. Cradling it in her withered hands like a precious newborn, the Crone turned it over, examining it, until finally, she lifted it to her face. As T.J. watched in horror, she tried to force it into the empty eye socket it had once called home.

A sudden flurry of wings filled the hallway, as a large black crow swooped in through the window arch and dove at the Crone. He attacked the fingers holding the powerful eye, biting into the thin, parchment-like skin with his sharp beak. The Crone screamed and swung at the bird, as he circled and came at her again. His razor sharp talons scratched her already marred face, and dove again at the hand holding the eye. This time he caught the eye in his beak and escaped high into the towering ceiling of the castle hallway. The Crone shrieked at him, red light pouring from her remaining eye as she tried to catch the crow in its powerful beam. Corvus dodged the stream of light and plunged toward the open window. The Crone leapt to block him, but it was too late. The large constellation soared into the afternoon light of the Spectre Lands, the Crone's eye shining brightly from his beak.

'Noooooooooooooooooooooooo!" she shrieked over and over. "I can't lose it again! Siglets! *Where are you?* Draco!" she screamed, calling over and over for her evil minions.

Twicket was whimpering from the floor not far from T.J.'s shoe. Mandy had stopped running. She came back, standing several yards away. Her mind was spinning. *What could she do to save T.J.?*

The Crone turned, her face effused in rage, and looked down upon the cowering boy. Some kind of red liquid was running from her remaining eye, and she was slobbering like a rabid dog. T.J.'s knees were shaking. His stomach had lifted closer to his mouth, and he felt bile salting his tongue. He was screaming on the inside! The light coming from her eye was making his head float, and strange visions were playing through his mind.

He suddenly saw himself in a well, crying and screaming, his hands bloody from clawing at the rough stones in an effort to get out. There was nothing but darkness around him. Somewhere in the distance he heard Markus's voice calling, "T.J.? Where are you?" Then he felt himself being lifted out by his wrists. He looked up to see an old man, grunting beneath the boy's weight, lifting him from the well. As T.J. reached the edge, his head hit the stone rim, and he didn't remember anything after that.

Mandy heard Twicket whimper again, and she had a sudden flashback to the Banshees, and the peddler. Taking a deep breath, she sprang for the troll and grabbed him up by his cane, brandishing him in front of her toward the raging Crone.

"Now!" Mandy ordered the troll. "Sneeze...NOW!"

The Crone glanced at the girl for a moment, and a ragged gasp escaped her gaping mouth.

"*You!* I know you even in this guise! You and your meddling sister!" She paused, still panting in her rage. An evil grin crossed the Crone's face. "Look at you now," she sneered. "Your fate has been meted out to you! I have no use for you...it is this boy I want!"

The Crone ignored the other two, as she returned to focus her powerful gaze on T.J. The blinding stream of red light from her eye pierced T.J.'s vision and he felt himself sinking. The Crone watched as his memories began flooding toward her. She saw him in the school hallways, and chasing Siglets down the stairs at the old house by the woods in the Human World. But as T.J. felt his world becoming darker, the Crone became more agitated. The boy's memories showed him finding Twicket in the attic room, feeding a reptile he kept in a tank by his bed, but no Orb! She inhaled sharply, as she saw his memory of himself retrieving her eye from the troll's mouth by the river, but it was of little use now! That crow had just stolen it away! Nowhere in the boy's memory was there anything useful!

Screaming with fury, she ripped through the back pack, sending the flashlight rolling along the stone floor. Fragments of brown, crumbling mushrooms fell out from the tattered bag, along with the boy's jacket and an empty, crumpled raisin box. But the Orb was not there! It had to be here! It was never far from her precious eye, and the boy had carried *that* inside this bag. Her rage shook the hallway, the stones feeding upon it. They pulsed, as strange faces swirled inside their granite facades.

"Twicket!" Mandy hissed at the troll. "What are you waiting for? *Slime her!*"

But the light from the Crone's eye was focused on T.J. Twicket tried with all he had to sneeze, but nothing was coming.

"Get ugly to look at me!" he whimpered. "Me need more light!"

It was then that T.J. let out a scream, as the Crone bent and grabbed him by his shirt, her face only inches from his own. The pure red light from her eye poured into his green irises, until all he could see was a crimson halo. The red glow turned to dark brown, and finally to black, as the last of his sight was funneled into her own.

"T.J.!" Mandy screamed, as the ruler of the Spectre Lands let go of the boy, his body slumping against the stones writhing all around him. The Crone floated away down the hallway, still calling to her Siglets; her eye's red glare preceding her into the depths of the castle.

Chapter Forty-Six

A GHOST IN THE SPECTRE LANDS

Another night has passed. Tonight the Dark Moon will rise. Tonight everyone's fate in the 5 Dimensions will be sealed for another 100 years.

These were the thoughts going through Corvus's mind, as he circled high above Haver's Wood, coming around again to see where the elderly ghost in the funny red jacket he had noticed earlier, had gone. It seemed everyone, and everything, was showing up in the Spectre Lands in time for the Dark Moon. The crow had watched earlier as that batty peddler Wheedle had pulled some old human from the Moaning River. He was at first surprised to see her show compassion to another living creature, until he saw her eagerly go through the poor guy's pockets. From where Corvus sat in the nearby pine tree, it looked like the man was pretty much dead.

After Wheedle had finished picking over him, the peddler had ambled off. The crow would have gone after her, but she must have hidden her cart somewhere in the depths of the trees where he couldn't get to it. He would wait until she pulled it out into a clearing.

Just then, the old man on the bank stirred. He turned slowly onto his side and tried several times to stand, only to fall back onto the ground again. Corvus almost felt sorry for him. He was badly cut and his clothes were stained with blood. He imagined the Crone's bats had made a meal of him, and then he had been casually tossed into the Moaning River to drown. Corvus had other things to do than watch some human try to escape his demise in this putrid land.

As he was about to fly off, a high keening wail sounded from the Lamberhook Forest behind him. The bird turned to see the two Banshees standing at the forest's edge, their song calling out to the half-dead human. The old man made it to his knees and struggled to stand on his feet. As Corvus lifted into the air, he glanced down to see the human stumbling toward the siren call of the Banshees.

Leonardo Da Vinci's ghost walked along through the woods looking for anything to show him where his friend Dillon might be found. The bright-red Boston Red Sox jacket he wore touched the bleak land around him with a rare scrap of color.

Being in this strange place did nothing to make him feel warm and fuzzy. The Renaissance artist's mood was dark as he rounded a corner in the woods and heard the sound of something creaking up ahead. He stopped and strained to see what was creating the rhythmic sound. *Creak, creak, creak.* A rare beam of sunlight had tenaciously punched its way through the thick tree tops, and fell onto one of the strangest sights Da Vinci had ever seen. Up the pathway, heading toward him, was what appeared to be a bent lizard, walking upright in a soiled apron, and pulling a weathered cart piled high with junk. The wheels turning on the cart were making the creaking noise.

Wheedle looked up, and spotted the ghost of a tall man, about the same time he noticed her. The small slits in her nostril's opened to take in his scent. Her eyes became watchful, as the stranger advanced toward her.

"Well Rider?" she rasped, taking in his strange jacket. The ghost's hair was long and curled, and he wore a quaint little cap. The jacket however was not ghostly; it was real—a red, shiny material. She licked her lips in anticipation.

"I suppose you could call me that," Da Vinci said, smiling. Lizard or not, it was nice to talk to someone after the darkness of the well, and his lonely travels through this cursed land.

Wheedle squinted at him suspiciously. Maybe the ghost was from the Void. Things going into the Void were stripped of their mortal forms, and often found their way into the human world in search of a soul. But, why was it here?

"Looking for someone, or some*thing*?" Wheedle asked smoothly, studying the patches on the ball jacket with interest. She would love to have the strange coat to keep her warm on the damp evenings near the swamp.

"Actually, I am," Da Vinci said, weighing his words. He wasn't sure how much information to give away to this strange creature, but what other choice did he have. "I am looking for a man...uh...a human, of about 79 years of age. He has graying hair, and is usually wearing clothes with paint on them somewhere."

Wheedle's eyes became hooded and her mouth drew back exposing her tiny sharp teeth. Da Vinci found it a very unpleasant look for a face already lacking in charm.

"What will you trade for the information?" she asked, picturing the jacket as already hers.

"I'm afraid I don't have anything to trade," Leonardo said, feeling slightly irritated. "It is a simple question...have you seen such a man or not?" He eyed her closely.

"I will trade your friend's whereabouts for the jacket," Wheedle said evenly, her heart thumping as she awaited the ghost's response.

"Sorry, it is not mine to trade," the artist said, and turned on his heel to leave.

"Wait!" Wheedle croaked. "I will offer you twice the asking price. I will give you the location of your friend *and* something from my cart! All for the red jacket. It is a good bargain!"

"Is anything in your cart of value?" Da Vinci asked, thinking perhaps the sneaky peddler may have picked up something of Dillon's, which would prove the elderly gentleman was really here.

Wheedle's breathing became labored. She could sense the close of a deal near at hand. She limped to the cart and threw back the ratty blanket, pulling a scarred pan from the pile of junk. She held it up for inspection.

"This is very rare!" she said panting. "Real copper!" She thumped the damaged pan with an arthritic knuckle.

"It is not copper, it is iron, and I am in no need of a pan," Da Vinci said, his eyebrow arched.

"This clock....this clock belonged to a wealthy Well Rider and it is worth a fortune!" she croaked, replacing the pan with a small tabletop clock, whose face was hanging halfway off, showing a missing sweep hand. It was marred and dirty.

"Tempting, but no," the artist said, beginning to think this was all a waste of time. He backed up a few paces, as if getting ready to leave.

"Wait! I can see you are not easily pleased with common things! I do have....*this!*"

Wheedle pulled a pocket knife from beneath a pile of tattered books and held it up, her orange eyes glinting in the sunlight. The initials D.F. were carved into the scratched metal. Da Vinci had seen Dillon Finnel use the knife on more than one occasion to sharpen an art pencil's lead. Wheedle saw the look of total astonishment on the man's face. *I've got him!* she thought, again licking her lips.

"Yesssssssssss," she hissed. "Beautiful isn't it? Have we a trade then?"

Leonardo stepped closer and took the knife from her eager hands. He could not believe his eyes! It meant Dillon really was somewhere here in this horrid place.

"Where did you get this?" he demanded.

"Ahhhh....Wheedle shares her secrets only with her bottle," she said mysteriously. "Have we a trade?"

Leonardo stood in the fragmented afternoon sun turning the knife in his hands. Finally, he made a decision. He hoped Dillon would forgive him for parting with the baseball jacket. Da Vinci pulled his arms through the slippery sleeves as the lizard watched him, panting like a winded animal.

"Give me!" she rasped, holding out both hands.

"Our trading is not complete," Leonardo said, holding on tightly to the jacket. "Where is my friend? The older gentleman?"

Wheedle licked her cracked lips again, and struggled to come up with a quick lie before the man changed his mind.

"I saw him on the banks of the Moaning River. He looked well enough to me," she lied. "I...uh...gave him a drink of water and something to eat. He gave me the knife as payment."

An image of herself taking the small knife from the man's pants pocket shot through her head. He was half-dead anyway. What did it matter?

"Indeed?" Da Vinci asked. "Well, that was kind of you. Did you see where he went?"

"No...um...no. I merely warned him about the Lamberhook Forest, and the Crone...that's about it."

The ghost studied the pinched face before him. He didn't believe the creature had parted with her food, but on the off chance the peddler really had seen Dillon by a river, and was only embellishing her story, he handed over the jacket.

Wheedle snatched the precious coat from his hand and rubbed it against her scaly face. She had never felt anything so wonderful!

"Which way to the...what did you call it...Moaning River?" Da Vinci asked.

Wheedle merely pointed off to the left and continued to stroke her new treasure. Da Vinci headed off down the proffered path, running his finger along his friend's treasured pocket knife. When he glanced back at the peddler, she was carefully pushing her spindly arms through the smooth sleeves of the baseball jacket.

Chapter Forty-Seven

POTIONS AND PROBLEMS

Frinkle walked through Drigmot's Passage, grumbling and kicking loose rocks that found themselves in his way. The weight of the useless silver ball could be felt from its place in his vest pocket, along with the Mind Snatcher he had found. It no longer buzzed or showed the face of the human man. He had spent the night inside a thicket where something kept nipping at his ear.

"I am doomed," he kept muttering to himself. "Once that danged well changes locations tonight, when that danged Dark Moon shows up, I will be stuck here with that danged Wheedle for the next danged one hundred years! I can't take it!" he yelled, and then quickly looked around for anything that might be looking for lunch.

"'This isn't what I want'," he squeaked, mimicking his friend's words. "'This is the wrong silver ball!' Dangit, how many silver balls does he think are floating around this stupid place? And then I'm 'posed to find some bloody eye, and a bottle of juice called Lunar Potion, or a white pod that makes the juice…what does he think this is…a Cosmic Flea Market?"

Suddenly, the little man stopped dead in his tracks; the memory of the Siglet attack in the woods came flooding back to him. He "saw" them ripping at his pockets, taking Wheedle's bottle, and then tearing the red stopper from the opening—the red stopper that was the red crystal his ex-new friend had wanted so desperately. The Siglets had dropped the bottle when Wheedle's whispers started coming out.

"What did she say?" Frinkle strained to remember the whisper that had leaked from the bottle. It came to him slowly—Wheedle's raspy voice whispering from deep inside the purple glass: *"Blue bag with white pod buried in hollow by yellow ragweed bed,"* Wheedle's whisper had said...or something like that!

A white pod! His new friend said a "white pod"! He may not have the right silver ball, or the eyeball, but he did know where the hollow with the batch of yellow ragweed was!

"I ain't done yet!" the little man cried, as he quickened his pace; his swollen knee still hurting from the Rictor gash. He hobbled into Haver's Wood and turned down a rutted path toward a small hollow at the base of a hill.

Corvus spiraled high above the Spectre Lands, looking desperately for a place to hide the Crone's eye. He had hidden it the night before, along with its tell-tale red glow, in the hollow of a stump near Ribhound Passage, packing mud on top of it with his beak until it no longer shone. Now it was daylight and he needed a safer place to put it. He could then retrieve the Dark Orb, from where he had hidden it the day before, after stealing it from the Queen. The red glow from the eye was making him nervous—there was no way to cover it! He had to hide it in a safe place until he recovered the Dark Orb and Lunar Potion from their secret hiding place high above the dark and twisted Spectre Lands.

He saw movement through an opening in Haver's Wood and circled back. It was the peddler's funny little assistant. It looked like he was in a hurry, as he scurried down another path and disappeared from view.

The crow circled the mutated shapes of the dark land beneath him. He needed a place that would hide the eye's beam! *Perhaps he should check on the Dark Orb's location one more time,* he thought. He had flown over the Orb's hiding place several times, and so far, no one had noticed it. *It was a stroke of genius to put it there,* Corvus thought proudly. He was not the imbecile the Queen took him for! Besides, the name of the hiding place held a wonderful irony.

Doubling back he swung out over Drigmot's Passage and headed for his destination. Something below him shimmered in the afternoon light. The bird's keen eye picked out the faint form of a tall ghost with a long flowing beard, making his way toward the Crone's castle.

"Him again," Corvus thought. "He's lucky to be a ghost, or he would have been in a Lamberhook tree by now...looks like he lost his fancy red jacket, though." The bird flew on, wondering what the ghost could possibly be looking for. *If he is looking for a soul, he has come to the wrong place!* the bird thought as it flew off.

Leonardo Da Vinci traveled throughout the day searching for his friend. Hours later he came to the Black River and stopped. His artist's eye was fascinated with the swirling mass of ebony-colored water. He found himself falling into the habit of determining how he could paint it realistically. It was while he stood there, studying the late afternoon's light playing among the eddying current, that he heard something that sounded like soft sobbing. He turned and walked away from the river toward the crying. The sobbing sound grew louder as he stepped inside a shelter of the trees. He walked toward the mournful noise, and found himself coming to a rocky area of woods.

"I am so sorry," he heard a faint female voice cry. "I never meant for this to happen to you! I was so focused on getting the Orb, and having everything ready for tonight, that I put you in danger. What will we do now?"

The sobbing escalated as Da Vinci rounded a large oak and saw the bent form of a purple creature doubled over, cradling her repulsive head in her hands. As the ghost got closer, he stopped, startled. There, seated on the ground, his back against a rock, was Dillon Finnel's grandson!

Barnacle slapped at the Dead Man's Eye, as it continued to bounce frenetically on its hook. The pirate ghost wanted to try to find the Dark Orb one last time before the Dark Moon slid into place in only a few hours. He had already sailed over Apparition Bay only to have Two Hook's eye get excited about a brass captain's bell laying buried in the fly-infested beach at the Cove.

"I don't need no stinkin' bell!" the pirate ghost lectured, as he reeled in the excited eye and turned the wheel leeward. But the eye would not quit dancing about on the hook, its iris looking toward the tattered ship's mast overhead.

"What the blazes ye keep lookin' up thar for?" the pirate said irritably. "Ye find more brass riggings? I don't need no brass....no stinkin' bells, I jest want that thar Dark Orb—now focus!" He slapped at the slippery eye, sending it swirling through the air, tethered to the fishing line. It swung back to within inches of Barnacle's face and began its agitated dance anew, still peering anxiously toward the crow's nest atop the leaning ship's mast.

"'Bout to lock ye below, Two Hooks!" Barnacle threatened, as he steered the ship toward the Crone's castle once more. "Gotta be in old Hag Face's castle," he muttered. "Only thing is…how to get at it!"

He sailed on with Volan's, burping periodically on his leash behind the ship, and an excited eyeball leaping about on a crusty fishing line.

A raspy shriek shot from the swamp area near Haver's Wood. Wheedle was cradling her precious Bottle of Whispers in her scaly hands. She could not believe it was back inside its burlap bag! She had found it nestled safely in its usual spot beneath the bench seat in her rickety cart. *Frinkle must have returned it in the night,* she thought, holding it lovingly in her hands. Though the Crone's eye had been replaced with a cheap human gemstone, it was still good to have it back!

Once her happiness at finding her bottle abated, her thoughts turned to the little man who had made off with the powerful eye. Wheedle turned to look at the stacked planets behind her. They were perfectly in place now, one positioned above the other, with Pluto sitting atop the tower like a human's Christmas tree angel. Within hours, the Dark Moon would complete its rise and she would be stuck here for another 100 years!

Wheedle snatched up the handles to her cart and headed for the woods with grim determination. She would hunt for the eye and the Orb until the final minutes! She strode off into the trees. The slippery fabric of her new red jacket made *swishing* noises as she moved her hands to get a better hold on the cart handles. She did not know where Frinkle was, but she would do her best to find him, beat him within an inch of his life, and retrieve the Crone's eye...*if* the little weasel still had it!

As Wheedle moved along, tugging at the heavy cart, the jacket became too warm for her. She paused and slipped her spindly arms from its sleeves, being careful not to tear the shining threads with her ragged fingertips. As she was about to place it gently into the cart, something in the coat pocket clunked against the weathered boards. Holding the jacket in one hand, she slid the other into its pocket, and pulled out a small blue bottle with a smudged perfume label. Wheedle laid the jacket softly into the cart and gently twisted the crystal stopper from the small bottle. Bringing it to the two small slits in her reptilian face, she sniffed at the opening. Her eyes dilated in surprise. She held the bottle up and stared at it, her mouth gaping open. She knew that smell! Beneath the fading fragrance of perfume, the peddler recognized what she was sniffing. She was holding a small vial of Lunar Potion!

Morble stood in Garglon's garden, and stared at the towering planets through an opening in the oppressive ceiling of Lamberhook treetops. Anger pulsed through her veins. All of her plans had failed. She had nothing with which to thwart the Dark Moon's passage this night. The Banshees had gone out and not returned. The old man they had captured earlier, and stuffed into the trunk of a Lamberhook tree, had nothing of value on him, merely an old human ring that was of no use to her. He looked barely alive. From the looks of it, the Crone's bats had been unleashed upon him.

It was time! Morble wanted her old name back. Cassiopeia, the Queen of the Glimmer Lands, looked once more at the tree hut she had called home since landing here through the well, and made a decision. She would leave the protective shelter of the Lamberhook

Forest and go in search of the Orb herself. She was sure the Crone's Siglets had flown into her hut and stolen the Orb high on the shelf above the table. She feared the Crone was probably in possession of it, and it was forever lost to her, but she had to try! Cassiopeia gathered up the tattered folds of her ruined gown and headed into the depths of the forest, choosing the path that would take her to the Crone's castle. It was time to leave the Spectre Lands, and the name "Morble", behind!

* * *

Chapter Forty-Eight

A SECRET IN THE CROW'S NEST

Leonardo looked sadly upon the young boy who sat huddled in the shadows of the trees, his eyes frozen in a sightless stare at nothing in particular. His shoulders hung in defeat and his hands were clasped loosely in his lap. There was no hope left in him. The night had passed and day was here, but to T.J., there was no difference...darkness was now eternal.

Mandy was still sobbing, continuing to beg his forgiveness. Twicket was silent in his spot against a nearby rock. Leonardo glanced at the troll-head walking stick, but took no real notice of him. He remembered seeing the cane among Dillon's sticks in the artist's studio. His thoughts were on the boy. He felt helpless to comfort him. Time was running out, and Mandy told the artist she not only felt responsible for T.J.'s blindness, but they had lost the Crone's eye to Corvus, and no one knew the location of the Dark Orb. They had escaped the castle and spent the night in the woods.

It had taken several minutes to explain all that was going on to the ghost. Getting T.J. back through the tunnels of the Crone's castle, and across the Black River had left her exhausted, Mandy told him.

Using T.J.'s trick with the river rocks had taken most of the Lunar Potion, she explained. She had placed him on a giant boulder beside her on the river's edge and done her best to navigate the bucking stone through the current. She lifted a scaly arm to show the ghost a large gash where something with a long snout and teeth had leapt from the water and taken a bite out of her. She finished by saying the only thing they had for all of their trouble was a small bottle of Lunar Potion the Crone had missed when tearing apart T.J.'s backpack. It was still in the small zippered compartment.

"I also have a bottle of the Potion, though I don't know how it will help us now," the ghost said, sliding his hand into the pocket of his tunic to retrieve the small bottle of liquid. Leonardo felt around inside the deep pocket. A look of horror crossed his face. He hurriedly shoved his hand into the other pocket, feeling around frantically. Finally, he stood and checked the only pocket in his short pants. Panic shot from his eyes.

"Oh no!" he groaned. "I put it in the baseball jacket pocket when I went into the well! That lizard has my bottle of Lunar Potion!"

A small clump of leaves spiraled down over the small group. Mandy looked up at the towering oak they were resting beneath. At first she saw nothing. Then, without warning, a glistening eye, attached to a fishing line, pierced the canopy of leaves, and descended toward her. Mandy yelped and jumped to her feet, scurrying away from the twirling eyeball.

"What in the name of Galileo?" Da Vinci gasped, as he stared at the swaying fish line with an eye pinned to its hook.

The eye continued to lower, as something unseen above the treetops let out more line. It came to a stop next to T.J., who sat blind and oblivious to everything going on around him. All at once the eye began bobbing up and down in excitement, swinging toward the boy's pant pocket.

A voice from above called out, "Hold, Two Hooks! Hold!"

With that, a giant fish, with a transparent pirate ghost riding side saddle, came crashing through the tree limbs. Barnacle was trying to keep the fishing pole he was holding from becoming tangled in the tree branches.

Leonardo stared open-mouthed, as the strange man steered the fish to his right to hover above T.J.'s head. Two Hook's eye was dancing about on the hook, staring excitedly at the boy's pants' pocket.

"Ye got treasure in dem pants, boy?" Barnacle asked, taking up the slack in the fishing line.

"Great...we now gots two ghosts," Twicket said sarcastically. "Regular Caspar reunion."

T.J. didn't answer Barnacle. He had no idea who, or *what,* was talking to him. He sat there in silence for a few moments, and then let his hand snake down to the pocket in the back of his pants. A look of confusion spread across his face. There was indeed something in the fabric, but he couldn't remember what. The boy slid his hand into the denim opening and came out with a gold watch dangling from his fingertips.

"That's the old man's watch," Mandy said. "Remember, T.J.? You found it by the well right before we came here."

Two Hook's was bobbing so hard on the fishing line, he almost came unhooked. Barnacle took the other end of the fishing pole and quickly ran it through the opening in the watch band before T.J. knew what had happened. The pirate hoisted the pole up toward him, and snatched the shining gold watch from the wooden rod.

"Nicely done, Two Hook's," the pirate said, quickly jerking Volan's reins to send the fish flying high above the group's heads.

Leonardo sprang to his feet.

"Just a moment, Sir!" he shouted angrily. "You can't go about stealing people's possessions. You return that watch to the boy immediately!"

"Yeahhhhhh.....that's not gonna happen!" Barnacle called down snidely. "Ye might want to look up the word 'pirate', Matey, cuz..."

Suddenly, the sound of something crashing overhead cut the pirate short. He looked quickly out over the top of the expanse of trees and gasped. The group below could not see what he was looking at. Leonardo and Mandy ran out into an opening that skirted

Drigmot's Passage, and looked up. Corvus, the Crow was attacking the pirate ship's crow nest, black feathers spiraling to the ground.

"Git away from my ship, you big gal-darned black magpie!" the pirate yelled, kneeing Volans to hurry him along. The large grouper belched and picked up speed, sailing higher toward the ship above the forest, which was anchored to nothing but air.

Corvus continued to dive repeatedly at the interior of the weathered nest sitting atop the main-sail's mast. He tore at the boards with his talons, trying to free an object stuck inside a rotted knot hole. The Crone's eye still shone from his beak.

"Git away!" Barnacle screamed, swinging the fishing pole at the bird before he was anywhere near it. Two Hook's eye was zooming through the air, precariously close to losing its hold on the hook.

As Corvus dove once more at the ship, his beak hit the mast protruding from the crow's nest. He squawked in pain, dropping the Crone's eye. It bounced off the rim of the nest, pinged against the rigging, and was jolted out into the air. Barnacle tried to dive for it, recognizing immediately what it was, but he was not within reach. Red light was streaming from the eye as it took two more bounces off nearby tree limbs, and landed with a plop a few feet from where Mandy was standing. She ran to it, scooping it up, and held it tightly in both hands. Its red glow seeped out between her misshapen fingers like oozing blood.

Chapter Forty-Nine

THE DARK MOON

A shadow fell across the marred face of the Spectre Lands. Mandy, Barnacle, and Corvus all stopped mid-action and turned to stare at the surreal sight of a moon, as black as a bottomless hole, rising slowly between the twisted shapes of the Lamberhook Forest. This sight had not been witnessed for one hundred years! In slow increments, the Dark Moon began eclipsing the full moon that was still in place, glowing softly upon the surreal scene.

Da Vinci stared in awe at the twin moons, one black, the other a fading shimmer of golden light, as the tower of nine planets stood like a celestial sentinel in the night.

"Holy Copernicus!" he whispered, his eyes bulging.

Mandy was the first to break the spell. Corvus had been momentarily distracted by the onset of the Dark Moon. Mandy took the opportunity to run back toward T.J., the Crone's eye cupped tightly in her hands. The crow saw her fleeing shape out of the corner of his eye, and with a loud cry, dove for her. Mandy ducked beneath the protective cover of the forest surrounding the nearby cave, where the ancient well waited in the fading light.

The bird was having a hard time finding an entrance through the closely seated trees. He tried swooping through the opening through which the girl had disappeared, but his wing span was too wide. Pine needles exploded from the low-hanging branches, blanketing the floor.

The ghost of Leonardo Da Vinci hurried into the forest after Mandy, as Corvus came for him as well. Da Vinci wondered just what the bird thought he could do to a ghost, but guessed that in the crow's current state of mind, the entire world was the enemy. He stopped as he came upon T.J., still sitting almost comatose on the same grouping of rocks. Outside the small clearing near the cave, the Spectre Lands were gradually falling into deep shadows as the Dark Moon continued to rise.

"We have to do something!" Mandy whimpered.

"Did you see it?" Da Vinci asked mysteriously.

"Did I see what?" she asked tersely. Panic was taking hold, and she was in no mood for half-formed sentences.

"The thing the bird was trying to get out of the Crow's Nest," Da Vinci said with authority. "It's a silver ball! A round silver ball lodged in a knot hole. I could see it peering out from between the rotted boards. That daft bird is trying to get the Dark Orb, and it is hidden up there at the top of that loony pirate's ship!"

Mandy gasped. "Are you sure?" she pleaded, her eyes bright with hope.

"Madam, I tell you, I could see the opening in the ball's side, just as you described it. Now...how do we get our hands on it? I really don't think that stinky pirate even knows it is up there."

"Do you think Corvus put it there?" she asked, risking stepping closer to the opening of the forest that looked out over Drigmot's Passage. Several yards away she could see the shadow made by the floating pirate ship, as the remaining patches of moonlight shone through its tattered sail.

A creaking sound came from behind a stand of trees. It gradually grew closer, and Da Vinci smiled. He knew that sound. He might be able to get his jacket, and the Lunar Potion inside its pocket, after-all.

Wheedle stopped and listened. Her small nostrils flared as she took in the unmistakable smell of a human. Letting go of the cart handles, she stepped gingerly over to a clump of bushes, and slowly parted their branches in an effort to see what was on the other side. She knew she was close to the well cave, and to the Crone's castle. *Tonight will be like a mad game of chess,* she thought, *with everyone trying to topple the other. It will be every creature for itself beneath the glow of the Dark Moon!*

Something suddenly struck her spindly legs. They let out a gut-wrenching cracking sound. The peddler found herself pitching forward, snatching furiously at branches to break her fall. She landed on the hard ground, face first, a loud groan breaking through her pointed teeth. A burning fire was throbbing inside her ankles, and she feared her legs were broken. She rolled painfully onto her side to look up and see the purple creature, with the wild orange hair, standing over her, brandishing the walking cane with the strange troll head.

"What are you doing?" Wheedle screamed. "Are you trying to kill me?"

"Why you upset?" Twicket asked, his face looking as though someone had just fed him a lemon. "Me cane touched you ugly legs! Me hurting more than you!"

Wheedle flipped up with surprising agility, lunging at the pair with fire shooting from her eyes. A guttural sound rose from inside her, as she grabbed Twicket's cane and tried to wrestle it from Mandy's grasp. Mandy cried out for T.J., and then remembered her friend was useless in his current state of blindness. *Where was that ghost?* she thought anxiously. It was he who had alerted Mandy to the peddler's whereabouts in the first place, sending the girl into the thicket to waylay the peddler. Mandy's first thought had been to temporarily put Wheedle out of commission by knocking her to the floor.

"Let go of him!" Mandy screamed, as Wheedle grabbed the troll by his small green head.

"Ma fass!" Twicket screamed, his words muffled beneath the scaly green hands of the peddler.

Wheedle planted her feet and yanked, pain exploding from the bruised area in her legs where Mandy had struck her with Twicket's cane. As Wheedle leaned back, pulling with all her might to wrestle the cane from the girl, her ratty apron strap slipped off her shoulder, exposing the skin clinging to her protruding collar bone like wrinkled turkey flesh. Mandy gasped as she saw the faint Zodiac symbol embedded in the peddler's skin that had been covered by the only garment Wheedle ever wore.

The peddler yanked one more time, and with a huge POP, Twicket's head came off. Wheedle fell back, the troll's head in her hands, as Mandy also teetered backwards from the force of the cane's release. Her stomach wrenched as she saw the decapitated troll head screaming in Wheedle's hands.

"Me cane!!!" Twicket screamed, his face effused with terror. "Mandy! Help Twicket!"

Leonardo suddenly appeared behind the peddler, and made a grab for the troll. But a ghost's grasp was no match for that of the strong little reptile, as she clung to Twicket's head with all her might.

"Give me the cane and you can have his silly head!" she spat, breathing hard as Leonardo came at her again. "I only want the black cane!"

A large mud clod shot out of the bushes directly into the peddler's eyes. She screamed and brought her hands up in an effort to cover her face. As she did so, Twicket fell from her grasp, his little head taking a bounce off the hard forest floor, and rolling a few feet, coming to rest at the base of a pine tree. T.J. stumbled from a grouping of trees, one hand feeling his way through the tangle of underbrush, while the other held the butt end of a large flashlight; the only weapon he could find inside his pack. He stopped, his open palm pressing into the rough bark of a towering pine, grateful to hold onto something solid.

Mandy dove for Twicket and snatched him up. The little troll was spitting dirt and pine needles from his mouth. Da Vinci took the flashlight from T.J. and turned it on, keeping the bright beam focused on the screaming reptile, who was cursing all of them in a language he was not familiar with, but the fury and inflection left little doubt that they were being verbally abused!

"Nice shot!" Da Vinci said to T.J. "I doubt a kid with sight could have aimed that mud clod any better than you just did!"

"I think my hearing has improved," T.J. said meekly. "I just aimed for the sound of her voice."

"Me cane," Twicket sniffed.

"We can put you back on your cane," Mandy said sympathetically. She turned the gleaming black wood with the strange markings over in her hands to determine on which end the little head belonged. As she rotated the Lamberhook wood, her eyes opened wide in surprise. There at one end of the cane, the end that Twicket's head had always covered, were three perfectly shaped holes.

"You're a flute!" she gasped, running a distorted finger along the holes. Then she looked along the black wood at the strange carvings and symbols, recognizing some of those she had seen on the well's rim. She turned to look down at Wheedle who was trying to crawl away from the flashlight's reach. The bright light was excruciating for a creature that lived most of its life in the dark.

"That's why you wanted the cane!" Mandy cried to the peddler, who finally stopped crawling, and tried to look up at the girl through the blinding ray of light. "You thought it was a clue to the wells!" She looked back at the three small holes. "Now I'm wondering if this is also the ancient flute...the one used to open the Lamberhook trees when Garglon lived in the forest!"

Da Vinci crossed over to Mandy and took the cane from her. He was now looking at it upside down.

"Look at this!" he cried. "I didn't really look very closely at this cane before in Dillon's studio, but these are ancient markings, some of them of constellations no longer around! There are also other symbols and numbers here. I wonder what this was used for!"

The ghost raised the cane to his lips and blew softly into the opening. Haunting strains of music came from the three holes in the black wood. It had a melancholy sound to it, like someone's soul slipping sadly away. He blew on it again, and the notes lifted up through the trees, and floated out into the night. Turning it in his hands, he studied the markings with interest.

Wheedle suddenly lunged for Mandy's ankles and the girl went down. The two rolled about on the ground, screaming and pulling at one another. Da Vinci stared in shock.

"You let go of me!" Wheedle cried, her anger pulsating in her veins. "You had my hand and you let me go!"

Mandy tried to release the death-like grip Wheedle had on her arms.

"I didn't mean to!" she cried, tears rolling down her face. "I held on to the end! The Crone was coming and you fell in! I told you to stay out of the Glimmer Lands' cave! I warned you that spying on the Crone, Scarflon, and the Queen would only end badly, but you kept going back. That's why I came after you that night…to stop you. But she caught us in the Well Room…and then you fell over the edge of the well. I tried to hold onto you! You're my sister! I never wanted to let go of you, but I couldn't hold on! I just couldn't hold on anymore!" Mandy cried, years of guilt flooding out of her.

"What?" T.J. said still standing, rooted to the spot next to the giant pine tree. "Mandy, what are you talking about?"

"She's my twin," Mandy sobbed. "I saw the sign on her shoulder just now when she was grabbing Twicket. She is wearing the Zodiac sign for the Gemini Twins! She's the main reason I came here…to find her and make it right! To take her home."

T.J. stood there, feeling both blind and mute, as he was too surprised to utter a word. He had seen Mandy's sign for the Gemini Twins back when they were trying to enter the Crone's castle. He knew then she had come from the painting in his grandfather's studio. But Wheedle? *Wheedle* was her twin?

"I saw your arm that day in the woods," Wheedle gasped, her right hand tangled in Mandy's hair. "I saw the Gemini sign beneath that bracelet you wear. When you reached for the Glimrocks, I saw it! You betrayed me! You should have saved me and you let me go!"

Wheedle tore at Mandy's face with her free hand, hate blazing in her eyes.

"I have lived like an insect hiding beneath a rock all this time because of *you!*" Wheedle screamed. "Look at me! I was beautiful! *We* were beautiful! This is all your fault! I loved you! *I loved you* and you betrayed me!"

"Get off her, you crazy fish head!" a squeaky voice called from the bushes.

Chapter Fifty

A MAGNETIC ATTRACTION

Frinkle hobbled from the seclusion of a grouping of trees, and lunged at Wheedle. He grabbed her by the arm and tried to hoist her off Mandy.

"Leave it, Frinkle!" Wheedle screamed, jerking her arm free. "This does not concern you!"

"Maybe not," the little man said, "but getting the beejoobies out of here tonight concerns me tons! We still have to finds that Orb thingie and that spooky eye, and some potion, and that moon is almost fully up! I'm not as dumb as you think. My friend told me all about it!"

In all the excitement, the group had not noticed that beyond the bright glare of the flashlight, the Spectre Lands were almost as dark as midnight. Only a small amount of moonlight lit the clearing past the fringe of the trees.

Leonardo walked over to the peddler's cart as Wheedle lay gasping on the ground. A sour smell escaped her lips, like that of dead fish, as she panted from exhaustion and anger. The ghost quietly looked through the contents of the cart, the beam from the flashlight illuminating the peddler's legacy of collected junk. He quietly pushed aside a pile of dusty books, and continued searching the cluttered wagon. He found his red jacket folded neatly near the pan Wheedle had tried to trade him. Being careful not to draw any attention to himself, Da Vinci lifted the jacket and slid his hand into the pocket. It was empty. He tried the other pocket...it too was empty!

"You really think I would be dumb enough to leave it there?"

Wheedle's raspy voice near his elbow made him jump. The peddler had hobbled over to him silently, still trying to calm her breathing, as she watched him with glowing orange eyes.

Before Leonardo could retort, Barnacle's raised voice thundered overhead.

"You danged sea gull!" he screamed. "Git your bony, feathered hide away from my ship!"

Corvus's angry cry answered him. Sounds of splintering wood could be heard as the bird continued to dive at the weathered crow's nest.

"We have to get the Orb!" Mandy whispered nervously, trying to compose herself as she brushed dirt and leaves from her hair. "There is no time left! How do we get it down from the ship?" She turned suddenly to Leonardo. "I don't suppose...as a ghost...that...you know...well...um...*fly?*"

Leonardo looked at her with a puckered countenance.

"No....Madam...I *do not*...fly!"

T.J. had been standing in silence...his world dark and unreal. It was terrifying to know only blackness. He noticed his hearing was more acute, as he relied on it now to compensate for his blindness. He could hear Wheedle's raspy breath, Twicket's whimpering over his cane, and the commotion overhead from the pirate ship. As he stood there, a thought came to him.

"What is the Dark Orb made from?" T.J. asked so quietly, that for a moment, no one was sure he had spoken.

"Did you say something, son?" Da Vinci asked, as he scanned the peddler's cart from the corner of his eye for the Lunar Potion's hiding place.

"The silver ball...what is it made of?" T.J. asked, slightly louder than before.

"I always heard it was made from a meteorite back when the Universe began," Mandy said. "Why?"

T.J. suddenly came to life. He had a plan, and one they would have to execute quickly.

"Ok," he said. "We need something made of iron. Mandy, where's my backpack? Get the wire I put in there that I found on the ground in the cave back home!"

No one moved…they only looked at him for an explanation.

"Now!" T.J. hollered, when he heard no movement. "Just do what I tell you to do!"

Mandy darted through the bushes for the backpack lying near the rock the boy had been resting upon.

"We need something made of iron," T.J. repeated, "And we need the flashlight batteries!"

Leonardo suddenly smiled. "My boy! You impress me! We are creating a magnet, are we not?"

"I sure hope so," T.J. said, and smiled for the first time since the Crone had taken away his sight.

Leonardo reached into the cart and lifted out the iron pan Wheedle had tried to pass off before as copper.

"Madam? I am *now* in need of a pan!" he said, smiling.

Wheedle jumped to grab it from him.

"You can either help us, or remain here for the next hundred years," the artist said to the angry peddler. "Your choice!"

Wheedle dropped her hands and remained still—her nostrils flaring.

Mandy dashed through the bushes, the coil of trip wire Old Man Harmon had used in the cave in Harmon's Wood, gripped tightly in her hand.

"Here!" she panted, and pressed it into T.J.'s outstretched hand. Da Vinci brought the iron pan to the boy and laid the heavy handle into T.J.'s palm. The boy began winding wire around and around the pan's iron handle, feeling his way. The ghost turned his attention to the flashlight. He began unscrewing the head of the metal torch.

The light went out. The forest was almost pitch black, and the sudden loss of light made it almost impossible to see. The artist fumbled with the metal case until the two 'D' batteries slid out into his hand.

"Ok...," T.J. said to the air around him. "Coil the two ends of the wire around the batteries, and make sure the wire is touching the bottom of the negative side of one of them, and the little positive nub on the other."

Da Vinci did as he was told, smiling at his admiration for the boy with his mind for science. As he worked on the battery set-up, Mandy gently pushed Twicket's head back onto the cane top, once more covering the flute holes.

"Tank you, Mandy," the little head sniffed.

"Now be really careful to keep the connections to the batteries intact," T.J. whispered as Leonardo let him know it was ready to go. "Let's do this! Mandy, would you mind guiding me out of here to where we can be under the pirate's ship?" He gripped the iron skillet, making sure the wire was wound snuggly around its handle.

Mandy took his elbow and began leading him slowly from the forest. Wheedle and Frinkle followed along at a safe distance, not sure what the pan-wire-battery-thing was all about.

"Might be 'nother Mind Snatcher," Frinkle muttered to himself.

Mandy stopped as the forest gave way to the open clearing. She was holding Twicket gently after his ordeal. Barnacle's screams were louder here, as he threw things at the circling bird, who was still making periodic dives at the crow's nest. T.J. stopped and felt around the iron pan handle, once again making sure the wire was tight. Da Vinci was next to him and set the batteries, with wires attached carefully, down on a flat boulder, checking to see if the negative base was touching one of the wires. T.J. swallowed hard.

"We have one problem," Da Vinci whispered, as the small group waited in the shadows of the forest's edge. "We can't lift that ball out with this magnet with the pirate and that crow right there. We need a distraction!"

"One distraction comin' up!" Frinkle squeaked. Before anyone could stop him, the little man dashed out into the clearing and went into a dramatic act that left the others astonished.

"What do you want me to do with this here silver ball?" Frinkle cried loudly, pulling Markus's silver baseball from his pocket, and holding it high for Barnacle and Corvus to see. "Does we just put it in the moonlight, or what?"

Wheedle's mouth dropped open. Where did he get *that?* she wondered in amazement. The moonlight Frinkle referred to was from the remaining half of the moon; its golden light tenaciously shining at the edge of the dark planet moving across its face.

Barnacle stopped screaming at the bird and lunged at the side of ship, gripping the railing with transparent fingers. Corvus circled around and looked down at Frinkle in confusion. The bird looked back at the other silver ball he could see still stuck in the rotted ship's boards. *Two of them?* The crow thought in panic. *There are two Dark Orbs?*

"Wow...this thing is surrrreee heavy!" Frinkle continued. "Yessir...must be really valuable."

Barnacle grabbed his fishing pole and was about to rip Two Hook's eye from the hook in preparation to snag the little man's arm, when the dead pirate's eye began hopping madly on the hook, its iris turned upward toward the crow's nest.

"Dadgummit, Two Hook's! Fer the last time, nothin' is up thar but that pesky bird! The Orb is right thar," the ghost said, pointing down to Frinkle. "You lost yer dang touch, ye meaty peeper!"

Barnacle plucked the eye from the hook and tossed it down the steps to the galley. The pirate grabbed the ship's wheel and brought the boat down a little lower, steering over to where Frinkle had hobbled, holding the baseball up like a carrot for a horse. Corvus was swinging down through the sky to get a closer look at the ball in the little man's hand.

"Now!" Da Vinci whispered to T.J.

T.J. held the pan handle high, pointing its end upward. Da Vinci moved the boy's hand until the magnet was aligned with the ship's crow's nest.

"Hold her steady, son," he whispered. Moments passed and nothing happened.

"It isn't working," Mandy whined.

"The current isn't strong enough," T.J. whispered anxiously. "We need something to ramp it up! Mandy, where's the Lunar Potion?"

"Take it," Wheedle said heatedly, pulling the small vial from her apron pocket, as she hobbled over to the ghost, and pressed the small blue bottle of Lunar Potion into Da Vinci's hand. "If it'le get us outta here, then just take it!"

"My bottle of potion!" Da Vinci said, as he recognized the blue perfume bottle belonging to T.J.'s mother that Markus had used for his magic show.

"Yeah, well, you ain't the only one that wants outta here!" Wheedle grunted.

Da Vinci took the vial and hurriedly unscrewed its stopper. Making sure the batteries were beneath the glow of moonlight, he dropped several drops of the potion onto the homemade magnet chargers. Moments passed. Suddenly light shot out of the wires. The coil vibrated, starting at the battery connections, and working its way up the wire until the handle in T.J.'s hands exploded with energy. He grasped it with both hands to steady it.

An invisible current of magnetic energy shot up toward the ship. Da Vinci grabbed T.J.'s wrists to help him keep the magnet on target. Iron riggings on the ship's mast began jumping as the electromagnetic pulse sailed past them. Finally it came to rest on the silver ball. At first the ball didn't move. It was lodged tightly into the crow's nest's knot hole. Then it quivered, jumped a little, and jerked to one side.

Frinkle saw the pirate look toward the group below, as light shot into the sky from the drops of potion.

"What am I bid for this most rare Orb?" Frinkle screamed, in an effort to distract the pirate. "I'm thinkin' its worth all the treasure you gots there in that flyin' shipwreck of yours!"

"What're ya callin' a shipwreck, ye freckled mutt? *Vela* is the finest ship to sail da skies!" Barnacle screamed.

"Flip the handle up and down a little to see if you can fling it out of that hole," Da Vinci whispered, keeping an eye on Barnacle, who was leaning so far over the ship to see the silver ball Frinkle was dangling in front of him, that he nearly fell overboard.

T.J. flipped the wire-bound pan handle up and down, and the silver ball bounced slightly. The boy tried it again, and the Dark Orb popped out of the hole and rolled across the weathered boards of the crow's nest, coming to rest against a folded piece of sail.

"Here...you do it!" T.J. said, passing the pan to the ghost. "You can see it...I can't."

Da Vinci maneuvered the iron handle up and around until the magnetic current snagged the ball. It rose slowly into the air as the artist turned the handle gently to guide the most powerful object in the Universe out of the tattered pirate ship!

Corvus was circling over Frinkle, eyeing the silver ball keenly. It did look like the Dark Orb! This one wasn't stuck in a hole. It was right in front of him, and he had only to steal it! Frinkle was trying to keep one eye on the pirate, and the other on the circling bird. He saw movement over Barnacle's head. The Dark Orb was rising out of the crow's nest!

"Yep!" he yelled loudly, hoping to keep the strange pair's attention, "I gots the Orb...and you knows what else ole Frinkle gots? He gots THIS!"

Triumphantly he produced the white pod he had unearthed in the hollow by the yellow ragweed from his pocket. "This here makes more potion! Lots and lots of potion!"

"My holey socks and garters!" Barnacle yelled out, as the small white pod caught the splintered fragment of moonlight. Its sticky whiskers swayed in the breeze.

"Where did you get that?" Wheedle screamed. "That's mine!"

Just then, the pod Frinkle was holding began to light up, as a strange green liquid pulsed through its veins.

"Throw it down, Frinkle!" Wheedle yelled. "It's poison!"

"Nice try, Wheedle," Frinkle said, sneering. "I gots it and…"

Before Frinkle could finish his taunting, he felt something thick oozing onto the hand holding the strange pod. He looked down to see green liquid dripping from the thing's open mouth. As he hurried to fling the pod from his hand, a burning sensation rushed through the little's man's veins. His heart stopped, and he dropped to the ground. The pod turned to black dust and was carried away on the breeze.

Da Vinci had not noticed what was happening to Frinkle. He guided the Dark Orb slowly past the main mast, through a hole in the tattered canvas sail, and out toward the stern of the ship. Suddenly the ball dropped, as the Orb passed behind the ship's other mast, the magnetic current temporarily blocked by the towering wooden pole. It plummeted toward the pirate's head. The artist gulped and gripped the pan's handle, catching the ball up again. The Orb wavered, only inches above Barnacle's head. Moving the pan carefully, Da Vinci pulled the silver ball over the ship's railing, and brought it floating toward him through the still night air. As it dropped toward the group, waiting breathlessly below, he flipped the pan around, and the Dark Orb landed neatly into the iron skillet.

"One Dark Orb, over hard!" he said, letting out a huge sigh of relief.

Chapter Fifty-One

ANCIENT SYMBOLS

Mandy stared at the prostrate form of the little man lying frozen on the parched ground. Corvus snatched up the ball that rolled from Frinkle's lifeless hand, and realized it was not the Dark Orb.

"We can't just leave him there," Mandy said tearfully. "He probably saved our lives."

Even Wheedle looked at her assistant with pity. "Help me put him in my cart," she said. "I won't leave him there for the creatures of this foul land to pick him apart."

She and Mandy managed to lift Frinkle into the wagon, where he lay among the treasures and trash he had so often pillaged through.

Mandy glanced at the Dark Moon. It had almost completed its rise. There was only a quarter crescent left of the golden sphere. Its light would be needed to activate the well before the Dark Moon rose closer to block out its face. It would soon be too late.

"Quick," she said, "Bring the Orb to the well! We'll put the Crone's eye in it there. Hurry!"

Da Vinci walked quickly back to the forest, holding the Orb carefully in his hand. Barnacle was still yelling at Corvus to "Hand over that bloody ball!" Corvus, knowing now the ball was useless, ignored him. Instead he flew up to the crow's nest to wrestle free the real Dark Orb. He found nothing but an empty knot hole. It was then he noticed the small group making a beeline for the forest entrance. Crying out in fury, the large bird flew toward the woods behind them, Barnacle's swear words glancing off his feathers like idle threats.

A red glow stained an area of foliage near a stand of trees by the entrance to the cave. The eye casting that glow had been watching with interest for the last several hours from its hiding place in the forest. The Crone smiled. She had bided her time and let the blind boy, that red-haired creature, and the ghost do all the work for her! They had the Dark Orb, and very soon it would be hers! The well would switch locations, its symbols change, and all the creatures she had worked so hard to send here would remain in the Spectre Lands for the next 100 years! Once she captured the Orb, she would travel the well's portal to other realms, and bring back more of each dimension's inhabitants, while unleashing her evil throughout the Universe. She would be the only one to know the new symbols once the wells changed tonight.

She had seen the Human Dimension now, thanks to that foolish old man painting her constellation into his painting with Lunar Potion. She had decided there was much she could do in the Human World to gain control. The smile grew across the scarred face. It was *her* time now…no insipid Scarflon to mess things up, or that worthless Queen. She would do things her way and control the Universe!

Moonlight fell dimly through the roof opening in the cave, and onto the well. Mandy (still carrying Twicket), T.J., Leonardo, and Wheedle hurried over to it. Mandy had been leading T.J. through the forest. She had scooped up his backpack, peeking quickly to make sure the Crone's eye was still inside, where she had hidden it only minutes before. The moment she unzipped the small compartment, red light shot out as the eye tried valiantly to find its owner.

The Crone saw the eye calling to her and hissed from her hiding place in the woods. She began floating excitedly toward the cave. Just as she was about to emerge from the sheltering trees, something lunged at her, and tackled her to the ground.

T.J. could smell the unmistakable odor of the well, and his nerves began jumping. He had been through a nightmare, and now he would have to enter the well again....and this time blind! Would that make it easier, or harder, he wondered, shuddering at the thought.

Mandy hurriedly removed the Crone's eye, and taking the Dark Orb from Da Vinci, forced the red crystal into its opening. The red stream of light was pouring out as if a flood gate of energy had been opened!

"Hurry," Mandy said nervously, looking around. "Who has the Lunar Potion?"

"I got it," Wheedle said, baring her pointed teeth. She had snatched it up again when Da Vinci had set it down after pouring it on the batteries. "Let's see the map and get out of here!"

Mandy looked at her suspiciously. There was something in the creature's smile that made her nervous. She felt her sister was up to something.

"What about Grandpa?" T.J. said, fighting to choke back the tears. "We can't just leave him here!"

"T.J., we tried!" Mandy said sadly. "I wanted to tell you, but I didn't know how...once someone is put inside one of those trees...."

"They will probably be itching termite bites for the rest of their days," a male voice boomed from the entrance to the cave.

T.J. recognized the voice immediately, and his face lit up with joy.

"Grandpa!" he cried. "GRANDPA! Where were you?"

"Studying bark from the inside-out," Dillon Finnel said good-naturedly. "I doubt I shall ever want to see a tree house again in my life!"

He was leaning heavily upon a strange man none of them had seen before. He was older than Dillon, his clothes shabby. Dillon stumbled over to T.J., and embraced the boy, who clung to him for dear life. The elderly man winced from his myriad cuts. His face was caked in blood, as was most of his body.

"Good to have you back," Da Vinci said.

"Well...," Dillon said ruefully. "It's not just me! Besides Ruther Harmon here, there are many more!"

He stepped aside to let the others see the large group of Well Riders who had also been released from the Lamberhook trees. Unbeknownst to the others, when Da Vinci played Twicket's flute earlier, the ancient tune had wafted through the treetops of the twisted forest. Beneath the fading moonlight and magic notes, the grotesque tombs had opened, releasing their prisoners. Now the tired Well Riders stumbled toward the well in a daze beneath the last vestiges of moonlight.

"Ruther Harmon?" T.J. asked in amazement. "Old Man Harmon's missing brother?"

"One of them," Dillon said. "I'll tell you all about it after we get out of here. We *are* getting out of here, right?"

There were dozens of other Well Riders, still brushing bits of tree from their hair and picking scabs of bark that had begun to take over their skin. They were trying to understand what was happening. Some were human...some were creatures from other dimensions, but all stood staring at the Dark Moon that was now completing its rise.

"If we hurry!" Mandy said. She motioned to Wheedle, and the peddler poured the drops of Lunar Potion over the Crone's eye. Light shot out from the Orb. As the astonished group watched, a hologram of a map spread out into the cave, filling the small room. Wheedle didn't waste any time. She dropped two drops onto the image of the well in the Glimmer Lands' section of the map, and watched as the symbol of Virgo, the Virgin, and the Star appeared in faded ink.

"Virgo!" she hissed, and darted for the well. Quickly she dropped two drops onto the symbols of the Glimmer Lands' Star, and Virgo. White light shot from the well, illuminating the cave like a spotlight!

"Wait!" Mandy yelled, "Let the humans go home first. Hand me the potion and let me see what their symbol is on the map!"

Wheedle paused and stared at her, her eyes glittering with hatred.

"The *humans?* Why my dear sister, perhaps you should take more thought for yourself...as always! This time you can be the one to live here, and *I* will go home!"

With that, Wheedle jumped up onto the well still clutching Da Vinci's bottle of potion. She turned once more to glare at the girl who had been her twin in another lifetime. As she paused on the well's rim, the white light from the portal washed over her, and Mandy gasped. For one second she was staring at the beautiful sister with whom she had shared the night sky—one half of the Gemini Twins. Her soft orange hair billowed behind her, and her dainty dress sparkled. Then the image was gone, as Wheedle dropped into the well, disappearing from sight.

The exploding light from the well bathed the group inside the cave with the healing warmth of the Glimmer Lands. Mandy felt her arm tingle and look down to see the open wound from the river creature disappear.

A moan came from the peddler's cart that was parked just inside the entrance. Before the group's astonished eyes, Frinkle stirred and sat up. He blinked several times in the glare of the well's magic light, and finally clambered clumsily over the cart's side. His legs were still numb from the poison.

"Krikeys!" he said, as he stumbled to the well and looked at the opening where Wheedle had disappeared. As the light washed over him, his deformity vanished for a split second, and Mandy saw his true form, the one he had been in the Glimmer Lands. She was staring at Cancer, the Crab!

Other creatures who had seen the light streaming up through the opening of the roof like a beacon came running for the well...all wanting their glory back. Many of the Toad Kingdom's inhabitants, along with a host of the humans who had been encased in the Lamberhook trees for years, had become the black twisted limbs and buried roots, unable to escape their fate.

Lepus, the Hare, shot past the group like a white cannon and jumped in, happy at last to be going home. Hiding from Canis Minor was better than hiding from all the ugly things in this dimension!

Frinkle looked at Mandy and smiled his twisted little smile. He held his small hand out toward her. In his palm was a strange black object with buttons.

"You can haves it," Frinkle said kindly. "I don't know whats it is—and I don't care! I is goin' home! Careful though, it might be a Mind Snatcher!" he said, tossing it to the girl.

Mandy caught the strange black object. She watched as Frinkle clambered clumsily onto the well rim, saluted them, and dropped into the white light.

It was then that a terrifying scream came from the forest outside the cave.

Chapter Fifty-Two

A MAP, A POTION AND A PORTAL

"You creaton!" the Crone screamed, as she pushed against Morble's hands that were clawing at her face. Morble shoved her hard, and in a flash of gnarled fingers, dug into the Crone's remaining eye. Blood gushed from between her fingers, as she triumphantly pulled the red crystal from its socket. The Crone screamed in agony and fell back. She clawed at the vacant space in front of her in an effort to find the fallen Queen.

"You will die for this!" the Crone screamed, pressing her hands to the ground as she struggled to rise. "There will be nothing left of you!"

Morble paused, panting. "Yeah, that's pretty much what your sister was probably thinking as she plummeted through the night after I pushed her from a cliff side," the witch said cruelly. "You and Garglon make a great pair...just not a particularly powerful one!"

Morble stood hidden in the forest, a few feet away from the cave's entrance, where creatures were scurrying to get to the well and return home. Her chest was heaving as she struggled to get her breath. She glanced down at her fingers that were smeared with the Crone's blood. In her left palm she clutched the severed eye she had just plucked from the hag's face, leaving the evil specter now entirely blind.

"Your threats mean nothing now," Morble gloated, staring at the powerful eye. "Both your eyes are gone, as is your power! I am

Cassiopeia! I was always meant to rule the Dimensions…and now, I will! You can remain here with Scarflon and Cepheus for the rest of your days! I know Scarflon lives in that hollowed-out ship in Apparition Cove, and I have heard rumors my *beloved* husband is locked away in one of those castle rooms of yours, along with a host of evil constellations from *eons* ago! They should all make for a rather happy little family!"

She laughed as she wiped the Crone's blood onto her tattered gown. Morble glanced at the darkening night, and turned toward the well.

"If you were going to hide in the woods you might have thought to wear a patch over that glowing eye of yours! I could see it from the Lamberhook Forest!" the Queen taunted, as she moved away. "But I suppose it is a moot point now! Adieu, dear Crone!"

Cassiopeia tiptoed silently along the path leading to the cave. Behind her she could hear the thrashing sounds of the blind Crone trying to find her way to the well.

The last of the Glimmer Lands' creatures had entered the well. Mandy's heart had soared as she watched Andromeda, Taurus, Centaurus, Chamaeleon, Scorpio, Cygnus, and so many others enter the well, leaving their distorted forms behind. The creatures who swam in Apparition Bay were unable to leave there, their fins and tails precluding a trip on dry land.

"Better hurry," Da Vinci said to her, as he watched the moonlight edging away from the cave opening.

Mandy reached into T.J.'s backpack and removed the small vial of potion they had been carrying. She handed it to the ghost.

"Wheedle didn't know we had this," she said with a sad face. "She thought when she escaped with your bottle just now that she was leaving all of you humans stranded. You might tell T.J's little brother that he is dabbling with very strong magic if he keeps using this stuff. Oh, and I don't know what this is that Frinkle just tossed to me."

Mandy held up the small black "Mind Snatcher" the little man had been carrying around in his pocket.

"That's my phone!" Dillon yelped, taking it from her. "How in blazes did he get it?" He turned it over in his hands, noting the familiar blue smear of paint near the pound sign on the keyboard.

Mandy turned and looked at T.J., her heart swelling as she stared at his face. "You're going to be alright," she said, touching his cheek. He recoiled slightly at the touch of the scaly skin, and then grabbed her wrist with affection.

"You be careful," he said, his voice cracking. "If it weren't for you, I wouldn't have my grandpa back."

"And if it weren't for that smart brain of yours getting the Orb out of that ship with a magnet, none of us would be going home. I believe the trip home through the portal will restore your sight, just as it will restore our forms," she said, pressing Twicket into the boy's hands.

As Mandy saw T.J. wrap his fingers around the shiny black cane with the strange symbols, she smiled.

"That's why the well didn't turn you 'ugly'", she said, using Twicket's term. "You were holding Twicket! There is more to his cane than we know," she said reverently. "I think it goes very far back in time to the ancients! Take care of him, T.J."

Glancing at the fading light, Mandy handed the Dark Orb to Leonardo and hurried to the well. The hologram of the map wavered as she walked through its luminous shape. She climbed onto the stone rim, and smiled back at them.

"Just drop the Lunar Potion on the map where the well for the Human World is drawn. It will show you which symbols on the well will open your portal. Good-bye," she said softly. "Bye Twicket...you saved us several times with that sneeze of yours."

With that, she jumped, and disappeared into the light of the well. Da Vinci caught a momentary glimpse of a beautiful girl with streaming red hair, before the portal's light claimed her.

Leonardo hurriedly took the stopper from the glass bottle and dropped two drops onto the section of the ancient map labeled the Human World. A shimmering image of two symbols appeared next to the drawing of the well. The image of a Globe appeared, and next to it, the Zodiac sign of Aries.

"Aries!" Leonardo yelled. He ran to the well and quickly added the drops to the two symbols. The ancient carvings lit up, erasing the signs for the Glimmer Lands which slowly faded back into the dark stone. "Let's go!" he called to Dillon, T.J. and all the human Well Riders who had been standing in the corner, watching in shock at the events playing out before their eyes. "Once that moonlight is gone, the well will be too!" He passed the Dark Orb to Dillon, along with the small vial of Lunar Potion. "Here, you be in charge of helping T.J. I'll help the others."

The Renaissance artist smiled at Dillon, and shouted, "See you at home!" He helped several of the frailer humans enter the well, turned and waved, and vanished into the depths of the white light.

"You best hurry," Ruther Harmon admonished Dillon and T.J. "You lose that light, you lose your ride home!" With that, the old man climbed over the rim of the well, and disappeared into the blinding light.

T.J. jumped. That voice! He knew that voice! It was the same one he heard as an elderly man helped him up from the well so long ago when he was only a child. *"Come on boy...push with your toes! Grab my other hand...there ya go."* Ruther Harmon had been the savior rescuing him from the well that day! How very strange.

"T.J.!" Dillon yelled, taking the boy by his arm. "Get over here, boy! Let's get those peepers popping and go home!"

"What about poor Twicket?" the troll suddenly cried out. He had been waiting to see when it would be his turn to find the symbols for the Treblin, and go home to Mudlin.

"There's no time!" Dillon said, sensing the urgency to get into the well before the light disappeared. He heard the troll sniff, and he looked about at the other strange, amphibian-like creatures. Twicket's lip was protruding, and he was making whimpering sounds.

"Not the lip!" Dillon screamed. "Alright! I swear we are going to lose that moonlight!"

Dillon had heard Mandy's instructions for operating the map. He dropped two drops of the potion onto the shimmering hologram, next to the image of the well in the Treblin. Two symbols—a Toad, and Lacerta, the Lizard appeared. He dashed to the well, the ancient map vibrating around him. He ran with the Dark Orb in one hand and the potion in the other. Quickly he dropped two drops of potion onto the well's symbols for the Treblin, also known as the Toad Kingdom. The images sparkled and light exploded again from the well.

"Hand him over," Dillon said quickly to T.J.

The boy reluctantly let go of the small talking troll cane.

"I'm gonna miss you, you dumb ugly troll," T.J. said, his voice shaking.

"Me no be flashlight with green mushrooms no more," Twicket said, his voice weak. "But me miss you too, you boy with big ugly feet!"

Several creatures from the Treblin, who had been waiting their turn, hurried to the well. Some still carried debris from their imprisonment in the Lamberhook trees. Dillon watched in awe as creatures with horned backs, webbed feet, and bulbous eyes, hopped, hobbled and crawled to the well. They scampered up the stone side and dove in.

"Be safe, little troll," Dillon said, as he held Twicket over the side of the well.

"Mudlin be there when me get to other side," the troll said confidently. "Tank you for saving Twicket out of cave in Human World!"

Dillon patted the little guy's head and gently lowered him into the light. Finally, he let go. Twicket vanished from view.

"Let's get outta here!" he said to his grandson.

Still carrying the Dark Orb, its red eye casting the interior of the cave in a crimson haze, the artist took his grandson by the elbow and led him to the well. He dropped two drops of potion onto the symbols of the Globe and Aries, and watched as the glow from the Treblin's images faded away. A blast of light signified the portal to the Human World was now open.

"I'm right here!" Dillon said, as he turned to put the Dark Orb into T.J.'s backpack, along with the small bottle of potion.

"As am I," said a determined voice from the cave's entrance.

Chapter Fifty-Three

BETRAYAL!

Dillon whirled around to see the second-ugliest creature he had ever seen before standing there, her bent form silhouetted in the darkness behind her. The moonlight coming through the cave's opening was all but gone, only a splinter of light hit the well.

"You have what belongs to me!" the creature said, the cruel gash of a mouth working with jerking, irregular movements.

Before Dillon could recover, the thing lunged at him, grabbing the Dark Orb from his hand. She held to her breast in a fierce hug, her eyes two small orbs of glittering madness.

"It's mine!" she screamed. "I will have it all back! Did you really think I would not prevail? Me? The Queen of the Glimmer Lands? You pathetic little humans!"

She held it up, bathing in the red glow of the Crone's eye. Suddenly a fury of wings exploded through the opening in the cave's ceiling. Corvus dove at his former mistress, and snatched the Dark Orb from her gnarled hands.

"Noooooooooooooo!" she screamed. "Give it to me, you idiot! We are out of time! We must go into the well now! Give me the Orb, you ungrateful, hideous bird!"

Corvus circled the well, and angled up toward the ceiling. He flew out through the opening and into the night to escape her grasp. He circled again, looking down through the cave's break in the rock, calculating his descent. The trip through the portal back home would restore his tattered body. Glancing at the last rays of

* * *

moonlight, he prepared to dive at the well, not realizing the symbols glowing on the stone rim were no longer those of the Glimmer Lands, but now shown with the images for the Human World.

Taking a deep breath, Corvus swung around and shot toward the opening in the roof. As he did, something hit him hard on the bone of his small skull. A sickening *Thwack* sound exploded from the bird's head, as Barnacle's fishing pole struck the crow soundly on his skull. The Orb fell from his claws and hit the side of the cave's opening. The powerful talisman fell to the well, bounced off the rim, and disappeared into the cavern's light, the red glow from the Crone's eye streaming behind it.

"My Orb! You idiot! Not this time!" Cassiopeia yelled, and ran toward the well. She scrambled up, and clutching the well's rim, dropped into the bowels of the stone cavern; the portal to the Human World pulling her under.

"Hurry!" Dillon screamed as the holographic map disappeared along with the Orb. He grabbed T.J. and propelled him harshly toward the well. The shadow of Barnacle's pirate ship fell across the cave's entrance, as the ghost searched for a way in.

Dillon grabbed T.J.'s backpack and prepared to help the boy onto the rim. T.J. felt the warm light, and for an instant, saw a pinprick of white funneling into his sightless eyes. At that moment, the Dark Moon completed its ascent. The well room went dark. Dillon felt the rough stone surface of the well's rim disappear beneath his fingertips, as the magic portal vanished, to resurface somewhere else in the dark kingdom. It would have different symbols in place to unlock its passageway, leaving the inhabitants of the Spectre Lands trapped here for the next 100 years.

Chapter Fifty-Four

A BIRD'S EYE VIEW OF THE SPECTRE LANDS

The Spectre Lands lay in complete darkness. No sound came from the usual stirring of bats, river creatures, and insects. It was as though the kingdom had been sucked of life.

Dillon stood completely still, with his grandson by his side. The boy stood motionless, the fleeting shaft of light he had seen moments before, gone. To T.J., in his current state of blindness, nothing seemed any different, other than the sudden quiet, and the heaviness he sensed coming from his grandfather.

"What's wrong?" the boy asked, uneasiness replacing the stark fear he had felt only moments before, as he thought about descending into the well again.

"Houston, we have a problem," Dillon said, trying to keep his manner light. "Our ride home has just been canceled."

T.J.'s heart hammered as he tried to understand just how bad their situation was.

"The well has moved," Dillon said, "to where...I have no idea. The Dark Moon is in place, and there is nothing but black everywhere. The Orb just disappeared into the well, along with the map, and that wretched Queen, so I have no idea what to do now."

"So even if we find the well, without the Orb, we don't know which new symbols will get us home, right?" T.J. asked, his mood as black as the world he was living in.

"Technically, we just need to know the new Zodiac sign for our world," Dillon said. "I think the image of the Globe stays the same. But I could be wrong."

Dillon looked down at the ground where the well had sat. Only a ring of scorched earth marked where the famous portal had been. He walked to the cave entrance, guiding T.J. carefully along with him. He peered out into a world straight out of a nightmare. The only sound he heard was the distant sloshing of the Black River, as its ebony waters licked the dark moss along its banks.

An idea suddenly hit T.J.

"Grandpa? Look in my backpack, and get out that little bag! It has Glimrocks inside. If we toss them down and say 'well', maybe they will lead us to it, and we can figure out what to do after we get there. At least we still have some of the Lunar Potion!"

Dillon reached into the pack and felt around. His hand fell on a flashlight, but he noticed its bottom was missing, and it felt too light to contain batteries.

"What happened to the flashlight?" he asked. "We could have sure used it about now."

"Let's just say it was used in an experiment...one that worked," T.J. said. "Do you feel the little leather bag?"

Dillon located it. He pulled it out and opened its drawstring neck. Carefully he let the jewel-tone rocks fall into his open palm.

"Do what now?" he asked, staring at the multi-colored rocks that gave off a soft glow in the darkness.

"Toss 'em down and say 'Find the well!'"

Dillon shook his head but did what he was told. He tossed them gently to the ground next to his feet, as not to lose them in the dark, and said, "Find the well!"

The Glimrocks did nothing. There was no movement at all.

"I think your rocks are broken," Dillon said softly, as he squinted in the darkness at the glowing stones. "They are not doing anything."

"Try again!" T.J. urged, but before the words were completely out of his mouth, a soft clanging sound came toward the pair in the darkness. As the noise grew closer, a foul odor grew as well.

"Oh no," T.J. muttered. "I think it's Barnacle."

Dillon looked up to see a soft glow of light breaking through the inky blackness overhead. Before his startled eyes, a pirate's ship sailed down toward them and landed softly on the hard ground of Drigmot's Passage. A candle's flame inside a broken lantern, dangling from a hook on the main mast, shed the only visible light in the darkened world. T.J. listened to the sounds of the fish burping and the stirring sounds the pirate ghost made, as he hoisted a rope ladder over the side of the broken ship. Dillon looked above him at the ghost leaning over the ship's railing, his filmy shape glowing in the darkness. Somewhere off to their left came the sound of something thrashing about in the bushes as the Crone struggled blindly to find her way out of the forest.

"Hope ye happy thar, ye dang humans!" Barnacle called out in the inky blackness. "Ye coulda been home by now if ye had held on to that dern ball! Not my night...couldn't even kill that dang magpie! I'm guessin' the well is gone, is it?" T.J. heard him spit.

"I don't suppose you might know where the well is?" Dillon asked, trying to calm his voice. The sight before him was unnerving.

"Me? Nope!" the pirate said emphatically. "Now, Two Hook's...Two Hooks could probably locate it fer ye. Magic wells, especially ancient portal-type wells, are always treasure, and that thar eye can find treasure. Stupid thing was tryin to tell me all long dat thar dern Orb was in me crow's nest!"

"I don't know what "Two Hook's" is," Dillon said uncertainly, "but if you can take us to the well, I will try and make it worth your while."

"Don't gots to try," Barnacle said smiling, showing mostly gum, and only two blackened teeth. "You can jest hand over that little ole bag of rocks you gots, and I will take ye to look for where the well is now."

Dillon whispered something to T.J. who nodded.

"We have an accord!" Dillon said, smiling.

"We have a what?" Barnacle asked, eyeing the man suspiciously.

"An accord...it means an agreement. I thought that was how pirates talked."

"Ye been watchin' too many movies, Bucko," the ghost said. "Oh, and dem rocks...coulda told ya, ya can't use dem rocks to find a well. There be a spell on 'em that don't let 'em do that! 'Side, de only work in real moonlight, not dat dark light we got shinin' right now."

Dillon scooped up the Glimrocks and returned them to the bag. He led T.J. toward the ship. The boy felt his way along the splintered planks of the hull. Finally, his fingers touched the rough hemp of the rope ladder, and he waited, as Dillion helped him grab hold. Little by little T.J. climbed up the swaying ladder, the rope smelling strongly of brine shrimp. Once the boy was onboard, Dillon climbed up after him; T.J.'s backpack hanging from his shoulders.

"Fare please," Barnacle said, holding out his transparent hand.

As Dillon reached into the backpack for the bag of rocks, he felt something glowing wash over his face. He looked up in surprise to see the Dark Moon slowly lifting away from the giant golden moon's face. The splinters of light shot out into the Spectre Lands, like accusing fingers pointing at fragments of landscape.

Barnacle glanced over his shoulder at the departing Dark Moon as it moved slowly across the golden sphere.

"Yessir...goin' away fer 'nother 100 years!" He spit over the side of the ship for emphasis. Dillon placed the leather pouch into the ghost's hand. Barnacle checked the bag of rocks and bit one of them. Satisfied they were the real thing, he tied the bag's drawstring to his belt loop.

"These'll do," he said, and walked to the galley doorway. He retrieved the fishing pole with Two Hook Mason's eye attached to the hook. As soon as the eye saw the bag of Glimrocks it began bobbing up and down.

"I KNOW!" the pirate spat. "I gots a treasure...I already KNOW! Pay attention!" He slapped at the milky eye. "We gotta find a well...that portal thing...understand? Good!"

"How do we know that eye can find the well?" Dillon asked.

"Ya don't," Barnacle said simply.

The pirate walked to the ship's helm and took the wheel in both hands. It lifted silently from the ground. Turning the wheel hard to the leeward side, Barnacle steered it off into the night, the glow of a golden moon silhouetting him in its halo.

As strange as the Spectre Lands were on a normal day, the sight of a flying, broken-down pirate ship with a ghost at the helm, a flying grouper sailing behind, and an elderly gentleman hanging over the port bow (dangling a fishing pole with a bouncing eyeball attached to its hook), ranked in the top five. Dillon Finnel held tight to the pole and let out, or reeled in, the line as necessary, trying valiantly to keep the eye from snagging on treetops or craggy cliffs. T.J. was seated on a weathered barrel, one finger under his nose, as the rank smell of the ghost and galley enveloped the ship in a perpetual stench of baked fish guts.

"Give him some slack!" Barnacle called back to the artist. "Two Hook's don't like a tight line when he's searchin' fer treasure!"

Dillon sighed, still trying to wrap his mind around his current situation, and let out a little more line. The eye swirled below him, looking left and right, and up and down, in search of something valuable. It "hit" on a few useless trinkets during the two hour voyage. Dillon was about to give up, his shoulders burning from staying hunched over the ship's side for so long. Just as he was about to reel in the line, the eyeball began spinning out of control, pulling excitedly on the crusty line.

Barnacle heard the whizzing sound of the line spinning from the reel, and hurried over to see what was going on. He leaned out to see the frenetic eyeball swaying toward an outcropping of rocks at the far edge of the Spectre Lands, where few creatures ventured.

"Whatcha got thar, Two Hook's?" he called over the side. "Better not be no more dang boat bells or pretty rocks!"

The pirate returned to the wheel and cranked it over, steering the ship about, and lowering it carefully toward the rocks. As the boat descended, a small entrance could be seen leading into the boulders.

"There's a cave in there!" Dillon called out excitedly. "Is the well always in a cave?"

"Can't land the ship here," Barnacle said, ignoring the man's question, as he surveyed the jagged rocks and encroaching trees. "Have to use Volans!"

"Use what?" Dillon asked, turning to look at his transparent host.

"That flyin' grouper back thar," the pirate said, jabbing a thumb toward the fish, who was floating quietly behind the ship. Volans merely burped at the introduction.

"You expect me to get on that fish?" Dillon asked in shock.

"I needs to steady the ship. You go see if yer well is in thar. If it is, ye can stay down thar, and send Volans up fer de kid. I only promised to get ye to the well, not be yer travel guide when we got thar!" Barnacle grabbed a rusted anchor and heaved it overboard; it hung uselessly in the night air.

"This isn't happening!" Dillon muttered, as he set the fishing pole against the ship's rail and began picking his way through the maze of rope, buckets, lures, lines, and broken ship parts. He reached the stern of the ship and looked out at the disinterested fish. Pressing his lips together in frustration, he took the tether line tied to the grouper and began reeling her in. Volans floated over to the ship, turned sideways so that Dillon could swing a leg over her saddle, and burped beneath the weight of the man, as the artist settled in, gripping the reins for dear life.

"He doesn't buck, does he?" Dillon called.

"It's a "she", and only if ye call her a "he"!" the pirate yelled back, chuckling.

Grasping the reins, the artist pulled the lead to the right, and Volans turned away from the ship, lazily sailing down closer to the cave entrance. Dillon tried to keep his weight even, and his knees away from the fish's stomach, so as not to entice another series of belches. The odor that came with each burp was making him nauseous.

He pulled up a little on the reins, as Volans lowered him close to the ground. Gently he swung his leg over and dismounted.

"Stay!" he said to the fish, as if speaking to a dog.

The cave entrance was only a few feet away. A pale beam of moonlight was falling just inside through an opening in the roof.

"Strange that it is always the same," the artist said, noting the cave, a roof opening with moonlight streaming in, and, he supposed, a well sitting dead center in its midst.

Dillon stepped into the entrance and smiled. There before him was the well. He could see some of the carved symbols illuminated by the moon's soft glow.

"It's here!" he yelled up to the ship, as he returned back to the fish. He took the reins and turned Volans around. He then gave the fish a pat to send her back up to her master. A disgusting burst of gas released from the fish's rear when Dillon swatted it.

"Good grief!" the artist cried, covering his nose. "What do you feed that thing?"

Volans floated back up to the boat. Barnacle left the wheel and took T.J. by the elbow, guiding him to the back of the vessel. The boy tripped several times over the debris strewn about the ship's deck, and nearly toppled over the side. Finally they reached the stern and Barnacle gave him instructions on how to mount the fish the boy could not see. T.J. fumbled with the reins the ghost placed in his hands. He could not bring himself to leave the safety of the ship and step off into thin air. Barnacle brought Volans in as close as he could, and placed T.J.'s fingers on the fish's head.

"Thar!" the ghost said, losing his patience. "She's right thar! Jest swing yer leg out, and ye will be sittin' on her saddle!"

T.J. gulped, felt along the fish until he found the saddle horn, gripped it tightly and swung a leg out. His foot hit the saddle, as he had not brought his leg up high enough, and he nearly toppled over the stern into thin air.

"I can't do this!" he cried, grabbing onto a line attached to the mast.

"Ye almost had it!" Barnacle yelled. "Here, I'll guide ye leg!"

T.J. was trembling, as he stepped up onto the stern again. The ghost handed him the reins.

"Now squat down, put dat hand...yeah, dat one...right thar...feel dat? Dat's da saddle. Get hold of the horn ag'in...thar ye go...now I'll take yer leg...quit kickin' at me!...thar....sit down! Ye's on her!"

T.J. felt the leather saddle beneath his rear end, and the sickening sensation of the fish sinking slightly beneath him. He gripped the reins in one hand and held onto the saddle horn with the other; his knuckles white.

"Turn her right," the ghost called, sighing. He was eager to be done with these humans. He had the Glimrocks, which would be worth some good bargaining. He turned and looked over his shoulder to see the Dark Moon releasing its final hold on the full moon. In a few more minutes the black harbinger would be gone for another 100 years. It mattered little to Barnacle, as he could fly back and forth between the Spectre Lands and the Glimmer Lands at will. It did mean, however, that without the Orb, he would probably remain a ghost for a long time.

T.J. pulled the reins to the right, and felt the fish turn and sink slowly down.

"You still there, Grandpa?" he called out in a panic.

"Right here, Teej!" Dillon called. "You're doing fine!"

The fish finally glided in next to the elderly gentleman, and Dillon put his hand on T.J.'s leg to assure him. He helped the boy swing his leg over the saddle and step down to the ground.

"Whatever you do, don't pat its fanny!" Dillon whispered.

The fish waited until Dillon had wrapped the reins around the saddle horn, and pointed it in the right direction.

"Shoo!" he said, not wanting to touch the thing again. Volans lifted into the sky and sailed home to the ship.

"Well, happy huntin'!" Barnacle called, as he tied the tether to Volans saddle ring. "Ye humans might want to keep to yer own land from now on…dangerous stuff 'round here!" He floated back to the helm, and grabbed the wheel. "Oh…and don't forget…ye get the symbols wrong and ye be in dat Void…just sayin'!"

Barnacle chuckled to himself, as he turned the wheel deftly to starboard, and steered the ship up into the night sky, with Volans burping quietly along behind him. Moonlight sparkled off a small bottle of Lunar Potion partially hidden in a folded, torn sail in the crow's nest where Corvus had hidden it. Two Hook's eye looked up and began jumping about on the line.

"Thar ain't no more treasure up thar!" Barnacle screamed at the eye. "That Orb is gone! Behave or I'll throw ya below!"

Dillon watched until he lost sight of the ship in the treetops, the pirate's threats disappearing on the night breeze.

"You ok?" he asked T.J., who was still trembling. "The well is in there, but son, I don't know what we do with it now," he said hopelessly. His body ached from myriad cuts. He was exhausted.

Taking T.J. by the elbow, he led the boy into the cave. The odor of cold, cloistered stones assailed their noses, and T.J. was instantly reminded of the damp basement's smell at the Finnel's house. Dillon stopped the boy as they reached the well. He laid T.J.'s backpack on the ground and walked around the cistern, running his fingers over the ancient symbols carved into its rim. He paused at the image of the Globe and probed at it with his forefinger, a ridiculous wish in his mind that by pushing on it, the well portal would open, like a flip-top can. Moonlight bathed the silent cavern, and Dillon sighed.

"Leonardo said the symbol for home was Aries," Dillon said. "Any chance that symbol will still work?"

"I don't think so," T.J. said. "Now that the well has changed locations, the symbols have changed too. Mandy explained a great deal to me about the portal thing. If you go into the well without the right portal opening...well...you end up in some forsaken place called the Void."

"Well, Teej," his grandfather said wearily, "who would have thought this would be our fate?"

At the word "fate", T.J. thought of the little blue flickering flame that had shown him a message in a rock. A thought suddenly occurred to the boy. "You don't see a well bucket lying around in here, do you?" T.J. asked hopefully.

"Well bucket?" Dillon asked.

"Yeah...this little blue guy, that Mandy said was an Oracle, showed me a rock with a message on it. It said, *'The Well Bucket is the Answer.'*" Mandy said he predicted the future. If there's a bucket around, I just thought maybe it had a clue in it or something." Suddenly T.J.'s face lit up.

"Grandpa!" T.J. exclaimed. "*The Well Bucket* doesn't have a clue *in* it....it *IS* the clue! Remember what you taught me about the ancient constellations...how different civilizations gave them different nicknames? *The Well Bucket* was the old Druid nickname for Aquarius...because he is pouring water from a bucket, or urn! *The Well Bucket is Aquarius!"*

"T.J.! That's brilliant!" Dillon yelled, clapping the boy on the back.

"But how do we know Aquarius is the symbol for *our* world?" Dillon said, some of the excitement leaking from his voice. "It could be for any of the dimensions. We don't know for what purpose your little blue guy showed you that. It could be a trick to send us to the

Void." He paused, staring at the well's symbols. "I sure wish we had that map back."

"We have to try," T.J. said. "If we don't, we are stuck here anyway. I say we put the Lunar Potion on the Globe and Aquarius!"

Dillon studied his grandson's face—and the frozen, blank eyes—and made a decision.

"I'm proud of you, Teej! No matter what happens, you are the bravest kid I know!"

T.J. heard the zipper opening on his backpack, and steeled himself. He knew his grandfather was getting out the Lunar Potion. He prayed it would work, but a part of him was still afraid to go back into the well. If they were wrong ...

Dillon slung the pack onto his shoulders, wincing from the pain, and crossed to the well's rim. He dropped a small amount of potion onto the symbol of the Globe and, taking a deep breath, let a single drop fall onto the carved image of *Aquarius, the Water Bearer*. If the well remained dark, the symbols didn't match any of the portals, and they would be stuck here for 100 years, perhaps longer. If it lit up, they had opened a portal, but to which dimension?

Tense seconds passed. T.J. was frozen, his breathing shallow.

"It isn't working is it, Gran...?"

Just then white light shot from the well, bathing the cave in brilliance. T.J. felt a blast of air on his face.

"It worked!" T.J. cried. "The portal opened!"

Dillon's first reaction of elation when the light blasted from the well was followed immediately by feelings of worry.

"We opened *something*...," Dillon said slowly. "...but to which world? Just because we lucked out and chose two of the correct symbols doesn't mean we just opened the portal that will take us home. The Globe might belong to some other place now."

T.J. pressed his lips together, and finally said, "We can't stay here...I can't stay like this. I say we risk it."

T.J. let his grandfather lead him to the well, both of them trembling with fear. He felt its rough stone rim with his quivering fingers. His throat was too dry to swallow, though he kept trying. He lifted himself onto the rim, gripping the edge, with the fear of falling in before he was ready, making him tremble.

"I'm right here, Teej!" his grandfather said. "I got ya, kid."

Dillon climbed up onto the rim and swung his legs over to match T.J.'s, who were dangling above the white light. T.J. felt his grandfather take his left hand into his own, and hold it tightly.

"Let's go home..." Dillon said hopefully, and taking a deep breath, they both jumped into the light.

Moments passed, the brilliant glow from the well pulsated in the quiet cave of the Spectre Lands. A scuffling sound came from the entrance. The creature's shadow cut through the light, as he walked cautiously to the well, and peered in. *They should be far enough ahead by now*, he thought. Stepping up to the rough stone, he placed two torn hands onto the rim and paused, listening for sounds from far below. Only a faint rushing noise could be heard. Holding a limb from a black Lamberhook tree he had just flown on to the well, Scarflon sat on the stone rim, and swung his legs over the edge. With a grunt, he pushed off and disappeared into the belly of the portal.

Chapter Fifty-Five

HOME IS WHERE THE ART IS!

"Awk! Tell Copperfield here this parrot is not part of his lame magic show!" Harper squawked, as Markus tried unsuccessfully to stuff the large bird into his magic hat.

"I lost the stuffed bunny!" Markus said, breathing hard, as he wrestled with the parrot in an effort to cram his wings into the lining of the stovetop hat. "He hopped out the window one night and I can't find him. You gotta be the new Disappearing Parrot Act!"

"Only thing that's going to disappear is your nose after I bite it off!" Harper cried, bobbing his beak toward Markus' face.

"Markus, let him go," Marsha Finnel said, her voice breaking. She was seated at the kitchen counter, working her way through bills with 'Overdue' stamped across them in bright red ink. The *Coven Bay Tattler* lay near her elbow. A large black-and-white photo of the planets stacked one upon the other adorned the front page next to a bold headline that read:

IS THIS THE END OF THE WORLD?
"Strange planetary movement and lunar eclipse baffles scientists."

The boy sighed elaborately and released the harried parrot. Harper flew to his cage, hopped inside, and slammed the wire door shut. He began preening his ruffled feathers and mumbling threats, that included midnight attacks on Markus' bed while the boy slept.

Marsha looked up at the clock. It was 4:10 in the afternoon. David had been out all day looking for Dillon and T.J. again, along with several policemen and volunteers. After T.J. had disappeared, along with the artist, the Coven Bay Police Department had finally taken the case seriously. They had combed the woods and neighboring towns for days. One officer had entered Old Man Harmon's house, finding the notorious hermit hiding in his basement. They had also checked Tabor's brother, Ruther Harmon's bordering property, but found only an empty, decomposing house, a newer barn, and a weed-infested yard. The latest report was that the famous well in Harmon's Wood had disappeared earlier that day.

The stress of the past few days had taken a toll on the family. David had lost weight and Marsha saw a woman five years older staring back at her from the mirror each morning. She had bags beneath her eyes, and her cheeks sagged.

"What if we never get them back?" she had asked her husband the night before, as they got ready for bed. "What if this nightmare never ends?" She had begun sobbing into his arms.

A loud bang sounded at the front door. Marsha jumped, and then immediately told Markus to stay where he was, noticing the boy was about to bound out of the kitchen toward the living room.

"It's probably more reporters," she whispered tensely to her son. "Do they never give up?"

But to her surprise, the next sound was that of the front door swinging open and feet tramping into the living room. Just as she was scolding Markus for leaving the door unlocked again, and grabbing up a broom in readiness to assault some aggressive reporter, Dillon Finnel and T.J. walked into the kitchen, with smiles plastered across their filthy faces.

"What's for dinner?" T.J. asked, his eyes dancing with happiness.

"Oh my gosh! *OH my gosh! You're here....you're both really here!*" She rushed at them with tears streaming down her face. The broom clattered to the floor, as she grabbed them and kissed their faces.

"Easy, Mom," T.J. laughed. "We both need a shower!"

"Crimination!" Markus yelled, grabbing T.J. around the waist. "Where the heck have you been? I had to hold this family together!"

Dillon laughed. "I'm sure you did, Mark." He hugged the boy tightly.

"Fine! Do the group hug without the family pet!" Harper called from his cage. "No respect for the bird...ya hear me? NO respect!"

"I'm even happy to see you," T.J. said, walking over to the parrot. "Heck, I'm thrilled to "see" anything at this point. Thank goodness Mandy was right about the portal returning things to normal!"

"Mandy? Portal? What are you talking about?" Marsha asked, wiping her eyes. She was gently checking the scratches and bruises on T.J.'s and Dillon's face and arms from their trip through the wells. "You look like you've been through a war zone," she said.

"If you had seen what I looked like earlier, these would be nothing!" Dillon said, happy to see the bat's destruction had vanished in the well's healing light.

The sound of a car pulling into the driveway could be heard. Markus ran to the window, and peered out.

"Dad's home!" he said happily. "He's gonna pee himself!"

"Markus we do not say "pee" in this family!" Marsha lectured.

"It's a lot better than the word I was gonna use!" the boy said, with an arched eyebrow.

The front door swung open again, and David Finnel walked into the room, his shoulders sagging. Dillon and T.J. had stepped out of sight to the side of the door to surprise him.

"No word," David said, reaching for a glass, and turning on the faucet. He took a sip of water. "Oh...you're going to love this!" he said acidly. "They actually had the audacity to ask me if I knew where the well in the woods back there had gone! Can you believe that? Now we are *well* thieves...I have half a mind to..." He turned toward his wife to make his point, and saw his father and T.J. standing there, beaming at him. The glass fell from his hand, as tears sprang to his eyes.

"We can tell you where the well went," T.J. said mysteriously, his face beaming.

"Yeah, we can pretty much give you the guided tour," Dillon said, smiling at his son.

David was speechless. He crossed to the two and felt their faces. He had to make sure they were not an illusion. Then he pulled them into a hug, and T.J. could feel his father shuddering. He had never seen him like this. He had always been so careful to show only his strength. He felt his dad's hand cup the back of his head and hold him tight.

"It's ok, Dad," T.J. reassured his father. "It's all going to be ok."

"Can we go out for pizza to celebrate?" Markus asked hopefully. He was sick of the leftovers they had been eating for the past four days.

"I would enjoy tasting your version of an Italian pizza," said a voice from the kitchen doorway.

They turned to see Leonardo Da Vinci's ghost standing there.

"About time you two got here," he said grinning at Dillon and T.J. "I thought you were right behind me in the well!"

"We...uh...had a few hiccups after you left," T.J. said, laughing.

"I will be heading back to Italy through the well in my painting," the ghost said. "I just wanted to make sure you are both alright."

David and Marsha Finnel were standing with their mouths gaping open, and their eyes threatening to pop from their heads.

"Oh, I forgot," Dillon said. "You have never met my mentor! Leonardo...this is my son and daughter-in-law. David, Marsha...this is Leonardo Da Vinci...well, his ghost anyway," he said good-naturedly.

"Pleasure to finally meet you," Leonardo said, smiling broadly.

David and Marsha stared at the ghost of the famous Renaissance artist with gaping mouths.

"Thanks for goin' on the adventure without me," Markus said grumpily to the ghost. "Next time, gimme a minute!"

Da Vinci smiled and looked at Mr. Finnel.

"I apologize for the trouble my appearances cost you in your efforts to locate employment," the ghost said to David, who was still standing open-mouthed in the middle of the kitchen. "I have been thinking about your situation and I may have an idea to help out. Just a thought, but what if we create an art gallery—a very special art gallery to showcase Dillon's work? I will make appearances, and autograph the paintings Dillon and I have worked on. For a price, the paying public can hear my series of lectures on oil painting, anatomy, structure, my *sfumato* effect, subject juxtaposition, and light. We can call it Finnel's Fine Art Gallery, and have Marsha here run it, since she has a decorating background. Didn't I hear you worked for a floral boutique?" the ghost asked kindly.

"Well, yes...I did. Oh! That would be wonderful! Maybe I could create floral arrangements for the Gallery to sell as well!" she cried happily. It was the first time she had felt hope, and excitement, for days.

"Of course, someone will have to do all the marketing, advertising, display set-up and bookkeeping. I don't suppose that would interest an old marketing exec like yourself?" Da Vinci asked David. "Any problem with working with a ghost, Mr. Finnel?"

"Ghost?" David finally spluttered. "Uh, no...no problem at all," he said feebly. Thoughts of the amount of money they would make with the world famous Renaissance artist being part of his very own gallery were running through the man's mind like a freight train.

"Hey...I could do magic tricks!" Markus said excitedly. "Gimme back the rest of my magic potion, and I can do some really amazing stuff!"

Dillon threw an arm around his younger grandson and laughed. "There will be no magic potion used around here," he said, laughing. "And the lip will not work!" he said, as Markus' lower lip protruded in a pout.

"Now then," the ghost continued. "I owe you an apology, Dillon. It would seem I left your baseball jacket inside the peddler's cart. Anyone feel like a trip back to Spookville?"

T.J. looked at him in shock, and seeing the wry grin on the ghost's face, burst out laughing.

"Maybe tomorrow," the boy said, and Dillon joined in with the laughter.

"I *can* return this to you," Da Vinci said, handing Dillon the small pocket knife he had traded the jacket to Wheedle to obtain.

"Is someone going to explain all this to us?" Marsha asked, her head spinning.

"Later," Dillon said. "We are starving, and I want out of these filthy clothes."

He pushed his hand into his pants' pocket to replace his knife, and pulled out the battered cell phone Frinkle had carried around the Spectre Lands. He flipped it open and looked at the list of phone calls. There had been five from his son and Markus the day of his disappearance, at the times he would have already been taken prisoner in the Crone's castle. The phone had obviously fallen from his pocket. The Siglets may have carried it off or the Crone could have tossed it from the window of her castle. Somehow, Frinkle had found it.

"That is what I call great cell phone coverage...," he said, grinning. "...all the way to another dimension. Perhaps I should do a commercial for the wireless company. Airways Cell Phones. We give new meaning to loooonggg distance coverage!"

T.J. and Leonardo burst into laughter, as the others looked helplessly on.

Dillon suggested they make a quick phone call to the Police Department to let them know he and T.J. were home, and safe. He joked he might even tell them the well had moved from Harmon's Wood over to Jackson County, New Hampshire. It had taken him and T.J. all night, and most of the day, to hitchhike from the well in the next state, three hundred miles away. He knew the cave out back would now be empty. It felt strange to think of all that had happened.

A smile suddenly creased his ravaged face.

"I believe I can now paint a realistic medieval castle for the museum mural I was about to start when all this happened," Dillon said, grinning. "You'll forgive me if I don't go and ask the castle owner permission to paint a replica of her abode."

The sun set in Coven Bay. Stars dotted the cloudless sky, and a golden moon hung low over the treetops of Harmon's Wood. Marsha called to order a pizza that Dillon said he could pay for. Harper was squawking that he wanted anchovies on his. David was hammering Dillon with questions, stopping the poor man each time he tried to go in search of a shower and clean clothes. Dillon explained to David how T.J. and his knowledge of the stars and science had saved all their lives.

Markus was asking Da Vinci if they could collaborate on a magic show, explaining to the ghost how authentic it would be to have a ghost *actually* disappear before the audience's very eyes. Leonardo said he would "think about it." He also told Markus the magic potion would have to be carefully hidden away. This statement was met with a pouting face, and then a thought hit him.

"Okkkk...," Markus said, slipping an arm through the ghost's transparent sleeve, as he led Da Vinci from the room. "I heard from the kids at school you are good at pranks. There's these two guys who are reaaalllly mean...the Marek brothers...and I was thinkin'... maybe you could..." His voice trailed off down the hallway.

David crossed over to T.J. and placed a hand on his shoulder.

"Is it too late for a dad to tell his son, "Well done?" and to ask for a second chance?"

"You have chosen wisely," T.J. said, grinning. At his father's confused expression, he said, "It's a deal. Besides, thanks to some basketball stuff you taught me, I nailed a snake pretty good!" He hugged his father.

As the commotion continued in the kitchen, T.J. stepped out the kitchen door onto the back patio, and closed it against the noise. It was eerily quiet in the sudden stillness of the back yard. He stood staring at the woods that once terrified him. Images of the night's activities filled his head.

His grandfather had exited the well last night ahead of him. He remembered looking up into the light filling the opening, as he ascended from the furious rush through the portal's passageway. His first thought had been one of ecstasy to see the moonlight streaming in...to *see* anything! His sight was back! His second thought was one of joy, as he saw the giant smile on his grandfather's face as he reached a hand over the well to help the boy up. That smile meant only one thing...they were not in the Void...they were home!

"Grab my hand," T.J. heard Dillon say. "It's ok, grab my hand!"

T.J. grabbed hold, as he toed the stones with his tennis shoes, trying to push his way up. Suddenly, it all came back to him—that day in the woods. Just as he reached the top of the well, he hit his head, and then it all went black. Somehow, during his game of hide-and-seek with Markus in the woods, he must have tumbled into the cavern, and some old man had been there; perhaps just exiting the well from another dimension, or preparing to go in. *Why had old Ruther Harmon been there that day?* he wondered. T.J. had been terrified of dark places, and the woods ever since.

It all seemed so surreal now; so many unanswered questions. He suddenly thought of Twicket, and smiled. Was he home with Mudlin, happy and annoying all the toad people? And Mandy....

T.J. looked up at the twinkling stars overhead and got his bearings. He followed the celestial landmarks he knew so well, tracing the sky with his finger. He noticed a void where Cassiopeia's constellation should be, as well as her husband

Cepheus's. They were gone. Scarflon's was also missing. Where were they now? A shimmering outline of a large sailing ship moved through the Milky Way, and the boy smiled. Barnacle was alive and well and hunting for treasure.

T.J. continued scanning the night sky, until he stopped, pointing at the constellation of the Gemini Twins. Only half of the famous constellation was showing. He figured Wheedle and Mandy had not yet reconciled. He looked up at the star cluster so far away and felt a strange sadness.

"So are you Wheedle, or Mandy?" T.J. asked quietly, staring at the half-filled constellation.

Suddenly, one of its stars twinkled at him, filling the night with a piercing light.

He smiled, and said softly, "Good night, Mandy!"

As he turned to walk back to the kitchen door T.J failed to notice the shadowy figure watching him from the darkness of the forest. The creature's scarred hand, bearing the symbol of a crown on its wrist, let the branch fall it had been holding back to peer out at the boy, and then disappeared into the shadows of the woods. Moonlight poured through the opening of a crude hut sitting on a cliff side high above Coven Bay, bathing a large towering plant with its magical glow. Luthor trembled in its warm embrace. Somewhere in the darkness beneath the trees, the glow of a powerful eye stained the foliage in blood-red hues, as something in a tattered gown moved through the trails in search of it. Night had come once more to Harmon's Wood.

About the Author

Rebecca F. Pittman has been fascinated with the world of ghosts for as far back as she can remember. This led to her researching and writing about some of the most-haunted venues in America.

The History and Haunting of the Stanley Hotel, The History and Haunting of the Myrtles Plantation, and *The History and Haunting of Lemp Mansion* are works of non-fiction and were spotlighted on TV and radio, including a two-hour interview on *Coast to Coast AM* with George Noory—the largest paranormal radio program in the world with over 3 million listeners. Similar books on the Lizzie Borden House in Fall River, Massachusetts, and the Crescent Hotel in Arkansas, are now in the works. Each of these venues are listed in the Top 10 Most-Haunted Places in America.

T.J. Finnel and the Well of Ghosts is Book One of a Five-Book series. *T.J. Finnel and the Treblin's Secret* is due out Spring 2017. Other works of fiction in the paranormal genre are also on the drawing board.

Rebecca makes her home in Colorado where you can find her golfing, boating, or enjoying her 4 sons and their families, when not painting murals or creating worlds of adventure at the keyboard. During the summer months, she is known as the Popsicle Lady to the neighborhood children —a title she proudly bears.

1418 BITTERBRUSH DRIVE

www.rebeccafpittmanbooks.com

65523801R00252

Made in the USA
Lexington, KY
15 July 2017